# ALSO AVAILABLE FROM BLOOM BOOKS

CANE BROTHERS

*A Not So Meet Cute*

*So Not Meant to Be*

*A Long Time Coming*

BRIDESMAID FOR HIRE

*Bridesmaid for Hire*

*Bridesmaid Undercover*

*Bridesmaid by Chance*

*How My Neighbor Stole Christmas*

*Merry Christmas, You Filthy Animal*

*Till Summer Do Us Part*

# JUST FOR THE CAMERAS

MEGHAN QUINN

Bloom books

Published by Bloom Books, an imprint of Sourcebooks
1935 Brookdale RD, Naperville, IL 60563–2773
(630) 961-3900
sourcebooks.com

Cataloging-in-Publication data is on file with the Library of Congress.

Printed and bound in the United States of America.
WOZ 10 9 8 7 6 5 4 3 2 1

*This book is dedicated to each and every baseball tournament hotel bathroom I wrote in while my daughter was sleeping in the room next to me. Special thanks to the Fairfield Inn in Brighton, Colorado, as your running toilet set the mood while the dim yellow lighting created the perfect ambiance.*

# PROLOGUE
# GRAYDON

"THERE IS A REASON YOU'RE all here today, and it's because you've single-handedly made every major sporting team in San Francisco unbearable to watch, unlikeable, and frankly, a mockery."

"Um, I was actually just traded here," the guy on the end says while raising his hand.

"Which says a lot about the trade, doesn't it?"

*Fuck, good burn.*

Gretchen Michaels, San Francisco's most sought-after crisis PR manager, picks up one of the three files on the desk in front of her and pushes her chestnut-brown hair over her shoulder. Wearing a bright-red pencil skirt and matching button-up shirt, she gives off the impression that if you fuck with her, she has no problem ripping your testicles straight from your body. "Graydon St. John. Defensive end for the San Francisco Foghorns. In nine years of starting, you've secured a losing record for your team, appeared in zero playoff games, and disappointed the fans to the point of having to promote half-price games throughout the year just to get fans to come and support you."

"Ouch," the guy on the end says while rubbing the tops of his thighs.

I flash a death-inducing glare his way, and he winces, shrinking back into his chair.

Gretchen sets my file down and picks up the one next to it. Flipping it open with precision, she says, "Bennett Brinkman. Third baseman for the San Francisco Bombers. Currently playing your second full year with the team, and because you were not with them during their infamous cheating scandal, you're one of the few faces on the team who could save the franchise at this point." She glances up at him and purses her lips. "But given your lack of personality, I think the chances of saving the team's catastrophic 27 percent drop in merchandise sales are disappointingly low."

*Jesus.*

She picks up the last file, and from the corner of my eye, I catch the guy fidgeting in his seat. Clearing her throat, she keeps her head down, but her eyes lift to look at him. "Oden 'OC' O'Connor."

"Present," he says, raising his hand like a dweeb.

"Put your hand down." He snatches his hand out of the air and rests it on his lap as she continues. "Left wing for the new hockey expansion team, the San Francisco Rogue. Created by a group of the most ruthless investors with the need to win, the team has brought together all the bad blood of the hockey scene. With a take-no-prisoners model and a number one goal of fighting with fists out on the ice, they haven't really been welcomed into the Bay Area, which is why you're here. Apparently, your connection to the Vancouver Agitators is supposed to help transition some good faith over to the team."

"Aw, I love being used."

Gretchen's brow rises. "Are you always this mouthy?"

"Are you always this...schoolmarmy?"

"Excuse me?" She sets the file down, and he straightens in his seat, then gestures to the room.

"Sorry, but don't you think this is a little much? Intense? I thought we came here to get assigned some after-work activities and be done, but I don't know, you're bringing down the hammer on things that are not our fault." He glances over at me. "Well, besides you. Given your team record, it seems like your defense might not be up to snuff?"

I nearly growl as I hold back the tongue-lashing I want to give him.

The Foghorns suck, but not because of our defense. We can't develop a franchise quarterback because our offensive line is so goddamn terrible that the fucking guy spends most games running around trying to save his own damn life from people like me rather than throwing the ball.

"Actually, the reason Graydon is here is because he's the one player on the team who knows what he's doing," Gretchen says before I can tear this new guy a fresh asshole.

He winces. "Whoops, wrong call on the jab, then." He offers me a thumbs-up. "Proud of you, big guy."

I cross my arms over my chest. "Can we get to the point, please?"

She moves toward the front of the desk, leans against it, and crosses her arms. "For the next few months, you'll be spending every hour off the field and ice attempting to change the public opinion about your team."

"What does that mean?" I ask, irritation flooding me because this is the last fucking thing I need right now.

"It means that your face will be plastered all over every form of social media available. There will be news outlets and media picking up your stories. Your daily life will be put under a microscope, just so your teams can make a few more bucks and salvage what shitty perception they're barely hanging on to."

The room falls silent as her words slice through all three of us.

When I was drafted to play football professionally, I knew there'd be a side of the sport that wouldn't mesh with my lifestyle, and that's being in the public eye. I grew up with a father who was a professional football player, and I saw what the public's opinion could do to someone.

I know the damage.

Lived the damage.

The nimrod on the end is the one to break the silence as he says, "Well, aren't you a ray of sunshine."

Gretchen's head snaps in his direction, causing him to shift in his seat.

She pushes off the desk and opens another folder, only to hand us each a piece of paper. "Your first assignment is with the San Francisco Zoo."

She has to be fucking kidding me.

"A zoo?" I deadpan. "How the fuck is volunteering at a zoo going to help with public image?"

"People like animals, my man," the hockey player says as he examines the leaflet.

"I'm not your man," I snap back.

Gretchen slams the folder on the desk, bringing all of our attention back to her. "It's best that you three get along, because if there's one thing I know for sure, none of you have a clause in your contract that prevents you from mandatory public service, which means all three of you will be spending a lot of time with each other over the next couple of months." She smirks and then moves around her desk. "Any questions?"

"What if we say no?" I ask, because this is the last thing I want.

Letting the public into my life brings questions.

Questions breach privacy.

*And privacy is everything to me.*

Gretchen smirks at me as she sits on the desk and crosses one leg over the other. "You don't have the option to say no."

*Fuck.*

# CHAPTER 1
# GRAYDON

THREE...TWO...ONE...

I drop the battle ropes to the ground, my shoulders burning. "Fuck!" I yell as my hands fall to my hips and I walk off the fatigue from the physical exertion I just put myself through.

"Jesus, man. I think the seagulls out on the bay just heard that."

Hutton Marshall, wide receiver for the Foghorns, and the only glimmer of hope for the offense, hands me my water bottle.

I squirt some water into my mouth and continue to pace, letting my shoulders take a break after a grueling workout.

"Any reason you seem like you're ready to rip someone's head off?"

I pick up a white towel with the Foghorns logo printed on it and wipe away the sweat dripping down my face, neck, and chest.

Turning to him, I ask, "Does your contract state that you can't be forced into any mandatory public appearances with the team?"

"Doesn't everybody's?" he asks, as if it's a dumb question. "And if I'm required to show up, I'm compensated. Why? Is that not in your contract?"

I shake my head, already dreaming up the email that fires my agent. "No, it's not," I growl before squirting more water in my mouth. "Which is why I have to go to the fucking zoo today for some new initiative to make the team look better."

"Wait...what?" he asks.

"Apparently, the owners of the Foghorns, Bombers, and Rogue came up with a bullshit plan to create a sense of community with the sports teams here, and I'm the lucky motherfucker who was picked for the job."

"Shit." He chuckles, which makes me shoot a glare his way. At six foot five and two hundred and eighty-eight pounds of rock-hard muscle, I'm not a fucker to be messed with. "I mean, uh…dude, that sucks. Can't your agent get you out of it?"

"No, he's the dickhead who got me into this mess."

And sure, I told him to lock me in with the Foghorns with a no-trade clause so I could remain here for the longevity of my career, but Jesus Christ, I didn't mean give away all my goddamn rights.

"What does that mean?"

"It means I'm going to a fucking zoo today."

He winces. "By yourself?"

I shake my head and move toward the mats, where I grab a band and start stretching my sore muscles. "No. There are two dickheads from the Bombers and the Rogue coming too."

"Is it Asher Peppers?" Hutton asks. "I went to school with him at Brentwood. When I moved back here, I tried meeting up with him, but he's been a recluse."

"No, some new kid. He didn't speak once the entire time. Bennett Brinkman."

"Oh yeah, he's the third baseman. Fucking killer of an arm. He has potential to be a franchise player."

"How do you know this?" I ask.

"I pay attention to what's going on in our city. Doesn't hurt to make friends with people other than me, you know?"

"I'm barely friends with you."

He clutches his chest. "You wound me, man." He helps me stretch my hamstrings as I lie back and he pushes at my ankle. "Who's the other guy?"

I roll my eyes. "Some clown who's going to test me."

A smile creeps over his mouth. "Is it Oden O'Connor?"

"How the fuck do you know that?"

He chuckles. "He's the only Rogue player I could think of who'd be even slightly marketable to the public. The rest of the team are a bunch of assholes, castaways, and players who are too much of a problem to deal with. The owners put them all on the same team. It's going to be a recipe for disaster, and I can't fucking wait to watch it play out."

"Well, he's a moron."

"I've seen his socials; he's more...lighthearted. He came from the Vancouver Agitators. I remember the uproar around the trade. I don't think the dude has a fighting chance on that team. They're going to eat him up."

"Why did they sign him if he's not like the others?" I ask, hating my curiosity because the less I know about the other guys, the better.

"Because they needed someone fast and someone who could score; he was the one."

"Well, he seems like a tool."

I switch legs and Hutton pushes at my heel, almost giving me more of a stretch than I can handle, but I breathe it out.

"So what do you think you're going to do at the zoo?" he asks.

"No fucking idea, but I can tell you one thing I won't be doing."

"Making friends?"

"That and picking up animal shit."

"They're not going to have you do that. If anything, they'll probably take pictures of you holding your arm out while a bird rests on you. People will think it's cute and then you move on with your life. Seriously, this public appearance shit is a breeze. Show up, smile, move on."

"Yeah, I fucking hope so."

---

**Gretchen Michaels:** Reminder: You're expected to smile, take pictures, and sign anything held your way. You are yes-men,

> you're there to help, show interest, and attempt to look like God's gift to San Francisco. Any other behavior, and you'll be fined by your respective teams.

I stare down at the text and hold back a growl. I don't think I've ever hated a woman the way I hate her.

Sign everything held my way?

That's easy for her to say. She doesn't have to protect the value of her autograph. I barely sign anything now unless it's for a kid because I learned from Daddy Dearest to limit autographs as much as possible. Looks like that's about to change.

Grumbling, I open the door to my truck and heft my sore body onto the paved concrete of the back lot of the zoo. Luckily, they allowed us the option of private parking to avoid any run-ins with fans.

As I lock up my truck, I glance down at the two text messages waiting to be opened.

One from Gretchen...and one from my dad.

> **Gretchen:** Meet up at Gate B, your zookeeper and Phil will be waiting for you.

Next I pull up the text from my dad as my shoulders tense just from his name popping up on my screen.

> **Troy St. John:** Don't let this zoo situation distract you from what the hell you're really supposed to be doing. You need to be focused, because I'll be damned if you embarrass me.

What a fuckwit.

As if I fucking care what he thinks.

Pocketing my phone, I start to head toward the gate but spot Oden O'Connor standing directly in front of me.

"Jesus," I say, taking a step back. "What the fuck is wrong with you?"

"Thought we could walk in together."

I adjust my black shirt before moving past him and saying, "I'm good."

"You know, I think we got off on the wrong foot," he says as he matches my stride. "Trust me, this is the last fucking thing I want to do as well."

Ignoring him, I keep pushing forward toward the green gate marked with a *B*.

"And it might not hurt to, I don't know, communicate since we're in this together."

"You can fuck off," I say, reaching the gate just as it opens, with Gretchen and Bennett standing on the other side.

"You're late," Gretchen says.

"The fuck I am," I say. "I'm five minutes early."

"Which means you're late. I wanted you here at least ten minutes early."

Who the fuck does she think she is?

"Then maybe you should say that," I shoot back, really not in the mood for her sass, or anyone's for that matter.

I'm a moody dick as it is, but put me in a situation I don't want to be in and you make me almost unbearable.

She purses her lips and gives me a slow once-over as she juts her hip out, looking to put me in my place. "Might I remind you about the attitude you're supposed to have at these outings?"

"We're still backstage," I say. "Out of the public eye."

"But there are employees all around." She clenches her teeth. "So plaster a smile on that disgruntled face of yours and act the part."

From the corner of my eye, I catch OC smirk, which of course makes me want to smack him right into the fence, but I hold back the urge, creating another layer of tension that tightens my shoulders.

"Follow me, boys." In her pencil skirt, she leads the way through the back area of the zoo. Dirty golf carts are lined up one right after the other, while dumpsters, shovels, wheelbarrows, and bins flank the sides of the worn-down, paint-chipped buildings. Seems like they only put their money into the publicly viewed spaces.

We zigzag through some alleyways and then pass through the door of a large building with a thatched roof. Impractical, but also not my problem.

When we enter, a balding man in a navy blue suit with an annoyingly cheery disposition greets us. His eyes light up with excitement as we approach—he's clearly a fan despite our terrible reputations.

Gretchen clears her throat and says, "I would like you to meet Phil Foreman. He's the VP of public relations at the zoo. We've spent a great deal of time on the phone and he can't be more excited to have you three here, helping and bringing more awareness to the zoo. Phil, please meet Bennett, Oden, and Graydon."

Phil steps forward and shakes our hands. I offer him a curt smile and try to erase the permanent scowl from my forehead.

"What an absolute pleasure to meet you," Phil says as he clasps his hands together in front of him. "When Gretchen proposed the idea of having you come out and help around the zoo, I must say, I squealed in excitement."

Squealed?

Who says—

"I might have squealed myself," OC says, rocking on his heels. "Love animals."

Oh, that's who.

What a fucking kiss-ass. Jesus, and he thought we were going to be friends and commiserate? Not going to fucking happen.

"Then you're in the right place," Phil says. He turns to Gretchen and asks, "Have you informed them of what they'll be doing?"

Gretchen shakes her head and smiles. "I thought I'd give you that honor."

"Oh, wonderful. Well then, follow me."

Follow him?

Why does this feel like a setup?

He leads us out of the building and straight into the main area of the zoo. I half expected a media session with cameras and a photo opportunity, but instead, he offers us a seat on a three-row golf cart.

Huh, maybe the media opportunity is somewhere else.

Since I'm the biggest guy here, I hop on the back of the golf cart on the rear-facing seat, only for OC to slide in right next to me.

"What the hell are you doing?" I snarl at him, trying to move my shoulder away from his.

"Catching a ride. Not going to fucking walk next to the golf cart."

"Sit next to that Phil guy," I reply, wanting to spread my goddamn legs. "There's a cooler up there."

"Are we fighting?" Gretchen asks, turning around from where she's seated next to Bennett.

"Nope," I say as I try to move my body as close to my side as possible, but I feel like a sardine next to OC. The guy isn't as big as me, but he's still fucking huge, and I'm sure it's a comical sight watching us try to fit into this golf cart together.

"Hold on," Phil says as he starts the golf cart and pushes forward. "Whoa, this baby has probably never carried around this amount of muscle."

I refrain from rolling my eyes as we move through the zoo, onlookers pointing as we drive by.

Camera phones point at us.

Visitors gawk.

And I can feel my defenses rising.

I'm already uncomfortable.

And it's been five minutes.

Phil pulls up shortly to another building and puts the golf cart in park. When he hops out, he gestures to us to follow him behind a fence, out of the public eye.

Once again, there's no media anywhere.

What the hell is going on?

We gather around, OC standing next to me, Bennett next to him, and Gretchen tapping away on her phone as Phil clasps his hands together looking like a proud motherfucker about to deliver us delightful news.

My guess is, I'm about to despise what comes out of his mouth.

Clearing his throat, he smiles at us. "This is an opportunity we never thought we'd secure, so to have you three here means so much to the board of directors, our staff, and most importantly, our animals." Yeah, because animals can sense three celebrity athletes in the confines of their captivity. "Since Gretchen didn't break the news to you, I'll bring you up to speed." Irritation creeps up my neck because I can feel it; I know it's coming. This is not going to be an easy media day. No, I think I'm about to be sentenced. "For the next two months, you will be the official liaisons for the zoo, focusing with zookeepers on a specific animal to raise awareness, generate funds, and create a habitat that enriches the visitors' experience."

The fuck did he just say?

Did he just say two months?

Two fucking months?

"Wait, two months?" I ask as Gretchen tears her eyes off her phone and stares me down, a warning in the form of a devil's gaze.

"Yes, I know, we wish it was longer too," Phil replies.

Not what I was getting at.

"But you are welcome to help out longer once you become acquainted. It will probably be hard to step away once you get into the swing of things and start interacting with the animals."

Trust me, I'm willing to step away right fucking now.

Phil rubs his hands together. "I know what you must be thinking..."

I hope my agent burns in hell—that's what I'm thinking.

"What animal are you going to be assigned to? Well, this is the best part." He pauses for effect, as if we're waiting for the results with uncontained glee. Between the three of us jackasses, my money is on OC to actually be excited.

"Bennett, you'll be with the lions."

I glance at Bennett, who nods with a soft smile. Such a newbie; life as a professional athlete hasn't scarred him yet.

"Oden, you'll be with the giraffes."

"I fucking love giraffes," OC says with way too much pep.

"Language," Gretchen warns.

"Right. Sorry."

"And Graydon..." He pauses, and I swear, for a fucking second, I can see an evil glint in his eye. Like what he's about to say is a part of some master plan to piss me off. "We paired you with the flamingos."

Flamingos?

OC snorts next to me.

The corner of Bennett's lip turns up.

And Gretchen doesn't even bother hiding her delight.

He's kidding, right?

I have to be paired with fucking flamingos?

For two months?

"Flamingos? Really?" I ask.

Phil nods. "Yes...flamingos."

No.

Fucking.

Way.

# CHAPTER 2
# MAPLE

"I DON'T KNOW, BIG HERMY, I think this could be a bad idea."

My light pink flamingo friend stares at me with his sand-colored eye, his head cocked to the side, waiting for some pellets.

"I really wish you could talk back. I think you would have some good advice for me. I can see the wisdom you hold in your one eye."

He squawks, and I nod. "No, no, I'm not making fun of your one eye. I think it's dignified. Having one eye is the new thing and actually trendy. It's why you're the king of the lagoon. No one is going to mess with someone who survived a jackal attack."

"Maple," Kylie calls out from the shack. "They're here."

Ugh, great.

I stand and brush off my butt. "That's my cue. Wish me luck, Big Hermy. I'm going to need it."

I pick up my bag of pellets and head over to the Flamingo Shack, also known as our office. I set the pellets on the table next to the door, then grab some hand sanitizer and work my way to the main office, where I pause as I hear some whispering on the other side of the swinging door.

"Flamingos? Fucking flamingos. Gretchen, you can't be serious. Bennett and OC get lions and giraffes, and I get a pink-feathered dipshit on stilts?"

Um...pardon me?

"The team thought it would be the best animal to gain the most sympathy and appreciation," the lady who I'm assuming is Gretchen replies.

"This is a fucking joke. What am I supposed to do for two months with these asinine animals? Does anyone even care about them? Are they even endangered?"

Um, I do.

I care about them like they're my own children.

"I have no idea, but get it together because this is not optional. This is mandatory."

"Jesus Christ," the guy mumbles. "You're doing this on purpose, aren't you? You know I can't fucking say no, and you're going to continue to twist the knife until I give in."

"I'm not twisting a knife. I'm attempting to help you gain a positive reputation."

"By pairing me with a fucking flamingo? What a goddamn joke. I mean, no offense, but I don't want to spend my days fawning over a pink bird."

A goddamn joke?

Um, sir, I take offense to that.

"Yes, and you're going to put on a smile while doing it. Now get it together," Gretchen answers before I hear them walk away.

I stand still, allowing his savage words to sink in.

He's...he's so rude.

How dare he insult flamingos like that? Pink-feathered dipshit on stilts? That's just so mean. They're anything but dipshits. They're ecosystem engineers and a vital component to the wetlands. And it seems like someone needs an education on the matter.

And I will be sure to be the one that gives him a first-class talking-to. When he's done at this zoo, he'll...he'll be composing sonnets about my precious birds. That's right.

Sonnets!

Head held high, I push through the door and come face to…chest with the largest brick wall of a human I've ever seen.

Good God, that's a lot of man in one body.

Slowly, my eyes trail up a tight black shirt where well-formed muscles pull on the threads, to a thick neck with traps that nearly touch his ears, to a square jaw covered in a five-o'clock shadow, and dark, menacing eyes that almost resemble the color of an obsidian stone. His full and tousled pitch-black locks are artfully shaped into a fauxhawk, making him seem incredibly dangerous. The shorter sides sharpen the angle of his jaw, while the style screams rebellious, flamingo-hating…douche.

"There she is," Phil says as he comes over to me. "Maple, I'd like you to meet your new partner in crime." I glance over to where two other very fit, very tall brickhouse men stand, one expressionless, the other nearly bouncing on his toes with joy. "This is Graydon St. John, the defensive end for the Foghorns. Graydon, meet Maple, one of our flamingo zookeepers and your liaison for the next two months."

A pained expression crosses his stern features before the corners of his lips slightly angle up. He holds out his bearlike paw of a hand and says, "Nice to meet you."

Because I'm not someone to stir up trouble, I plaster on a smile and shake the flamingo-hater's hand. "It's very nice to meet you. We're excited to have you here helping with our precious birds."

He shifts on his feet and sticks his hands in his pockets. "Yeah…same." Ooh, I really felt the excitement. Gretchen elbows him in the side, causing him to stand taller and mutter, "Really excited."

Yeah, I can tell.

Insert eye roll.

Why? Why is this the guy I had to end up with? Why not the smiling fool behind him? Or even the silent one next to him? No, I get the annoyed, brooding asshole.

"Well, I'll let Maple catch you up on everything flamingos while I take Oden and Bennett to meet their zookeepers. So glad that you're here, Graydon."

Phil guides the other two out the door right before Gretchen exchanges a challenging look with Graydon. She mutters something under her breath and then takes off, leaving me alone with the intimidating giant.

"So," I say, feeling incredibly awkward. "Do you happen to know anything about this project?"

"No," he says, his voice curt, uninterested.

Boy, is this going to be fun.

"Well, maybe we should take a seat somewhere, and I'll give you a rundown of what's going on."

"Sure," he answers, his eyes studying me for a second longer before he moves.

With that riveting start to the conversation, I guide him to the small bistro table we keep near the fridge that holds some of the brine of shrimp, krill, flies, and mollusks that we feed the flamingos.

He stares down at the wrought-iron chair for a beat too long and then grumbles something under his breath as he squeezes into the space, his shoulders kissing the wall and the side of the fridge, causing them to turn in, and his hands to forcefully rest on his lap in front of him. His legs, long and as sturdy as freaking tree trunks, stretch well beyond the confines of the table's width and into my personal table space. *If only I had a camera.*

Just for the hell of it, I ask, "Uh, are you comfortable?"

"I'm fine," he scoffs as he shifts, trying to make the best of what little space he has. Not wanting to make him too comfortable since he verbally assaulted my friends, I sit and cross one leg over the other, completely content. "As you know, we're looking for help here at the zoo because we're trying to expand our facilities. Not sure if you were able to see it or not, but our flamingo lagoon is quite small, and our facilities are incredibly dated."

He glances around the room at the scuffed-up walls and chipped cabinets. "I've seen better."

Way to not sugarcoat it.

"Well, yes, I'm sure your facilities are much better than ours, which is one of the reasons we need your help. A series of events, fundraisers, and grants are coming up in the next two months that could really help us grow and expand, add a few updates here and there that we're desperate for. A celebrity endorsement can help our chances, especially at certain events."

"Okay, so what? I need to go to a few parties?" Could he be any more uninterested?

"Well, yes, but also, we're putting together a campaign that doesn't just show you at events but shows you helping out at the zoo as well, almost like a vlog. We know it can't be daily, but weekly is what we're looking for. I believe the Foghorns offered two to three times a week, depending on your schedule."

His eyes nearly fly out of his head as he says, "Two to three times a week? Doing what?"

If only Gretchen were here to elbow him and tell him to watch what he says. Doubtful she would like his most recent response.

"Well, cleaning the—"

"Cleaning?" His brow rises. "Cleaning what?"

"If you'd let me finish," I answer, the tension between us growing, "you would have heard me say, cleaning the enclosure, feeding once trained, and basic animal care, as if you were an intern."

He rubs his lips together, avoiding all eye contact with me. "Don't you have employees to do that?"

"We're actually short-staffed at the moment. We're looking to bring on someone else, but finding someone with the experience we need has been hard. After the avian flu broke out, there was a decline in flamboyance all around the country, leaving zookeepers to focus on other animals."

"Flamboyance?" he asks with a quirk of his brow.

"That would be a group of flamingos."

"Ah." He blows out a heavy breath. "Okay, so what, I just show up here, do some chores, and then leave?"

"Well, yes, but—"

"Great." He lifts from the table. "Then send me a schedule." He holds his hand out to me, and I study it for a second, insulted at his abrupt departure.

So that's that?

He's just going to shake on it and leave?

You know, if I had half the courage I wish I did, I'd swat his hand away and tell him to sit back down because I'm not finished with him. But I'm afraid to admit I'm weak and haven't quite established a backbone yet, so demanding that a man four times my size take a seat is not in my wheelhouse.

Instead, I stand as well, reach out and take his hand in mine to give it a shake, but he looks at me as if I've grown three heads, two of them being flamingos, before he shakes me off.

"What are you doing?" he asks.

"Giving you a handshake? Or were you looking for a high five?"

"I was looking for your phone so I could give you my number so you could send me the schedule."

Well, that wasn't obvious at all.

Grumbling, I reach into my pocket and say, "Words accompanying the hand would have been helpful."

I unlock my phone and hand it to him, only to find him staring at me with mild curiosity.

"What?" I ask.

"Nothing," he replies as he punches his number into my phone. When he hands it back to me, he says, "I put my number under Graydon St. John."

"Wow, novel idea, since that's your name."

The smallest of twitches appears around his lips, which only pisses me off even more because I find nothing about this funny. Not a single thing. When Phil came to me about the prospect of attaching a celebrity to my efforts to upgrade our facilities, hope and ideas bloomed inside me. I know that with a big name attached to your events, more people pay attention. But now that I see that the person I'm going to have to work with is only willing to give the bare minimum, all of that hope has been quickly extinguished.

"Is there...a problem?" he asks, folding his massive arms over his equally massive chest. Dear God, the muscles on this man. I think if I told him to, he could lift the crustacean fridge with one hand right over his head.

"No," I answer.

He studies me for a moment, his dark gaze swooping over me, intimidating me, making me want to shrink right back down into my chair.

"You're lying."

He just calls it like he sees it, huh?

Well, maybe I will do the same.

Holding my chin up high, I say, "You know what? Yes, I am lying. Because this program means a lot to me and those...those birds that you seem to think are pink-feathered dipshits on stilts, they mean the world to me too." His brows rise. "Yeah...I heard what you said. And you might not want to be here, but I do, and I want nothing more than to help out these birds that have done nothing to the human race other than grace us with their beauty. So...buck up, mister." I clear my throat, my nerves getting the best of me as I shakily hold my finger out to him, attempting to give him the scolding of a lifetime. "Because I'm here to say that you...you are now under my jurisdiction, and we...we work here. This is not some cushy job where you can roll in and pretend to put in the work. Unlike the Foghorns, I intend to win."

My finger shakes as I lower it back down to my hip.

I know nothing about the Foghorns other than that they don't win a lot.

I know nothing about him other than that he's the largest man I've ever seen in real life.

And I know nothing about his work ethic other than that he clearly has no problem insulting things before he even gives them a chance.

But there is one thing I do know: my insult does not go over well.

When my eyes meet his, I wince as I watch his expression grow dark and angry. And for a moment, I get the sense that the look he's giving me is the same one he gives his opponent right before a match.

Is that what they call it?

A match?

Honestly, I know nothing about football.

What is a defending end, anyway? Is that what Phil called it?

Either way, his nostrils flare, his teeth grind together, and his chin juts out in anger.

Oh boy…

He steps in closer, my eyes even with his nipples, causing me to have to crane my neck back to look at him.

Speaking in a dark, rather deathly tone, he says, "You know nothing about my work ethic."

My legs shake under me, his intimidation factor winning, because boy oh boy, do I wish I was anywhere but here, in the path of a goliath of a man holding back his transformation into what I can only imagine to be a beastly, snarly mythical creature that eats chest cavities for a snack.

But to my credit, I don't back down.

"Yeah, well…prove me wrong," I say, the need to pee my pants as we stand nose to nipple very evident.

"I don't have to prove anything to you."

"But you do have to prove something to the public, right?"

"I do what the fuck I want."

Still shaking, I respond, "Ah, so it was your idea to come here and play with pink birds?"

His nostrils flare even wider, and he takes a step back, his jaw tight and his anger billowing. I think I know why this man plays football. It seems like he has a lot of aggression built up inside him.

"Just send me the schedule when it's ready." He blows past me and tears open a door, walking right into a closet.

"Exit is that way," I say, pointing to another door as he swears under his breath.

Wow, this is going to be so much fun…

# CHAPTER 3
# GRAYDON

MY LEG BOUNCES AS I wait outside my coach's office.

We're not in season yet, given that it's July, but we are about to start training camp soon, which means I don't have time to dedicate two to three days a week to fucking flamingos. There has to have been a mistake, because this won't work for me, and my coach is about to hear about it.

A pair of heels clicks across the hall, pulling my attention, and when I see Gretchen head in my direction in a red power suit, I groan out loud.

Jesus.

Christ.

What the hell is she doing here?

"Well, if it isn't my least favorite player. So glad I was called into your stadium on a day that I should be working in my office."

"I didn't call you in here," I say.

"Yes, but I apparently have to be present for whatever you're about to whine to your coach about."

The door flies open, and Coach Keenan gives me a disgusted once-over before offering a smile to Gretchen. "Shall we?"

"I think we shall." She walks in, and I lift from my chair with a grunt before entering the large room covered in accolades...from when he was coaching other teams.

Gretchen sits in one of the chairs across from his desk while I choose to stand and lean against the far wall, crossing my arms indignantly.

Coach Keenan's bald head reflects the light from the window behind him as he leans back in his chair and picks up a pen. Whenever you have a conversation with him, the man always needs to fidget with something. A pen, pieces of paper...his underwear. Yeah, I was present once when he picked a wedgie from the depths of his ass.

Incredibly unpleasant experience.

"Care to explain why you called this emergency meeting about your new assignment?" he asks.

"How do you know it's about the assignment?" I ask.

"Because you were just assigned it yesterday, and you immediately asked for a meeting. I'm intelligent, *Saint*. I can put two and two together."

"Don't call me that," I say through a clenched jaw.

He fucking knows not to call me that.

That there is only one person on this earth who is allowed to call me that.

And yet, he likes to push my goddamn buttons the minute I get into his office.

He shrugs. "Oops."

The smile that tugs at his lips shows me that he's nothing but an indignant fuck who doesn't want the best for his players but rather plays politics to keep his job. It's one of the top reasons I hate him.

Not wanting to stay here any longer than I have to, I say, "I can't dedicate the time they need for me to be there at the zoo with training camp coming up soon."

"Training camp isn't for three weeks," Coach Keenan counters. "That gives you plenty of time to help out at the zoo."

I attempt not to crack my teeth from how irritated I am. "You know I have a training schedule I follow to get ready for camp. I'm not going to show up not in top physical form and let my boys down."

"Pretty sure your training sessions aren't all day, and if they are, I need to speak to the training staff because maybe your fatigue is one of the reasons we can't win a game."

This...mother...fucker.

The only reason we're not annihilated out on the field is because of my defensive line and the pressure we apply on the opposing team's quarterback.

Then again, he's always been a cocksure asshole who thinks his game play is the only way to play the game. Seems like our record has a different opinion.

Sensing the tension, Gretchen steps in. "It's only a few hours a week, Graydon. I'm sure you can swing it."

I shoot a glare in her direction. "And was it your idea to pair me with the fucking flamingos?"

"No, that was your coach's and Phil's," she answers. "I asked him what animal he thought would best boost the team's image, and he and Phil picked the flamingo."

Coach Keenan clicks his pen. "They're something that just stuck out to me. Seeing you care for such...delicate birds. It would really put a smile on my face."

My anger roaring to life, I shoot my arm out to the side. "This is bullshit, and you know it. I shouldn't be the one parading out there in the public eye. It should be Marshall or Trivet...or how about Bateman, who can't seem to get the public on his side since he gets sacked every other play? Someone from offense to gain the public's trust."

Coach Keenan straightens up. "Please inform me, *Saint*, when you became the coach of this team. Because it seems that you're under the impression that you're the one who makes the decisions."

"Someone needs to be fucking smart about this," I shoot back, unable to rein in my temper.

It's true though, there seems to be a lack of intelligence in this organization. Why would they choose me to try to gather some "team spirit" when I'm not only one of the least personable players on the team but also the one that doesn't need to prove himself to the fans?

The offensive line should be the ones going on some sort of "apology/please like us" tour. Not me.

I make no sense as the chosen one.

Sure, I might not want to do this, and when it comes down to it, do I really have a hatred for flamingos? Honestly, I'm indifferent, but take away my time and force me to hang out at a zoo doing God knows what. . .yeah, I'm going to be a cranky ass about it, because I have better things to do with my life.

This is not a job for me, this is a job for someone who has a personality like. . .like OC.

Coach Keenan slowly nods. He's calculating. I can see him plotting, and honestly, I don't give a shit what he might be thinking in that pea-sized brain of his. I don't have many years left in the game. Retirement is around the corner for me. I won't be traded because we made it clear in my contract that this is where I will rot. San Francisco is where I end my career. I banked my money, saved it, and when I do retire, I won't have to worry about one goddamn thing. I can tuck away into an abyss and block myself off from the rest of the world.

Just the way I fucking want it.

"I suggest you leave my office before I ask the front office to leave you on permanent assignment with the damn flamingos throughout the season." His eyes latch onto me. "And if I hear one more complaint about this, consider your sentence doubled."

And there he goes, solidifying my thoughts on the intelligence in this organization. He's running this team with his ego, not what little brain he has.

And his ego has been attempting to tear me down since the moment he got here.

Unfortunately, there is nothing I can do about it.

Growling, I tear the door open, ready to slam it shut when Gretchen calls out, "I touched base with Maple. She said she'd be sending you a schedule. I asked her to send it to me as well so I have an idea about your visits. We want to make sure you put in the time we promised the zoo."

Irritated, I slam the door and start heading down the hallway just as there's a ding on my phone.

I pull my phone out of my pocket and see that it's a text from a strange number. Attached to it is a picture of a schedule that says I'm due to be at the zoo today at three.

Fucking perfect.

---

I slam my truck door and work my way to the green gate with the letter *B*. The sounds of birds chirping mixed with humans and what I want to believe are monkeys fill the air while the smell of manure engulfs me.

Unsure of what the day would entail, I chose an old pair of jeans and a gray Foghorns shirt because I received a text from Gretchen reminding me to dress the part.

I snidely replied, asking her if that meant my jersey, pads, and helmet. And she said if I wanted to look like a jackass, then I should go ahead.

Hands stuffed in my pockets, I close the space between me and the gate just as it cracks open. Expecting to see Maple, I instead find OC on the other side with a stupid fucking smile on his face.

Jesus.

Christ.

"Dude, why the scowl?"

"Don't call me 'dude,'" I say as I move past him, only to see Bennett standing on the other side of the gate as well.

Not sure what his deal is, but he seems like a goody-two-shoes. Someone who will do what he's told without a complaint. I hate that kind of person.

"You know, I was thinking," OC says, clearly not reading the room. "Since we're all going to be in this together, don't you think we should start a group chat?"

"No," I answer as I look around. "What are we doing just standing here?"

"We were told to wait. Our zookeepers are coming to grab us," Bennett says while he leans against the fence.

Huh, so he does have a voice.

"Back to the group chat," OC answers. "I think it would be beneficial—"

"What is your deal?" I ask, turning toward him. "Read the fucking room, man. We don't want to be here. Don't make it worse by wanting to start a group chat."

"Bennett was into it."

I glance over at Bennett, who just shrugs.

"Well, then keep it a duo," I reply just as Maple and two other zookeepers step out of the building.

There she is.

My chest constricts as she heads in my direction, my eyes betraying me as they slowly work their way up her legs, over the curve of her hips, and right to her stunning face, where they remain.

And just like the first time I met her, the back of my neck heats up as I'm greeted with a soft, unsure smile.

She's...gorgeous.

Breathtaking.

Not at all what I expected when I was told I would be working at the zoo. I had pictured in my head that I would be working with an old crotch of a man who was a fan but had an opinion on how I could improve my defensive line.

Since the moment I met her, I've wished she would transform into an older man with nose hair, but instead, I get her...beautifully stunning *her*.

The other two zookeepers flank her sides; one is a tall man in khaki shorts, a sun-stained green polo, and a safari hat with the strings closed in tight under his chin. The other zookeeper is younger like Maple, but with a short pixie haircut, brown hair, and a fanny pack around her waist.

Safari hat speaks first. "You ready, Mr. O'Connor?"

"Dude, call me OC." He pats the tall guy on the back. "I'm more than ready. Bring me to those giraffes."

I hold back an intense eye roll. Not sure what glitter bomb crawled up his ass, but I plan on staying far away.

"Ready, Bennett?" the other zookeeper says as she pulls some ChapStick out of her fanny pack and coats her lips.

"Yup." Bennett heads in her direction, leaving me with Maple.

Just like the other day, she's wearing a pair of khaki pants, a green polo, and hiking boots, with her blond hair pulled back into a high ponytail, the loose strands braided. Her jet-black eyelashes highlight her electric blue eyes, while her cheeks are sun-kissed with a pink hue. There's a spot on either side of her mouth where it seems like she has dimples, but from the scowl in her glare, I'm going to guess I won't be able to find out if that's true or not.

Not that I would want to.

Sure, she easily has one of the prettiest faces I've ever seen, and one hell of a curvy body, but that means nothing because she holds the key to my torture. And from the set in her shoulders and the attitude brimming in her body language, I can tell she's going to have fun torturing me.

"Do I need to call you Mr. St. John, or can I just call you Graydon?"

I push off the fence and move toward her. "And here I thought you were going to call me douche bag."

"Don't tempt me," she answers. Yup, she's ripe.

I offer up one insult to a flock of fucking birds and now she has a vendetta against me?

Not that I really care.

I don't care how people feel about me.

I don't need to win over their affection or friendship. It's better if they hate me. Actually, I prefer it since it means I don't have to talk to people I don't care about.

She opens the door to the building in front of us, and I grab it from her, allowing her to step under my arm and into the building.

Her eyes widen in surprise at the gesture, confirming that I've been an asshole. She didn't expect something so simple as holding a door open for her.

And I hate to admit it, but that makes me feel...kind of shitty.

I'm the first to acknowledge, I'm not the nicest guy.

I'm grumpy.

I'm hard to work with.

And I have a truckload of baggage that no one wants to unpack, leaving me grouchy most of the time.

But not holding a door open? I'm not that big of an ass, right?

She slips past me and Jesus, for someone who works with bird shit on the daily, she smells fucking amazing. Like so fucking good that I find myself wanting to get another whiff.

She heads into the building, her braid swinging across the top of her shoulders, and I can see that she wants to thank me, but instead, she snags two Nalgene water bottles full of ice water off a table.

As she hands me one, she says, "Here. In case you get thirsty. You can leave it here or you can take it home with you. Just know that if you forget it, it's the water fountain for you."

I take the bottle with the zoo logo etched on it and my name scrolled across a piece of tape right below the logo. Whereas mine is brand new, Maple's looks like it's been through hell and back, with scrapes and gouges across the top, bottom, and sides.

"This way," she says, directing me out a door and to a two-person golf cart with a flatbed on the back. She takes a seat and nods at me. "Hop in."

As if it's that easy.

I move to the other side of the cart and bend down to try to fit my body inside the damn thing. My shoulders nearly take up the entire width of the bench seat, my head kisses the top, and my right leg has to hang off the side because there is absolutely no way I can squeeze into the minimal space provided.

When she glances in my direction, her eyes widen in surprise before they find humor in my situation and she stifles a laugh.

"Okay, taking note that I'll have to ask for the Gator to better accommodate your size."

I adjust, gripping the hood and attempting to get comfortable, but there's really no use.

"Can we just walk to the flamingo exhibit?"

"Normally," she says. "But today, I have to give you a tour of the zoo."

"Is that necessary?"

"I would think so since you're probably going to have to talk about it at some point, but if you're confident enough to just wing interviews without an education on the topic, then I'm more than happy to hop out and walk to the flamingos."

Smart-ass.

"Just drive," I huff, hanging on to the cart and my water bottle as she jolts it into motion.

Jesus Christ.

We make a left-hand turn, tilting on two wheels as she directs the cart toward the front of the zoo, braking haphazardly by a rather large, blooming bush.

Visitors move in and out of view along the walkways, some with strollers and freshly purchased stuffed animals clutched in children's arms, others exhausted and decked out in reusable cups dangling from their necks by lanyards. It's giving amusement park vibes without the rides.

"We house over two thousand animals here, with two hundred and fifty species."

Shit, that's a lot of animals. I keep that to myself.

"The San Francisco Zoo is best known for Koko the gorilla. Are you aware of Koko?"

"Does it look like I'd be aware?"

She scoffs. "Right, what was I thinking?" She shifts, her shoulder touching mine. Even with how petite she is, there is absolutely no room to spare between us in this fucking thing, which also means I get a front-row seat to her scent. What the fuck is that? Jesus Christ, it smells so damn good. "Koko was born here and was an avid communicator in American Sign Language. A real treasure on this earth."

I nod.

"She also loved kittens and adopted and cared for many throughout her life. A very popular, sweet, loving animal." She glances in my direction with an irritated gaze. "Not that it seems like you'd care, but she passed away in 2018. It was a devastating loss to so many." She somberly sighs.

Unsure of what to do, I clear my throat. "Sorry for your loss."

"I can tell you really mean that," she says with sarcasm as she puts the golf cart into drive again and jolts us forward.

I mean, I sort of did mean it. Probably not as much as someone else would, but you know...a gorilla dying is sad.

"The zoo spans over one hundred acres, making it the biggest zoo in Northern California."

"One hundred acres? That's it?" I ask as my fingers dig into the top of the roof, keeping me locked into this miniature golf cart while she jolts around, moving from side to side like a madwoman. Who gave her the keys to this thing?

"That's a lot of acreage."

"Yeah, but not for a wild animal. They're used to all the land they want."

Her head snaps to look at me with those devastatingly beautiful eyes. Jesus, they're even more blue when she's angry. And crazed while driving.

Please look at where you're going. For the love of God!

"Do not be one of those people."

"What do you mean?" I nod toward the front of the cart, letting her know that she should be paying attention.

"The kind of person who puts down zoos by claiming the animals could be better off not held in captivity."

"I mean...can't they?" Why am I distracting her?

"For your information...*Graydon*...most of the animals we host here have been rescued from the human species, given a second chance in life to thrive, and provide us with the opportunity as zookeepers to educate others on the importance of conservation." She brakes harshly at a four-way stop, nearly slamming me into the windshield, and then she pushes forward again, flinging me back in my seat. What kind of horse-power does this thing have? "But then again, maybe your football-addled brain can't quite comprehend such a thing."

Hey, that's fucking rude.

"And I'll have you know, we've spent hundreds of hours studying these animals, creating an environment for them that is natural to what they're used to." The cart skitters across the pavement, making my stomach drop as we tilt at another turn, her anger clearly turning her into a crazed Cruella de Vil driver.

"Hey, maybe you should slow—"

"And we're constantly studying them, coming up with ways to assist in their population growth and making sure they don't go extinct because of ignorant people like yourself." She snorts at me and tosses her hand to the side in disgust.

Then, with a whip of her head—I'm sure her version of a mic drop—she sharply maneuvers the cart, making a left-hand turn and jolting me so much to the side that I lose my grip on the roof, my entire upper half whipping out of the cart.

Like one of those wind sock guys at a car dealership, I thrash around, arms flailing, feet pressed into the floorboard while my hands grasp for anything solid, anything to keep me from having to perform a tuck and roll in front of a stroller brigade.

But I come up short.

And just as I'm about to fly out the side, right into a child eating Cheerios from an elephant-shaped container, my hand connects with a rope and I grab hold of it, hanging on to it like a lifesaver.

"Ahhhhh!" Maple cries as I yank myself back up and the cart comes to a halt. We both fly forward against the plexiglass windshield and then bounce back in our seats.

"Jesus Christ, I almost flew out of the cart. Who gave you permission to drive this thing?"

She grips her head and turns to me, fury in her eyes. "That was my hair you pulled on."

"When?" I ask, adjusting myself back in the seat and trying to figure out a way that I can wedge myself in to guarantee I stay in the cart at all times.

"Just now." She rubs the side of her head.

"That wasn't rope?"

"No, that was my hair, and I do not appreciate having my hair pulled."

I pause and slowly give her a once-over, letting my eyes travel over her khaki pants, up to her tucked-in shirt, to the curve of her breasts, and all the way up to that gorgeous face of hers. "Clearly you haven't had the right guy tugging on your hair, then."

Her eyes widen in shock as she flips her ponytail away from me. "Ew, don't be disgusting."

"There's nothing disgusting about pulling on a woman's hair. Especially when done correctly."

Chin held high, she counters, "Well I can tell you right now, there isn't a snowball's chance in hell that you know how to do it correctly." Leaning in a touch closer and lowering her voice, she adds, "Instead of arousal and excitement, all I feel is animosity and exasperation."

That response grates on my nerves, because I know how to pull on a woman's hair. I know how to wrap it around my fist and tug just right to make her back dip and her head arch back. I know how to make a woman scream my name while I hold on to her tightly and fuck her until she comes.

I know what the hell I'm doing...*Maple*. "Anyone ever tell you there's a thin line between love and hate?"

She scoffs. "Ugh, get over yourself." Straightening up, she brings her attention back to the zoo, clears her throat, and says, "This is the Exploration Zone. It's a family-friendly area of the zoo where kids can roam and explore our more human-friendly animals such as chickens and goats." So she's just going to act like she didn't almost send me flying off the golf cart? Okay. "Be grateful this is not where you were assigned. You could have been assisting with coop revitalization, cleaning the kid disease off every touchable surface, and battling it out with the goats for superiority."

"Yeah, but does the family farm come with an irritable shrew?" I ask under my breath as I gaze out toward a carousel.

"No, but it's surrounded by booger-eating children."

"Can't decide what's worse."

She huffs something under her breath and slams her foot down on the pedal.

"Whoa." I grip the roof again. "Can you rein in the crazy-ass driving?"

"Just attempting to get this done so I don't have to sit close to you anymore."

"I would prefer the same, but if you run down a child licking an ice cream cone, it's not on me."

I feel her glance in my direction and then, to my surprise, she slows down while driving us past a small theater before she pauses in front of the Flamingo Lagoon.

"This is where you'll be spending all of your time. As you can see, there's room to expand the exhibit, but as discussed before, we need to find the funds first. That's something we can discuss later."

She continues to drive to the left side of the park, taking her time now and pointing out sections of the zoo, rattling off facts, and attempting to keep me interested as I scan the exhibits, watching kids pointing their sticky fingers, parents scolding children for licking ropes that section off areas of the zoo, and trash being tossed toward a trash can and not quite making it. Jesus, it's not that hard.

When we reach the African region, I spot OC on a golf cart as well, chatting it up with his zookeeper. The man is animated, using his hands as he speaks, clearly entertaining the zookeeper as he dips his head back and laughs.

"Shame he wasn't assigned to me," Maple mumbles.

"Yeah, shame. You would have had to learn how to fake laugh to deal with his company."

Her eyes fall on me right before she lets out a roar of a laugh, one so obnoxious that it rattles the windshield of the golf cart, only for her to quiet down within an instant. With zero emotion on her face, she deadpans, "I think I could have handled it."

Fucking cheeky smart-ass.

Continuing with the tour, she says, "This is the African savanna, one of our most notable exhibits because of its size. It allows animals like our giraffes, zebras, and ostriches to live in a more natural setting. I'm unsure why it's included in the fundraising race, since they have so much more space and better resources, but I'm not running the zoo."

Sensing some bitterness toward the savanna.

Noted.

In silence, she drives back to the flamingo building and puts the golf cart in park. "Any questions?"

"Nope," I answer as she gets out of the cart while I unfold myself and stretch out, letting my body twist from side to side so my back doesn't cramp up on me.

"This way." She brings me to the lagoon and a tall fence lined with chicken wire. It's an odd addition that seems to have been erected temporarily to create distance between the flamingos and the visitors. The barrier feels out of sorts, haphazard, like an afterthought rather than a planned feature. "We house just over—"

"What's with the fence?"

"What?"

"This fence." I give it a little shake, wondering if the entire thing will collapse under my grasp. "What's with it?"

"Oh. It was added during the outbreak of the avian flu. We were trying to protect our birds, and it hasn't been dealt with since."

Well, it's a fucking eyesore.

And if they want visitors to be more in tune with the flamingos, this is one way not to do it.

Then again, what do I know?

Absolutely nothing, nor do I care.

"As I was saying, we house just over twenty-five flamingos here."

"Just over? Why not just say twenty-six or twenty-seven, or whatever the exact amount is?"

Her nostrils flare and Jesus, even angry she's fucking gorgeous. Not that I'm paying attention to that. "Why does it matter?"

I shrug. "Just seems weird to put it that way."

She looks up toward the sky as if she's begging for patience, then continues, "We house twenty-six flamingos here. We use bands on their legs to help track them so we can perform medical checkups much easier, as we keep a detailed log of their daily health. The guy with the lime-green band in the back, patting the water—that's Big Hermy. He's the oldest in our flamboyance and also my favorite. He's missing an eye, but that doesn't stop him from loving shiny things, so make sure to never wear jewelry around him unless you want him pecking at you."

"That won't be a problem," I say.

"The one off to the right with the red band and the number eleven, that's Dinkle. He was one of our first-born flamingos here at the zoo."

"Dinkle?" I ask. "Couldn't have picked a better name for him?"

"The public voted for it."

"Why was it even an option?"

She shrugs. "I like it. Think it fits him perfectly because he's just...always been off." She points toward the back of the lagoon, her attitude gentling as she speaks about the creatures she cares for. I'm not sure I've seen anyone light up the way she does, especially about birds. "And the one back there, that's Gwendalyn the Great. When the krill come out, she makes it known that she gets first dibs, and even though Big Hermy is clearly the king of the flamboyance, he allows it. But I think it's because he has an eye for her."

Okay, so...she's writing flamingo fan fiction in her spare time. Got it.

"And number four over there by the big rock, that's Kevin Malone, because the team is convinced that if he had to carry a pot of chili, he'd definitely spill it. Such a clumsy bird." She chuckles to herself, now leaning against the fence, admiring her...I want to say friends? Because that's what it seems like.

"Oh, and the one over there standing on one leg, that's Tribbs."

"Tribbs?" I ask.

"Yeah." She chuckles. "As in Joey Tribbiani because he's the horniest of all the flamingos. When it's mating season, his dance moves, a.k.a. the bobble of the head, are very eccentric and out-there. I have so many videos of it." She starts bobbing her head and then laughs at herself.

Dear God.

What the fuck is happening?

"That's, uh—"

"Oh, and the one with the sixteen on her band? That's Martha Stewart."

This ought to be good.

"Let me guess, because she teaches the other flamingos how to garnish their krill with lakeweed and make swans out of a simple stick and dollop of mud?"

Maple looks me up and down with insult written all over her face. "No, because she likes taking thirst traps while lounging in the water." She rolls her eyes and then moves away from the fence, as if I'm the insane one. "This way."

I follow her, glancing back at the flamingos that, let's be honest, smell fucking terrible, as she walks into the flamingo building. For a brief moment, as we make our way through the small hallway, my eyes fall to her backside, where her khakis cling to her heart-shaped rear and cinch around her waist, meeting her unflattering, tucked-in polo. A worn black belt is wrapped around her waist, keeping her pants in place, while the hem of her pants sits just half an inch off her hiking boots, making them almost high-waters.

It makes me chuckle. I don't really know anything about her other than it seems like the flamingos are her friends, she doesn't seem to take much shit, and she has one hell of a nice ass. Deceptive almost with her small frame, but she has a lot of curve in her backside. The perfect amount to grip onto.

To fucking ride.

To spank.

To...

"This is where we clean—um, hello?" Maple says, pulling me out of my thoughts. "Were you just looking at my butt?"

Shit.

"No." I casually lean against the wall, lying through my teeth, because yeah, I was looking at her butt. Her really nice butt. Although because I'm not one to show my cards—ever—I say the first thing that comes to mind. "I was looking at your high-water pants."

Her cheeks flame red as she looks down at her pants, pressing on the fabric like she thinks it will make them grow longer, but failing as she adjusts them. "They aren't high-waters."

"Sure," I say, feeling slightly bad about calling her out on her pants. I'm sure she gets paid shit for writing fan fiction about flamingos and feeding them, so she can't afford many pants, but before I can attempt to find the words to apologize, she clears her throat and moves toward the sink.

"Um…what was I saying?" She clears her throat again, looking out of sorts…and embarrassed.

Shit.

I'm an asshole, I know this, but making someone feel bad who doesn't technically deserve it is not the kind of asshole I tend to be.

"Maple—"

"You know what, let me just, um…" She spins around in a circle, looking every which way but at me. She's so flustered, her cheeks burning red, her hands fidgeting while attempting to find something to do. My apology is on the tip of my tongue because I can tell I hurt her, but she says, "Oh yes, these, um…these are some dishes that need to be cleaned. Use soap and water and rinse thoroughly." She brings me toward the sink, placing me right in front of the washing zone.

Uh, hold on one goddamn second.

She starts to step away, but I stop her. "You want me to clean these?"

She looks back at me, her eyes glistening. "I do, because they're not going to clean themselves, and I have more important things to do than wash them."

With that, she takes off, leaving me alone with a sponge, some soap, and the disgusting smell of bird shit.

# CHAPTER 4
# MAPLE

"HE THINKS I'M A DORK," I say as tears fill my eyes, attempting to hold them back, but now that I'm off duty and in the comforting presence of a friend, I know it's impossible.

"What?" Everly, my good friend, says as she sets down her milkshake with a stern look crossing her features. "Did he say that to you?"

I shake my head as I twirl my straw around the chunks of Oreos in my drink. One of my favorite days of the month is Milkshake Monday with Everly. We meet every second Monday of the month at the Milkshake Bar and catch up on everything that's going on in our lives. Funnily enough, she's married to my ex-boyfriend—long story short, they are perfect for each other, and I don't think I could be happier for them. But that's how I met her, through my ex-boyfriend, and it's a friendship I've clung to ever since moving back to the States, especially since my college friend Polly moved out of San Francisco.

"He didn't say it, but he implied it."

"Walk me through the conversation," Everly says as she crosses her legs in her chair.

After work, I went home, changed, showered, and then put on a pair of comfortable yoga pants and a baggy zoo shirt, not caring who I ran into because I had one thing on my mind—talking with my friend.

Plus, I have zero intention of running into anyone of the opposite sex who would catch my interest. My perspective on life changed after living in Peru for several years, studying flamingos and sleeping in a permanent tent with no running water. I want a simple life where I can share a milkshake with a friend and spend time with my flamingos but then go home to the quiet of my apartment and work on sudoku while listening to moody music.

"Well, I showed him around the zoo, almost sent him flying out of the golf cart—"

"Uh, what?"

"He made me mad and I might have been driving erratically. The first time I saw him jolt forward, I chuckled to myself and, well, I kept it going until he lost his grip and nearly flew out the side. My braid was the only thing that kept him inside the cart."

She taps her chin. "Care to elaborate on the braid thing?"

"He grabbed my hair."

"Ooh, really?" Her eyes light up.

"Everly, please. A little decorum. You're just as bad as him."

"Did he make a comment about pulling your hair?" She's far too excited about the prospect.

"Yes, and it was immature and crass. I don't wish to revisit the comment."

Because I hate to admit it, but...the way he talked about tugging on a woman's hair, it made me have thoughts.

Dirty thoughts.

Thoughts I shouldn't have about such an insufferable man.

"Fine. Continue," she says with a wave of her hand.

"Thank you. Where was I? Oh yes, I showed him around while he exhibited zero interest in the zoo, he made a comment about wishing he was with the giraffes—"

"Ass."

"I know. Then when we got back to the flamingos, I might have gotten a little ahead of myself and was telling him all about them, including their names and charming characteristics. After I spouted off about Martha Stewart being a thirsty bitch, I realized he was judging me from his unamused expression, so I cut it short—"

"Even though you could have kept going."

"Exactly, I would have talked about all twenty-six of them. But I wasn't going to subject myself to his visual harassment, so we walked back to the flamingo building, where he took the opportunity to point out that I was wearing high-waters."

"What?" Everly roars as she sits taller. "He said that?"

"Yes. I got so embarrassed, I've never felt my cheeks flame hotter. I didn't know what to do, so I told him to wash the dishes, and then I vanished into the bathroom, where I told myself not to cry."

"Oh my God, Maple." She reaches out and takes my hand. "I'm so sorry. That's terrible. Ugh, I hate him."

"I do too," I say. "Seriously, I've spent maybe three, four hours with the man in total, and I don't think I've ever disliked someone so much. Like he's going out of his way to be a dick. And I told you what he said about the flamingos, right?"

"Uh, yeah. He seems like a giant douche. Like, dude, you're on assignment to raise the public opinion of your team, and you're not doing yourself any favors."

"I know." I lean back in my chair. "We need this money, Everly. It's important. I know Phil could drop the flamingos anytime and build a different exhibit. He's even talked about making a merchandise building in that area. The stupid chicken-wire fence surrounding the exhibit ensures that making a connection with the birds is impossible. And I just feel like teaming me up with Graydon is a slap in the face. Almost as if Phil knew Graydon would be useless."

"I told you, JP has hounded Hardy and Hudson, and they're willing to make the donation to shut him up."

I chuckle, thinking about the billionaire flamingo advocate who was dropped in my lap one day. JP Cane, one of the three Cane brothers who rule the real estate market, is a champion for flamingos, pigeons, and penguins. And there's been a rumor that another bird has been catching his attention as of late, but he's been keeping it a secret, saying he wants to reveal it to his followers when he's ready. But he's already donated a lot, which has paid for some much-needed, upgraded equipment, including a new fridge, and he's pressuring his friends, a.k.a. Everly's husband and his brother, to donate. But I told them no.

I wasn't going to go down the slippery slope of asking friends for money. JP is doing enough by bringing awareness.

"You know my rule," I say. "They can spread the word, but I don't want their money. It will feel…tainted, forced."

"I understand. I would feel the same way, but it's there if you need it."

I shake my head. "It's not there, because it's not an option."

Not to mention, it would feel really weird getting a donation from my ex-boyfriend even though he's a good friend now.

"I just need…I need the freaking football man to cooperate and not make me feel like a high-water-wearing dork."

"'Freaking football man' has a nice ring to it." Everly always knows how to make me smile.

"That's what he is. And you know what, did I make fun of him for the way he couldn't fit his body in the golf cart? No. I held my tongue even though I had some serious thoughts about it. Because I have manners. Not him, he doesn't have any manners. He's just…he's a jerk."

"That's right, you get it out," Everly says.

"He's a big jerk."

"Enormous jerk. The jerkiest of all jerks."

"Exactly." I sip my milkshake. "And his…his fauxhawk is stupid. Just do a real one if you want it so bad."

"Ooh, good burn. Maybe you can say that to him next time you see him."

"Yeah, it would be a good comeback. I could say..." I hold my finger up to the air and stare at the ceiling as if I'm talking to him. "By the way...*man*...your fauxhawk is stupid, just, uh, just get a real one."

"A little less shaky," Everly says.

"I'm just pumped with adrenaline right now."

"I can sense it."

I pause for a moment, thinking about the man behind the shit day I had. Freaking high-waters.

Wincing, I look my friend in the eyes. "The pants were kind of high."

She snorts, covering her nose.

"Maybe I should get new ones."

"No." She slams her hand on the table. "Absolutely not. You wear those high pants with pride. If anything, you hike them up so high that not only does he see your ankles, but he sees a camel toe too."

I grimace at the thought. "Uh, no, thank you. That's not necessary, but the ankle thing..."

"Yeah, and wear low socks so when he sees the smooth, pasty lumps of your ankles, he gets all flustered."

"This isn't the eighteen hundreds, Everly. Trust me when I say he has no desire to catch a glimpse of my ankles."

"What? No way. I bet he took one look at you and those high-water pants and was like...'I wish she were wearing low socks because—bites fist—fuck, I want to marvel at her ankles.'"

I shake my head with a chuckle. "He definitely didn't think that." I let out a sigh, depleted from the day. "Feels like high school all over again. He's the hot jock, and I'm the nerdy girl in the corner, reading books about birds."

Everly blinks. "Umm...hot jock?"

I roll my eyes. "Please don't even get any sort of inkling of a romantic connection in that mind of yours. The only reason I said 'hot jock' is because I'd be lying if I said he was anything but hot. It's a no-brainer."

"Let me see." Everly pulls out her phone and starts typing away on it. "I can't remember what the freaking football man looks like. He can't be that—oh my God." She brings the phone closer to her face, clicks on a picture, then turns it to face me.

Graydon stands in a gym, wiping his face with a towel, wearing only a pair of navy blue shorts that ride high on his thighs. His chest glistens with sweat, the lights above him almost making it seem like glitter as droplet after droplet drips down each and every divot of muscle along his chest and stomach.

Mother.

Of.

God.

I don't think I've ever seen such…such athleticism encompassed in one singular body.

Are those muscles real?

I mean, he's a huge man, but look at his side, you can practically see the sinew wrapping around each individual rib. He's bulging and expertly carved in every section of his body.

Is that sort of physical form obtained by strictly drinking protein drinks all the time? I doubt he knows what a milkshake even is—I think this as I sip harder on my churned ice cream drink.

I swallow, my mouth growing dry as I gesture to the phone. "See? Hot."

"Yeah." Everly stares at the picture longer. "God, why do I like the fauxhawk?"

"Ugh…I like it too."

We both look at each other, then burst out in laughter. She sets her phone down and then picks her shake back up. "Sucks to be that hot but have the ugliest personality."

"For real, what a waste."

"Hey, at least when he's at the zoo, being a grump of a man, you have something nice to look at other than analyzing the color of bird shit."

"That's true." I pull my leg up and wrap my arm around it. "Ugh. What am I going to do, Everly? I'm so embarrassed. He clearly thinks I'm the king of dorks, and I have to see him three times a week and do events with him at night to gain support from possible donors."

"Do what you're supposed to do." Everly shrugs. "Be yourself. Teach him about flamingos and show him that you won't take his shit. If he's rude, you snap back. If he's kind, pat him on the head and tell him he's a good boy."

I chuckle. "I'd need a ladder to be able to pat him on the head."

"That tall?" she asks.

"When I say he barely fit in the golf cart, I'm not kidding. He's gigantic. Also, I think his hands are bigger than my face."

"Wow…that's…that's nice," she replies, staring off into space.

I snap my finger in front of her. "Um, hello, you're married to my ex-boyfriend."

"That I am," she says dreamily and then snaps out of it. Eyes focused on me, she continues, "You're going to go into your next meeting with him, and you're going to show him who's boss and that he can't treat you with disrespect. And your pants, if they're not at least five inches off the ground, showing off your ankles, I don't want you stepping outside your apartment."

I smirk. "I think I can do that." I sip my drink. "Give him hell."

"But also…teach him the way of the birds, because at the end of the day, we are really here to use his celebrity to help save the flamingos."

"Have you been reading JP's emails again?"

Everly shrugs. "They're catchy."

# CHAPTER 5
# GRAYDON

**OC:** Got your number from Gretchen. Thought I would start a group chat with all of us. So...how're the zoo chores going for you?

I STARE DOWN AT THE text message and groan because no. This is not happening. I'm not doing this whole bonding thing.

My phone dings.

Christ.

**OC:** I ask because yesterday I fell into a pile of giraffe shit, and I can still smell it.

On the other hand...hearing about OC falling into shit *is* appealing...

**Graydon:** Face-first?

Please say yes.

**OC:** You wish!

Yeah, I really fucking do.

**Graydon:** So you didn't eat shit?

**OC:** Ha...HA! <—note the sarcasm. No, but thanks for your concern. I sat in it.

**Bennett:** At least sitting in it made your ass smell, which is better than your face.

My lip tugs up because look at the young one chiming in. Didn't even think he had a personality.

**OC:** Don't want my ass smelling either. Don't want anything smelling.

**Graydon:** Maybe stop playing in giraffe shit then.

**Bennett:** That would be my suggestion as well.

**OC:** Normally, this kind of chatter would piss me off, but...look at us bonding.

**Graydon:** And you just ruined it.

**OC:** No, don't leave. I think...I think we need to help each other out. I don't know about you, but doing zoo chores wasn't on my list of ways to improve the public perception of my team. It only feels like a way to make people laugh at us.

Well, look at him. He does have a fucking brain.

**Bennett:** Yeah, I'm not doing much. Just sitting and reading facts about lions.

Grumbling under my breath, because I don't want to bond but it seems like they're in the same headspace as me, I text back.

**Graydon:** I washed dishes yesterday.

**OC:** How dare they make a man of your stature perform such an inconsequential task that could wrinkle your fingertips.

**Graydon:** Seconds from blocking you.

**OC:** Fine, but I want you to remember just how concerned I am for your fingertips. Washing dishes...preposterous!

**Bennett:** I'm not concerned about your fingertips.

**Graydon:** That's how I prefer it.

**OC:** Stop, we need to focus. This is serious. I think we need to hold a meeting, get a grip on what's going on.

**Graydon:** Already tried that with my coach, didn't go over well.

**Bennett:** I'm in the middle of my season. I can't be wasting time reading facts about lions.

**OC:** Exactly, there needs to be structure, there needs to be accountability, and above all else, if I'm sitting in giraffe dung, there at least needs to be a camera crew following me so I can get the public on my side.

**Graydon:** You think they're going to get on your side from watching you sit in shit? That's laughable.

**OC:** You know what I mean. I thought this would be a vlog thing, but it doesn't seem that way right now. It seems like we're just doing dirty work.

**Bennett:** I mean, I wouldn't mind a meeting with Gretchen.

I blow out a heavy breath because I feel like I know how this meeting is going to go, but then again, the last thing I want to do is cut out my training time to go wash dishes, so...what could it hurt?

**Graydon:** Fine. Set it up.

**OC:** It would be my pleasure.

---

Gretchen shifts on her heels, hip jutted out, looking at all of us in her office. Her lips purse, and her stare would probably wilt a lesser man, but I hold strong.

"Well, isn't this a pleasure for me, seeing all three of you in here?" She sits on the edge of her desk, her villainesque stance revealing she's ready to strike.

OC, wearing a goddamn necktie like he's about to go on trial, sits taller in his chair and says, "We have concerns."

Gretchen's eyes shoot to me. "The same concerns I already spoke to *St. John* about?"

"It's Graydon," I correct her.

OC clears his throat, bringing her attention back to him. "I'm just going to say it. This assignment is bullshit. You know it, we know it, and the zoo staff knows it. We are glorified fetching boys for them. I don't see how this is helping the way the public perceives us."

She picks up her phone and flips through it. "It's been...ah, yes, two days." Her eyes find us again. "Two days and you guys can't cut it. It's no wonder we don't have any championship titles."

"Hey, this is our inaugural year," OC states. "You can't throw that in my face."

"True." She looks him up and down. "But from the way you're crying about sitting in giraffe dung, it doesn't bode well for your chances at winning."

"How did you know I sat in giraffe dung?"

"Because." Gretchen pushes off her desk. "We didn't want cameras following you all the time, so we had some cameras installed around the facilities you'll be working in with the hope that we can capture some real interaction and then bring it all together for the public."

From the corner of my eye, I can see OC's mouth drop.

"You don't think we should have been told that?" Bennett asks in a calm voice.

"Well, if you had given me a moment to collect everything, you would have seen that I was sending you an email today about our goals for the zoo visit. Excuse me if working with someone unreliable like Phil has pushed me behind in delivering information. There seem to be a lot of moving parts with a lot of unintelligent individuals. Therefore, I'm chasing information."

I have to hand it to her for at least telling it like it is, because I agree with the unintelligent individuals part, especially pertaining to Coach Keenan.

"Oh." OC crosses his ankle over his knee and picks a piece of lint off his jeans. "Uh, care to elaborate, then?"

Gretchen folds her hands together and looks between the three of us. "Although it's charming that you three came in here together as a united front, I don't need to elaborate on anything. You can wait for my email."

She pushes off her desk, then rounds it, sits down in her chair, and starts tapping away on her computer. After a few seconds, she looks up and shoos us with her hand. "You can be gone now."

I guess that's that.

Grumbling, we all stand like a bunch of fucking idiots and take off into the hallway, then make our way to the elevator.

I knew this was going to be a waste of time.

It was a waste of time when I brought it to Coach Keenan, and it was a waste of time now. No matter what, they have us in a choke hold because of our contracts. There really isn't much we can do, yet I allowed myself to get sucked into possibly attempting another challenge to get the hell out of this nightmare.

The elevator doors part, and we all shuffle in, Bennett pressing the button for the lobby floor. When the doors shut, we stand there, leaning against the elevator walls as we descend.

After a few short moments of silence, OC says, "I think we might have pulled the protest card too soon."

"You fucking think," I say, hating him all over again.

---

Mindlessly, I watch the Bombers game, keeping an eye on Bennett. Even though he's fucking young, the guy has made some insane plays, launching the ball across the baseball diamond from his goddamn knees, getting the runner out every time.

Up at bat, he has a double to left center and a triple down the third base line. His last at bat, he struck out on a breaking ball, but Jesus Christ, the kid is good.

And the announcers wouldn't stop jabbering about it either.

A prospect from their farm system, he came up two years ago to join the team before the playoffs. Last year was his first full year with the team, and he's already made a strong impression.

They flash his face on the screen for what seems like the twentieth time, and there's no doubt in my mind that it's a PR move from the team. Not only is he apparently liked by the public, but he's also—I'm not fucking shy to say it—a good-looking guy. He could build more muscle on his bones—he's still in that phase of moving up from the farm system to the major leagues—but he's not as scrawny as he used to be.

He's old enough to grow some scruff on his face, and his blue eyes almost seem darker under his baseball cap. And the camera is taking full advantage of it as they keep showing him off.

Over…

And over…

And over again.

Look at the Bombers working overtime to save their image.

I take a sip of my beer as my phone dings with a text. I glance down to see it's from OC.

What does this motherfucker want now?

**OC:** Are you watching the Bombers game? I swear it's half baseball, half pornographic display of Bennett. The way they slowly slide up his body with the camera while he's on deck. Tell me that's not intentional.

I drop my phone. No need to respond, because I can tell you right now, this is not a build-a-friendship moment.

No fucking way.

But of course, my phone dings again.

**OC:** Have you gotten an email yet? Because I haven't. Do you think she just said that to get us out of her office? I fell for it. Did you?

I drop my phone to my lap and drag my hand over my face.

A week ago, I didn't have this annoyance, this stress. I didn't have this extra thing to worry about. And now look where I'm at, getting irritating texts from someone I don't care to know.

Blowing out a heavy breath, I check my email, and when I see nothing, I text OC back.

**Graydon:** Smoke and mirrors. Nothing.

He texts back immediately.

**OC:** What the actual fuck! I say we riot at dawn.

Does he realize when he says stuff like that it makes me want to shove my palm straight up his nose?

My phone dings again, but this time, it's a notification from my inbox. I glance down at my email and see something from Gretchen at the very top.

My phone dings again with a text.

**OC:** Oops, never mind, looks like we have a very comprehensive document to look over now. Huh, pulled the trigger early on that too. Anyway…how about those Bombers?

**Graydon:** Lose this number.

I open Gretchen's email and glance over it, barely giving her intro the time of day as she scolds us for not trusting the process.

My eyes roam over the details of what we are doing at the zoo, each of us helping bring awareness to individual animals, cameras in the facilities, needing to learn about the animals before the production crew arrives, galas and fundraisers and all that bullshit.

But the thing she emphasizes at the bottom is growing trust with our zookeepers because they will be helping us with our public image the most.

I roll my eyes and toss my phone to the side because it's the same bullshit that they've said before. Not sure how this is going to help us in any way, but whatever. I'll fucking do my time and be done with it. Not like they can fire me if they don't like how I perform off the field.

Some of my teammates have done way worse…and hell, they get bonuses. I'm the best defensive end in the league, headed for the Hall of Fame, and no one can take that away from me.

Not a flamingo zookeeper.

Not Gretchen Michaels.

Not Coach Keenan.

And not his best friend…the asshole I despise most in this world, my dad.

# CHAPTER 6
# MAPLE

IT'S GOING TO BE A good day today.

I'm wearing pants that hit my shoes.

I'm sporting my favorite navy blue polo because it's actually fit for a woman, not a man. My hair is pulled back into a tight ponytail on the top of my head, my hair curled on the ends, and I made sure to spray a touch of my favorite perfume before I came into work.

And I know what you must be thinking...but, no, it's not for the benefit of Graydon St. John.

For all I care, he can rot.

It's for me.

It's for my confidence.

It's so when that brick wall with a scowl akin to Geralt of Rivia's appears—God, Henry Cavill is so hot—I will be poised and ready to take him on.

"Changed out the water," Harriot says as she comes into the flamingo building. "When does the football guy get here?"

I glance up at the clock. "Five minutes. I should probably go meet him."

"What are you going to have him do today?" Harriot asks while she takes a seat at the bistro table.

"Not sure yet. Guess I'll have to see what kind of attitude he walks in with."

"Good luck," she calls out as I head toward the exit.

Yeah, I'm going to need it.

I make my way toward the back lot of Gate B, picking up a few pieces of trash on my way and depositing them in the garbage cans. You would think being at a zoo would stop people from littering, because you know, we should keep animals safe from plastics and all, but that's so not the case. I'm always picking up trash as I walk around—it's infuriating. *Do they not know how many animals die each year due to human trash traveling out to sea?*

When I reach Gate B, Travis and Callie are already waiting.

Travis offers me a nod, his neck so long that it makes me giggle. They sometimes say that zookeepers take on the characteristics of the animals they care for, and Travis is no exception.

"Ready for today?" he asks.

"Ready as ever," I answer as I remove the top on my water bottle and take a sip.

"I hope OC doesn't sit in giraffe shit today." Travis shakes his head. "That was not a fun cleanup."

"Maybe Bennett will actually say more than two words to me," Callie says on a sigh. "It's been really hard trying to have a conversation with him. I mean, he asks me questions, but that's about it. There is no bond there." She leans in close and says, "I even watched his game last night to see if I could strike up a conversation about his sport."

"How did that go for you?" Travis asks.

Callie winces. "I fell asleep."

I chuckle and then cap off my water bottle. "At least you're not working with an asshole. I would take OC sitting in poop and Bennett not talking over Graydon any—"

My words are cut short as the gate opens and, lo and behold, Graydon is standing on the other side with that signature scowl of his.

Today he chose a pair of worn jeans, white shoes, and a navy blue

Foghorns T-shirt. The scruff on his jaw seems to be even thicker today, while his hair is styled in a more tousled way, still taking the shape of a fauxhawk. When his eyes land on mine, his jaw works over the gum that must be in his mouth as he says, "Don't let me stop you from finishing."

Dammit.

He heard me.

I clear my throat and attempt a shaky smile as I say, "Um...I'd rather not."

He slowly nods as he glances at Travis and Callie, who both take a solid step back. "Right. Let's get this over with."

He takes two steps forward, propelling himself right past me, and doesn't glance back as I'm forced to chase him.

Looks like it's going to be another great day with my celebrity advocate.

Travis and Callie both offer me sympathetic smiles before I chase the giant of a man who is plowing through the door.

"Hey, hold on," I call out, only for him to whirl around on me, nearly scaring me half to death with his size. I gulp as his menacing eyes meet mine.

"What were you saying about me?"

"I, uh, I wasn't, I mean...I was just, you know...lamenting."

"Lamenting?" He crosses his arms over his chest, and that's when I notice he's carrying the water bottle I gave him. If I wasn't so terrified about what he might say, I'd probably think it's nice to see him using it. "What exactly were you lamenting about?"

"Well, I didn't really get a chance to lament about anything before you arrived."

"And what were you going to say if I didn't show up?"

"You know, I really don't think that's important at the moment." My legs tremble beneath me. "I think what's important is that we focus on the flamingos."

"Why? Do more dishes need to be washed?" he asks, disdain dripping from his voice.

"No," I drag out. "I thought that maybe I could sit you down and educate you about the animals."

"I don't need an education."

"Don't you want to learn about them?"

"No," he growls as Bennett and Callie walk by us, clearly tiptoeing around the negative energy between me and Graydon. "I couldn't care less about the flamingos."

And just like that, my hackles are raised.

My anger takes hold of my tongue.

And my sense of decorum is erased.

Because he couldn't care less about flamingos? That is so…that is so…

Rude!

And mean.

It disgusts me.

To have a platform such as his and say something like he doesn't care about flamingos—how dare he!

"Yeah, brought a spare pair of pants to keep here," OC says as he walks in with Travis at his side.

"Great idea, man," Travis answers, walking by us. "But maybe try not to sit in giraffe dung this time."

"That's the mission," OC answers before they exit as well, leaving me alone with Graydon.

Trying to speak in a steady tone, I say, "I find it extremely offensive that you don't care about the flamingos, especially when you haven't given them a chance—"

"The first day I was here, you made me wash dishes. Excuse me if I'm lacking a connection."

"It's because you made fun of me for my pants," I snap back. "And I wasn't in the mood to hang around and give you the lowdown on my favorite things in this world."

His face remains expressionless as he asks, "Do you think that's professional?"

Excuse me?

Do I think that's professional? Look in a freaking mirror, sir.

I don't think I've ever met anyone as rude as him before.

"Do you think it's professional to make fun of someone's pants?" I ask.

"I was pointing out the facts."

"Just because it was a fact doesn't mean you needed to point it out," I counter, hands on my hips.

He drags his hand over his face, clearly bored of this conversation. "Can we just start this fucking jail time so I can get on with my day?"

Jail time?

Wow.

Just wow.

"You know this is important to me, right?" I ask. "Like there is a lot riding on you being here and helping?"

He's barely listening. His eyes aren't even on me.

I poke his shoulder. "Hello, I'm talking to you."

"Yeah, I know, and it sounds like you're gaining the courage to go on a tirade. Not interested in hearing it."

Anger consumes me, and when I get so angry, I start to cry. It's a horrible attribute, I hate it and wish it wasn't something I was prone to do, but unfortunately, that's how my body and brain work.

So as tears well in my eyes, I say, "You are so…privileged. You know that? You have the opportunity to make a change, to help, and you're choosing indifference."

His eyes finally land on my watery ones, which don't seem to affect him one bit. "Privileged life?" He shakes his head. "You know nothing about my life. Don't make assumptions you can't back up with facts."

He's right; I don't know what his life was like or is like, but I do know he's a self-centered ass, which makes a tear fall down my cheek. I quickly wipe it away, but I know he saw it.

Catching my breath, I say, "Either way, you have to be here, so don't you think it's worth trying to make something of this rather than wasting your time? It's not going to hurt you to learn about flamingos and possibly help a group of animals that are floating close to the endangered list. You are blessed with a celebrity profile because you can toss around a ball—"

"I don't toss around a ball. I fucking annihilate grown-ass men."

"Whatever, same thing."

He takes a step forward, his menacing stare eating me alive. "It's not the same thing. My specialty on that field vastly differs from what you have in your head."

"Honestly, I have nothing in my head because I don't know anything about football."

His tongue pokes against his cheek as he slowly nods. "So what I'm hearing is that you want to use my platform that I built from a sport that I've been playing my whole life, a sport you know nothing about, and use me by having me become a goddamn encyclopedia for Double Bubble Bubble Gum birds? Tell me how that computes."

"They're flamingos, so you can call them that."

He shakes his head. "Pretty ironic that you want to use me while knowing nothing about what I do but insisting I know everything about what you do. Not an even swap."

"You're getting good publicity out of this."

"It's not guaranteed," he says. "But if I learn your shit, then you will get grants and benefits, some new facilities. It's not an even swap."

I go to protest, but then I shut my mouth and consider what he's saying, because he's right. It's not an even swap. He can wash dishes for the flamingos all he wants, but that doesn't mean he will earn the public's trust.

I mull it over, my mind racing with a possible idea.

No…I couldn't.

But…what if…

"You're mumbling to yourself," he points out, stalling me in my thoughts.

"I was just thinking, what if…" My teeth pull on the corner of my lip.

"Please, I don't have all fucking day."

Ugh, I hate him.

I really hate him.

But I also need him. I know I do. Phil favors Travis and Callie. He also favors money, and what makes money? Merchandise.

And what does he need for merchandise? A central store.

And where would be a great place for a large central store?

The Flamingo Lagoon.

So as much as I hate to admit it, I have to make the most of this "partnership," even if it pains me.

Gathering all my courage, I say, "What if we do something a little different from what Travis and Callie are doing with OC and Bennett?"

He eyes me. "Like?"

"Well, what if…instead of doing a vlog thing where cameras follow us around, why don't we treat this as a partnership…a trade-off of sorts?"

"Not sure how I could possibly benefit."

No, you couldn't, could you?

Ass.

Grasping at straws, I say, "What if we went for a whole…social media approach instead? Where we start an Instagram account together. It could be about our unlikely pairing. You helping out with the flamingos and me…attempting to train as a football player?"

His brows shoot up, and then slowly the corners of his lips tilt to the sky. It's not quite a smile, but I think it's the most I'll ever get from him.

"You…a football player?"

"I mean, I wouldn't go out on the field, but you're right, it's only fair. If you have to learn about my love for flamingos, then I should learn about your love for football. An even trade. We can post about our days together on socials, create a following, build a love for you while people are hooked on watching me make a fool of myself attempting to trudge around a football field and bring awareness to the flamingos."

From the slight glimmer in his eyes, I almost feel like I have a shot at a winning idea.

Do I want to do it? No.

Am I desperate enough to do it? Absolutely.

"So...I come here, do flamingo things, and then you're going to come to my work, my training camps, and do football things?"

Training camp? Oof, never seen what happens there, but I can only imagine after being an avid watcher of *Friday Night Lights* what kind of torture that could bring me. With someone as vindictive as Graydon, I can see a lot of sore muscles in my future. But...I would do pretty much anything to make sure my flamingos are cared for and safe.

Chin held high, I look him in his dark eyes and say, "Yes, you help me here, and I will train for football with you."

He mulls it over, his tongue pressing against the side of his cheek as he looks away. Is he really going to turn this down?

To me, it seems like a golden opportunity.

"Listen, you have to be here no matter what, so let's make the most out of it," I say.

He glances down at me. "Do you even know anything about social media?"

No.

I lived in Peru for many years and came back to a world where social media rules the universe, but that doesn't mean I can't learn.

"Absolutely," I say, lying right through my teeth. "Some might say that I'm a social media wizard. A czar. A savant of all things socials."

"Why don't I believe you?"

"Maybe because you have trust issues and that's something you need to deal with on your own?"

His eyes narrow, and I nearly wet myself.

"What would the account even be called?" he asks.

"Great question. And you know, I think we could be really clever, something that could combine both of our interests in a unique and punny way."

He lifts a brow in question. "Like...?"

"Putting me on the spot, okay, well, let's see..." I think about it for a second. "Um, maybe something like...Flamingo Formation." His expression sours. "Yeah, not my best work. Um, what about...Clash of the Titans and the Flamingos?"

"Really?" His brow quirks up even higher.

"Don't judge, this is hard." I tap my chin. "What about Flamingo Hating Is a Personal Foul, but spell 'fowl' F-O-W-L."

"That's fucking terrible."

"Fine, you give it a try."

"Nope, not my idea."

God, why is he the worst?

"Well, if you're not going to try, then you're not going to have a say in it."

"If I don't get final approval of the name, then I'm not participating," he counters.

"Aha." I point at him. "So you want to participate."

"'Want' is a strong word."

"Either way, you are a yes."

"I'm a 'Let's just get this the fuck over with so I can move on with my life.'"

"Great," I say with a smile. "Then it's settled, we're starting a social media profile together to show off football and flamingos, and it's going to be called Flamingo Hating Is a Personal Fowl."

"That's not what it's going to be called."

I move toward the door and say, "Come up with something else, and we'll talk. Remember, I'm the social media expert here."

He follows me but takes his leisurely time, letting me know that I'm on his watch and not the other way around.

"What social media do you manage?"

"That is none of your concern," I say as I hold the door open for him, but he takes it from me, letting me walk through first.

Ah, look at that, maybe there's a pinch of kindness in him.

"What are you hiding? Do you have some secret foot fetish account?"

"If I did, I wouldn't be wearing high-water pants," I shoot back, and for a moment, I see a drop in his "couldn't care less" facade. And I want to say that maybe I caught a glimmer of guilt, but that irritated glare fixes itself right back on his face.

"How do I know you won't embarrass me on social media?"

"Don't you think a little humility goes a long way?"

We head in the direction of the flamingos as he curtly says, "No."

"Well, it does. Also, it's not in my best interest to embarrass you because I need people to take you seriously. Serious people with serious money like to donate to serious things."

"Couldn't think of another way to say serious?"

"I was getting a point across. Can't think of another way not to be an ass?"

Now his brows really shoot up, and I realize that I might have gone a little too far.

Nervously, I laugh and then clear my throat. "Um, anyway, I think we can make a pact that we use the platform for good, not for anything else, and we both approve what we post. Deal?"

I stretch my hand out to him to shake, but he just stares down at it. "What's the name of the account?"

This again.

Groaning, I retreat my hand as we make our way to the flamingo building, and I just start shooting out anything that comes to mind.

"Flock and Tackle. Uh...Fowl Play. Two Can Play That Game, but Only One Ruffles Feathers." He's so unamused. "Foghorns and Flamingos. Feathers and Football. Pink You Stink."

He shakes his head. "'Pink' and 'stink' should not be in the same sentence...at all."

"Why? I don't—" I pause and think about it, my cheeks flaming with embarrassment. "Oh, right. Umm...Flamingo Fiasco. He's All Tackle, and I'm All Talons. Flamboyance Football. Pink Wings and Brown Balls."

"Once again...no. Brown balls, pink and stink. Do you not see what you're doing?"

I huff. "I'm sorry that I'm not as perverted as you."

"Not perverted, just aware."

"Fine, then you pick."

"Just go with Flock and Tackle."

My mouth falls open. "That was one of the first things I said. Why didn't you just stop me?"

He shrugs. "Wanted to see what else you could come up with."

I purse my lips, looking him up and down. "You really are an ass."

# CHAPTER 7
# GRAYDON

I LEAN BACK IN MY chair, staring out at the quiet coffee shop that's close to my house. It's not frequented by tourists or football fans, which makes it the perfect place for me to sit, grab a cup of coffee, and find some peace.

It also makes it the perfect place to have a meeting.

Not to mention, the chairs and booths accommodate my body size.

It's just past six at night. Commuters are making their way back home outside, a few stumbling in for a cup of caffeine before they probably head off to their workout classes. One of my favorite things to do is lurk in the shadows in the back, watching, hearing what people order, seeing what kind of twist they're going to put on their coffee.

My phone, resting on the table in front of me, dings with a text message. Casually sipping my coffee, I lift up my phone to see a text from Hutton.

> **Hutton:** Uh, did you see this article? [Link] Graydon St. John Owes Everything to His Father

Bristling with immediate anger, I click on the link and skim the article, letting my eyes linger on quotes from my dad telling the reporter how he's the one who raised me into the man I am today. How he's the reason I'm succeeding on the field because of the countless hours he's spent practicing with me. He's the reason I have such a level head on my shoulders. And he's the reason why I grew up in such a stable household…

He's got to be fucking kidding me.

My phone dings with another text.

**Hutton:** You should ask for a retraction given that everything in that article is fiction.

Furiously I type out a response.

**Graydon:** The only thing that's going to need retraction is my fist from his face.

**Hutton:** Probably not the best approach.

**Graydon:** He's taking credit for everything I did to get to where I am.

**Hutton:** I know, man. I'm sorry, but I thought it would be best if you saw it before you were approached about his words.

I wipe my hand over my face and take a deep breath, attempting to calm my anger even though I know it won't help, because this…this is overstepping. This is the kind of shit that pushes me over the edge.

This is what turns me into a goddamn beast, ready to sink my claws into the next victim that attempts to talk to me, because how the fuck dare he, after everything he's put me through. After the neglect, the passing me off, the…the…

The door to the coffeehouse opens, and Gretchen walks in.

Fuck, she's here.

I stuff my phone away and clench my teeth, keeping the anger pulsing through me at bay while I take her in.

She is wearing a pair of dangerously high high heels, a black pencil skirt, and a purple blouse tucked in at her waist, and her hair is curled, looking fresh like she just got it done, but I know that's not the case because she works more hours than most. Somehow, she is just able to keep it looking like that. Her tight expression is framed by her intense makeup, dark bronzer, and long lashes.

One look at her and you know she busts balls for a living.

The door opens again, and I catch Maple walking in, hands clasped together, looking around nervously with her teeth pulling on the corner of her mouth.

She is not in her zoo uniform, and my eyes trail up her short legs, which are encased in a pair of yoga pants that flare toward her ankles. Looking at her side profile, my eyes land on her round, pert ass before trailing up to the tight white V-neck shirt that molds around her chest. Her hair is pulled back still, but instead of a tight ponytail, she's let it hang loose in a clip in the back, a few tendrils of hair framing her face.

Jesus, she really is fucking beautiful.

This is going to make me sound like an ass, but given my status as an athlete, I've seen my fair share of beautiful women, many of them offering up whatever the hell I want. I've taken a few bites, but nothing has interested me...ever.

But there is something about Maple.

Something different.

Her features are soft while innocence radiates from her as she fidgets, looking nervous and unsure. But there is also a toughness to her, an underlying ability to stand up for herself or, better yet, the things she cares about.

And that's attractive. So goddamn attractive that she catches my attention, a lot.

More than she should.

She catches my attention the minute I walk through those zoo gates and I find her attempting to plaster on a smile even though I know she can't stand me. Even though...I make her cry.

Jesus Christ, seeing those watery eyes, it nearly broke me, though I maintained a calm, unfazed exterior. I don't like upsetting her the way I did, but there is just something inside me, something that can't stop my mouth from saying hurtful things, something that keeps my expression emotionless.

Hell, who am I kidding, I know exactly what that something is. It's the shield I have raised whenever I interact with anyone. Given my past, those shields have been firmly set, never to be lifted so I won't ever get hurt again.

Instead, I just hurt innocent people like Maple.

Maple, who...who...Well, it doesn't matter because I don't have any goddamn interest in starting anything romantic with anyone.

I fuck when I need to expel leftover adrenaline, but that's about it.

And I'm not about to fuck around with Maple, despite how attracted I am to her.

She's not someone you screw and leave cold in bed. She has *relationship* written all over her. She's perfectly innocent and beautiful and doesn't need an unruly asshole disrupting her life more than I already am.

I watch carefully as she accidentally bumps into Gretchen, apologizes, and then pauses as she recognizes her. They exchange pleasantries, Maple clearly trying to be kind while Gretchen is terse and all business.

Their personalities could not be more opposite...or their attire, for that matter.

They both order drinks, then continue to look around for me before Gretchen pulls out her phone and texts.

I glance down at my screen, looking at her message.

**Gretchen:** You here?

**Graydon:** Back left corner.

When she reads my response, she looks up at me. She rolls her eyes and points in my direction to Maple, who's holding an iced tea.

I remain where I am as they approach.

"You could have said something," Gretchen says as she takes a seat but does not get comfortable. No, she's one high-heeled step away from ditching us, on to the next thing on her to-do list.

"Why are you in the shadows? That was creepy when you came into view." Maple takes a seat, and a wave of lavender hits me all at once, her scent infiltrating my peaceful coffee aroma.

She must have taken a shower before meeting up with us because once again, she smells amazing. I don't blame her—if I had to hang out with those birds all day, I'd do the same thing. Hell, I'm there for a few hours, and I feel the need to scrub myself raw.

"Don't like to be recognized," I answer as I lift my cup of coffee to my lips.

"Well, it's weird." Maple hangs her bag on the side of her chair and then crosses one leg over the other before taking a sip of her iced tea.

Gretchen looks between us, those cunning eyes attempting to understand the dynamic between me and Maple. She doesn't need to think long and hard, as it's clear we don't get along.

Maple confirmed it after calling me an ass twice yesterday before she made me wash fucking flamingo water bowls again. I swear she did that just to piss me off.

"Let's get to the point." Gretchen sets her drink on the table. "You two want to start a social media profile together?"

"Her idea." I nod at Maple, who glares at me.

She clears her throat and turns to Gretchen with a smile. "Yes, it was. You see, the athlete I've been paired with dislikes the program he's in, and therefore it's made things rather difficult." Gretchen flashes me a disappointed glare, but I shrug it off, because really, at this point, I don't give two shits. "And I thought that maybe we could make the most of this plan by doing things a little differently than what was originally laid out."

"So you don't want him representing you at fundraising events and bringing awareness?"

"Oh no, that will still happen."

I grumble under my breath while Maple continues, "But I was thinking that maybe it could be an even trade. Why not make the most of it by bringing more attention to both of our causes? We want to make the Foghorns seem more approachable and well-liked, and create more love for the flamingos, so why not do both simultaneously?" She takes a deep breath and says, "I thought we could make a social media account that can benefit both of us. It can show Graydon helping out at the zoo with little snippets here and there, and it can show me learning around the football field."

Gretchen leans back in her chair, bringing her drink with her as she eyes Maple over the rim. "You want to learn about football?"

"I mean, not really. I couldn't care less about the sport, but he couldn't care less about flamingos, so I just thought it was an even trade."

At least she's honest.

Gretchen moves her jaw back and forth, mulling over the idea. When her eyes land on me, she says, "And you're good with this?"

"If she's going to torture me, might as well torture her."

"Mature," Maple says before sipping her drink.

"And who will be running the social media?"

"Me." Maple raises her hand.

Disbelief in her expression, Gretchen runs her eyes over Maple. "You?"

"Yes." She nods, not looking even the slightest bit confident. "I'm quite knowledgeable with the social media."

"With *the* social media?" Gretchen questions.

"Yes." Maple gulps, a telltale sign that she's lying.

"Let me see your accounts."

Maple bristles and says, "That's neither here nor there. I think we should have you approve the name of our joint account, and we can move ahead with the plan. Let's be honest, the fact that we could get the big guy to agree on something is a miracle in and of itself. We don't want to lose such an opportunity over semantics."

Gretchen glances down at her watch, her lips pursed, and then, to my surprise, says, "Fine."

"Fine as in we can do it?" Maple asks, looking far too excited.

"Yes, but don't make me regret this. Anything posted must be mutually agreed upon and must show Graydon in a good light."

"What about me?" Maple asks.

Gretchen waves her hand dismissively. "Your reputation doesn't matter."

Maple's expression morphs into a deep scowl. "I beg your pardon, but I'd say my reputation does matter. I have a board of directors who'd be very unhappy with me if I showed up on social media looking like a deranged psycho bird lady."

"Might want to cool it on the flamingo fan fiction then," I say, taking a sip of my drink, only to have Maple whip her scowling gaze in my direction.

"I do not write flamingo fan fiction."

"Could have fooled me with all the personality facts you were laying down the other day." I raise a brow. "Martha Stewart thirst traps..."

Insulted, she sits taller. "Pardon me for wanting you to feel connected to the birds."

"Yeah, not interested."

Gretchen's eyes bounce between us, a small smile tugging on her lips.

"What?" I ask her.

She shakes her head. "Nothing."

"You're going to clam up now? You have an opinion about everything. So I repeat: What?"

Her smile grows wider. "You know, I don't care what you name the social media account." She stands and gathers her things. "I think this is a brilliant plan. Keep me updated. I can't wait to see how this turns out."

Then she takes off, without another word.

After a few seconds, Maple huffs out an annoyed breath. "What a waste of time. That could have been resolved over text." She glances off toward where Gretchen retreated and then brings her attention back to me. "Why was she smiling? It seemed unnatural."

Her assessment makes me want to chuckle, but I hold back. Don't want to give her the impression that we can bond over someone like Gretchen.

Or bond at all, really.

No, I need to keep my distance, as much as I can afford.

"Are we good here?" I ask while her eyes dart to mine.

"Are we good here? Umm, I don't know, are we?"

I shrug. "Seems like we got permission. Not sure we need to do much more."

She leans forward on the table that's between us. "Not sure we need to do much more? Um, don't you think we need to talk this through? Don't you think we need to come up with a plan? A schedule? Maybe limits?"

"You looking for a safe word?" I ask her, causing her to blush in embarrassment.

"What? No. I wasn't. That's not what—"

"You can unclutch the pearls," I say, her flustered look nearly making me smile. "Just send me a schedule." I start to stand, but she holds out her hand.

"Hold on a second." Sitting taller, she continues, "Contrary to what you might think, I'm not your personal assistant, therefore I'm not going to just send you a schedule. We can sit here, look at our calendars together, and work out something that favors us both."

That's where you're wrong, because the longer I sit here, smelling whatever heavenly scent you're wearing, staring at your drop-dead gorgeous face, the more likely it is that my shields will fucking weaken.

And I can't have that.

"I'm late for something else."

"What can you possibly be late for when you're the one who scheduled this appointment?"

"Dinner," I answer.

"With someone?"

"Yeah, myself." I stand and take down the rest of my drink before setting it in the empty dishes tray.

Time to get the hell out of here.

I move past her, but clearly not fast enough, as she quickly gathers her stuff and plasters her body right next to mine, her lavender scent wrapping around me like a vine.

I glance down at her in mocking distaste. "What are you doing?"

"I'm late for dinner too. Why don't we just be late together?"

"I eat alone, Flamingo Girl."

She moves around me, placing her hand on my chest. When my eyes gaze down at her touch and back up to her eyes, they widen in fear as she quickly removes her hand and clears her throat.

Nerves get the best of her vocal cords, but it doesn't stop her from saying what she wants to say. "Don't...don't call me that. My name is Maple. Maple Baker. And I believe you should respect that, because even though you're here to help me, I'm...I'm here to help you too. I think there should be some respect passed between the two of us."

"You have to earn my respect," I say, moving past her and out the door of the coffeehouse.

She's trailing right behind, catching up to my long strides as I make my way to my favorite sandwich shop a few blocks down.

"Well, you have to earn mine too," she says, her voice still shaky. "And right now, you...you deserve the same amount of respect as a...as a bottom dweller."

"Is that supposed to insult me?" I ask as I look both ways before crossing the street.

She trips over the sidewalk, and I almost hold out my hand to help her, but she catches herself, still stumbling to keep up.

"What is your problem?" she shouts. Her voice is loud enough to gather the attention of other people. When they see who she's talking to, I immediately notice the whispering between strangers.

Great.

"Keep your fucking voice down," I say, just as realization crosses her eyes, an evil glint in her pupils.

Fuck.

"I said, what is your problem, Graydon St. John?" Her voice is nearly shouting again as someone takes their phone out and starts recording.

Double fuck.

I turn to her, lean in close, and whisper, "Keep your voice down and we can meet up another time to go over the schedule."

Whispering, she says, "I want dinner tonight, you pay, and to go over schedules while we eat, or I will shout to the rooftops just how much of an asshole you are."

I grind my teeth, irritation spiking up the back of my neck because she's got me.

The last thing I need right now is some asshole to capture a viral moment of me on the streets of San Francisco acting like a dick to a petite blond with a charming disposition. That will guarantee me a visit to Keenan's office, which will grant me a call from my dad.

Can't have that.

I can't.

Just hearing his voice makes my skin crawl.

So, I grit my teeth and say, "Fine."

A smile lights up her face as she says, "Great! I prefer Italian."

# CHAPTER 8
# MAPLE

VICTORY!

If I wasn't trying to remain cool, calm, and collected, I would jump up in the air, my arm leading the way in a fist pump, only to land in the splits while whooping it up like I just won the lottery.

Because…AHA!

Got him.

I freaking got him.

He thought he could mess with me?

Ohhhh no.

He has no idea who he's—

"Are you fucking coming?" he asks, pulling me out of my thoughts.

"Oh, yeah, sorry." I tuck away my smile and follow the grumbling giant next to me as he leads me to our dinner location.

It took him a second to find a place, mumbling the entire time about wanting a sandwich, but I didn't give in. I said Italian, and we're getting Italian.

God, it's so freeing, knowing that I beat him at his own game, and in all honesty, I wouldn't have had to go to such lengths if he didn't act like what we had to talk about wasn't important. Because it is.

I'm a planner. I like to know what's going on. I don't think it was asking too much to have him figure out a quick plan with me, but he refused, and that meant I had to take matters into my own hands.

At first, the plan was to follow him and sit on him until he listened to me, but that turned into a free meal, which, I mean, don't mind if I do.

He turns right down a block, then stops in front of a red storefront and pulls open a door to a quaint restaurant. A matching red awning hangs over a three-table seating area outside with wrought-iron bistro tables. When I step inside, I'm immediately assaulted by the smell of garlic and tomatoes just as a hostess greets us with a charming smile.

"Two?" she asks, her eyes fully taking in the height of Graydon.

I don't blame her. Even if he wasn't famous, it would be hard not to glance his way.

A single one of his pecs is the size of my head, he towers over everyone, and I'm fairly certain, every hour, on the hour, he swallows at least four eggs whole, shell and all.

"Yes," he says in a gruff voice.

"Would you like to sit outside?"

I'm about to say how lovely that would be since it's a nice day out and it's not foggy or raining, but Graydon quickly says, "Your most private table, please."

Okay, I know he's saying that because he doesn't want people listening in on our conversation, but for some reason, the rasp of his voice when he says "private" sends a shiver down my spine.

Sounds so...naughty.

Like something scandalous will happen in the privacy of said table while consuming an immaculate plate of eggplant parm.

But you and I both know that's not the case. Nope. The only thing scandalous between me and Graydon will be the sharing of calendar details and going over the ground rules of our new social media endeavor. And correct me if I'm wrong, but there is nothing scandalous about that, other than the possibility of revealing an appointment he doesn't want me to see. Like...laser hair removal.

"Of course," the hostess says as she leads us to the back of the restaurant, where the sound of a small voice pulls me from my thoughts.

"Graydon. Graydon, I love you."

I glance to the right where a little girl with curly hair is bouncing up and down in her booth, waving dramatically for Graydon's attention.

I wince, gearing up for the kid to get the cold shoulder, but to my surprise, Graydon's shoulders visibly relax as he heads over to the girl's booth and then squats next to her.

Holy. Shit. He knows how to be nice?

"What's up, little lady?" Graydon asks, giving the girl a ruffle on the top of the head. "Can I get my picture taken with you?"

Stunned, the girl just nods, unable to form words.

Graydon slips his arm over the girl's shoulder and then faces her parents, who are both in awe as well. They take a picture of the two of them before Graydon turns back to the girl and grips her shoulder.

He picks up the girl's fork and taps her uneaten broccoli.

"Listen, little lady, I'm going to need you to eat these vegetables, okay? It's important. If you want to get big and strong like me, you better not skip out on this stuff."

The girl nods, mouth still agape.

"Good." He stands now. "I'll let you get back to your dinner. Have a good night."

He offers the parents a wave as they profusely thank him.

Me...I stand there stunned.

Probably more stunned than the family because what the hell did I just witness?

Graydon can be...nice?

Not just nice, but actually go out of his way to be kind?

Consider me floored.

"You coming?" Graydon asks in a grumbly voice as the hostess leads us up a set of stairs.

"Uh, yeah," I say absentmindedly, still trying to process.

When we reach the top, we are met with a private room and a booth positioned toward the front of the building, bathed in candlelight.

Oh boy.

I think he ordered us the lover's special.

Before us is a red booth with a dark mahogany table. Battery-operated votives softly illuminate the area, while grapevines dance along the back of the booth and along a partition that closes the table off from the rest of the restaurant.

He wanted private. Well, he got it.

We both take a seat, him adjusting the table so it's closer to me while the hostess places menus down in front of us.

"Your server will be with you shortly."

"Thank you," I say as she walks off, shutting the partition a few inches more. "Well." I look around. "This is. . .intimate."

He stares down at his menu, scouring the beer and wine list.

"So, you and that little girl, that was really—"

"Do not say 'nice.'"

"Why not?"

"Because."

Well, that answers that.

"I just wasn't expecting—"

"Drop it, Maple."

Ohhh-kay. I can see that he can converse with others, just not with me. Noted.

I bring my attention to the menu, looking for the wine list because it seems like I'm going to need some to get through this evening. "Going to order something alcoholic?" I ask.

"Several," he answers, never lifting his gaze.

"Maybe you can hold back on inebriation until we're done with our scheduling and planning?"

"Not making any promises," he says as a server joins us.

"Hello." She sets down some bread on our table as well as some water. "Can I get you started with something to drink?"

"Guinness," he says, making me cringe.

Yikes, that's some thick beer.

"Tall," he adds.

Looks like I'm going to need to work fast. Then again, his body mass is large, so he might be able to guzzle down three of those and not even feel a hint of a buzz.

"And you?" the server asks.

"Um, could I have a glass of your chardonnay, please?"

She nods and takes off.

When I glance up at Graydon, he studies me for a moment before turning back to his menu.

"What?" I ask. When he doesn't respond, I nudge my foot against his leg, which causes him to raise one brow. "Why were you just looking at me like that?"

"Surprised is all," he answers.

"Surprised about what?"

"That you drink."

"Do you think I'm not old enough or something?"

"No, you just seem like a goody-two-shoes is all."

"How so?" I ask, slightly offended.

He leans back in the booth, assessing me. "You just give off that kind of vibe."

"Well, I'm not. I've done some pretty crazy things. And I've gotten drunk several times."

"Wow, several?" He presses his hand to his chest. "Jesus, I better watch out."

My eyes narrow. "You're so...rude."

"Would you rather I fake it?"

"I'm sure you know how. You've probably learned from every woman you've ever been with."

The insult flies past my lips before I can stop it, and I almost let out a burst of laughter, because man, that was a quick one. An old one-two punch I wasn't expecting to escape my mouth. Then again, Graydon St. John has been able to get under my skin faster than anyone, which means I think he pulls the snarky out of me.

I'm half tempted to pull my phone out and text Everly, let her know that I just burned Graydon to the point of being—

"If they were faking it, it's only because they couldn't handle the real thing, something I'm sure you know plenty about."

My mouth falls open in shock, my brain short-circuiting because... how?

I thought I had him.

I thought—

"Trying to show me what you can offer with your mouth open like that?" He shakes his head. "You're going to have to pop that jaw wider if you want any chance...*Baker*."

I snap my mouth shut, my eyes stinging with tears. It's not because he hurt me, but because he angers me.

He angers me so much that the back of my neck heats up, my stomach twists in knots, and my body goes into fight mode, something I rarely feel.

And I don't like it.

I don't like the way it makes me feel.

I don't like the spike of adrenaline. It's not...it's not for me.

Before I came back to San Francisco, I led a very simple life. A life where I slept under a blanket of stars every night, where I shared common interests and goals with the people surrounding me, where I spent every day with people who didn't insult me but rather praised me for the work I was doing.

So this...this *lack of respect* is so foreign to me that I don't know how to handle it.

But I will be damned if he sees me cry, so I lift my menu and focus on the entrées.

If my stomach wasn't so twisted in knots and my heart racing from adrenaline, I would consider getting the most expensive thing on the menu, along with an appetizer and a dessert since he's paying, but I don't want to prolong this meal any more than I need to.

So a main dish and that's it.

When the server comes back with our drinks, we put in our orders. I go with an eggplant parm, and he picks a pepperoni pizza.

I pick up my wine and take a large gulp before setting the thin glass back on the table, my mind reeling with how he can be so nice to a child out of the blue but can't treat me with the same respect. And to be honest, I hate that for a moment, a very brief moment, I saw him as a decent human being. I hate that I saw a kind side to him, because before that it was almost easy to just chalk up his behavior to a personality that makes him a constant dick to society. But that's not the case; he's just a constant dick to me.

He leans back, twisting his pint glass as he stares me down.

"What?" I finally ask, breaking under his gaze.

"Are we going to proceed with why we're here, or are we just going to stare at each other all night?"

"I'd rather stab my eyes out," I say as I remove my phone from my purse and pull up my calendar.

"Hey, you were the one who wanted to have dinner with me. This is the company you chose."

"Way to make it unbearable."

"I can make it worse if you want," he taunts.

"Please, restrain yourself and pull out your phone."

He reaches into his pocket and retrieves his phone, unlocks it, then shoves his calendar in my direction. I partly want to push it right back at him and tell him to work in tandem with me, but honestly, what's the point?

I glance down at his calendar and start pressing on the days that have events highlighted on them. I half expect them to be meetings, but they're all training sessions and his zoo meetups.

"I thought you'd be busier." Pure observation on my part.

"I will be when the season starts. So get in your precious time now."

"You don't do any like...commercials or filming?"

"Funny thing," he says before taking a sip of his beer. "No one wants you slinging their product around when your team is trash."

"Well, that makes sense," I say as I scroll through his schedule and mine. "What do you have planned for me? Because how you plan to teach me will depend on how often I want to be at your training facility."

"I have to be at your zoo, so you should match it with my football."

"I can hardly see how they're the same thing," I deadpan.

"You're right. Mine is more interesting." He sets his beer down and pulls his bottom lip over his top lip, wiping away the foam from his beer.

I punch down the irritation that spikes up my spine. "If you actually have me training, it's going to be much harder for me to keep up, whereas you just have to—"

"Wash dishes? My hands get pruney quickly, and you haven't taken it easy on me."

I press my fingers to my brow and say, "Can you just...God, can you just be nice for one second?"

"Did you want to work over a schedule, or did you want me to be nice?"

"Can't you do both?"

"Never been good at multitasking." He takes another drink of his beer, this one bigger.

"Fine, be a jerk." I start typing away on his phone. "What time do you want me at your facility?"

"Whatever time it says in my phone."

I check out the time, and my eyes nearly bug out of my head. "Some of these are at six in the morning—like be there at six."

"Exactly."

My nostrils flare because I know this is just him being a jerk and trying to get back at me for something that wasn't even my idea in the first place. Trust me, if I had a choice in all of this, I wouldn't have asked for him to be an advocate for my flamingos, but here we are.

"Fine." I'm going to have to talk to Phil about my schedule to make these times work, and the early mornings are going to be a rude shock to my system, but a deal is a deal, so I plug in some dates for the next month and then do the same for him, including the fundraiser events.

"What are you adding?"

"We have a board of directors event this coming weekend that you need to attend."

"Says who?"

"Says Gretchen," I shoot back. "It's on the list of events that you haven't plugged into your calendar."

"I thought those were optional."

I shake my head. "Nope. Mandatory." I push his phone back to him and smile. "Looks like you'll be seeing me almost every day for the foreseeable future." I circle my finger around my head. "Get used to this face, because I'll be everywhere, even in your dreams."

"More like nightmares," he mumbles.

"Yeah, well, you're going to be in my nightmares too."

He lifts a brow in my direction. "Great comeback."

I lean back in my chair, planning an exit strategy. I could ask for my food to go because sharing a meal with this man is the last thing I want to do, but guess who is just stubborn enough to stick around to make things uncomfortable?

This girl.

If I have to eat my meal in silence, I will.

I will sit here until every last bite of my meal is consumed.

And that's what we do.

We don't talk.

We just sip our drinks, quietly avoiding eye contact.

I grab a piece of bread and put some butter on it while he picks up his phone and starts looking through some emails.

I cross one leg over the other, studying him, wondering what possessed him to become such an asshole over the years of his life.

How old is he, anyway?

I lift my phone and do a quick internet search of Graydon St. John. One of the first pictures I see is of him with his shirt off, the same one Everly showed me. I ignore it and look up his age.

Thirty. Huh, my age.

Doesn't seem like he's thirty. From the crinkles next to his eyes—which most definitely are not laugh lines—I would have said maybe mid-thirties. Then again, doesn't football age people?

Next thing I notice is his net worth.

Over $50 million!

What?

My eyes shoot up to where he's sipping his beer, reading something on his phone.

Uh, he's definitely buying dinner tonight. He probably makes as much in a minute as I do in a year.

I scan farther down and see that he was born in California, and his dad is a famous football player.

Huh, didn't know that.

"Your dad played football?" I ask, causing his eyes to shoot up to mine.

"What are you doing? Are you googling me?" His eyes turn dark and menacing as his paw of a hand pushes my phone down to the table where he can see what's on my screen. His gaze lifts to mine, and for a moment,

I feel like he's about to flip the table as fire spews out of his eyes. "Don't fucking google me. If you have a question about my life, ask me."

Flustered, I exit the Google search and say, "I'm sorry, I just...I was curious about your age."

"Thirty," he answers.

"Yes, I saw that."

"You could have asked."

"You've been a jerk the whole time we've been here, so I'm sorry if I didn't want to talk to you."

His jaw grows tighter. "If you have a question about me, ask. Don't fucking look me up."

"Okay," I say, feeling embarrassed.

Heat trickles up the back of my neck as I can feel a bout of tears spring to my eyes.

No.

Do not cry.

Not in front of him.

He doesn't deserve to see how his words, his demeanor, and his overall assholery affect me.

I blink back the sting of tears and keep my head tilted down, my eyes studying the grain of the table as silence stretches between us.

He doesn't seem to be moving either, and if I were even remotely brave enough, I would look up to see what he's doing, but instead, I keep my eyes locked on the table. If I look at him, I know these tears will flow over, and I'm doing everything in my power to keep them at bay.

Why is he so...angry? Why does it matter if I look him up on the internet? He's a public figure, there are probably a ton of things written up about him, and yet I get chastised for trying to figure out his age.

He's just so...awful.

And even though I want to stick it to him and make him suffer through this dinner, I think it's going to do more damage to my self-esteem and confidence if I stay.

Thankfully, the server brings our food to the table, and because I need to get the hell out of here, I ask, "Um, can I actually get a to-go box?"

The server pauses and looks between the two of us, as if trying to gauge the issue. Good luck, lady, bet you can't even come close to guessing what's going on here. Smartly, she nods and delivers a box almost immediately. If I were paying, I would leave her a nice tip just for how speedy that was.

"Thank you," I say before she leaves, and I put my meal in the box as quickly as I can.

All the while, I hold back my tears, training my mind to focus on the smell of the food and not the embarrassment rolling through me. When I'm done filling my to-go box, I stand and fit my purse over my shoulder. "Well, it's been a pretty shitty evening, and to be honest, I don't want to share air with you any more than I have to."

His eyes are cast down at his food as he picks up a piece of pizza. "Same," he says as he bites into a meat-loaded slice.

What I wouldn't give to have the courage to kick him in the shin, right here and now. If he says one more mean thing, I very well might.

"Great, at least we can agree on something. I'll be sure to start some social media accounts under Flock and Tackle tonight, and tomorrow, while we're at your football thing, we can take a picture for our profile and introduce ourselves."

"Just take a picture now."

"Honestly, not in the mood. I don't want to be scowling in my picture."

"Can't make any promises that I won't tomorrow."

*Hold back your foot.*

*Do not kick him, Maple.*

*Do not freaking kick him.*

"All right, then, please don't have a good night. I hope you burn your tongue on your pizza."

"Don't trip on your way down the stairs."

"Dick."

"Bird lover."

I look over my shoulder as I walk away, only to catch him glance at my ass on the way out.

Ugh, disgusting.

# CHAPTER 9
# GRAYDON

**Coach Dickwad:** She's not to leave your sight. If she gets into any trouble, you're the one who'll pay the consequences.

I STARE DOWN AT HIS text, wanting to reach through the phone and strangle him myself.

None of this was my idea.

Not a single second of it. And here I am, not only caught up in some insane social media ploy, but now I have to babysit as well?

Christ!

Gretchen must have let Keenan know about what was going on, because I got his text this morning, warning me about making smart decisions.

As if I need the warning.

Maybe he should worry about making smart decisions as a coach and not worry about me.

After Maple bolted last night, which thank God she did us both a favor, I sent her a quick text as to where to park, where to meet me, and what to wear.

I considered taking it easy on her, giving her a general understanding of football and my position, but then when Coach Keenan started going off about how it was insane that I needed my own social media campaign to make the Foghorns look better because I couldn't just follow instructions, I decided to ditch my plan and give her the works.

Yup…she's training with me today. Let's see if she can keep up.

I lean against the stone wall, watching as a sedan pulls past security and finds a parking spot. That has to be her because it's the only car in the parking lot that is at least ten years old.

Although, mine is about eight, so it's not like I can say much. I just don't care to spend my money like my teammates do.

I watch as she steps out of her car and slings a bag over her shoulder before locking up.

Under the parking lot lights, I catch a glimpse of her in a pair of leggings that cling to every inch of her legs, making them seem longer than they actually are. Her tight-fitting tee shows off her full chest but grossly masks it with a fucking flamingo on the front—of course. Her long, blond hair is pulled back into a tight ponytail like normal, swishing across her shoulders as she makes her way across the parking lot.

And for a second, and I mean just a second because it's all I'll allow, my eyes wander over her curvaceous body and the way her hips swell just past her narrow waist, sexily swaying with every step. Then there's the slenderness of her neck, unmarked, ready to be claimed, while the fullness of her lips nearly drives me to the point of wanting to take a few more seconds to stare longer.

But it's a fleeting moment because as she approaches, it's hard to miss the scowl on her brow and the disdain for me in her body language.

She might be sexy as fuck, but the feeling is mutual.

When she reaches me, I dangle a lanyard out in front of her and say, "This is for you. It's your key card to get into the facility. You're allowed to open the door, but you are to wait by it until I come to retrieve you."

She takes the key card and studies it for a moment before slipping it in her bag. I push off the wall and flash my own key to the door before opening it for her.

We're at the practice facility, a large dome field with training equipment, a weight room, and everything you could possibly need when it comes to catering to a shitty-ass football team that hasn't even made it to one playoff game in over a decade.

I will say this, though—even though we don't win, our facilities are top-notch.

State-of-the-art training room with every physical therapy device you can think of, which is great for me as I start pushing toward the older end of football players. The kitchen is fucking phenomenal, and I always stop by for at least two meals and snacks. The weight room has everything I need and more. And the practice field is a soft turf that doesn't leave you scratching at the end of practice.

For a losing team, we have it pretty good.

Kind of feel bad for someone like Maple, who has to work in a building that smells like bird shit and seafood.

"This way," I say, nodding toward the field, where I plan on warming up before hitting the weight room.

She follows me closely, her eyes scanning every inch of the facility as I lead the way to an empty practice field, which is just the way I like it. No one likes to wake up as early as I do, especially when we're not in season, so it's the perfect time to get my work in without others bothering me.

"Wow, I expected a whole lot more people."

"Just us," I say as I walk over to my zoo water bottle and take a sip. I watch her study the water bottle, the smallest of smirks on her lips. She probably loves that I use the damn thing, and not that I want to admit it, but it's a pretty nice water bottle. "Don't think much of it. It was left in my truck, and I forgot my other one." At least that's what I'm telling myself...and her.

She grumbles under her breath, then sets her things down on one of the benches that line the field. While she gets situated, I take a peek at her ass in her leggings because, well...I apparently have no self-control, and she has a really nice ass. She fishes through her purse for a few seconds, then pulls her phone out.

Turning toward me just in time for me to lift my gaze without getting caught, she says, "Before we get started, we need to take a picture so I can make a post."

"What kind of picture?" I ask.

"Well, it can be a selfie, or it can be a video of us waving, or we can stand side by side, not touching, and stare at the camera like vampires. You tell me what the almighty Graydon St. John wants to do."

Sassy this morning.

"Glad you have my title correct." She rolls her eyes. "Just do a quick selfie and get it over with."

"Are you going to smile?"

"Do you want me to smile?"

"Do you know how to smile?"

"Sneering is more my forte."

"I've noticed. But for social media and the image you're trying to portray for your team, maybe you can muster up, oh, I don't know, a smirk?"

I grumble under my breath and then say, "Fine." I take her phone and pull up the camera. I snap a picture of us, then toss the phone back to her. Simple.

She fumbles to catch it as she says, "Wait, hold on. I wasn't even smiling." She pulls up the picture, and I lean over to find that it's blurry, her mouth is open, and I'm not even looking in the right direction.

Oops.

She stares up at me, irritation laced in her expression. "Do it again, and this time, count to three before taking it so all parties are ready."

I take the phone back from her and hold it out, attempting to get her in the frame. "You're going to have to get closer."

"I'd rather not."

"Do you want this to be a weird picture or something you can use?" I ask.

"Fine, but don't think this is me lowering my defenses. I don't like you, and I need you to know that."

"Feeling is mutual, Baker."

"I don't see why." She moves in closer to me. "I haven't been rude to you."

"You made me wash dishes."

She turns to me, disgust in her expression. "Oh my God, the famous, rich football player had to wash some flamingo dishes. Yes, all the more reason to hate a nice lady who was attempting to welcome you into the flamingo family." She leans in and sniffs me, causing me to take a step back. What the hell is she doing? "Yup, just as I suspected, you smell like an entitled ass."

My eyes narrow. "You know nothing about me."

"I know enough," she huffs and then steps in closer. "Now take the picture. If I stand too close to you for too long, my skin might melt off my face."

The image that conjures up in my head makes me smirk, and it stays there long enough for me to take a picture of us both and then hand back her phone.

Skin melting off her face. . . if only.

"Now, was that so hard?" she asks as she pulls a tripod out of her bag and then sets it up.

"What are you doing now?"

"Gathering content. What does it look like I'm doing?"

"You're going to record us?"

"That's the whole point, Graydon." She sets up her phone and then angles it toward the field. "We're here because we need content. We need to put on a show, demonstrating to the people that flamingos and football can mix in the best way possible. I'm not just here to torture myself by being in your presence."

The insults are flying this morning. That's fine, I've heard worse. Hell, I've said worse.

She hits record, then moves next to me, her lavender scent floating in my direction. I hate that I like the way she smells. It's annoying, because it makes me want to lean in closer just to get another whiff.

"What are we doing?" she asks, looking far too ready.

I snap out of my thoughts and look her up and down, gauging her athletic ability. This could go two ways, and we're about to find out which way it's going to go.

"Warming up," I say. "Down and back, let's go."

"Down and back where?" she asks as I take off.

"The field," I call out and leave her in my dust.

"Wait, don't you think it would be better if we did this together?"

I ignore her and run my way down the field. When I hit one end zone, I turn around and find her at the fifty, her little legs no match for my long ones, her arms pumping at her sides, a steady effort on her end that doesn't even come close to matching mine.

When I hit the other side of the end zone, she does the same, so I go in for one more lap and end up finishing right behind her.

"You going to go down again?" I ask.

"Uh, no." She puts her hands above her head, catching her breath.

"Does that mean I get to say no when you ask me to do things?"

Her eyes narrow, and to her credit, she turns and takes off down the field, jogging all the way to the end and back. While I wait, I continue to warm up my legs by performing some dynamic stretches, focusing on the drills that my trainer has given me.

"You're behind," I say as she gets close again.

"Maybe you can...wait...for a second," she says, breathless.

I shake my head. "I don't have time to wait. I'm on a schedule. So... keep up."

"Jerk," she mutters as she starts copying the way I open my legs up and step to the side. "What the hell is this doing?"

"Waking up the hip flexors, getting us ready for the weight room."

"Weight room?" Her eyes widen. "Like...lifting weights?"

"That's what usually happens in a weight room."

"But I've never lifted weights before."

"Have you ever worked out before?" I ask. It comes off more dickish than I intended it to, but I'm genuinely curious so I know how hard I should push her.

"I've done some things," she answers. "Definitely not to your extent. But I have to lift things at the zoo."

So no lifting experience.

My plan to be her own personal hell slowly subsides because even though I want this experience to die as quickly as it was formed, I'm also not going to put someone at risk of hurting themselves. Looks like I'll have to take it easy.

"What's that look for?" she asks as I start shuffling side to side. She's trying to copy me but is having a hard time keeping up.

"What look?"

"Like you were...feeling pity for me."

"Not pity, just realizing that I can't do what I wanted to do with you today."

"And what did you want to do?"

I do knee-highs, and she does the same. "Put you through my workout."

"Oh, I'm doing the workout."

I roll my eyes. "With no experience, you're not doing the workout. It wouldn't be safe."

"I'm not some incompetent peasant that you found on the streets." She walks up to me, determination in her eyes as she flexes her bicep. "Look at that muscle."

I stare down at her slender arm, holding back my smile.

"Go ahead, feel it. It's steel. Cold, hard steel." When I don't move, she thrusts her arm closer. "Go ahead, don't be shy."

Christ.

With a roll of my eyes, I reach out with my forefinger and thumb and I grip her muscle, squeezing down on it.

"Ouch." She shakes her arm free of me.

"Yup, cold, hard, *bendable* steel. Never felt a muscle like it before," I say with an eye roll.

"All muscle is going to bend like that when you push down on it," she counters.

"Really?" I ask with a quirk of my brow. "Want to test that theory?"

"Why yes, I do. I'll show you." She gestures to me. "Go ahead, flex."

I pull back the sleeve of my shirt and flex my arm for her, my bicep bulging into a solid rock right in front of her face, causing her eyes to widen.

"Go ahead, show me how it bends."

Chin held high, she says, "Don't mind if I do."

She steps up and tries to put her forefinger and thumb around my bicep like I did to her, but her hand isn't big enough, and I watch as her expression contorts in disappointment. It doesn't stop her, though, because she wraps her hand around my bicep and attempts to push down, growing frustrated when she doesn't get the right angle.

"If it wasn't so big, I could wrap my hand around it."

"Are you talking about my arm, or something else, Baker?"

Her eyes widen for a moment before narrowing. "Don't be disgusting."

"You're the one who said it."

"Clearly, I'm talking about your bendable bicep."

"It's not bendable."

"Oh yeah? Watch this," she says with a grunt before wrapping both hands around my bicep and lifting her feet off the ground, dangling from my arm. "Is it...bending?"

I do a bicep curl as she hangs off me. “Nope, just getting stronger.”

“Ugh, fine.” She releases me and straightens out her shirt. “Maybe not all muscles bend.”

“Glad we had to go through that to figure it out.” I nod toward the camera that’s still recording us. “At least you’re getting the content you wanted.”

She huffs and then turns off the video. “Are we warmed up or what?”

“We are. Time to hit the weight room.”

# CHAPTER 10
# MAPLE

WHEN I LOOK BACK AT my life one day and think about the choices I made, good and bad, I'll remember this moment as one of the worst.

Sweat is dripping down my face.

My legs are noodles.

I have no power left in my body.

And we have two more sets of overhead presses to complete before we're done.

Graydon has been pacing through this workout like it's a regular walk in the park. He's shifting from one exercise to the next with ease, while I've been dragging my body along, begging and pleading every muscle within me to hold out until I'm in private and I can collapse in shame.

"What, uh…what are those? Twenty-fives?" I ask, trying to seem nonchalant as I engage in gym talk.

Graydon glances over at the two water bottles in my hand that I've been using as weights because the facilities don't carry small enough weights for a lady like me. "They're fifties."

Fifties?

Dear God in heaven.

I'd be lucky to even drag that across the gym floor, let alone have one in each arm and lift them over my head.

Clearing my throat, I say, "Yeah, I'm working up to those." Then I lift my water bottles over my head as we start the second-to-last round.

And it's the most pathetic thing I think I've ever seen.

Us both sitting on angled benches, our backs pressed against the vinyl at a ninety-degree angle, me with my water bottles, bright-red face, and tongue nearly hanging out of my mouth, giving the impression that I'm seconds away from death. Him with his burly chest pushing against his threadbare, soaked T-shirt, his rock-hard arms and massive weights hoisting over his head, acting like the god of the weight room. Quite the scene.

I made sure to get this in the video because in all honesty, it's comical and I'm never one to shy away from honest self-deprecation.

We finish up our set, and I rest the water bottles on the ground, letting my arms have a break while he rests his weights on the ground as well and leans forward on his thighs.

"So this is fun for you?"

"Some days." He then looks over his shoulder at me and asks, "Is cleaning flamingo shit fun for you?"

"No, but it has to be done."

He nods and turns back to focus on the floor in front of him.

Seeing that there might be a moment of peace between us, I ask, "So what does a defensive person really do? Like...what is your position in charge of?"

"I'm a defensive end," he says, keeping his focus on his weights.

"Right. Defensive end. And what does that entail? Like, do you run after people, like someone who catches a ball?"

He glances at me again, and this time, there's a hint of humor in his eyes. And I mean a hint.

"Do you know nothing about football?"

"Zero. And anything I might know is from *Friday Night Lights*, but in real life, I think maybe I've watched a second of a single game ever. There's a ball being thrown to score points, and that's the extent of what I know."

He slowly nods and then picks up his weights. "Last set."

Okay...so we're not going to talk about the game? Good to know.

I grab my water bottles, and then together, we lift the "weights" over our heads, my arms numb to the point that I'm surprised they keep moving up and down because I can't recall telling them to do such a thing.

Exhaustion rips through me as we finish up our workout, my body thanking me for the reprieve from hell.

After the last rep, I dramatically drop the bottles to the ground and let my arms hang to my sides as he gracefully stands with said fifties and puts his weights back on the weight shelf where he got them.

Hope he doesn't ask me to pick up my water bottles, because I don't think I have it in me. I have depleted any and all resources I've stored in my body.

"Time to stretch." He nods toward an open area with extra cushioned mats on the floor and giant rubber bands hanging next to them.

"Do you want a bonus workout that could perhaps involve picking me up and setting me on the mats?"

His razor-sharp eyes fall to mine. "No."

"You sure? Might be a nice opportunity for you."

He doesn't respond to that, instead tugging one of the bands from a hook and handing it to me.

"What's this for?"

"To stretch," he says and then effortlessly gets on the floor, hooks the band over his foot, and lifts his foot toward the ceiling, stretching out his hamstring.

Ugh, looks like I'm going to have to drag my body to the ground on my own.

I stare down at the ground, willing my body to gracefully get into the same position, but every muscle holding my skin and bones together whimpers in pain, begging me to end their misery and never use them again. From squats to lunges to some weird box-jumping thing to more squats to this bench press thing-a-ma-bob to every which way you can move your arm with a weight in your hand. Nothing was left out of today's workout.

Nothing.

It's why when I slowly start to lower my body, attempting to curtsy down to the ground, it instead decides to give out on me, seizing in every which way.

Oh no.

Lady down...

I barely have enough time to pinpoint where I'm landing before I flop straight on top of the chest of the one and only Graydon St. John.

"Oof, fuck, what are you doing?" he asks.

Great question.

The only answer that comes to mind is...death.

I'm dead.

The fish has flopped and has found the end of its life.

There is nothing left inside me.

There is no shame.

There is no humiliation.

There is no...stamina or fucks to give as I lie lifeless on top of Graydon.

Nope, this is where I live now.

This is my new home.

Pull up a potted plant and a picture of a flamingo, because I don't see myself moving in the foreseeable future.

"Hello?" he pokes, trying to get me to answer him.

Mumbling, I say, "I live here now."

"The fuck you do."

To my surprise, he lifts me by the shoulders like I'm a pool noodle and flops me to the side so my head is now right next to his hip.

"Jesus Christ, why aren't you...folding properly?"

I stare up at the fluorescent lights, angels singing to me, pulling me into the heavens where I know I will feel no more pain.

"Is this what death feels like?"

"For fuck's sake," he mutters as he slides away from me, stands, and then looks down at me. "Are you serious right now?"

I blink a few times, his dark gaze breaking me away from my attempt to fly into a safe space where I will no longer feel. "I. . . I don't foresee myself getting up from here. Please tell Phil to find someone worthy enough to look after my pink-feathered friends."

He rolls his eyes and then bends down and drags me by the legs, straightening me out across the mat. Then he lifts one of my ankles, kneels between my legs, and holds one down while pushing the other up.

"What on earth are you doing?" I ask as his entire body crowds the juncture between my thighs. "I tell you death is knocking on my door, rigor mortis firmly taking hold, and you get me into a sexual position?"

His brow cocks up. "I'm stretching you so I don't have to explain to my coach why there's a woman face-planted in our weight room."

"I am not face-planted."

"You will be in a second." He switches legs, making me holler in pain as he stretches the muscles that I thought no longer existed inside me.

"Just leave me for dead. Have them scoop me up with a shovel and deposit me in the back of a garbage truck. Please put my pitiful savings toward a bench that sits in front of the flamingos. And for the love of God, tell Big Hermy he was my favorite."

He rolls his eyes once more and then, in one fell swoop, he turns me on my stomach and starts stretching my quads.

"Mother of God!" I shout, burying my head into the mat, a mat that is probably infested with things like ringworm and imprinted with sweaty man balls. But it's my solace right now, my peace, the only thing keeping me from losing all sense of control.

*Oh, dear sweet mat, please swallow me into your sanctuary where hairy backs and moist ass cracks find solace.*

Graydon spends the next few minutes stretching me out, maneuvering me around like his own personal lump of Play-Doh, and then, when he's done, he lifts me to my feet and holds me by the shoulders, keeping me in place until he finds that I'm steady enough to walk on my own.

"You good?"

I sway for a few moments, and when the darkness around my vision recedes, I slowly nod. "I think so."

He grumbles under his breath and then takes off for the exit, but when I don't follow him, he stops. "For the love of God, keep up."

I take one step forward and feel that my leg can handle it, so I take another, and another, and find myself very slowly walking toward him.

*Thata girl.*

"I told you not to do the fucking workout," he says in a terse voice.

"And I said I could do it, and I did. I did it."

"With water bottles."

"Hey." I point my finger at him. "That was good content, showing people you don't need a state-of-the-art weight room to get in a good workout—water bottles will do the trick."

"Whatever you need to say to make yourself happy."

I reach out and tug on his arm, barely grasping him. "Can you...can you please not walk so fast?"

He sighs but slows his walking, and it makes me think maybe...just maybe, he's not all that bad.

"And you said you worked out," he huffs.

Actually, change of mind. He's bad.

He's the worst.

And I hate him.

He's rude and inconsiderate, and sure, he might have stretched me out and deposited me on my feet, but he's still a jerk, and I hope he steps in gum today.

"I lift things at the zoo. I'm not training to get rammed in the head by another human."

"We don't ram each other in the head."

"Really? Because it seems like you're missing a few brain cells."

"Is that supposed to be funny?"

I mean, I kind of thought it was.

"You tell me."

He jerks his head to the side. "It's not." His lip curls into a snarl, and I fear I might have woken the beast. I blame my exhaustion, mental and physical.

I shall never recover from this.

Never.

He pushes a door open, and we enter a cafeteria where chefs wait behind the counter to serve whoever walks in.

"Two protein smoothies, please. A four-egg omelet with spinach, cheese, and bacon, and a bowl of fruit." He glances at me and asks, "Do you have any allergies?"

"Uh…no."

"Do you want anything else other than a smoothie?"

Any donuts lying around here? Because I know that would truly soothe my battered and beaten soul.

"Um, I think I'm good."

"Want a bacon omelet?"

"I'm a vegetarian."

He pauses for a moment, as if he's recording that information before saying, "Then a cheese omelet? You should have some protein."

"Isn't that what the shake is for?"

"You should have more."

"I'm good." I hold my stomach. Could I actually hold anything down?

He turns back to the people behind the counter and says, "That's it, then."

They nod and get to work as he takes a seat at a nearby table. I follow right behind him and take a seat as well.

"You just have people making you food all the time? That must be nice."

"It is," he says as he leans back in his chair, studying me, those dark eyes penetrating any sort of protective shield I might have up. "Do you want to call this quits?"

"What?" I ask, my brow pulling together.

"You really think you can keep on doing this?"

"It was one day and my first time. I'm sure I can keep doing this." If by "this" he means feeling like a sweaty, slightly ripe noodle, then I *doubt* I can keep doing this. But I'm not a quitter, and I can be quite stubborn when I want to be.

And this...this is a moment where I want "stubborn" to be my middle name.

"You can barely walk, and you have no idea the kind of pain you will be in tomorrow or even the day after that, when you're back out here with me. Just call it like it is—you can't keep up."

"Oh, I can keep up," I say as I lean forward, my body screaming at me for making any movement. "Just...just need to get used to it is all."

Two smoothies are set down in front of us, and we both politely thank the human being who served us, only for me to have to turn my gaze back to the rotten tomato in front of me.

"No amount of torture that you put me through will end this contract between us. And I don't even know why you're trying to end things in the first place."

"Because I don't want to do this," he hisses at me.

"You don't have a freaking choice," I hiss right back. "The sooner you realize that, the better." I get that he doesn't *want* to help me out, but it's not a lifelong commitment. It's a few weeks and then he can just go on with his football-loving life. *What's his deal?* "No matter how much you complain and whine and groan about helping out the freaking flamingos, nothing's going to change. This is it, this is what you have to do, so why don't you just suck it up and be nice?"

"Because that's not who I am."

"Clearly," I say as I throw my hands up to the sky, lean back in my seat, and take a sip of my smoothie. "Oh wow, this is delicious. Is it strawberry banana?"

"Yeah."

"Delightful." I suck in some more and then turn my snarly gaze back on him. "Can we come to some sort of truce? An agreement that doesn't make us both want to keep badgering each other? Because listen…*man*…I'm not the one who did this to you. Your team did. And I'm just the one you have to deal with, and if you ask my friends, I'm a pretty nice person. So if you could just drop the asshole persona to realize that, maybe we would get along better."

"This coming from the person who said I'm lacking in brain cells."

"Okay, I can admit when I'm wrong, and that was not nice to say," I reply in a calm voice as the rest of his food is delivered. There's a giant chunk of pineapple on the top of his fruit salad, and without even thinking about it, I snag it for myself, only for him to eye me and then pull his bowl closer to him. "But maybe we can start over. Okay." I clear my throat. "Hi, I'm Maple Baker. I'm a flamingo zookeeper over at the San Francisco Zoo, I'm thirty years old, I have zero knowledge of the sport of football, and I really like music by Ed Sheeran." I gesture to him. "Okay, your turn."

"Not participating," he says as he sticks some omelet on his fork and takes a huge bite.

"Fine, I'll answer for you." I take a sip of my smoothie, swallow, and then say, "Hi, I'm Graydon St. John, and I play defensive tackle—"

"Defensive end," he grumbles.

"Oh, right." My cheeks flame. "Hi, I'm Graydon St. John, and I play defensive end for the Seattle Foghorns—"

"San Francisco."

"What?" I ask.

"You said Seattle. Last time I checked, we're in San Francisco."

"Did I? Huh. Maybe all the sweating and exertion has gotten to my brain. Not used to such a taxing effect being placed on my body."

"Shame," he says. "Sweating and exertion is all I fucking crave…"

When my eyes connect with his, all I see is darkness and innuendo…

*Sexual* innuendo.

Visions of him sweating…

Exerting…

Sweating and exerting…

They both viciously flash through my mind like an erotic theater, causing a wave of sweat to break out on my lower back because I bet he knows how to sweat and exert properly.

Not that I've thought about it or anything.

But let's be honest, one look at the man and you can gather he knows what he's doing. No man with hands that large doesn't know what he's doing.

Flustered, I say, "Um, well, that's…that's information I didn't know. So…good thing we are doing this, right?" I clear my throat, then nervously laugh. "So to sum it up, you like sweat and exertion, and you're a defensive tackle, I mean end. Defensive end. And you eat a lot of protein and, umm…you like the combination of strawberries and bananas. Oh, and you live in San Francisco, not Seattle. Did I miss anything?"

He lifts his fruit bowl up and starts chomping away on fruit. "Nope."

"Anything you want to add?"

"Nope."

I sigh and take a bite from my pineapple chunk.

What's the use?

---

"Okay, so does everything look good there?" I ask Everly, showing her the caption I made for my first post on Flock and Tackle.

For the past hour, Everly has given me a crash course on social media. I took notes like a lunatic, writing down all the things so I can make sure this social account does well. She assured me that once I start posting more pictures of Graydon, it will pick up because people will love seeing him. I hope she's right, because if this idea works, maybe he'll lighten up and trust that I'm not in his life to make it unbearable.

"I think it looks great." She stares at the picture a touch longer. "God, he's so hot."

"Wouldn't know," I say, even though that's a blatant lie. He's hot. Incredibly hot. "So I should post?"

"Yes, post."

I hit the post button and then hold my breath, as if I'll get instant feedback.

"Okay, now that you made your first post, let's go back to the whole 'you wouldn't know he's hot' thing."

"Must we? I really don't want to think about him in any capacity at the moment."

I stretch out across my couch, thankful for the long Epsom salt bath I took after work because it helped ease some of the pain that's already been building up. I'm going to be in a world of hurt tomorrow, which is fantastic, because he's coming to the zoo, so he can see the results of the torture he made me endure.

There's a knock on the door, and I turn to look at Everly, who says, "It's Hardy." She hops up from the couch and lets him into the apartment. I hear him whisper something to her before the telltale sound of a kiss rings through the apartment.

Is it weird to hear my ex-boyfriend kissing someone else?

No, actually.

I'm really happy for him.

We weren't meant to be together. He and Everly, though? That's a completely different story.

They walk into the room, holding hands, and Hardy offers me that boyish grin of his. "Hey, Maple. How are you?"

"Great. I would stand and give you a hug, but my body is hanging together by a thread."

He chuckles. "I heard. Graydon St. John's giving you trouble in all aspects of your life?"

"What do you mean, 'all aspects'?" I look over at Everly, who looks guilty.

"Work and love," Hardy says nonchalantly as he takes a seat on my couch and pulls Everly onto his lap.

"Uh...not love. There is no love."

"We were just talking about that," Everly says. "She doesn't want to mention him at all."

"Sounds like something someone who is in love would say," Hardy taunts jokingly.

"There is absolutely not one shred of any sort of affection for that man in my body. None. He's rude and inconsiderate and mean and selfish, and I can't wait for the moment that I can take the money he helped me raise and run without looking back."

"So things are going well, then," Hardy jokes.

"He stretched her," Everly says.

Hardy's eyes light up. "In what way?"

Deadpan, I answer, "In a 'her legs are seizing, I better stretch them out before I have to take her to the hospital' kind of way."

"Sounds hot." Hardy smiles.

"It wasn't."

"He was between her legs," Everly continues.

Why on earth did I say anything to her in the first place?

"Ooh, really?"

I press my fingers into my brow. "Listen, as much fun as this is, I'm getting a headache because my muscles don't know what to do with themselves. I think I should take some pain relievers and call it a night."

Not to mention, I'd rather not talk about how Graydon was between my legs today. Or how my leg twitched when his hand pressed into my thigh. Or how there were moments, although fleeting, when I caught his eye in the mirror while we were lifting before we both looked away.

But that's neither here nor there.

"Okay, fine, we'll leave you alone, but just remember, hate sex is so much fun if you get a chance."

"Dear God, there will be no sex with that man. He's enormous."

"All the more reason to do it," Everly says with a wiggle of her brow.

"Okay, this is getting too close to crossing my boundaries," Hardy says, lifting himself off the couch alongside Everly. "Do you need anything before we leave?"

"Yes, can you please follow my new social media account, Flock and Tackle?"

Hardy smirks, pulls out his phone, and taps away. "Hey, you have fifty followers."

"Really?" I ask, sitting up. "That quickly?"

"Yup." He taps. "Just liked your picture." He stares at it for a second. "I don't know, Everly, I think they make a cute couple…and so does everyone else."

"What?" I shout as I pull up the account and go straight to the comments.

Ten.

There are ten comments.

My eyes travel over them.

Graydon has a girlfriend? Since when?

OMG he's so hot. Who is he with?

I'd let him tackle me.

Ahh, that smirk.

I think I just got pregnant, but don't tell my husband.

Who's the girl?

Are they dating? They're so cute together.

New couple alert!

What a way to hard launch a relationship.

Um, this is my new obsession.

I look up at Everly, fear prickling the back of my neck. "Oh God, we did not think this through."

# CHAPTER 11
# GRAYDON

**OC:** Umm, what's with the hard launch?

THIS MOTHERFUCKER, SERIOUSLY, WHY DOES he think—

**Bennett:** Yeah, I saw the same thing.

What?

What the hell are they talking about?

I rest my feet on the coffee table in front of me and respond.

**Graydon:** What the hell are you talking about?

**OC:** Uh, your relationship.

Relationship? Has he lost his mind? I know it's late, but it's not that late. Maybe he's been drinking.

**Graydon:** Put the fucking drink down and go to sleep.

I shake my head and turn off my TV. Jesus, there's something wrong with that guy. My phone dings with two more text messages.

**OC:** Are you really going to deny it?

**Bennett:** It seemed like maybe it was a hard launch. I'm guessing no?

What in the actual fuck?

I scoot to the edge of my couch.

**Graydon:** Spell it out for me, because I have no idea what you're talking about.

**OC:** With the flamingo girl. What's her name again?

Flamingo girl? Huh?

**Bennett:** Maple, right?

**OC:** Oh, right. Maple. The whole joint Instagram account. The picture. Ring any bells? It's blowing up.

Uh…what the hell did she post?

**Graydon:** What's the account?

For the life of me, I can't remember what she landed on—in all honesty, I really wasn't paying attention when she jabbered on about it because I didn't care.

OC sends another text with a link.

I click on it, but the app has to update because I'm never on the damn thing. I wait impatiently, and when it's ready, I click on the link again and am brought to a profile with one picture posted. It's the same picture that is used for the profile picture.

It's Maple and me, smiling at the camera while standing in the practice dome. There isn't much distance between us, and I'm holding the camera up just enough to make it seem like I'm crowded around her when, in reality, I was trying to angle the damn thing to fit our height difference in the frame.

Jesus Christ.

She's smiling brightly, her dimples on display while a faint spattering of freckles dot the bridge of her nose and her cheeks. Despite her aversion for me, she is giving off the impression that she's happy to be snuggled in next to me.

Snuggled in close…

*Christ, don't think about it like that. Do not even fucking go there.*

I click on the picture she posted of us, and the caption says: "He's teaching me football, I'm teaching him flamingos. Come along for the ride." And then a bunch of hashtags. My name being one of them.

Holy shit!

Over three thousand likes? And three hundred comments?

I glance back up at the profile, and there are already over ten thousand followers.

What the hell did she do? I was certain she'd been lying when she said she was awesome at social media. *And yet.*

**OC:** From your silence, I'm guessing that maybe you didn't know about this?

**Bennett:** Does Gretchen know?

**Graydon:** I did, and Gretchen approved, but I thought it would just be some stupid thing that didn't gain any traction.

**Bennett:** Oh, it gained traction. People are already planning your wedding.

**OC:** Me being one of them. I'm thinking a summer soiree. By the way, you two make a good couple. Don't you think, Bennett?

**Bennett:** I'm not answering that.

**Graydon:** WE ARE NOT A COUPLE.

**OC:** Are you shouting at us? Dude, this is a chill place.

**Bennett:** Why are you poking the bear? Didn't he tell you not to call him dude?

**Graydon:** Why are you both even talking to me?

**OC:** We like you. We want to form a bond.

**Bennett:** Bored in a hotel room.

**Graydon:** Well, we are not hard-launching anything. There is no relationship. This was just a stupid PR ploy to get people to like the team.

**Bennett:** Seems like it's working.

**OC:** Now you have to give the people what they want.

**Graydon:** And what would that be?

**OC:** A romance!

---

I lean against Gate B, arms crossed, murder on my mind.

When I checked the profile this morning, we already had over one hundred thousand followers—how?

Who cares that much about a zookeeper and a football player?

And the comments, likes, and shares? Astronomical. One picture—that's all it was—and now I feel like I have all eyes on me...which is dramatic, but fuck.

The door to the building in front of me opens and Maple walks out...slowly.

Almost hobbling as she moves, pain etched all over her face. It's oddly adorable.

When she looks up and spots me, she stops walking and lets out a sigh of relief.

"I'm not making it all the way to you."

I push off the fence and walk up to her. "Sore?"

"What the hell do you think?"

I run my tongue over my teeth. "Is that any way to greet your boyfriend?"

Her brow twists together, and a scowl forms. "What?"

"Your boyfriend? Isn't that what you set us up as last night? Romantically involved?"

Recognition falls over her face. "You saw the post?"

"Half of San Francisco saw the post, Baker."

She twists her hands in front of her. "Yeah, I feel like people are taking the account the wrong way."

"You think?" I gesture with my arm. "People think we're practically engaged."

"Which was no fault of my own. That's just an assumption on the public's behalf. Please tell me you don't have a girlfriend."

"I don't have time for a girlfriend."

"Oh, okay." She sighs in relief. "At least I'm not some homewrecker. I was sweating about that this morning when I checked the account." The smallest of smiles creeps over her lips as she leans in. "Did you see all the follows?"

"Yes, I did," I practically growl. "I saw all the bullshit comments too."

She stands taller. "Why are you so angry? Isn't this what we wanted?"

"I can't be romantically attached to you," I say, my anger getting the best of me before I realize *how* I said that.

Maple leans back, as if she was just slapped. Her lip quivers for a moment. "Well, I understand that looking like you're romantically involved with someone like me might tarnish whatever reputation you have, but I'll be sure to focus our social media attention on the cause and not the perceived relationship."

"Maple, that's not what I meant." I sigh, feeling like a fucking dick.

"It's fine," she says, turning away from me and doing her best to walk away, despite her physical pain.

"Wait," I say, catching her by the wrist and turning her around. When her watery eyes look up at me, a weird sense of...pain ricochets through my chest.

Again...I made her fucking cry again?

I know I can be a dick, but to make someone cry? Multiple times? That's...that's not the man I am. It's not the man my mom raised me to be. So why am I so lost, so unable to control my emotions when I'm around her?

Regardless, it's not okay.

"Maple—"

"There you two are," Gretchen says from behind us, interrupting me before I can apologize.

I glance over my shoulder to see her walking through the gate, her heels clacking against the concrete.

"Glad I caught you before you headed over to the birds." She clasps her hands together and looks between the two of us. "Wanted to let you know that the Foghorns front office was flooded with press this morning from your social media idea. Everyone wants to know the scoop on what's going on over here." She smiles brightly, as if this entire thing was her idea. "I told them that I'd discuss with you two how we should proceed."

"What do you mean?" I ask.

"How about we sit down so we can discuss?" She gestures toward the building in front of us that I've found out is used for receptions and parties. Maple painfully makes her way toward the building and I hold the door open for her and Gretchen before we find a table off to the left, offering us a little privacy.

I glance Maple's way as she slowly lowers herself to her chair, her face attempting to remain neutral, but I can tell from the grimace pulling at her lips that she's in pain. I have an overwhelming urge to help her, to hold her hand while she lowers herself down, but I know for a fact that she would deny it, even possibly swat my hand away.

"Well." Gretchen folds her hands, looking far too pleased to be here.

"This was a pleasant little surprise, waking up to a whole lot of followers on an account with one picture. It's a great start, but how we proceed is what will really keep people interested."

I'm not appreciating the words she's choosing, because it seems like things are about to get way more complicated.

"First of all, I'm holding off on all press requests at the moment, not only because I don't think you're prepared for such attention just yet, but also because we want to edge everybody."

"Edge?" Maple asks.

"Yes, we want to give them little breadcrumbs, small insights into what you're doing, but not give them the relief they need."

"Can you not use sexual terms when it comes to this?" I ask.

"Yes, please," Maple agrees. "Graydon is quite disgusted by being tied to me intimately, so please spare him."

"I'm not...that's not what I said," I almost growl, but it doesn't get Maple's attention as she avoids all eye contact with me.

Gretchen pauses and leans back, her black-lined eyes studying us as her red-painted lips purse. After a few seconds, she motions between us. "What's going on here?"

"Nothing," I say.

Maple folds her arms over her chest. "Nothing's going on."

"I sensed tension last time we met, and I thought that maybe with the success of this account, there might be reduced tension, but that's not what I'm seeing now."

I remain quiet because there's no need to get into this. Gretchen just needs to say what she needs to say so we can move on with the day.

But Maple has other plans.

"He's upset because people think we're a couple, and the thought of him being romantically attached to someone like me makes him shiver to the point of vomiting."

Jesus.

Christ.

"That is not what I said," I growl.

"Well, that poses a problem," Gretchen says as she shifts in her seat, crossing one leg over the other. "Because the front office loved this attention so much, they wanted to discuss a possible PR relationship."

And there it is, the thing I feared the moment Gretchen sauntered in here with that smirk on her face.

"Wait, what is that?" Maple asks, sitting taller now.

"No." I shake my head. "Absolutely not. Not happening."

Gretchen eyes me. "Everyone already signed off on it."

"That's fucking great for them, but it's not their life or their decision and it's not fucking happening."

A PR relationship?

That's just asking for fucking trouble. They're always messy. Someone ends up getting hurt, and I haven't seen one where it's rolled out smoothly in both parties' favor.

"You don't really have a choice in the matter," Gretchen says. "So let's not make a big deal about this and just lay down the guidelines."

"Hold on, what are you talking about?" Maple asks, her eyes searching both of us.

I can't do this to her.

I don't know her really well, but what I do know from the short amount of time I've spent with her is that she doesn't have a thick skin. She takes everything to heart, and there is no way in hell that she'll be able to handle something like this. Jesus Christ, when I came here today, I was going to talk about shutting down the entire account because of how it took off; the public is far too fascinated by one picture. So rolling out a PR relationship seems like the last thing we should be doing, especially with highly sensitive Maple.

Gretchen turns to Maple and says, "A PR relationship would be alluding to a romantic relationship between you and Graydon for the public eye. It's beneficial to both parties."

"You want people thinking we're in a romantic relationship?" she asks.

"Yes."

"No," I reply. "Once again, not happening."

Maple's eyes shoot to mine and grow insecure in a flash, the pain I saw just a few moments ago reemerging all over again.

*It's not like that, Maple. I'm protecting you.*

"He's right." She clears her throat. "Not happening. I don't want to make him uncomfortable, and clearly, I'm not the type of person he'd want to be seen with in a romantic sense."

Actually, she's exactly who I would want to be seen with romantically. Blond hair. Beautiful eyes. Killer ass. Dimples that will bring you to your knees. Cute and innocent but also feisty. If I were actually on the hunt for a relationship and I weren't so fucking annoyed with the entire situation that I'm in, I'd ask her out. But that's not the case.

"Oh stop, you two look great together." Gretchen waves her hand in dismissal. "But listen, we have to go about this in the right way."

"We're not going about this," I say. "There's no point in adding the burden of a PR relationship. I don't see how this will favor the team by any means. If she were a well-liked celebrity, sure, that makes sense, it's done all the time, but she's just a zookeeper."

Maple's eyes fall to her lap as she says, "He's right. I'm *just* a zookeeper."

My teeth grind together, because once again I've made an insult that I apparently didn't know I was making.

"That's the brilliance of it all," Gretchen says. "There's relatability there because she's not a celebrity. Trust me, by just scrolling through the comments, we can tell that this will be a big win for the team, especially if we get her involved at training camp and have her attend games."

"Um, not that I want this to happen, but there needs to be something for the flamingos too," she says.

"Of course. That's why he'll be attending all the fundraising events as previously discussed. Also, Welcott was telling me that he's so enthralled with the potential of this that if it goes well, he'll be making a sizable donation to your cause."

Of course he would.

I drag my hand over my face. Jesus.

"Who is Welcott?" Maple asks, looking between the two of us.

"The owner of the Foghorns," I answer, knowing that there is no chance in hell I'll be able to get out of this now.

When Gretchen said, "front office," my initial thought was that it was just PR and marketing. I had no fucking idea this went all the way up to Darby Welcott.

"Oh, he's...he's aware?" Maple asks.

Gretchen nods. "Very aware and loving it. We've already seen an uptick in follows on the team account. Therefore, we're riding this, but like I said, we need to be careful. We need to go at this slowly, not confirm or deny anything, continue to post from Flock and Tackle and keep followers on their toes, feeding them what they want, and then when the season starts, possibly go public after she attends one of your games."

No, I will not let this happen. There is so much that comes with a PR relationship that will hurt her, that will mess with her mind. I might be an asshole, but Maple...she...she deserves so much more than being roped into a shitstorm like this.

I shake my head. "This is so fucked up. She should be able to live her own life. She shouldn't have to—"

"How much of a donation?" Maple asks, her eyes landing on Gretchen.

*No, Maple.*

A slow smile pulls on Gretchen's lips. "I'm not sure, but he said significant since he knows what he's asking of you. I do believe he'll want some form of acknowledgment, like a building named after him, but no, I don't know how much."

Maple looks out toward the zoo, clearly considering this.

She can't be serious.

I don't think I can back out of this, and they can't force someone into pretending to date me for good press, but *her* choice forces my hand.

"Maple, this is ridiculous," I say. "You realize what they're asking of us?"

Her eyes land on me, and her expression is devoid of all emotion. "I understand."

"Okay, so then, tell her no, and we can just...we can figure out something else."

"Why would she want to figure something else out?" Gretchen asks. "This will bring awareness to the flamingos, secure fundraising, and, if all goes well, procure a significant donation from Welcott. It's a win-win for her."

"She's putting her personal life on hold. She's putting herself in the public eye."

"She did that the moment she created the Instagram account. I think she's aware of what's going on."

"That was supposed to be a friendly thing. That wasn't supposed to pick up so much steam."

"Well. It did, and here we are. So what do you say, Maple?"

"She's not going to—"

"I'm in," Maple says, not looking at me, causing Gretchen to nod.

What the fuck?

"Great, I'll get some NDAs prepared and sent over to you to sign electronically. Let me know if you have any questions." She stands. "Until then, keep doing what you're doing. Please no public appearances until this weekend at the fundraiser. Maple, do you have a dress to wear?"

"Yes," she says, almost looking insulted.

"Great. No PDA, no answering questions from press, and please continue to post pictures, but nothing that looks like you're dating just yet. Keep it platonic. We're edging the public, don't forget."

She pushes her chair in and then offers us a wave before taking off without another word. When she leaves, I turn to Maple and ask, "What the hell?"

She takes her time standing and winces with every movement. She heads toward the door, so I pop out of my chair and grab her by the wrist. "Maple, I'm talking to you. You're just going to agree to that?"

She glances over her shoulder, her eyes darker than usual as she says, "Yes, I am."

"You realize what you're agreeing to, right? This isn't just some social media posting. This will get real, and it will flood your life. The press will be unstoppable, and you're going to be torn apart online because the public will be relentless. They'll say things about you, make up lies, pick apart your life, your appearance, the way you act and present yourself. You're opening yourself up to the public in a way that you're not ready for."

Her eyes slowly lift to mine, the blue swimming with unspoken emotion. She wets her lips and says, "But I'll be able to help the flamingos, so I guess it's worth it." Then she moves away and pushes the door open. She glances over her shoulder and asks, "You coming? Or are you skipping your duties for today?"

Irritation plucks up my spine as I head in her direction.

This is not over.

I will not let her do this.

I will not subject her to public scrutiny.

And I most certainly won't allow her to attach herself to me, someone who...who...doesn't deserve to have someone like her at his side.

# CHAPTER 12
# MAPLE

"MAPLE," GRAYDON SAYS, HIS VOICE laced with anger. "Stop ignoring me."

"I'm not ignoring you. I'm trying to take care of the flamingos," I say as I prepare vitamins for some of our birds.

He moves in right next to me. "You're ignoring me."

Seeing that he's not going to quit with this badgering, I turn to him, one hand on the counter, the other holding a vial of supplements. "I'm not going to talk to you about this in my place of work. We have things to do. I'd like to take a picture of you looking at the flamingos today, and then you can be on your way."

"We need to talk about this."

"Text me later," I say, turning back to the vitamins, only for my shoulder to be pulled back so I have to face his dark gaze again.

"This is not a later conversation," he snarls. "This is a now conversation."

Just then, Harriot walks into the building and pauses when she sees me and Graydon staring each other down.

Slapping on a smile, I ask, "Harriot, do you mind finishing the vitamins? I need to speak with Graydon."

"Certainly," she answers as she comes up next to me and starts taking over the duties.

"Thank you."

I wash my hands quickly, dry them, and then take Graydon by his gigantic arm and move him toward the back of the flamingo building, out the door, and off to a corner surrounded by foliage.

Speaking quietly, I ask, "What do you need to talk about?"

His nostrils flare as he leans in close. "We're not pretending to be in a public relationship."

"Doesn't seem like we have much of a choice, now does it?"

"You do," he whisper-shouts. "You have a choice. They can't force you to do anything. You don't have a contract with them, so you don't have any attachment whatsoever. Tell them no and end this misery for us."

"For us, or for you?" I ask, shifting on my feet. Just as the comments have said on repeat, Graydon St. John is hot…to look at. Personality? Not so hot. But people don't know that. And me? Well, I'm definitely not in the same league. The only other stupidly handsome man I've dated was Hardy. So even I can see why Graydon's molars are grinding with distaste. "I know you wouldn't typically be seen with someone like me, but I can…I can get new pants if you're worried about the high-waters. If that's what's going to eat away at you."

He drags his hand down his face. "That's not what I'm fucking worried about. This isn't a smart move, Maple."

"It seems like it is. You're already looking favorable to the public. Gretchen believes this will change people's perception about the Foghorns and offer some good press. Isn't that what you want? Isn't that what you're looking for? Why are you so against it? Is it because it's me?"

"No," he snaps.

"Then what is it? I can't seem to figure out any other reason as to why this would be such a horrible attachment when it benefits you greatly."

His clenched jaw ticks just below his ear as he studies me, mulling over his answer. After a few seconds, he says, "You know what? Fine. If you want this, then you can have it."

"I don't want this," I say, wanting to make sure he understands he's not doing me any favors. "This is one of the last things I want, but I'm also desperate not to lose my job, not to lose a home for these flamingos. I will do anything to keep them around, which means saying yes to a plan that could grant me money to keep them around."

"It's not just a plan. It's an invasion of privacy."

I shrug. "I don't have much of a life. People can search, but they're not going to find anything."

He pulls on his neck, standing taller, actually seeming distressed about this. "They're going to eat you alive, Maple."

"That's a risk I'm willing to take," I answer, even though fear starts to prickle along my skin.

He slowly nods, then blows out a heavy breath. "Fine, but don't fucking say I didn't warn you."

"I've been warned," I say, not wanting to talk about it anymore. "Now, if we can get on with what we're here for, I'd appreciate it. I'd like to educate you about our flamingos before the event this Saturday."

He scrubs his hand over the back of his head. "Yeah, sure."

With those two words, I make my way back into the flamingo building, Graydon coming with me. I grab some pellets for enrichment and then say, "This way."

We walk back out to the exhibit, where I open the gate for both of us. Last time he was here, I went over safety with him around the birds, but this will be his first time in the exhibit.

I shut the gate behind me, locking it, and then bring him to the edge of the bushes, giving the flamingos some room. Stiff and uncomfortable, he shifts next to me, clearly out of his element, which amuses me slightly as I think about how out of my element I was yesterday.

When one of the flamingos starts moving toward us, Graydon takes a step back. "What's that fuck doing?"

"Can you not call the flamingos 'fucks'?" I ask as he moves behind me.

"Well, the fuck has a look in its eye."

"Once again, do not call them 'fucks,' and people are watching."

I look over at the windows and flamingo outlooks. People are holding up their phones, taking pictures and videos.

"Why the fuck are we doing this?" he asks.

"Because you need to get comfortable with them." Lester, one of the more curious flamingos, walks up to us, and I hand Graydon some pellets. "Here, toss Lester a pellet."

It's barely out of my hand before Graydon is tossing it on the ground behind Lester and causing him to turn away.

"This is fucked up. I don't want to be in here with food and them stampeding toward us."

"They're not stampeding toward us. They're barely interested." I step to the side and toss some more pellets before pulling my phone out of my back pocket. "Now squat down so I can take a picture with you and the flamingos."

"I'm good."

Growing frustrated, I turn toward him and quietly say, "Graydon, this is for social media. Now squat down and take a picture."

"No."

"Graydon," I say sternly. "I did your stupid workout, now you take a freaking picture with the flamingos."

He stares down at me.

I stare up at him.

And after a few seconds of silence, he rolls his eyes and then squats down a few feet from the flamingos, and I snap a picture of him looking out toward them like he's studying their beautiful feathers and quirky long legs. I stare down at the picture for a moment, taking in the juxtaposition of the imposing man with impenetrable muscles wrapping and weaving over his body next to the delicate pink feathers of an innocent flamingo. A very odd pairing, but also…it sort of works.

"Okay, can we leave?" he asks while standing.

"You realize you're scared of birds, right?"

"Have you seen the size of their beaks? You're just doing this to get back at me for yesterday."

"No, I'm just trying to educate you."

"You have yet to say anything educational since being in here."

"I haven't had the chance because you can't stop crying about being next to them," I shoot back.

His eyes narrow before he says, "Fine, educate me."

A smile tugs at my lips because I find it so much fun to talk about the birds that bring me joy and to educate people who might think they're not worth anything.

"I'm glad you asked. There are six species of flamingos globally. The greater flamingo, lesser flamingo, American flamingo, Andean flamingo, Puna flamingo, and Chilean flamingo, which is what we have here at the zoo. Four of them are found here in the Americas, while the other two reside in Asia and Europe. Currently, there are no more than two hundred thousand Chilean flamingos left in the wild, making them nearly threatened as a species. This is due to human disruption of their environment." Graydon glances out at them, taking them in. "They're very smart, they have great hearing, and although their eyesight suffers at night like an octogenarian's, they have great color perception, allowing them to recognize me from someone in the crowd."

He nods. "And their pinkness is from their food, right?"

Oh my God, look at him showing an ounce of interest.

"Yup," I answer. "They're actually born gray or white, and as they grow and feed on carotenoids, their diet reflects in their color. We try to offer them a diverse diet that helps them maintain their color but also offers them the nutrients they need to stay healthy."

Big Hermy squawks over in the corner, pulling our attention. Ugh, I love him so much. I toss him a few pellets to satiate him. "They're also loud. They'll growl and they'll bray like a donkey too."

"And they smell."

I roll my eyes. "Any animal's going to smell, especially when it comes to captivity. We try to offer them the most natural habitat. When I was in Peru observing them—"

"You were in Peru?" he asks, surprised, the tension between us easing for a moment.

"For a few years," I answer. "I was studying them in the wild." I stare off at the flamingos. "Best few years of my life. I miss it so much. I miss the chilly early mornings, the dew just lifting off the mud. I miss the sounds they make at night, the stars above us being the only glimmer of light. I miss the people…"

"The people?" I can feel his eyes on me. "What, did you have like a boyfriend or something out there?"

I push my hand through my hair. "No."

"Well, that's a lie. I could see right through that bullshit answer."

"He wasn't a boyfriend, just…just a guy who I got along with."

"Who liked flamingos as much as you."

"Yes," I grumble and try to remain neutral. People are watching us. "Other people like flamingos just as much as I do. I know that's hard to believe."

He scratches the back of his neck. "Yeah, it is."

God, what an ass. And here I thought we were getting along for a moment.

"But I do understand that the work you're doing is important. I don't know why anyone would volunteer to be around these fucks, but you're brave to do it. It's admirable that you want to protect them."

Did he…did he just give me a compliment?

Unsure what to do or how to react, I remain calm and steady and hand him some more pellets and direct him to toss them toward the center of the lagoon. I snap a few pictures of him. I might hate the man, but if I'm going to do something, I'm going to do it properly.

When he's done, he looks up toward the crowd that's formed, taking pictures not of the flamingos but of him. He turns toward me, his back to the crowd. "This is what I'm talking about," he says. "You're going to end up in a fishbowl, people watching everything you do, taking pictures to share on the internet."

I lift my gaze to his dark one. "I understand the ramifications."

"Yet you're still going to do it?" he asks quietly.

I glance behind him, at the chicken-wire wall that separates the visitors from the flamingos, the painted wall that's supposed to look like a natural habitat off to the right. They deserve so much more than this. If they have to live in a fishbowl, why can't I for a moment in time?

Bringing my attention back to him, I say, "Yes."

He nods. "Okay, just…just be warned, Maple."

The sincerity in his voice almost makes it seem like he cares.

But that can't be, right? He can't possibly be caring toward me.

I let my eyes trail over him for a short moment, his eyes connecting with mine as well.

What are you thinking inside that head, Graydon St. John?

Snapping away from our eye contact, he turns back around, only to find Lester inches away. "Mother of fuck," he squeals, quickly moving behind me and using my body as a shield. "Get me the hell out of here."

Chuckling, I lead him out of the habitat, hoping and praying that someone caught the *Matrix*-like move he just made to scramble away from an innocent bird.

I'll be scouring social media tonight, hoping the algorithm finds me.

---

I slide into my tub, the hot water seeping into my worn-down muscles as I lower myself to the bottom, my limbs straining, begging to be put out of their misery.

Candles are lit.

*Folklore* is playing on my Bluetooth speaker.

And there's a glass of wine waiting to be consumed while I pick up my phone and pull up Instagram.

I click on the profile for Flock and Tackle while the Epsom salts do their job.

"Holy shit," I whisper.

Over five hundred thousand followers. That's...that's insane.

After one picture.

That's all it took.

One picture.

Imagine the impact one picture could make if it was geared toward the right thing...like bringing awareness to flamingos.

That's exactly what I'm going to try to do.

I click on the post button, then pull up the pictures that I took today of Graydon. God, he's such a large man. He looks like a giant compared with the birds. I scroll through to find which one would be best. All are great options.

I narrow it down to two: one of him with his back toward the camera while looking off at the flamingos, and then one of him in profile, squatting down and tossing a pellet.

Unsure what to go with, I send him a text with both pictures.

**Maple:** Trying to decide which picture to post tonight. Do you have a preference?

I set my phone down on the tray that runs from one side of the tub to the other and pick up my glass of wine. I lean my head back and stare at the lights dancing across my ceiling from my light orb—highly recommend.

I'd never been a bath kind of girl until I had a hard day at the zoo and needed to ease my muscles. I talked to Everly about it, and she set me up

with all the things that I would need when it came to relaxing. Spending years in Peru living in a permanent tent makes you really appreciate luxurious things such as a bathtub...a nice glass of wine...running water.

My phone pings with a message, so I set my wine down and pick up my phone.

**Graydon:** Don't care.

I roll my eyes. God, why did I even ask? He's so not helpful.

My phone pings again.

**Graydon:** Maybe the one of me squatting down.

I snort.

**Maple:** I thought you didn't care.
**Graydon:** I don't, but if I have to choose, the squatting one.
**Maple:** Didn't say you had to choose.
**Graydon:** Why are you testing my patience?
**Maple:** Unsure.

I open Instagram again, but my phone pings with another text.

**Graydon:** Are you going to be able to work out tomorrow morning with me? It was uncomfortable watching you walk today.

My expression falls flat, because this freaking jerk.

**Maple:** Yes, I can work out with you tomorrow.
**Graydon:** If you get hurt, I'm not responsible.

**Maple:** I'm not going to get hurt.

Although my hamstrings are so tight that I worry if I bend forward, they might snap, but he doesn't need to know that.

**Graydon:** Maybe we'll do something different.

**Maple:** Do whatever you want, just know, I can hang.

**Graydon:** Sure.

**Maple:** Was that said with sarcasm?

**Graydon:** Really up to you to decipher.

**Maple:** You just keep finding ways to irritate me, don't you?

**Graydon:** You tell me.

**Maple:** God, you're so infuriating.

**Graydon:** Yet you keep texting me.

**Maple:** Because I was trying to be nice and post a picture of you that you thought was flattering. Next time, I'll make sure to post an extremely unflattering picture.

**Graydon:** Good luck finding one.

Oh yeah...challenge accepted.

I pull up the internet on my phone and type in his name, then go straight to images. Immediately it's an inundation of shirtless pictures of Graydon.

Dear God.

Him shirtless and in the gym.

Shirtless on the field wearing just his football pants with his hands on his hips.

Shirtless and sitting on the ground, looking out toward the stands.

Shirtless at a photo shoot.

Pictures of his biceps.

His butt.

His intimidating stature.

I pick up my wine and take a large gulp as I scroll and scroll...and scroll.

Even when he's angry, he looks hot.

There isn't one single thing I could use for fodder.

How is that even possible?

It takes me at least ten pictures of smiling to get one with my eyes open, and he's over here, taking candids like he's a *GQ* model attempting to sell you his grass-stained white football pants.

My phone dings with a text.

**Graydon:** Trying to find an unflattering picture?

I gasp in annoyance.

**Maple:** As a matter of fact, yes, and I'm just trying to decide which one to send you.

**Graydon:** Send them all.

Annoyed, I save a few pictures of him that are not the least bit unflattering and send them to him in a text.

**Maple:** Your muscles are too big. Very unflattering.

There, he can chew on that and rot.

I pick up my glass of wine, take a large sip, and then wait for his message. It takes longer than I was expecting, but then he pings back with a text...and a picture.

I sit up in the tub, pull up the picture, and feel my jaw drop.

It's him, in his bed, shirtless and showing off his chest and abs. The sheets are just below his belly button, and his hand is resting behind his head, making his bicep pop. The man is carved, so perfectly proportioned that it's almost hard to look at.

And his comment…

Graydon: Never had any complaints before.

Yeah…can't imagine he would.

My mouth goes dry, and I tip the rest of my wine back as he texts again.

Graydon: Feel free to use that picture if the others aren't satisfactory.

Maple: The others I have are fine.

Graydon: Then feel free to use that picture for personal use.

I purse my lips together—the audacity.

And yes, I might have felt a dull throb erupt between my legs from the sight of him in his bed.

And yes, I might have wondered what it would be like if he tugged those sheets down another inch.

And perhaps I thought about feeling his abs, running my fingers over them just for scientific purposes.

But that doesn't mean I'll use it for anything.

Maple: Already deleted it.

Ha, take that, you—*ping*.

Graydon: Here's another, then. Don't be scared to keep it.

My eyes nearly bug out when I see that he lowered the sheet an inch, making my mouth water from the sight of him.

Why?

Why is he doing this?

Between the compliment he gave me today, the concern he showed, and now this…I could not be more confused. What is he getting at? Is he trying to get on my good side to get me out of this PR relationship he so desperately doesn't want to be in? In any case, I need to have my defenses up, because I don't trust what's going on.

And after the way the back of my neck heated up from the picture he sent, I don't trust myself to not react stupidly either.

**Maple:** Not needed, I have my own stash of photos that keep me very occupied.

**Graydon:** Same…

Ugh, gross.

I exit the text thread and then go back to Instagram. I click on the side-profile picture where he's squatting down and choose that one as the picture to post. I make a caption that says, "Find someone who looks at you the way Graydon looks at flamingos," and then I post the picture.

There, done.

I set my phone down once again, only for it to ping.

Knowing exactly who it is, I think about not looking, but curiosity wins.

**Graydon:** Surprised you didn't put "The way Graydon looks at me" in the caption.

What is happening?

What has gotten into him?

**Maple:** Well, then, that would require a picture of you snarling.

**Graydon:** Clearly, you haven't seen me look at you enough.

My breath catches in my throat as I stare down at his text because...is he drunk? That's a very unlikely comment coming from him. Is he...is he flirting?

No, he can't be flirting.

There's no way.

*Ping.*

**Graydon:** Because it's not a snarl, it's a grunt of displeasure.

My face falls flat, and I toss my phone on the ground.

Ass.

# CHAPTER 13
# GRAYDON

**OC:** You know, I've been doing some thinking, and this might be a bit early, but I think we have a good vibe going and thought we should consider a name for our group chat.

I STARE DOWN AT THE dipshit's text, wondering what kind of glitter bomb crawled up his ass. Does he have to be so…upbeat all the time?

**Graydon:** No.

**OC:** I knew you were going to say that, but just hang on a second. When I was with the Agitators, we had a group chat, and we called ourselves the Frozen Fellas. And whenever we called in on the Frozen Fellas, we all appeared and helped each other out, kind of like Ted Lasso and the Diamond Dogs.

**Graydon:** The difference is they probably liked you.

**OC:** Are you saying you don't like me?

**Graydon:** Surprised you're just figuring that out.

**Bennett:** I don't know, seems like it might be good to have a place we can chat.

I groan and drag my hand over my face as I lean against the training facility wall, waiting for Maple.

She's late.

And her tardiness is irritating me.

**Graydon:** Bennett, you're not supposed to give in to his ridiculous ideas.

**Bennett:** Seems like he needs friends.

**Graydon:** Because he drives them away with asinine text messages.

**OC:** You know that I'm still here in the group chat, right?

**Graydon:** Yes, and I'm hoping you'll get the hint.

**OC:** I'm getting the vibe that you're not in the mood to talk about this at the moment.

**Graydon:** Try never.

**Bennett:** Just out of curiosity, what was your name suggestion going to be?

**OC:** I'm glad you asked. *Clears throat* I was going to suggest we call ourselves the Gladdy Daddies.

**Bennett:** Dude...that's not great. We're not dads—not that I know of.

**OC:** But we're "daddies," as in hot pieces of dick, and we're glad to be linked together. What do you think, big guy? You in?

**Graydon:** First of all, don't ever use the term "hot pieces of dick." Jesus fuck. And once again, lose this number.

I pocket my phone and shake my head.

Gladdy Daddies.

What the actual fuck is wrong with that guy?

The door to the facilities opens, and Maple walks in, head slumped, bag hefted over her shoulder, avoiding eye contact.

"Glad you finally decided to show up," I say as I push off the wall. "Thirty-five minutes late is inexcusable. And with no response to my texts. I'm fucking behind now."

I make my way down the hall toward the dome and she trails me.

"Are you going to explain why you're late, or are you just going to shuffle behind me?"

When she doesn't answer, irritation claws at me.

When we reach the dome, I pause in front of the door and snap, "Hey, I'm talking to you."

Slowly, she lifts her head, and when her face comes into view, my entire body stills.

"What the fuck happened?" I ask, taking in the bruising and swelling on the left side of her face. Concern rips through my chest and a need to protect her overcomes me.

A tear trickles down her cheek, and she wipes it away with a swollen wrist.

Holy fuck.

"Maple." I squat down and lightly press my hand to her jaw, examining her and using a gentler tone. "What happened? Did someone hurt you?"

She shakes her head, another tear cascading down her face. "I…I was in a car accident."

"What?" I nearly roar. "Jesus, are you okay? Have you had anyone check you out?" My thumb glides over her soft skin, her tears creating a ball of anger mixed with anxiety inside me.

She shakes her head. "No. I just grabbed an Uber and came here."

"You left the car accident scene?" I ask.

"When I was pulling out from my street, a cop ran into me. Dented my entire driver's-side door. I had to climb out the other side. He took down all the info and reported it, and I grabbed an Uber here. I'm sorry I'm late."

Jesus fuck. She's sorry she's late? Why is she even apologizing? She needs help.

I shut the door to the training dome and then carefully take her uninjured hand in mine and walk her back down the hallway.

"What are you doing?" she asks.

"Getting you medical attention."

"I don't need any. It's just bruising."

"Your wrist is swollen, Maple. Your face is bruised. You need someone to look at you. Don't fucking argue with me."

"I can't afford any medical bills right now since clearly I need to save for a new car."

I don't say anything as I walk her back toward our training staff and our excellent medical facilities.

When I push open the door, I catch Hutton on one of the tables, getting his ankle wrapped. "What's up, man," he calls out with a head nod, only for his eyes to land on Maple. "Oh shit, what happened? Did you do that to her?"

"Are you fucking insane?" I snap at him and bring her in closer to my side. "Of course I didn't. She was in a car accident, and I need someone to look at her because she's too stubborn to seek medical attention."

"I got it," one of the trainers says as she walks up to us. "I can see her on this table."

I take Maple's bag, sling it over my shoulder, and then carefully help her up on the table.

"You good?" I ask.

Her eyes cautiously glance up at mine, and for a pulse, I get the chance to study the depths of her blue irises and how they're not too dark, but not too light either. The purest blue, just like her soul.

She wets her lips, confusion forming in her expression. "Um, yeah."

I nod, not wanting to pull away, but knowing I have to. "I'll be over there if you need me. Don't lie to them about the pain. I know you're not okay."

Then, I step to the side to give Maple some privacy, but I keep my eyes on her the entire time, the instinct to protect and guard her overtaking any other thoughts right now.

Hutton places his hand on my shoulder, startling me as he says, "I thought she dropped a weight on her face or something. Car accident. Jesus."

Maple swipes at her cheeks again, probably really fucking embarrassed and shaken at the moment. It's taking everything in me not to walk back over there and stand by her side.

And it's a weird fucking feeling because no one has ever made me feel that way. Absolutely no one. And I can't really figure out how to process these sensations.

"You good?" Hutton asks. I can feel him studying me. I just hope he can't see into my thoughts.

"Why the fuck would I not be?" I grumble, my eyes latched on Maple the entire time the trainer carefully moves her hand around while another brings some ice over for her face.

Whispering, he says, "Because it looks like you're about to crack a tooth from how goddamn tight your jaw is set."

Because they better not hurt her.

"Just fucking stupid. She should have gone to a hospital, but she thought she was going to train with me instead. Carelessness."

"Uh-huh, and why do you care so much?"

Great question.

Keeping my voice to a whisper, I say, "Because now she's attached to me publicly, and I can't have her looking like she's all beaten up."

I let the words fall past my lips, but deep down, I know that's not really the reason. No, when she looked up at me and I saw her bruised face, nausea rolled through me, followed by an immediate flood of desire to murder whoever did this to her. She's not really my girlfriend, I know this, but ever since I laid eyes on her this morning I've felt like...hell, I don't know what I've felt. Just different.

And seeing her hurt, it doesn't settle well.

"Why don't I believe you?" he whispers back.

Because I don't even believe myself.

"I think she needs an X-ray," the trainer says. "I'd suggest taking her to an urgent care."

"You have an X-ray machine here," I argue. "Just take it here and don't waste the time."

"That machine is for the team," the trainer says, looking uncomfortable.

"It's fine. I'm fine." Maple starts to slide off the table, but I stop her before she can get very far.

Staring down the trainer, I slip my arm around Maple's waist and say, "She's with me."

The trainer looks between the two of us and then nods. "I understand that, but team rules."

Yeah, I'm not going to accept that. Running my tongue over my teeth, I pull my phone out and send a text to Darby Welcott.

**Graydon:** Sorry to bother you, Mr. Welcott, but I'm in the training room right now with Maple, my "girlfriend," and she got banged up in a car accident. Nothing too serious, but she needs an X-ray. I'm nervous if I take her to an urgent care it will cause a scene. Trainers won't give her an X-ray because they said it's against team rules. Can I get some support here?

Hutton looks over my shoulder. "Oh shit, you went there?"

"Of course I fucking went there."

My phone dings with a response.

**Darby** Welcott: Anything she needs. The trainers are required to treat her, so make sure they follow up with care.

**Graydon:** Thank you.

I look up at the trainer and show her the text from Welcott. She nods and then says, "Right this way...uh..."

"Her name is Maple," I say. "And she's my girlfriend."

Maple's eyes shoot to mine, confused and embarrassed.

"Of course, right this way, Maple."

The trainer takes her back to the X-ray machine and then Hutton turns toward me with concern and amusement. "Graydon, do I even need to ask?"

"Don't," I answer. "Please, just fucking don't."

---

I stare down at Maple's pink-wrapped left wrist as she receives instructions from the trainer.

The X-ray identified a minor fracture of her ulna where the car door was pushed into her wrist. Since it was a nondisplaced fracture, she didn't have to cast it, but it needed to be splinted. I asked if they had pink wrap, and when they said no, I told them to get some.

It took about thirty minutes, but they rushed back with some pink wrap and took care of business. Gretchen, of course, made her way into the training facilities, probably hearing about the accident from Welcott. I also saw her taking pictures of me hovering over Maple while they wrapped her arm.

It made me fucking irate, to expose something like this, but then again, that's what she signed up for, right?

"Any questions?" the trainer asks.

Maple shakes her head. Thankfully, the swelling on her face has gone down, and she just has some bruising.

"Great, and you said you have ibuprofen at home?"

"I do."

"Good." The trainer looks up at me. "I'm sure you have this handled and will take care of her?"

I swallow. "Of course."

"Great. Then just rest and immobilization of your arm—keep it in the sling as much as you can—and then check back with us on Monday."

Maple nods. “Thank you, I really appreciate it.”

“Feel better.”

Maple starts to scoot off the high training table, but I quickly grab her by the waist, her eyes snapping up to mine as I gently lift her off the table and help her to the ground.

I can feel all eyes on us, Gretchen’s specifically, as I let go of Maple’s waist and let her straighten out her shirt. “You good?” I ask quietly.

“Yes,” she answers, glancing up at me, those blue eyes of hers swimming with questions.

Questions I know I don’t have answers to.

Or that I’m even close to willing to give.

“Well, I’m glad you’re okay,” Gretchen says, breaking apart our gaze. “If you don’t mind, I’d like a moment with both of you.”

I pick up Maple’s bag for her and sling it over my shoulder. She tries to grab it from me, but I snarl at her to leave it. Thankfully, she listens.

Gretchen leads us down the hallway and to the second floor, where my coach’s office is.

Fucking great.

I remain silent, my eyes falling on Maple in front of me while we walk along the hallways. Her bandaged hand pulls at my chest, the thought of her bruised face making me irate all over again.

What was that cop even fucking doing?

Did he apologize? Is he taking the blame?

It’s his front that rammed into her driver’s-side door, so it’s likely he’s going to be at fault. And what the hell is she going to do now for a car? She said she’ll have to save up, and from what she said earlier, I know she doesn’t have a lot in savings.

Worry ticks away for someone who I don’t even fucking know, yet it feels like a wave of responsibility has enveloped me, like this is my problem to solve. I would lend her my truck if it wasn’t so goddamn big.

And if I knew she’d actually take it.

Gretchen knocks at the door of my coach's office, and he calls out, "Come in."

Gretchen opens the door, and Maple shuffles in. When I lift my gaze, I stop in my tracks, because sitting down in a chair, looking far too pleased with himself, is my father.

"What are you doing here?" I ask.

"Aw, is that any way to greet your dad?" He stands and moves in front of me, pulling me into a hug that I try to resist, but he's just strong enough to hide the fact that I want nothing to do with him.

He gives me a few pats on the back and then turns to Maple. "And you must be his little friend."

"Her name is Maple," I say, my voice terse, my entire body on edge.

Dad holds his hand out to her, and Maple takes it. "Um, it's nice to meet you, Mr. St. John."

"Call me Troy," he says as he lets his eyes rake over her. I nearly black out with rage. "Aren't you a cute little thing?"

I press my hand to my dad's chest, backing him away from her and offering him a warning glare that makes him chuckle.

"Miss Baker, why don't you take a seat?" Coach Keenan says. "Looks like we need to talk."

Unsure, she takes a seat in front of Keenan's desk. I stand behind her protectively as my least favorite people in the world smirk at her with wide grins, like she's their prey.

And she's about to be devoured.

*What the fuck are they up to?*

# CHAPTER 14
# MAPLE

NOTE TO SELF: GETTING SIDESWIPED by a police car hurts.

I already sent a text to Phil letting him know I was in a car accident and that I wouldn't be able to make it to work today. Thankfully, he was kind about it.

But the three people right in front of me seem like they couldn't care less about the pounding in my head, the heated bruises on my face, and the aching fracture in my wrist.

Gretchen, Coach Keenan, and…Graydon's father all carefully study me as I shift uncomfortably in my chair, Graydon directly behind me.

And even though all of them have their eyes on me, it's hard not to let my gaze float over to Troy St. John.

Just like Graydon, he's a powerhouse of a man, even in his older age. Maybe an inch shorter than Graydon, his chest and shoulders are wider than the average human's, with muscles wrapped all around them. His hair is thick and buzzed, dotted with salt and pepper, along with his short beard. Besides the eyes, he looks exactly like Graydon. Troy's eyes are blue, and even though they are a light version compared with Graydon's dark and stormy eyes, Troy's seem to be full of so much more sin.

"We wanted to bring you in here quickly because it seems as though Graydon made an announcement in the training room that was quite impactful," Coach Keenan says.

I know exactly what he's talking about because the moment Graydon told everyone I was his girlfriend, I felt the direct impact of that statement all the way to my fractured and bruised bones.

"Really playing up the role of a PR relationship, are we?" Troy asks, looking at his son.

"Again, why the hell are you here? This doesn't pertain to you."

An evil smirk passes over Troy's features. "Was visiting with my good friend when news broke out, and it just seemed like too much of a fun opportunity to pass up."

Not that I can see Graydon, but boy, oh boy, can I feel the tension and anger rolling off him from behind me.

Without even having to do a deep dive into Graydon's personal life, I can tell you right now that there's no chance in hell these two celebrate holidays or birthdays together. From the sound of it, they only see each other in forced circumstances like this.

Nothing's planned.

And not an ounce of love is passed between them despite the hug Troy offered his son when we first entered the office.

"Why don't we stay on track?" Gretchen asks as she looks at her watch. "I have some NDAs to check on with the training staff to make sure none of this has leaked just yet."

"Then why were you taking pictures of us in the training room?" Graydon asks.

She was?

I didn't even notice.

"Because you're going to an event tomorrow together. There will be questions about her wrist, so why not use this as an opportunity for the public to see how generous the Foghorns are with their medical attention?"

"Don't you think that's a little...invasive? Opportunistic?" I ask. "It is my medical information, after all."

Coach Keenan and Troy both chuckle while Gretchen crosses her arms. "Miss Baker, need I remind you what you signed up for? There is no more privacy where your life is concerned."

Oh, right.

"And if Graydon didn't just announce that you're his girlfriend after I told you to edge the public, maybe we would have given you the choice to back out of this agreement one last time, but it seems as though he stole that chance from you. I'm working on a post about your injury and will send you a caption along with the picture to post. Something that not only makes the Foghorns shine but doesn't involve you getting in a car accident."

"Don't you think people will figure it out?" I ask.

Gretchen waves her hand dismissively. "Already contacted my friend down at the precinct. It's all taken care of."

"What does that mean?" I ask.

"Nothing will be charged. You're good to go. No record of it will be shown."

"But she wasn't the one who fucked up," Graydon says. "A police car ran into her."

"But she pulled out on the street without looking," Gretchen says.

"This is bullshit, and you know it," Graydon says, stepping in closer behind me. My eyes catch on Troy's as he regards his son with humor. And not the kind of humor that screams pride, more like, *look at this fool...*

"It's fine," I say, trying to put a blanket over the sizzling rage brewing behind me.

"It's not fine. Gretchen just erased any chance of you getting money from your insurance company to get your car fixed."

Coach Keenan smiles sardonically. "Good thing she has a capable *boyfriend* who can drive."

"Oh no, that's not necessary," I say. "I can, um...I can figure things out. No need to bother Graydon."

"He got you into this mess, sweetheart," Troy says, those blue eyes piercing right through me, filling me with darkness. "He can be bothered."

"Don't fucking call her that," Graydon snaps, making Troy laugh and causing the tension to become suffocating.

Wanting to get out of here before Graydon blows a gasket, I say, "Um, okay, if that's all, I guess I'll just wait for the picture and caption."

"No, you're not posting that bullshit," Graydon says.

"She is," Gretchen says with a nod. "Sorry, but if she doesn't post it, then I will. Don't forget, she gave me the password information. So she can either do it herself, or I will."

"It's fine. I can do it," I say.

"Great." Gretchen smiles. "Now, tomorrow, I have a team going to your house to do your hair and makeup for the event."

"Oh, I can do it myself," I say. Although, that will be trickier with my left hand out of action.

"I'm sure you can, but like I said, we have control over things now, so we will have the team there by four." Gretchen checks her watch again. "Unless there are any other things that need to be discussed, I have some other fires to put out."

When no one says anything, she smiles and takes off.

I turn my attention back to Coach Keenan and Troy, waiting for them to add something, but when they don't, I stand and offer them a curt wave. "Nice, uh, nice meeting you."

I turn away from them and head out of the office, Graydon following as he places his hand on my lower back. Shocked, I glance back at him only to find his jaw in a tight set and an incredibly unhappy expression on his face.

He doesn't say a thing as he guides me through the halls, waits for the elevator, rides the elevator to the first floor, and then moves me toward the exit where the players' parking lot is located.

Once we're outside, I pause and turn toward him, reaching for my bag. "I can take that now."

"Leave it the fuck alone," he snaps, his rage looking like it's about to tip over any second.

Oh boy. How far can I push him? And when I say, "push him," I mean get my way, because it's looking like he's about to take control.

"I can just call an Uber from here and—"

"You're not calling a goddamn Uber." Gently, he takes my unharmed wrist and tugs me toward a large black truck with a double cab and shortened bed. The windows are tinted, and when he pulls the passenger-side door open, I take in the crisp, clean black interior, despite the truck clearly being an older model. "Get in," he says.

"You don't have to—"

"Get. In."

Not wanting him to actually pop a vein, I step up on the footer of the truck and then hoist myself in. He sets my bag next to me, and to my surprise, he takes the seat belt and leans over me, buckling me in before shutting the door.

Okay, well, looks like he's driving me home.

He moves stiffly around the truck and then effortlessly climbs in. For how old his truck is—I know this is not the latest model—I'm really shocked by how clean the interior is and how well it is taken care of.

The truck roars to life, and he pulls out of the parking lot.

"Where do you live?"

"Um, is your phone hooked up for GPS?"

He pulls his phone out of his pocket and hands it to me. I quickly type in my address and hand it back to him. The GPS directs him where to go as silence falls between us.

I don't know what to say, and I don't know how to calm the raging inferno of a man next to me. Although, I can't say I'm surprised by

Graydon's reaction. His dad…he seemed like pure evil. Like his duty in life is to find ways to piss his son off. Well, mission accomplished today.

Graydon's grip on the steering wheel is so tense, it almost seems like he's about to bend the circle in half. The tightness in his pecs is making it seem like the fabric of his shirt is about to bust open. And the sturdy set in his jaw is giving his facial features a dangerous, menacing expression that I don't want to mess with.

So I don't.

I keep my mouth shut.

I'm sure he's dealing with a myriad of thoughts right now. One being why I signed up for this PR stunt in the first place. Another probably involving regret over announcing that I was his girlfriend. And then there's his father.

There's something seriously complicated going on between them, and I dare not even whisper a thought about it because I know he'll put me right in my place and tell me it's none of my business.

It makes me wonder if that is the reason he slammed my phone down that one night when we were attempting to share a meal together. Is there something about his relationship with his father that he doesn't want me to know…or the public, for that matter?

From the anger steaming off him and the way he spoke to his father, I'm going to guess yes.

We pull onto my road, and just to be helpful, I say, "It's the white building on the left, with the damaged car out front."

His eyes narrow, his forehead so creased with irritation that I think I could stick a quarter in his brow and it wouldn't budge.

He finds a parking spot and puts the truck in park. I'm about to tell him I can hop out from here, but he snags my bag and gets out of the truck.

Looks like he'll be helping me.

I turn to the side, using my other hand to unbuckle, and it takes me a second, so when I go to open the truck door, Graydon's already there, holding it wide for me. He holds his hand out to me, and for a second, I stare down at it, wondering why he's being so kind. It's not like I hurt myself at his facility, or during something that we were doing, but ever since he saw me, saw the pain I was in, his attitude has changed from irritated manbeast to irritated yet protective.

And don't get me started on the pink wrap. I didn't have to ask to know why he demanded it.

He did it because of my love of flamingos, and I've spent the entire time since he put in the request not thinking about how special that request was to me. How much such a simple gesture meant to me.

Because it's stupid and nonsensical...and yeah, it makes my heart pound just a little faster.

I take his hand, and he helps me out of his truck before quickly letting go of my hand. I turn to him to take my bag, but he doesn't budge.

"What apartment?" he asks.

"You don't—"

"What apartment, Baker?"

I should have known that was coming.

With a sigh, I lead the way, bringing him inside the multifamily building split into six different apartments.

I lead him to the back where my door is located and reach into my bag—that he's *still* holding—and grab my keys, then unlock the door. I push it open and allow him inside, letting him take in my very plain apartment.

White walls meet sand-colored carpet. White curtains fall over the tall windows, and very minimal tan-colored furniture completes the small one-bedroom apartment. There's nothing special about it, not many decorations, and it never bothered me until Graydon St. John stepped into my apartment. As he takes in the meager dwellings, insecurity pulses through me in an instant. There's no doubt in my mind that his place is probably ten times nicer than mine.

Embarrassed, I say, "Uh, I got rid of everything before I moved to Peru, so I really don't have much." If there was one thing I learned being away from Western civilization for three years, it was that we have far more than we need. Our clothes, our food, our *things*...there's just such an excess. So I didn't reclutter my life upon returning. I live simply, I eat simply, and it's been...freeing. At least that's what I like to tell myself.

He sets my bag down on the kitchen counter and turns toward me. "Where is your ibuprofen?"

"In my bathroom, but you don't need to do anything. Seriously, I can handle this."

"Tell me to back off one more time, Baker, and see where it gets you," he says as he charges toward my bathroom.

I guess I won't be getting rid of him anytime soon, so I move over to my couch, where I take a seat and curl my legs into my chest, resting my bandaged wrist on top of my knees.

He reappears with a small bottle of ibuprofen, clearly not happy about it. Then he moves to my kitchen and pops open my fridge.

Crap, I haven't gone grocery shopping recently, so it's really bare in there.

He grumbles something under his breath and pulls his phone from his shorts pocket before tapping away on it.

"Um, what are you doing?" I ask.

He doesn't answer as he continues to tap away, opens my fridge again, and then does some more tapping.

So I wait.

He goes back to my room, comes back out, and looks in my cabinets.

Then back into my bedroom.

When he returns to the living room, he tugs on the back of his neck, staring down at his phone before he pockets it and then looks up at me.

"Care to share what you were just doing?"

"Do you need to shower or anything?"

"What?" I ask.

"Do you need help showering?"

"Uh...no. I'm good. I took a shower before I left this morning."

"You showered before a workout?"

"Yes, I didn't want to smell like early-morning human."

"Is that a thing?"

"It is."

He goes with it. "How's your face?"

"Sore," I say.

"If you had any sort of ice, I'd offer you some to help with the bruising, but since it seems like you have nothing, I'll have to wait until my order is delivered."

"Your order?" I ask, my brows shooting up.

"Yes, my order." Then he hops up on the kitchen counter and starts scrolling through his phone again, blocking me out.

Well, this is fun.

---

Graydon walks back into my living room, taking care of the trash accumulated after his "delivery."

I'm going to tell you, it was anything but a delivery. Because while I clumsily attempted to check emails on my phone and update Everly and Phil on my injuries and current state—very awkwardly typing with one hand—he bought an entire department store along with a grocery store.

I opened my mouth to protest, but he growled at me, so I just sat back, iced my face with an ice pack that he found in the back of my freezer I forgot about, and watched him move around my apartment, unloading food into my fridge and cabinets. Then he unboxed a brand-new coffee maker, a few mugs, and coffee pods on my counter. He moved into my bedroom and took out brand-new fluffy white bedding and light pink sheets, along with towels, a bath mat, and whatever else he thought I needed. He came back into the living room, grabbed the side table he purchased, and set it next to the couch before sticking a potted plant on it.

He draped a few Foghorns T-shirts on the couch arm, a Foghorns tumbler, and of course a mug.

When he was done, he answered the door again for a food delivery that he plated and brought over to me.

I watched him work in silence, my mouth agape as I thought about all the ways I could return the things he purchased, the things I didn't need, but the things that made this apartment look so much more...homey.

From the light pink area rug to the throw pillows to the freaking candle on the coffee table.

I don't even know what to say.

What to do.

I don't know how to respond because with the snap of his fingers, he just turned my entire living situation upside down. *And what mammoth football-playing mortal buys pink throw pillows for a virtual stranger's bedroom? What's with that?* Let alone a potted plant. What is going on?

After he gives me what was inside the food delivery—a bowl of soup and a plate of grilled cheese—he goes back to the kitchen to grab his plate, then makes one final trip for drinks and the bottle of ibuprofen. He wordlessly hands me a napkin and dives into his food, not even bothering to look at me. I can't just stay silent anymore.

"Um, what's going on here?"

He doesn't answer but instead shoves his sandwich into his mouth.

"Graydon, I'm talking to you."

He chews, swallows, and then sips from his bottle of Gatorade.

"Hello." I poke him with my finger.

He glances down at where I poked him in the shoulder and then turns his gaze back to his food.

"Graydon!" I yell, not holding back anymore. "Stop." I move his plate away and force him to look at me. "What the hell is happening? Why did you get me all of this stuff? Why did you march around my place like Joanna Gaines, decorating my apartment? Why are you sitting here, eating lunch with me in silence?"

He drags his napkin over his face and then, without looking at me, says, "I have a sense of responsibility to protect you now that we're in this agreement. I might not fucking like it, but it's part of the agreement."

"What agreement? Because I don't recall signing anything that says you need to take care of me."

"It's unspoken."

"Uh-huh, and what else is unspoken? Because I'd really like to know what I need to do to hold up my end of the bargain."

His eyes flash toward me, the darkness creeping into his pupils. "What the hell is that supposed to mean?"

Uh, I don't know.

I don't even know what I said to have made him turn on me like that.

"It's...not...there's nothing—"

"Because if you're alluding to sexual favors, I don't need to fluff someone's fucking pillows in order to get head."

My jaw nearly falls to the ground because, oh my God, that is *not* what I was talking about at all, and the fact that he'd even think that is highly insulting.

"That is not what I meant."

"Then why don't you just shut up, eat your food, and be grateful?"

"Excuse me?" I ask, turning toward him. "Did you just tell me to shut up? I don't care what you've done for me today, Graydon. But no one, and I mean no one, talks to me like that."

He pushes his hand through his hair, making the strands stand on end as he lifts himself from the couch.

He's quiet for a second, his body thrumming with anger.

Pacing.

Pulling.

Actually distressed.

"You're right, I'm sorry." He stares down at his plate, still tugging on his hair. "I'm not…I'm not in a good headspace right now."

"Oh, can I help?"

He shakes his head. "No, can you…just…can you just be quiet right now?"

I'm about to protest, but then his dark, hurt eyes meet mine and I clamp down on my response. He's hurting.

Actually hurting.

But why?

If it wasn't for the fact that I experienced the pure distaste and anger that Troy and Graydon shared today, I might have stood my ground and fought with him some more, but those six words—*I'm not in a good headspace*—hold me back.

It's the only thing stirring a sense of empathy in me toward him.

And the only reason I didn't just toss my soup in his face.

He moves over to the counter, sits on top of it, and starts eating again.

I stare at him for a few moments, taking in his turned-in shoulders, the crease in his brow that hasn't left since I showed up with my injuries, and the tightness in his jaw. I don't think there's anything, and I mean anything, that I could do or say that will make this any better.

He's a closed book, and I'm not about to open it. That's not my job.

Finding out who he is as a man is not my job.

Nor am I here to be friends with him.

I'm here to work with him to benefit his team and my flamingos—that's it.

In some respects, he's lucky I'm as pragmatic as I am. I have no doubt that someone else might want to work out his feelings, unpack him and see if they could help heal his hurts. But that's not what this is. Our time together has a dual purpose, and despite how we have to work together, we can still stay in our lanes.

But because I'm not a jerk, I say, "Thank you...for everything."

He grumbles something under his breath but then leaves it at that.

I guess we're done with conversation.

# CHAPTER 15
# GRAYDON

"I'M GUESSING YOU DON'T WANT to talk about it," Hutton says as he takes a seat next to me, returning from the bathroom, at the bar that's walking distance from my place.

"What gave you that impression?" I ask as I tip back my fourth beer of the night.

"Well, we've been here for about a half hour, sitting in silence, just drinking, and nary a mention about the girlfriend proclamation that happened in the training room, so..."

"So what?"

"So...I guess we're not talking about it."

"I guess you're right."

"Cool." From the corner of my eye, I see him nod. "Well, if you're not going to talk about it, then I think I might just go home and fuck my wife, if you don't mind."

"Do whatever the hell you want," I answer.

He stands from the barstool and pats me on the back. "When you need to vent, you know where to find me."

"Between your wife's legs."

"Precisely." He squeezes my shoulder and then takes off, leaving me alone at the bar, feeling like a steaming pile of shit. I appreciate that he sat with me, but he's right. I'm in no mood for company. *Not that that's unusual.* And I don't begrudge him going home to be with his wife.

Christ, today was a compilation of fuck yous.

From Maple being late, to seeing her hurt, to her tears that gutted me, to wanting to shield her from the pain and impending firestorm on her privacy, to seeing my dad, to him being a fucking slimeball all over her, to needing to do something, anything, to make it up to Maple after she had to meet him. *She has no real idea how messy this will get.*

It's why I needed to drive her home to her apartment. Then, once I caught sight of her meager dwellings, I just wanted to...make it better. Can't say I've ever shopped for someone else before. *I doubt I'll ever repeat it either.* How did she have so little? She's...she's so bubbly and feisty...Shouldn't she have all that pretty shit?

Like, Jesus, she didn't even have a coffee maker.

A plant.

Her bedding looked like it was from middle school, pulled straight from a trunk in the attic.

And her apartment was so bland that I couldn't imagine her going through all of this bullshit she's about to embark on and retreat to that... joke of an apartment.

And I shouldn't care. I really shouldn't. She grates on my nerves, there's far too much tension between us, and the last thing I want her to do is feel any sort of...empathy toward me. But I couldn't just stand there and not do anything when I feel this impending need to do *everything* for her.

I drag my hand over my face. What a goddamn mess.

And then there was my dad. I can't remember the last time I saw him, probably at my last game of the past season. Disappointment was written all over his face then, and even though I did my job, it wasn't good enough for him.

I was a disappointment to him. He's told me over and over again I was wasting my time with a front office that wouldn't know how to draft and trade players if their life depended on it, but I couldn't leave. I had to stay here.

I fucking had to stay here…

I down the rest of my beer and plop down a one-hundred-dollar bill on the bar, nodding at the bartender. He offers me a nod back, and I head out the door and walk the block back to my apartment.

It's a calm Friday night, not many people out and about, the wind whipping around off the bay more strongly than it normally does, cutting through the streets of San Francisco. And as I walk, my mind goes to Maple and how she's only four blocks from my place.

Fucking four blocks. I didn't mention that to her because she doesn't need to know, but how are our apartments so different with just a four-block distance in between? It's not that my place is anything to write home about, but it's newly renovated, offers me a sizable garage for my truck, and doesn't have chipping paint coming off the walls.

I bought below my means, but that doesn't bother me. I don't buy fancy things, nor do I care to own them. I live a simple life with a truck that gets me around, an apartment that keeps me warm and dry, and a job that lets me get out my rage.

And when I can't get out my rage because I'm attempting to play nurse on a white horse, I have a bar a block away that allows me to drown all the rage and confusion with a pint glass.

I jog up the steps to my duplex and unlock the door. I flick the lights on, take off my shoes, then head into the living room, where I flop down on my couch and turn on the TV so I can watch the highlights from the day.

I fish my phone out of my pocket and notice a text from Gretchen.

**Gretchen:** The inundation from press after today's post has been insane. You're bringing the team positivity up faster than the other two. And you were the one who I thought would fail.

Wow.

Isn't she fucking sweet.

Also...what post?

I pull up Instagram and go straight to Flock and Tackle, where I see a picture of me watching over Maple as she gets her wrist wrapped with a splint.

It's a candid shot of us together. Maple's face is tilted down so you can't see the bruising, and my eyes are concentrated on her, like if she's not okay, I might find my last breath.

Jesus Christ, was I really that concerned?

I mean, thinking back to it, I was concerned, yeah, but I was angry. I was irritated that she thought she was going to work out with a fractured wrist.

I was a whole bunch of things.

And I was also really pissed that Gretchen was seizing the opportunity, which clearly she had no problem doing.

I read the caption and feel my barely suppressed anger resurface all over again.

"Things got a little intense over at Flock and Tackle, but thankfully the Foghorns training staff was more than happy to help me out. A fractured wrist won't slow me down...just the big guy watching over me."

No doubt Gretchen wrote that.

I'm about to pull up my text thread with Maple when I hear a ding and a text shows up on my phone from Maple herself.

**Maple:** Um, sorry to bother you, but we never discussed if I'm meeting you at the venue tomorrow?

Sorry to bother me?

She's not bothering me.

This entire thing is a fucking bother, but she's not bothering me.

**Graydon:** I'm picking you up.

**Maple:** Where?

**Graydon:** At your apartment. Where else?

**Maple:** Oh, I didn't know. Okay, so you'll just come here then?

**Graydon:** That's usually how picking someone up works.

**Maple:** Right. Okay. Around 6?

**Graydon:** Yeah.

**Maple:** Hair and makeup should be done by then. I hope they are at least. I really don't want that much.

**Graydon:** For what it's worth, you don't need it.

And I fucking mean that.

Even with her face bruised, she's easily one of the most beautiful women I've ever fucking set my eyes on.

**Maple:** Oh, thank you.

**Graydon:** How do you feel? Do you need anything?

**Maple:** I'm fine. You've done enough.

**Graydon:** I'm serious. If you need something, tell me.

I swipe my hand over my face, hating this desperate feeling I have to make sure she feels okay and safe. It's driving me mad, leaving me feeling unsettled, like I can't quite get comfortable in my own skin.

**Maple:** I appreciate that, but I'm okay. And um...thank you for today. Sorry I ruined your training plans.

**Graydon:** Don't apologize.

**Maple:** Well, I am sorry. I know you have training camp next week, and I'm the last thing you want to deal with.

**Graydon:** Stop apologizing.

**Maple:** I'm being serious, Graydon.

**Graydon:** So am I.

**Maple:** I don't want you thinking you need to take care of me. I know you don't want to talk about it, but I don't want to be a burden to you. So, yeah, I'm sorry you missed your training today.

And here I thought the beer calmed me down. She's getting me riled up all over again. She needs to stop apologizing about things out of her control.

**Graydon:** Don't call yourself a burden.

**Maple:** I wouldn't if maybe you didn't make me feel like one most of the time.

I pause, staring down at her honest words. Fuck. How do I respond to that?

Because she's right, I do act like she's a burden most of the time, but not because *she's* the burden. At least, I don't think so.

The situation is a burden. Taking on the responsibility of trying to boost the fans' perception of the team, now that's a goddamn burden. But *she's* just wrapped up in it.

Then again, she didn't say no to the whole PR relationship.

*Yeah, and I was the jackass who proclaimed it this morning.*

I drag my hand over my face again, disgruntled and confused.

It's not even the official start of the season, and I already feel like I'm about to fucking blow.

How the hell will I deal with this for the next five weeks during training camp and then beyond?

**Maple:** From your silence, I assume you agree with me. It's fine. I'll try to make this as easy as possible for you. I'll meet you at the event tomorrow, and I'll put on a show.

Brows turning down, I type her back.

**Graydon:** I said I'll pick you up.

**Maple:** Don't sweat it. See you at the venue.

Growling, I toss my phone to the side and push my hand through my hair.

I'll be damned if she meets me at the venue.

# CHAPTER 16
# MAPLE

"YOU'RE A LIFESAVER," I SAY to Everly, who walks through my door carrying several gowns. "I can't thank you enough."

"Hey, this is what friends are for—" She stalls and looks around the space. "Umm, what's going on? An area rug? Throw pillows? Is that a candle?"

I didn't tell Everly about yesterday, other than that I fractured my wrist. It wasn't that I didn't want her to know. After last night's text messages, I'm still trying to process.

I've never met anyone so hot and cold in my entire life. There are moments when his stern expression takes a reprieve, and I'm met with a man who has a heart, a kind and caring heart. But then it's as if he snaps back into a trance and remembers that he's supposed to be a brooding asshole who makes everyone around him feel like trash.

"Yeah, so Graydon did all of that."

Everly slowly turns toward me, her brow comically raised. "Uh, care to explain? He bought you throw pillows?"

"And new bedding and a coffee machine, and filled my fridge and cupboards with high-protein food, fruits, and veggies. I have a very balanced diet at the moment, along with some ice cream sandwiches, which was a nice touch."

"Okay, you need to fill me in on the details while you try on these dresses."

When I was told I needed a dress for tonight—told several times—I knew Everly would be my girl. She works for Magical Moments by Maggie, which has a wing of the company called Bridesmaid for Hire where they help brides find extra help for their special day. There are always dresses being moved in and out of their office.

I lift an ice-blue dress and take it into my bedroom, where I undo my robe and change into it, the splint on my hand making things harder. I manage to shimmy into the dress. As I'm trying the dress on, I give her the quick version of what happened yesterday.

I step out into the living room and notice how the dress flares out at my hips, feeling more prom dress than fundraiser gown.

Everly shakes her head. "Yeah, not that one."

"Can you take a picture of it with my phone? I'll post the options on stories for Flock and Tackle, and people can decide which one they think I will go with."

"Ooh, look at you being a social media wizard." She picks up my phone from the coffee table and gives me a good pose before taking a picture. "Try this one." She hands me a deep green dress, and I take it back to the bedroom. "So basically he played knight in shining armor yesterday, but then made you feel like shit about it?"

"Basically," I say as I drape the ice-blue dress on the bed, then slip inside the green halter top. "I need help zipping this one." I exit the bedroom.

Everly winces. "Yeah, this isn't great, but we need the picture." She zips me up, takes a pic, then hands me a red cocktail dress.

"This is a bit short, don't you think?"

Everly rolls her eyes. "No, and it wouldn't hurt to flash him those ankles he's so worried about seeing."

I chuckle. "Imagine his horror if I showed up in high-water pants and a zoo shirt."

"After what you just said, he might steal you away and fit you for a dress, then make you feel bad about it later."

I laugh. "Why does that feel like the most accurate thing ever?"

"Because it is," she calls out. "At least you got throw pillows out of all of this."

And they're actually really nice throw pillows. Soft, fluffy. The man weirdly has nice taste.

I slip on the red dress, the fabric hugging my every curve and hitting me mid-thigh. It's scandalous, short, and there's no way I can wear this in public.

I open the door, and Everly's eyes widen. "Oh my God, that one."

"Are you crazy?" I shake my head. "There is no way I'm wearing this."

"Oh yes, you are," she says. "I refuse to let you wear anything else."

"Everly, it's too short, too tight, and I look like I'm about to go out for a night on the town, where I prowl the street corners looking for company." Leaning in, I whisper, "Company that pays me for certain services."

She chuckles and shakes her head. "No, you look hot."

I glance down at the simple dress with an off-the-shoulder sleeve, form-fitting bodice, and short hem.

"I don't even have shoes to wear with this."

Everly picks up her bag from near the front door. "I knew you were going to say that, so I came prepared." She pulls out a pair of matching red high heels. "These will do, and oh look, matching lipstick too."

"Why do I feel like you planned this all along? Is this even a bridesmaid dress?"

"That's neither here nor there." She claps her hands and then makes me turn around so she can finish zipping me up. "This is perfect. He's going to pass away when he sees you in this."

"'Pass away'? Isn't that a bit extreme?"

"Well, at least you wouldn't have to worry about him being an ass anymore. Death by red dress, what a way to go."

I move back into my bedroom and look at myself in the mirror. "I don't know, Everly, it doesn't seem...appropriate."

"Believe me, it's entirely appropriate." Everly stands behind me and pushes my hair to the side. "This is so pretty on you, and you'll really stand out. Isn't that what you want?"

"No," I say. "I don't ever stand out. I'm always the girl in the background, and I like it there."

I've always felt more comfortable around animals than humans. Birds in particular—no surprise there. I wasn't interested in the junior or senior prom, didn't join a sorority in college, and apart from Everly and Polly, my friend from college, I don't have many friends. And I'm quite happy with that. I'm a happy people watcher...on the periphery. Standing out, *in a red dress*, has never been my desire.

"Well, you're not that girl anymore, not when Graydon will be by your side at this event." She places her hands on my hips and talks to me while looking at the mirror in front of us. "Not that we need to change for society, but you can make it easier for yourself to thrive."

"What do you mean?"

"I mean, keep your vibrant, sweet, loving personality, but dress the exterior in something the public can't possibly hate. Don't give them fodder to troll the girl who's hooked to Graydon St. John. Give them all the reason to cheer you on."

"But don't you think a short red dress screams...hussy?"

"No, it screams bold and confident."

"What about that black dress?" I say, moving to the living room. "Don't you think that will look nice?"

"The bodice is rippling with jewels. I brought it as a joke."

I sigh and lean against the doorframe, looking my friend in the eye. "This is not me."

"Neither is the girl who would be seen romantically with someone like Graydon St. John. Sometimes we just need to play the part." She smirks and adds, "And make them drool while you do."

I roll my eyes. "Trust me, Graydon's not going to drool over this dress. The day Graydon drools over me is the day I sprout dragon wings and fly."

---

"Oh, um, my friend gave me this lipstick to wear tonight," I say to the makeup artist, Marty, who's finishing up. My hair is done as well, pulled back into a low bun—something I could have easily manufactured if I didn't have a splint, but hey, not my money spent.

"Oh, thanks," Marty says as she takes the lipstick and lines my lips. When she's done, she sprays what I learned is setting spray all over my face while her friend packs up everything else. She hands me a mirror. "What do you think? We kept it neutral, didn't go heavy, and just accentuated your eyes. Your skin's flawless, so I didn't have to add much foundation, just a little to even your skin tone and to cover the light bruising."

I take a look at myself in the mirror, and honestly, I'm blown away. She really didn't add much, which I appreciate. She did a very thin line of black around my eyes to make them pop, coated my lashes with mascara, and added some blush and bronzer. Honestly, the red lips are the real highlight.

My hair is slicked back, but in a higher bun than I expected, giving me more shape.

Huh...I look...I look really nice.

"This is lovely. Thank you."

"Of course." Marty finishes packing up, and I glance at the time. Fifteen minutes before I need to leave.

"Umm, should I tip?" I ask awkwardly, unsure how this works.

Marty waves her hand. "It's all taken care of. If you ever need us for another event, you have our card."

"I do. Thank you."

They let themselves out, and I go to my bedroom, grateful Everly helped me with my strapless bra before she left because that would have been a bitch to get on myself with this stupid splint.

"Oh shit," I say just as I remember I need help zipping up the rest of the dress. I was going to ask Marty to help but completely forgot.

Maybe they haven't gone far. I quickly put the dress on and head toward my door, just as there's a knock.

Oh thank God, they must have forgotten something.

I open the door and say, "Thank goodness—" My words fall short as Graydon stands in front of me in an all-black suit, black button-up shirt, and black tie. His hair is styled into that perfect fauxhawk of his and he smells like he just climbed out of a fancy parlor where business dealings take place.

His dark, smoky eyes roam over my body as he takes me in, stealing my breath right from my lungs as they stutter over my legs, at my waist, and then all the way up to my eyes.

"Umm…you're, uh, you're here," I say, really unsure how to handle this because, wow, he looks so freaking good in a suit.

A suit that must be bespoke because it fits every part of his body perfectly.

"I told you I'd pick you up," he says, his cologne penetrating every functioning brain cell I have.

"You did." I nod. "Yup, that's right, you did say that. I just thought we landed on something else, but you know, who cares, you're here now, so, um…do you want to come in?"

"Would rather not stand out here and wait."

My expression falls as my brain cells start functioning again. "A simple yes would have sufficed."

God, insufferable.

I turn around, about to head back into my bedroom when he moves in behind me and gently tugs on my good wrist, keeping me in place.

Stunned, I whirl around to look up at him when my hand lands on his chest, and his expression softens.

Not saying a word, he slowly and deliberately turns me around so my back is to his chest. I suck in a sharp breath as his knuckles rub against my bare back right before his fingers close around the zipper of my dress. With his other hand on my waist, he glides the zipper up slowly until the dress is firmly in place.

My breath ceases to exist as his hands gently slide down my sides, to my waist, and then turn me around to face him again.

"Need anything else?" he asks, the darkness in his eyes penetrating, but no longer bordering on angry.

Oh my God, why does it feel like my heart is about to pop out of my chest?

I wet my lips, my nerves jumping around inside me. "Umm, no. Just going to slip on my shoes quickly."

"Okay," he says as he takes a step forward, crowding my space and then shutting the door behind him. I stand there, staring into his eyes, the energy coming off him powerful, intimidating, making me feel broken, like I don't know how to walk anymore.

He wets his lips as well, not breaking eye contact, just slipping his hands in his pockets, his chest moving up and down.

It's the longest few seconds of my life, just me and him, tension, electricity bouncing between us. I have a deep awareness that we're in my apartment, dressed up, but all I am thinking about is how much I want to undress him.

And that's new.

Because I haven't thought of him that way.

I've always thought of him as *the ass.*

The beautiful ass, but an ass nonetheless.

I've never considered what it might feel like to undo his tie, to unbutton his shirt, to take off his belt. And yet, here I am, all those thoughts pulsing through my head, all because he shows up at my place in a suit...and zips up my dress.

What the hell is wrong with me?

After a few more seconds, he finally breaks the silence. "Are you going to put your shoes on or just stare at me?"

Yup, that snaps me out of it.

"Shoes," I say, spinning around, but then tripping over my own feet and tumbling forward.

I wince as I tip over, but he's quick to my side, catching me by the waist and pulling me back to my feet and right against his rock...hard...chest.

Dear God in heaven, I'm sweating.

"Jesus," he mutters. "Don't go fucking up your wrist even more."

His tone suggests I planned on doing that.

"I didn't mean to," I say, shrugging away from him, but he still holds on to my waist, checking to make sure I'm fine. When I take another step back, he releases me but doesn't look happy about it. *What is going on with him?*

*And me, for that matter.*

"Be careful," he says in a darker voice. Wait, is he...reprimanding me?

"I will," I say back, unsure how to respond to such a demand.

And weren't my thoughts just a second ago about wanting to undress him? Yes, those are long gone as he thrusts me back into reality with his prickly disposition.

Well, not long gone. I am a human with eyes.

As I start to walk away, he leans against the door, his large body taking up all of the space in the entryway as he folds his bulky arms across his thick chest, his eyes not leaving me as they follow me through the apartment.

Never straying.

Just...hungry.

Very, very hungry.

Graydon St. John *is* a man of few words, and that silence he loves to keep, well, it's saying a whole lot right now.

*And I have no clue how to interpret it.*

# CHAPTER 17
# GRAYDON

"DUDE, YOU LOOK LIKE SECRET service, ready to murder with your own hands," OC says as he comes up to me, wearing a navy blue suit with a white shirt underneath, the top few buttons undone. Next to him is, fuck, what is his name? Trevor? He's wearing a full-on safari outfit minus the hat. But he's making khaki his bitch tonight, that's for damn sure.

"Don't call me 'dude.'" I sneer at him.

OC winces, then directs his attention to Maple. "How do you deal with the grump on the daily?"

She takes a sip of her champagne. "Alcohol." This causes OC to let out a wallop of a laugh.

Fucking idiot.

Bennett isn't here because he's out of town for an away game, but his zookeeper is zooming around from group to group, chatting it up while I stand off in the corner with Maple, trying to avoid talking to anyone.

Gretchen would have a fucking fit, but I don't give a shit. The last thing I want to do is engage in small talk, especially with a bunch of people I don't know or care to know.

"Oh, there's Wallace. I'm going to go say hi," Khaki Man says before he takes off, leaving me with OC and Maple.

OC rocks on his heels, hands in his pockets, looking around with what seems like a million questions on his mind, but for once, he's reading the room as he says, "You know, I think I might go get a refill on my drink."

He takes off, leaving me alone with Maple.

Maple in a short, tight red dress.

Maple in heels that define her legs in a way I didn't even know was possible.

Maple with her blue eyes looking like endless pools of solitude.

And those goddamn red lips.

Like a siren, calling to me, testing me.

It's driving me fucking nuts.

When she opened her door, I honestly didn't know what I expected her to be wearing, but that dress...I swear she's taunting me. Not that we've ever interacted in a way that involves sexual taunting, but it fucking felt like that.

She's basically giving me a middle finger about my high-water pants comment. The way the fabric hugs her curves, making my vision go dizzy as I narrow in on her waist, her hips, and her ass...fuck, when she turns around I'm going to have to look away.

It's taking me fucking effort to keep my eyes straight ahead.

To not drool.

To not constantly check her out every goddamn second we share the same air.

It's been an effort since day one, when I first met her, but I've been able to control it—for the most part. Now that she's in that dress, Jesus, it's as alluring as the goddamn yoga pants. At least she was sitting down when she was wearing those, hidden under the table.

She's not hidden at all tonight.

Nope, out in the open for my goddamn wandering eyes.

And I hate myself for it.

I really fucking do.

I wish I had more goddamn control.

But I don't. The only control I had was exerted when zipping up her dress in her apartment and not taking it off. I also was able to hold back the onslaught of drool and inappropriate compliments that rolled through me. Like...

*Christ, you look hot.*

*And...lock the door, get undressed, you're not leaving this apartment.*

*And...bend over, ass up, underpants off.*

Maple clears her throat, waking me up from my red-dress reverie. "You know, I think we're supposed to mingle, talk to people, not be silent brooders in the corner of the event space, but what do I know about fundraising events?" she asks, a bit of snark in her voice.

"Then go mingle," I say, nodding toward the crowd.

"It would help if my celebrity counterpart came with me."

"Wouldn't that require you to drink more alcohol...spending that much time with me?"

Her eyes fall on mine. "Yes, it would, but I don't believe emptying the adult watering hole is going to help the situation, therefore, I shall suck it up and stick to this one drink."

"That's awfully big of you."

"Well, someone has to be," she says with a shrug and then takes another sip of her drink.

I step toward her, my voice dark as I say, "Pretty sure you can guess how big I am."

At a snail's pace, her head tilts as her eyes scan me. When our gazes meet, she wets her lips. "That's...that's not what I meant."

"Seems as though you don't mean a lot of the things you say when you're around me." I reach out and take her glass of champagne, only to down the rest of it.

"Hey, I was drinking that."

"And I finished it," I say, setting it down on the tray of a server going by. I place my hand on her lower back and add, "Now, you want to talk to people, so lead me to people to talk to."

"What are you going to say to them?" she asks, worried.

"I'm going to talk about the stilt-legged dipshits…Is that what I called them?"

Her eyes narrow, and she fully turns toward me, rage simmering behind those stunning eyes of hers. "Don't you dare."

"Or was it knobby-kneed nitwits?"

She backs away from me, her finger ready to rise as she prepares to lecture me.

"Better check the body language, Baker. People are watching, and they might think we're in a lovers' quarrel. Wouldn't want that, would we?"

Her back stiffens, and she tucks her finger back into her tiny fist before moving closer to me. I keep my hand on her back but tug her in just a hint closer so she's almost pressed completely against me.

She doesn't smell like her normal lavender self tonight. Instead, she must have sprayed some sort of fancy perfume, something feminine that I can't quite put my finger on. Whatever it is, it smells phenomenal.

So fucking good, I'm tempted to run my nose along her neck to try to pinpoint exactly what kind of scent it is.

Between the dress, the way she highlighted her eyes, and her perfume, she has me wrapped around her angry little finger, and it's taking everything in me to attempt to remind myself that I'm not interested.

That nothing good could come of making a move.

That this is strictly business.

But…fuck…why does she have to smell so goddamn good tonight?

To my surprise, her hand lands on my chest as she looks up at me, a smile crossing her red-painted lips. But the darkness in her eyes says she's anything but interested. "We are here to bring awareness to flamingos. It's part of the deal. Now, if you don't want me posting embarrassing things about you on Flock and Tackle—"

"I'm not hiding anything embarrassing."

"Oh yeah, then why won't you let me google your name?"

My entire body shifts, like an earthquake of fear and anger colliding together. All thoughts of how she smells and how beautiful she looks quickly vanish. "Do not fucking joke about that," I sneer.

"Body language," she singsongs.

I'll show her fucking body language.

So I lay my hand on her cheek, pushing her chin up with my thumb as I lower ever so slightly. I'm mere inches away from those red-painted lips. "Do not fucking threaten me, Baker."

"Isn't that what you were just doing to me, *St. John*?"

"I was joking."

"Ooh, that joke fell flat. You should try—"

"Maple?" Someone interrupts us.

Together, we turn to the side, where a nerdy-looking man grins excitedly, wearing a simple suit that unfortunately fits him poorly. He has brown hair with a middle part falling over his forehead, while stupidly thin-framed glasses sit perched on his nose.

Maple gasps as she turns. "Oh my God, Hank? What are you doing here?"

Who the hell is Hank?

I can barely process the question before Maple is dropping me like a piece of trash and securing her arms around the strange man's neck, pulling him into a hug. I watch as he loops his arms around her waist, picks her up, and starts spinning her around.

What.

The.

Fuck.

Spinning her? Seriously? He has about two fucking seconds to put her down before I do it for him.

"Holy shit," he whispers while he sets her on her feet and looks her up and down. "Wow, Maple, you look incredible."

"Thank you," she says, beaming. Like, actual light is seeping from every pore in her face as she stares at this fucking nimrod. "You, wow, have you been working out?"

*Have you been working out?*

*Uh, fucking excuse me?*

He shamelessly flexes his bicep. "Oh, you know, a little."

"Well, you look great." She wets her lips, letting her eyes roam over him.

"So do you."

He does the same, staring far too long at her curves for my liking.

And then silence falls, an unspoken exchange passing between them.

He smiles.

She smiles.

He shakes his head in disbelief.

She coyly tucks a loose strand of hair behind her ear.

I stand there watching the entire exchange, my fist clenching at my side, ready and willing to break bones.

*What the fuck is going on?*

He laughs. "Wow, when I moved here, I thought—"

"You moved here?" she asks, bouncing on the goddamn tips of her toes.

"Yeah, about a week ago. I thought about calling you, but I didn't know...wasn't sure of your situation."

"There's no situation. I'm totally—"

"Unavailable," I say as I step in, only towering over this guy by a few inches. I wish it was fucking more. I *wish* I was so much bigger than this fuck that when I stepped up next to him, his stupid little fucking knees quivered with fear.

"Yeah, I was going to say, looked like you were very much... unavailable."

Maple stiffens next to me as I slide my arm around her waist, letting my fingers dig into the fabric of her dress.

"I'm available for coffee, though, with a friend," she says, hope in her eyes.

"I'd really like that." He then lifts her arm and asks, "What happened?"

"Oh, you know—"

"Things got away from us one night," I answer for her. "Not going to use those handcuffs again, right, babe?"

I swear I can actually feel the heat building under her skin, ready to explode on me. It's practically burning my palm and melting my fingerprints off my fingertips.

Glasses Boy looks between us, his cheeks flushing as he clears his throat. "Well, lesson learned," he says awkwardly. "Anyway, I have an interview on Monday with your zoo."

Maple grows stiff. "Wait, are you serious? To work with the flamingos?"

A large smile crosses his cheeks as he nods.

Hold on a fucking second.

This dude just happens to run into us at a zoo fundraiser, acts surprised to see Maple, pretends like I don't fucking exist for at least a minute, and then just drops the bomb that he's going to possibly work with Maple?

What kind of con artist is this guy?

"Ahhh!" Maple squeals before pulling him into another hug. "Oh my God! I'm so excited."

Christ.

A con artist that Maple seems to believe.

And she didn't even introduce me to the dweeb. What's with that?

---

I hate tonight.

I hate everything about it.

I hate that I had to dress up. I hate that I had to mingle with a bunch of people I don't care about. I hate that Maple looks so damn good that for seventy percent of the evening, I thought about ways to slip her dress off her. And mostly, I hate the way I'm feeling right now…like someone lit some sort of jealous bomb in my chest and walked away, leaving me to deal with this unsettling and foreign feeling.

And you know what? I'm not going to admit that it bothers me that another man, who has more in common with Maple, talked to *her* the entire night as if I didn't exist.

I'm not going to admit that when he was sucking an olive from his martini, I wished he would choke on it.

And I'm not going to admit that when we parted ways, my fucking skin crawled as she touched him three more fucking times, ending the night with a quick kiss on the cheek.

Nope, it's fine.

Everything's fucking fine.

I'm not irritated, I'm not jealous…I'm not about to find out where Glasses lives and threaten his life if he ever goes near Maple again.

Nope, I'm good.

I pull up in front of her apartment and put the car in park. I'm about to open my door to walk her up to her place when she stops me. "Don't bother," she says, opening her door herself.

Don't bother?

Yeah, that's not how this works.

I get out of my truck and follow her to the steps of her apartment, where she turns around, almost coming face-to-face with me as she stands on the first step.

"I said don't bother."

"And I chose not to listen to that," I reply.

"Do you ever listen?"

"It's rare."

She huffs and then turns away from me and charges up her stairs. I follow until she reaches her apartment. She ignores my domineering presence, opens the door, and quickly slides in, trying to shut the door on me, but I slide my foot in the crack and prevent her from doing so. She has nothing on my strength, so I slide the door open and let myself in before shutting it behind me.

"Graydon, I'm not in the mood to get into an argument with you right now."

I lean against her door, watching as she nervously crosses her arms over her chest, attempting to look tough, but I see right through her.

I don't want to get into an argument either. Not because I don't have things to say, because I do. I have so much to say about that fucking prick who thought he could just show up and put himself between Maple and me as if he had the goddamn right. I really don't want to get into an argument because I don't know what the hell I'm doing here in her apartment in the first place. Any sane man would have just dropped her off and left, but I'm anything but sane right now.

I feel downright jealous.

Angry.

Betrayed, which is so fucking stupid, because what did she really do?

Nothing.

So why do I care about Flamingo Boy?

Why did I feel this insane, possessive pulse thrumming through me when he got near her?

Why did I desire to bring her back to her apartment to make sure she came back alone...with no one else?

All questions I'm not prepared to answer.

"I don't want to argue either," I say.

"Okay, so...why are you here?"

She wets her lips and my eyes track the movement, my stomach aching from the sight of her glistening red lipstick.

I don't answer her, because I really don't have an answer. I don't know why I'm here other than I want to be. I want to make sure she's here, alone. I want to make sure that no other fuck has the privilege of seeing her right before she gets ready for bed.

So I push off her door, close the space between us, and then gently place my hand on her waist before slowly turning her around, her back to my chest.

Surprised, she looks over her shoulder and shakily asks, "What are you doing?"

"Helping," I say as I rest my hand on her hip and then take her zipper and slowly slide it down her back until it reaches the very top of her black lace underwear.

Jesus.

My mouth goes dry at the mere sight of the delicate fabric, at the way the gentle slope of her back leads to a pair of dimples right above her ass. Her round, pert ass.

"Oh," she says breathlessly. "Um, thank you."

"You're welcome," I say, not moving away, my hand still on her hip, her scent clouding my thoughts and judgment.

She slowly looks over her shoulder, and when our eyes meet, a beat of electricity pushes between us, a wave that almost tastes palpable, like something is brewing that I'm not ready to accept.

But something my body desperately wants.

I swallow the saliva building up in my mouth as she blinks up at me, her lashes framing the depths of blue in her eyes, her innocence reflecting like endless pools, inviting me in to corrupt the calm waters.

"Do you need help with anything else?" I ask, my thumb betraying me and skimming across her exposed lower back.

"I...I don't think so."

She doesn't need anything else, so step away.

And yet, I don't.

Glancing down at her back again, I feel this fiery desire to caress my finger over her spine, from the nape of her neck to the delicate slope of her...

Jesus Christ, what is happening to me?

Snap the fuck out of it.

But...I can't.

My eyes travel back down to the clasp of her bra, my mind working on all the different ways that I could take it off. How I could push her up against the wall, right here, right now, and pull down the cups of her bra, exposing her.

I bring my fingers to the black lace bra, my mind racing, and quietly say, "I can take care of this for you."

Her short intake of breath collides with my thoughts—my muddled, confused, fucking scary thoughts—and when her eyes meet mine again, I can see those thoughts mirrored in her pupils.

Muddled.

Confused.

Scared.

Because something *is* brewing.

Something different between the two of us.

Something that has my body buzzing with lust.

With need.

With so much pent-up energy that if I'm not fucking careful, I'll do something really stupid, something I won't be able to take back.

After a few short, agonizing seconds, she says, "Um, is it weird if you help?"

Maybe, but I want to.

I want to be the one removing her clothes, no one fucking else and especially not Glasses.

I shake my head. "No."

"Then, um...sure. Thank you."

She turns her back toward me, and it takes everything in me not to drag my fingers along her soft skin as I reach for the clasp. Instead, I hold back my natural instincts, and slowly, one prong at a time, unhook her strapless bra until it falls loose. Maple holds the front of her dress close to her chest so nothing falls, which is a reminder that if she were possibly feeling the same way as me in this moment, she would let her dress and bra fall to the ground.

But she doesn't.

So I pull away to avoid the temptation standing in front of me. I take a step back, putting just enough distance between us so I keep my hands off her, and as she turns toward me, her dress hangs loose, ready to fall at any second. I raise my gaze to hers. All she would have to do is lift her arms and she'd be bare to me, and for some stupid reason, I find that really fucking appealing.

This is dangerous.

Very dangerous.

I need to fucking leave.

I tug on the back of my neck, taking another step back. "Anything else you, uh, you need?"

She shakes her head. "No, I think...I think I'm good."

"Okay." I glance at her one more time, those eyes huge as they stare up at me. *Drop your arms, Maple. Let me see your fucking gorgeous body. Let me kiss your soft skin like we both want. Let me show you what a real man would do with you. Let me own you...like you're owning me in this moment.*

*Just one taste...*

But that one taste would ruin me. I know it would. And I can't...I can't risk being ruined, not right now, not by her.

"See you, uh, Monday," I say.

"Right, first day of training camp."

"Yup," I say with a nod. "I'll pick you up."

A surprised look crosses her face as she says, "Oh, that's not necessary."

"Maple, I'm picking you up. Be ready by five thirty." And then with that, I use every ounce of energy that's not pumping straight to my dick and force myself out of her apartment, my chest heavy and my mind whirling.

What the actual fuck is happening?

# CHAPTER 18
# GRAYDON

**OC:** So…tonight was fun.

**Bennett:** What happened tonight?

**OC:** Fundraising event where Graydon stood in the corner, brooding. Really represented the zoo well.

**Graydon:** Are you trying to ensure my fist touches your pint-sized brain through your nose cavity?

**Bennett:** Yeah, not sure why you're angering him more.

**OC:** Not trying to anger, just trying to figure out what the hell you're doing, man. It might not seem like it, but we're all in this together, and if we can't figure out a way to help our teams' reputations, then we're going to be at this for a long-ass time.

**Bennett:** To be fair, Flock and Tackle seems to be picking up speed.

**OC:** Agreed, it's a golden opportunity, but if he's brooding in the corner during an event because some guy was talking to Maple, then it's going to be useless.

**Bennett:** Wait, why does it matter if she talks to some guy?

**Graydon:** I wasn't brooding about her talking to some guy.

**OC:** I took a picture. You tell me what you see. [Picture]

**Bennett:** Not wanting to make things more difficult, but that's brooding.

**Graydon:** That's my normal face.

**OC:** There's more crease to your brow.

**Bennett:** Jaw is tighter.

**OC:** Fist clenched at your side.

**Bennett:** A snarl in your lip.

**Graydon:** Are you two fucks done?

**OC:** It would just be great if you could acknowledge the brooding.

**Graydon:** Fine, I was brooding, but it was because some asshat thought he could steal all of Maple's attention.

**Bennett:** Wait, did I miss something? Do you like Maple?

**Graydon:** No.

**OC:** Um, I think that's a lie, but we'll let you live in denial and embarrass yourself later when you realize you need the Gladdy Daddies' help because you're in love with a zookeeper.

**Bennett:** When did we agree on the Gladdy Daddies?

**Graydon:** We didn't. That's not what we're called.

**OC:** So you're open to talking about what we're called, then?

**Graydon:** No. This is not a thing.

**Bennett:** Kind of seems like a bit of a thing.

**Graydon:** Bennett, you're letting him get to you.

**Bennett:** I'm not, I just…I don't mind having friends. I might need the Gladdy Daddies at some point.

**OC:** Now there's my boy!

**Graydon:** We are not the Gladdy Daddies!

**OC:** Are you having girl problems, Beanie Baby?

**Bennett:** Don't fucking call me that.

**Graydon:** See how quickly he can turn on you? Don't let him control this text chain with his absurdity.

**OC:** God, everyone is so goddamn sensitive. Just trying to create a rapport.

**Bennett:** Do it by using our regular names.

**Graydon:** And don't call us the Gladdy Daddies.

**OC:** Come up with a new name, and I'll change the group text name.

**Graydon:** The Three Fucks. Done.

**OC:** Although I appreciate your willingness to participate, if we're going to move forward with a podcast and merch once we become more comfortable with each other, the Three Fucks really doesn't lend to commercial appeal.

**Graydon:** Over my dead body will we have a podcast.

**Bennett:** I think we're getting away from the topic at hand. Graydon was brooding over Maple. He doesn't like her but doesn't want some "asshat" talking to her.

**Graydon:** It's not just some asshat talking to her. It's some guy she knows who loves flamingos and wears stupid little glasses.

**OC:** What kind of glasses?

**Graydon:** Why does it matter?

**OC:** Because if they're slutty little glasses, then that's a problem.

**Graydon:** How on earth is that a problem?

**Bennett:** Oh, you know, Bower was telling me about slutty little glasses.

**OC:** Who is Bower?

**Bennett:** My sister's best friend.

**OC:** *Pausing conversation about slutty little glasses* Um, do we have a crush on your sister's best friend?

**Bennett:** This is about Graydon.

**Graydon:** Oh, please, no, take the front seat. I'm more than willing to step back.

**OC:** Holy shit, you like your sister's best friend and Graydon likes his zookeeper who likes Slutty Little Glasses and I've wanted to get back together with my ex for so long but was torn away from her when I was traded to the Rogue and my heart has been bleeding ever since. Look at us...pining Gladdy Daddies!

**Graydon:** We are NOT THE GLADDY DADDIES! Also, I'm not pining. My situation with Maple is different. We're in a PR relationship. I just don't want her making me look dumb by talking to Slutty Little Glasses.

**OC:** Okay, so we're going with the name Slutty Little Glasses. I appreciate you acknowledging that.

**Bennett:** Not that I want to make you angry or anything, but the picture of you brooding is telling me something else. You might not want to be embarrassed by another man, but you're also pining. I could see it in your eyes, and if anyone knows that look, it's me. Because I've been pining for years.

**Graydon:** I'm not pining.

**OC:** You might not think you are, but the moment Slutty Little Glasses steps in, you're going to realize just how much you've been pining this whole time. Mark my words.

---

With flowers in one hand and chocolates in the other, I head into the recreation room. The smells of cleaning supplies and a freshly mopped floor flood my senses as I look over the facility I helped pay for with a very generous donation.

Expansive windows run from floor to ceiling, making it seem like the room is bringing in the beautifully landscaped gardens and the massive weeping willow tree that I've spent hours studying. To the right are tables with matching chairs and puzzles spilled across the tops. To the left, couches and seating for conversation, all of the furniture oversized and comfortable. And close to the window, my favorite part of the building, an entire art section with easels, canvases, paper, paints, charcoal, markers, scrapbooking supplies, clay, yarn, and crayons: anything you could possibly think of when it comes to creating.

And that's where I see her.

A canvas in front of her, her knitted wrap around her shoulders as she studies the weeping willow, her hand stroking over the blank white board in front of her with a pencil.

With an ache in my heart that will never go away, I move through the room, eyes all on me. Not because they know who I am but because of my size.

From the corner of my eye, I catch her nursing aide and pause for a moment. When she gives me the thumbs-up, I continue my approach until I'm right behind the person I love the most.

Squatting low, not wanting to seem intimidating, I turn my baseball cap that's on my head around so it's facing backward like I used to have it growing up and softly say, "Hey, Mom."

She startles for a moment but then turns toward me, her aged face dressed in confusion as she takes me in. I let her process as she looks me over, observing the man I've become, the man that she doesn't know. To her, even though I visit regularly, Graydon St. John is sixteen years old. *And in her mind, I forever will be.*

When I was sixteen, she was taking riding lessons and decided to hop on one of the horses for fun without a helmet. The horse knocked her off and she slammed her head against a pole. She was rushed to the hospital with a traumatic brain injury and was placed in a coma for a week before she came back to us. At first, we thought she'd escaped without harm, until she was examined and a devastating diagnosis was made. Anterograde amnesia. She wouldn't retain any new information from her accident on.

So seeing me as a thirty-year-old man, when the last time she saw me

before the accident I was sixteen, doesn't quite register. The only good thing was that she and my dad were divorced, so she never asks for him, ever.

But me…

I'm much bigger.

Thicker.

With a square jaw and menacing features that have hardened over time as I've tried to hang on to my mom and my dad's tried to push her out of our lives.

She shuffles her shawl over her shoulders and leans farther back, looking nearly horrified, and something in the pit of my stomach grows nauseous as I consider that this might be the third week in a row where she turns me away.

"Mira," Mom's aide, Rhonda, says quietly. "Remember the letter we just read, and the pictures I showed you? This is Graydon."

Mom's almost lifeless eyes flash to me again, her mouth slightly parted as she searches me. I keep my gaze fixed on her, begging, pleading, hoping she can process what we're trying to tell her. I know it's not easy. I know she thinks I should still be sixteen, but a small part of me believes she can do this and break free.

If not, next week I might just have to be the nice guy who paints with her, even though it kills me emotionally, shreds me to pieces that she doesn't know who I am. But at least I can spend time with her.

"I…I don't know," Mom says skeptically, her body language pulling away from me as an ache splinters through my heart.

Rhonda rubs her arm in a comforting way and says, "Would you like to see the pictures again?"

Mom peers at me, her eyes looking directly into mine, and I take that moment to try to push aside all of the anger and hate and let the inner boy come out of me, the one she loves.

Come on, Mom, you can do it.

"M-maybe," Mom answers, giving me hope as I remain in place, not wanting to move, not wanting to scare her.

Rhonda brings over the album and shows her a picture of Mom and me when I was sixteen, then shows pictures of me throughout the years, how I grew every year until I became the man I am now.

It's the first time in three weeks that she's gone through all the pictures in front of me. And when she's done, her eyes look up at me, and tears start to fill them.

"Oh...baby boy," she says, holding out her arms. A world of emotion crashes into me as I pull her into a hug, wrapping my arms around her and letting my body sink into the mind of that little boy who lost his mom fourteen years ago.

Tears immediately fill my eyes as I squeeze them shut, and the world around us fades away as I just let myself feel. Let myself hurt. Let myself mourn.

And let myself soak in every second of this, because it's rare.

"I love you, Mom," I say, burying my head into the crook of her neck.

Her hand cups the back of my neck, and she holds me even tighter.

"I love you, too, Gray, my little saint. I love you, too."

# CHAPTER 19
# MAPLE

I CHECK MYSELF IN THE mirror one more time, hating that I woke up extra early to make sure I looked decent and not like I rolled out of bed and threw some clothes on.

I put on a little bit of mascara to coat my long lashes but left everything else free of makeup. I threw on one of the new sets of workout clothes I purchased this weekend with Everly. We went to an outlet mall, scoured the clearance racks, and were able to find five cute workout sets of sports bras and leggings for fifty dollars. Yeah, fifty. It was crazy. I've never bargain shopped so well in my life.

I told myself I was getting clothes because I'd be on camera and not because I didn't want to look like a poor zookeeper trying to fit in.

And sure, I'm not poor, but I'm not about to spend five hundred dollars on some new leggings just for the hell of it. I use and abuse my clothes until they are just threads on the ground because I don't see the need to keep buying new ones.

After the outlet, we went to the thrift store, which was a jackpot for all Foghorns gear. I got T-shirts—even though Graydon bought me some, I wanted to cut these up—a cool jean jacket, a sweatshirt, and even a T-shirt jersey with Graydon's last name and number on the back. Sixty-eight.

I spent twenty dollars and was so excited about them that Everly and I immediately cut them up when we got home, fitting them so they were sleeveless and more like crop tops, without showing any skin.

Today, I went with my navy blue set of leggings and bra, and the neon yellow T-shirt jersey with Graydon's name and number. I thought about not wearing it as nerves took ahold of me, but Everly thankfully was up early and told me to do it. Do you know how hard it is to put on sportswear with only one good arm? Hard! No one prepared me for that. I was sweating before I had everything on.

So, here I am, waiting for Graydon to pick me up, wearing his number on my back, my leg bouncing up and down with nerves. Nerves because I'm still trying to make sense of what happened when he dropped me off after the fundraiser. He was so...rude and dismissive at the fundraising event. The event was something I was looking forward to, because after getting kicked out of Peru for lack of funding, I realized how important fundraising is. After the event, it was like I was dealing with a different man, and I'm not sure which one is going to show up today.

There's a knock on the door, startling me out of my thoughts, and I hurry to open it.

Standing at six foot five is Graydon, wearing gray sweatpants, a navy blue Foghorns shirt, and a backward hat. He didn't shave, so his scruff is extra thick, his lips look like he just applied a balm, and his eyes almost seem...clear, not clouded in anger like they usually are.

"Morning," he says, holding out a cup of coffee from Roads, the coffee shop where we met with Gretchen. I realize it's just around the corner from here. I can't believe I never noticed it.

"Um, good morning," I say, slightly disturbed that he's not scowling at me or yapping at me to get a move on. I take the to-go cup from him, the smell of caffeine waking me up. "Thank you."

Eyeing me over his lid, he sips his coffee and I watch the way his thick throat contracts as he swallows. Why is that so annoyingly hot? He nods at my outfit and says, "Nice shirt."

Oh my God, was that a compliment?

Consider my pearls clutched, because did Graydon St. John pull the stick out of his ass this morning?

I think he very well did.

And because he's in such a jovial mood—for him; anyone else would probably equate this to deadpan—I turn around and show him the back. "I found it at the thrift store. Is it too much? Should I change?"

I glance over my shoulder to catch a blaze of heat lighting up his pupils as he takes in his name and number printed across my back. A flutter of nerves erupts in the depth of my stomach as his roaming eyes take their sweet time gazing up and down my backside. *Your name is a bit farther north from there, Graydon.*

"Do you not like it?" I ask, his silence making me feel incredibly insecure.

He sips his coffee, his eyes meeting mine again, and after what feels like minutes, he finally says, "My name looks good on you."

"Oh." My cheeks flame into an inferno. "Um, so you...you like it."

"No need to trip over your words, Baker," he says in an exasperated tone, then pushes the door open wider. *There he is.* The asshole. The one I fight against every time I gain more confidence.

God, for a second there, I thought that maybe things were changing, that there was some light at the end of this bickering tunnel, but maybe it was just a hiccup in the road.

I duck under his arm and head out of my apartment, Graydon shutting the door behind him. I lock up and then he leads me down the street where his truck is parked and my car...

"Oh my God, someone stole my car," I say, panic wrenching through my chest.

"No one stole your car," Graydon says in his annoyed voice. "I had a friend come pick it up. They're fixing it."

"How did you get the keys?" I ask, stunned.

"When I was in your place." He shrugs as if it's nothing and opens his truck door, but I don't move.

"You took my keys, gave them to a random stranger, and had them take my car without my permission?"

"Yeah, because if I asked, you would have said no, and as much as I'm enjoying this early-morning rendezvous, I would prefer not to have to be your chauffeur."

"I told you I could have taken an Uber."

"And I told you, that wasn't an option."

"Who put you in charge?" I ask as I sip the coffee he bought me, a raise to his brow.

"I did. Now get the fuck in and buckle up. I don't like being late."

And there you have it, the man I thought went missing this morning. Nope, there he is, hyped up on a double shot according to the label on his to-go cup, ready to eat humans for breakfast.

This should be fun.

---

"Listen up. No one touches her, no one comes close to her, if I even see you bump her, you're fucking with me," Graydon says as I stand next to him in a pair of football pads, a bright pink practice jersey, and a helmet that feels like a ten-pound weight just sitting on the top of my head.

We took a picture together for Flock and Tackle, me next to Graydon, ready to take on the first day of training camp. I'll be honest, I looked ridiculous, but it's also going to make some good content.

We spent a good portion of the morning getting fitted for equipment and warming up, but now that it's over, we're about to get into some agility drills. Since Graydon is one of the captains on the team, he's letting every defensive player know that I'm not to be touched, just in case they happen to actually take me for an itty-bitty rookie who's lost.

FogHorns

"Did you hear me, rookie?" Graydon asks, getting in some poor kid's face.

God, he looks like he's about to shit himself. *Hold on, little fella, don't show fear now, it's only day one.*

"Understood," the rookie says, his voice cracking.

God, I want to hold him to my bosom so I can tell him everything is going to be okay.

"Good, now line up."

Graydon directs me in front of some cones and says, "Watch me, replicate."

Oh yes, it's just that easy, because I have the best coordination on this field.

Honestly, it's shocking that I'm even here. Day one of training camp? The Foghorns must be really hard up for good press. These early training days are sacred. Trust me, I know, because I scoured YouTube looking for what I could expect from today. All I saw were long, hard days of agility, films, and weights. Thankfully, I'm only here for a few hours, and then I'm off to my real job.

When we were getting our equipment, I asked Graydon how the schedule would work for him, and he said that because we're in a "special situation," the team is allowing him a few hours a week to be at the zoo. Lucky for everyone.

Graydon zigs through the cones in front of me while a line of giants stack up behind me, and I realize just how humiliating this is. Like. . . what has my life come to that I thought it would be okay to impersonate a freaking professional football player?

"Got to keep the line moving, Baker," the guy behind me says.

"Oh, sorry."

Hoping the coordination gods are in my corner today, I start zigzagging through the cones like Graydon, really concentrating to make sure I don't trip, and then follow Graydon when he goes to the back of the line.

"Pick up the pace," he grunts to me.

"Uh, still trying to remind my legs they're attached to my brain," I shoot back. "I can't be all speedy like you."

"You can try."

"And what, fall down and fracture my wrist again?"

Before he can answer, he weaves through the cones again and sprints to another set of cones.

Jesus.

I do the same, but my sprint is more like a little corgi galloping along because I have zero athletic talent. I make walking look hard sometimes.

I jog back behind Graydon and take a breath just as we move up to the front again.

You have got to be kidding me.

If this is the pace we're keeping, I'm going to get lapped.

Graydon steps up, does the zigzag, and then sprints to the cone, only to veer left and push at some giant pad thing.

Great.

I work my way through the cones, "sprint" to the far one, and lean my shoulder forward, pushing into the pad like him, but I'm met with a rock-hard brick wall. I go flying backward, right into a strong pair of arms before I fall flat on my ass.

"I knew that was going to happen," Graydon says as he rights me back on my feet and then takes off toward the end of the line.

"You going to catch me if I fall?" some big, bearded man asks.

"No, but I'll cut off your balls while you're showering if you joke about her again, Hendrix," Graydon snaps, causing the big dude to clamp his mouth shut. "And that goes for every single one of you fucks."

If I didn't dislike him so much, I might find his protectiveness sweet.

Graydon takes off, repeating the same movement, and I follow him, my breath labored as I lightly tap the giant pad this time. I know my strengths, and ramming into that thing is not one of them.

---

"Does it look bad?" I ask as I sit on a medical bench, looking up at Graydon, the spot above my right eye throbbing.

His lips thin, and his nostrils flare as he angrily stares down at me.

"It's not great, Baker." He huffs. "What the hell were you doing?"

"I don't know. I thought I saw a frillback pigeon and was interested in categorizing it. I was putting my helmet on at the same time, and then bam, I hit my head with my helmet. You know, these things are bigger than they seem." I squirt water in my mouth and try to smile up at him, but I know it's no use. He's not happy with me at the moment.

I've been a bumbling mess the entire practice, and I'm not really sure how intelligent it is to have a newbie out on a practice field with a bunch of children-eating barbarians.

Granted, they don't eat children, but from their size and the weight they carry, it seems like they could.

They've actually been pretty nice. One guy even slapped me on the ass, which of course caused Graydon to pin the guy to the ground and tell him to "never fucking touch" me again. The guy held his hands up in defense and said he always slaps butts as a sign of a job well done. Graydon informed him my butt was off-limits. God, that conversation still makes me chuckle every time I hear it again in my mind. Everly's going to love that one.

Graydon's eyes go to my forehead again, where I have a butterfly strip above my eyebrow. Then his eyes fall down to my wrist, and he noticeably gets angrier.

"It's not a training camp without a few injuries," Coach Keenan says, coming up to us.

"Looks good on her," Troy says, causing Graydon to grow even more tense.

"What the hell's he doing here?" Graydon growls to his coach.

"I invited him," Coach Keenan says. "Do you have a problem with that... *Saint*?"

Graydon's jaw grows even tighter, and I swear if Keenan wasn't his coach, Graydon's arm would be around his neck right now, squeezing all the air from his lungs until he was nothing but a pile of skin and bones on the ground.

"You know," Troy says, "if you worried half as much about your footwork as you do about your little *plaything*, you wouldn't be barely making the sprints."

"What did you say?" Graydon snaps at his dad.

Uh-oh.

I look between Troy and Graydon, the tension between them so palpable, so hungry that it's sucking all the air within a ten-mile radius.

"You heard me," he says.

Graydon steps up to his dad, his posture barely imposing over his father.

"I'm hoping for your sake I didn't hear you properly."

"No, you heard me. You're so worried about your little plaything that you're already a liability on the field."

Graydon's eyes nearly turn black, and within a flash, he cocks his arm back and punches his dad right in the freaking ribs, causing him to groan and bend over.

Oh shit.

"She's not my plaything. She's an intelligent woman with a heart of fucking gold. Show some goddamn respect," Graydon says as everyone turns toward us. Just as my mind tries to process what he said about me, fear also rips through my chest as I look around, grateful cameras are not allowed at the first week of camp so they can't record and spread this interaction.

A few of the larger guys run up and grab Graydon by the arms, pulling him back a smidge as Troy straightens, laughing the most maniacal laugh

I've ever heard. He pushes his hand through his hair, bent to the side, nursing his ribs as he says, "Finally, some fire in those eyes." He then nods toward Coach Keenan and says, "Make him pay for it."

Oh God. I don't like the sound of that.

Unsure what to do, I quickly say, "I...I thought his footwork was impressive."

Troy turns to me and lets his lips turn up even more. "Of course you did, sweetheart." And then he takes off with Coach Keenan at his side.

Graydon stares off at their trailing backs, his hands flexing at his sides. One of the big guys pats him on the shoulder and says, "Let it go."

Then they take off to finish their water break, leaving me alone with a heavy-breathing, ready-to-snap defensive end.

"Um, I didn't mean to—"

"Don't fucking say anything," he says as he pushes his hand through his sweaty hair before his eyes lock on mine, a hint of worry in those tortured pupils.

"Graydon, I—"

"Don't," he snaps, and then that worry, or any concern he might have had, vanishes. "I sent you a link for a ride home. All you have to do is click on it, and the car will come and get you."

"Oh, I can call my own car."

He leans in close, almost nose to nose with me. "I'm well aware of your ability to take care of yourself, Maple, so you don't have to keep reminding me. But as the person you are currently attached to, it is my goddamn responsibility to make sure you have everything you need. Don't fucking fight me on it."

"But we're not really attached." Why am I fighting with him? No idea. Seems like a recipe for disaster.

"We are," he growls. "If you don't use the link I sent, it will tell me. So fucking use it."

Then with that, he grabs his helmet and takes off toward the group of guys finishing up their waters before heading back to the field.

I guess that's that.

*An intelligent woman with a heart of fucking gold.*

Did he mean that? Because once again, that's a compliment from Graydon St. John and I don't know if I should be happy or concerned.

Before taking his directions, I allow myself to observe Graydon in his element and the way he stands with such dominance among some of the largest men I've ever seen. All the guys are tall, but he's by far the tallest and most muscularly cut. With his football pants landing just above his knees and his socks pushed all the way down, bunching at his ankles, his muscles glisten under the sun, flexing with just the smallest of shifts in his body. The sleeves of his jersey ride up high, unable to move over his biceps, so his arms are nearly on full display. His pants cling to his muscular ass, a part of his impressive body that I stared at a lot today. And his nearly permanent scowl meshed with the way his hair is mussed and sweaty make it incredibly hard to look away. It's hard not to notice him.

Especially when he's punching his dad in the ribs for disrespecting me.

Or carefully placing his hand on my back as he maneuvers me through the drills at training camp.

Or how he nearly bit a guy's head off for slapping me on the ass.

I should not be attracted to such barbaric behavior.

And yet, when he looks in my direction, the scowl on his face lessening as he takes me in one last time before he places his helmet on his head and gets to work, I can't help but feel…almost like there is something blossoming between us. Like there's something deep in my bones telling me he might not be the asshole I think he is.

---

I really need to work out more because even now, after another long bath, I'm sore.

I can only imagine what tomorrow will bring.

Wrapped up in my robe, my hair wet around my shoulders, I pick up a cup of decaffeinated coffee I made with my new coffee maker, then sit on my couch for some much-needed rest...and cookies.

After work, I swung past By the Dough, one of my favorite cookie places in town, and purchased half a dozen cookies: two pistachio, one cookies and cream, and three chocolate chip. I froze some and placed one giant chocolate chip cookie on a plate to have with my coffee.

The brace on my wrist is so much better than the splint, and I'm grateful for that. At least something good happened today. The cookie and coffee are to quell the nerves that keep racking my throat every time I think about Graydon and what might have happened to him at practice today after I left. What kind of things did he have to do because he punched his dad in the ribs?

I really hope it wasn't much.

But from the look in Graydon's murderous eyes, it seemed like he would have done it again.

From the moment he saw his dad, any ease from the morning washed away. Sure, when we were running drills and he was threatening the lives of his teammates, he was more intense, but there was still a lightness about him. Not when he saw his dad, though. Any jovial mood he might have been in dissipated, and it was like this dark cloud hung over him and he turned into pure, unfiltered anger.

What happened between the two of them that would spark such a reaction?

I break off a piece of my cookie and plop it in my mouth as I pick up my phone and connect it to my Bluetooth speaker to play some Ed Sheeran. Once I pick my favorite playlist, a text from Graydon appears.

My stomach somersaults at the sight of his name. Not sure how to handle that reaction, so I'm going to act like it never happened.

**Graydon:** Thank you for using the link.

Thank you?
Huh, didn't know he had manners in him.

**Maple:** Thank you for sending it.
**Graydon:** I'll have one set up for you tomorrow to get to work.

I'm about to text him back that I don't want him to do that, but I know he won't listen. The request will fall flat, and there's no point in arguing with him, not when I know it won't make any difference. So I concede.

**Maple:** Thank you.
**Graydon:** And I'll be in later, an hour or so before you leave work. I have to be here in the morning and through the afternoon. We have individual team meetings.
**Maple:** Don't worry about it. If you can't make it in, it's fine.
**Graydon:** I'll be there.

Of course he will, because he's the type of guy who keeps his word, and I'm having a hard time deciphering if that's a good thing or a bad thing. Keeping his word means he's trustworthy and that he won't back out on things, such as his ridiculous notion that he needs to take care of me.

**Maple:** Okay. Um…can I ask you a question?

I nibble on the corner of my lip, hoping he says yes, because I really want to know how he is and what happened at the end of practice.

**Graydon:** You can always ask. If I answer is up to me.

I roll my eyes. Of course.

**Maple:** Are you okay? I've been worried about what happened to you after practice and if your coach really made you pay for what you did to your dad.

**Graydon:** You worried about me, Baker?

**Maple:** I mean…kind of.

**Graydon:** Kind of or you are?

**Maple:** Are you really going to make me say it?

**Graydon:** If you want me to answer truthfully, then yeah.

**Maple:** Fine. I care about you.

**Graydon:** Wow, didn't think you would say it.

**Maple:** You might piss me off and I might swear at you under my breath, but we are in this intense thing together so, yeah, I care about you.

**Graydon:** Good to know.

**Maple:** So…are you going to tell me what happened?

**Graydon:** No.

**Maple:** Hey! You said you would tell me what happened if I said I cared for you.

**Graydon:** No, I didn't. You asked if I was okay, and that's the truth I will tell. I'm fine.

I grumble to myself, irritated with his little game.

**Maple:** Why won't you tell me?

**Graydon:** Because you don't need to know.

**Maple:** But why? What does it matter if I know?

**Graydon:** Because I don't need you feeling sorry for me.

**Maple:** I wouldn't feel sorry for you.

**Graydon:** Bullshit.

**Maple:** Fine, but I was the one who caused this, and it's eating away at me.

**Graydon:** You didn't cause anything. My father did.

**Maple:** But I was the reason.

**Graydon:** You did nothing wrong…other than not know how to fit a damn helmet on your head. Don't lose sleep over it, Baker.

**Maple:** I will, though. I feel guilty.

**Graydon:** Would it help if I sent you a picture of me, showing you that I'm fine?

**Maple:** I mean…maybe?

After I send the text, I immediately want to take it back, because what am I doing? Am I flirting? No, I'm not flirting. I'm just…I'm trying to make sure he's okay. That he didn't, I don't know, come out of practice with a brain injury or something. The last thing I need is for him to come to the zoo with said brain injury and accidentally fall into the shrimp fridge because his brain isn't working. We just got new fridges, and his goliath of a body would for sure demolish them if he tripped and rammed into them.

So yes, I'm just looking out for the safety of the fridges over here by asking for a picture.

Nothing else.

My phone dings, and I scramble to open the picture.

Graydon comes into view, once again in more of an aerial shot where I can see his handsomely carved jawline and dark eyes framed by a black eye. His thick chest and flat pecs are on full display while a pack of ice rests on his ribs.

What the hell happened?

Then I read his text.

**Graydon:** See? I'm fine, Baker.

I type back furiously.

**Maple:** Besides the black eye and the ice on the ribs. What happened?
**Graydon:** Put my helmet on wrong.
**Maple:** I'm being serious, Graydon.
**Graydon:** And I'm telling you I'm fine. So don't worry about it. Okay?
**Maple:** I'm worried. Is this how you're always going to be treated?
**Graydon:** No, if I refrain from punching my dad. But if he says shit about you, then yeah, this is how I'll be treated.
**Maple:** He's just going to goad you now.
**Graydon:** Yeah, he will.
**Maple:** I'm not worth the pain.
**Graydon:** Trust me...you are. See you tomorrow, Baker.

I stare down at his text, the butterflies in my stomach fluttering like crazy as I attempt to process it. From the dark, dangerous glares he offers me to the sensitive, supportive texts, to the compliments in front of his dad, I don't know how to read him. And the more time I spend with him, the harder and harder I'm finding it to dislike him.

# CHAPTER 20
# GRAYDON

"DON'T FORGET TO ICE," MY trainer calls after me as I move out of the training room, freshly showered with an ice pack strapped to my ribs from where I took a brutal beating at a late-night individual practice.

I won't get into the details, but Coach Keenan kept his word, and I know if we were any closer to the season starting, I wouldn't have had the same treatment. I might have been fined, if anything, but he knew what he could get away with, and he went for it, letting his assistants know what exactly to put me through. Hit after hit as I had to run sprints against their blocking pads…with no protective gear.

I didn't back down, though. I took it without a grimace or a shred of pain showing in my face.

And I think it only pissed him off more, which made it that much sweeter.

I grab my keys from my pocket and head out to the players' parking lot. The rest of the team is reviewing film, something I will have to do later tonight on my own and report back in a quiz the next day, because that's how much Coach Keenan doesn't trust me. Then again, they're the ones putting me in this situation.

I checked Flock and Tackle last night, and the account is growing so much and getting so many shares that it's unbelievable. Yesterday's post of Maple and me in our gear, ready to train, has been the most commented on so far, besides our first post. Gretchen texted and said they're already teasing merch and are putting together a website to purchase. I made it known that any and all proceeds will go to the zoo.

She agreed. Thankfully.

She also informed me that there will be media at the zoo today, talking to me and the boys. Since Maple and I have been able to bring attention to what we're doing, they want to loop in Bennett and OC as well and shine light on what they're doing, meaning today's post is going to include them.

I hop into my truck and make the quick twenty-minute drive to the zoo, happy that it's not that far away from the training facilities, or my place for that matter. What I hate most is driving in traffic.

When I pull into the back parking lot and put my truck in park, I grab the water bottle that Maple gave me on day one and head over to Gate B, where I can hear OC's dumb voice.

"Shit, that's a pretty nasty bruise," he says. "All from a helmet, huh?"

I push through the gate and find Maple on the other side, her arm in her brace and her eye swollen, a black ring around it, her eyebrow puffed up from the cut.

"Jesus," I say as I move in close, ignoring everyone around us. I grip her face and examine her. "Did you ice this last night?"

Her eyes widen as she takes in me and the nasty bruise around my eye. "Oh my God, Graydon. Your eye."

"I asked you a question, Baker. Did you ice this?"

She takes a step back, and I can see OC look between the two of us, studying our every move. "A pair of black eyes. If I didn't know any better, I would have assumed you got sick of his grumpy ass and he fought back."

"You think I would hit her?" I round on him, causing Maple to move in quickly, pressing her hand to my chest.

"Just a joke, man. Just a joke." OC backs up.

"Stop," Maple says, pushing me...well, attempting to push me, but her soft disposition is no match for my angry, ready-to-murder one. She runs her hand up to my neck, where she hooks it and brings my attention to her. "Stop."

Something about looking in her eyes, her hand on my chest, her body so close to mine, makes me ease the tension coiling inside me.

"Now, let's go talk for a second." She surprisingly slides her hand into mine and tugs me toward the events building just as OC calls out.

"Good to see you too, man. Catch up with you later."

That fucker, always pushing his boundaries and my buttons.

When we're in the building, Maple brings me to the completely deserted back kitchen. She turns toward me, and I prepare for her to tell me what an asshole I am, but then she surprises me as her expression softens and she says, "Are you okay? That looks…it looks bad, Graydon."

"It's fine," I say as she leans against the counter behind her, studying me. Wanting to see her more eye to eye, I step in close, then lift her up by the waist and set her on the counter. A surprised gasp parts her lips as my hands remain on her sides. I tell myself to take a step back, but my body doesn't listen.

I cup her cheek, inspecting her eye. "You didn't ice this."

"I did," she says.

"Then why is it still swollen?"

"Maybe because my body is trying to heal a fractured wrist too?" She shrugs. "It's fine. Reminds everyone not to mess with someone like me." She attempts a menacing expression, but it just makes my lips tilt up in a smile, because nothing is menacing about her. "Oh my God." She sits taller. "Oh my God, did I just make Graydon St. John smile?"

I roll my eyes dramatically.

Continuing, she says, "Call the papers. Alert the town crier. Tell the gossip rags. Graydon St. John knows how to smile."

"Are you done?"

"Do you want me to be done?"

"Yes," I answer.

"Then I'm done."

"Good." I study her eye some more. "Have you had any headaches or dizziness?"

"None. What about you?"

"Yeah, my headache is sitting on a counter right in front of me."

Her face falls flat. "Not funny."

"I thought it was."

I touch the bruising. "Is it sensitive?"

"A little, but nothing bad. I think it just looks like shit. I seem to bruise easily. Although from the look of it, you do too."

"No, this is well earned, yours is from knocking your head with a helmet. Big difference."

"Are you going to tell me how it was well earned?" she asks.

"Nope." My eyes connect with hers, and she presses her hand to my ribs.

"Does this hurt?"

Didn't think I would like it as much as I do. How I wish it was skin on skin, though. Now that would feel better. Maybe rip her T-shirt off and mine—

*Stop.*

This is Maple, not some hookup. *Jesus Christ, when was the last time I got laid?* I think back for a second, trying to remember, which means… it's been awhile.

That must be why I'm liking her touch so damn much.

"Does it?" she asks, looking concerned.

"No," I answer.

"Are you sure? Because you looked pained for a second."

*Yeah, because for some asinine reason, my body and my stupid brain are telling me that I like you touching me, and I really don't know how to process that.*

"Positive."

"And this is the—Oh," Phil says as he enters. The position Maple and I are in is not a position that screams sex, but it doesn't scream acquaintances either. "Pardon, I was just showing Hank around."

Hank.

Why is that name so familiar?

Maple pushes at my chest and squeals as she hops off the counter, just as Slutty Little Glasses appears at the door.

No fucking way.

I watch as Maple launches herself into his arms and hugs him tightly. Well, as tightly as she can with a fucking brace on her arm. "You got the job? Oh my God, this is so amazing."

The job?

What job?

And amazing?

I could actually think of many more adjectives to describe this moment. *Amazing* is not one of them.

"I did." He hugs her tightly, his hand splaying across her lower back, and this innate need to rip him off her squeezes at my chest, begging me to make a move.

He has about one second to fucking pull away before I force him to.

Luck is on his side because she releases him and steps back. "You hired a good one," Maple says with so much excitement that I wonder where this girl has been hidden this whole time. She sure as hell isn't that excited around me. Then again, do I give her anything to be excited about? "When we were together in Peru, I learned so much from him. He cares so much for the flamingos."

Wait...this is Peru Boy?

Slutty Little Glasses is Peru Boy?

That...that's information that I didn't want to fucking hear because I remember the look in her eyes when she spoke about Peru Boy, the dreamy stare. The yearning. The dreaming. And this is him?

Irritation claws at me.

A low, pulsing panic erupts in my chest.

And for the first time since I met Maple, I have the distinct sense that maybe…fuck, maybe I have "feelings" for her.

Jesus Christ.

---

"If I haven't mentioned it, you look really great," OC says as he leans against the wall of the building where we are waiting for our last shoot of the day. We're all wearing our team gear and jeans, looking like a bunch of fuck boys being bent over by their team ownership, and the only thing on my mind right now is how Maple is with Slutty Little Glasses. Probably laughing it up and touching each other and talking about old memories of being in Peru.

What are the goddamn chances?

"They're going to Photoshop my eye," I grumble as I take a sip from my stupid zoo water bottle.

"Wasn't talking about the eye, man."

"Yeah, you seem kind of…down," Bennett says as he peels a banana, then takes a big bite.

"I'm not down," I say, even though I kind of feel down. Jesus Christ, I need to get my head checked. Shouldn't I be angry? Shouldn't I be spitting fire? Should I have already kicked over one of the godforsaken lights they shined on us during the interviews?

"Uh, you kind of are. What's going on?" OC asks just as Maple walks by, Slutty Little Glasses walking beside her.

"Hey," she says, waving and then turning her attention back to him as they head toward the front of the zoo.

I watch them, studying their body language, attempting to force them apart with sheer mental power. But they don't budge as she laughs and bumps into his shoulder while he places his hand on her back for a mere second before laughing as well.

And just like that, a spark of anger fires off in the pit of my belly, and I can practically feel myself snorting, ready to charge the asshole.

"Um, I think it has to do with that guy over there," Bennett says, clearly able to track my inability to hide my feelings.

"Yeah, I think you nailed it, dude," OC says. "So who is he?"

I stare off at them and in a low voice, I say, "Slutty Little Glasses."

"Nooooo," OC drags out, turning to watch them.

"Fuck, really?" Bennett says, turning as well.

And together, we watch them all the way until they take a turn out of view.

"Shit," OC mumbles. "This is not good. I think we need to assemble the Gladdy Daddies."

I turn to him and nearly reach out to choke him. "We are not calling ourselves that."

"But you want to call us something..." He smiles brightly as Bennett cuts in, turning me around.

"From the way you reacted to seeing them together, I'm going to guess you've started to realize that you might have feelings for her."

I adjust the hat on my head, huffing out in frustration. "I don't know what the hell I'm thinking. I just know I don't like what's happening between them. He's such a fucking weasel. Like, way to be a stalker and find a job in the same zoo as her. Get a fucking life."

"Could not agree more." OC nods. "Screams pervert."

"Exactly. The zoo just hired a fucking pervert. How are we supposed to support a zoo that hires a pervert?" I gesture to where Maple and Slutty Little Glasses walked away.

"It's a great point," OC says, feeding into my anger. "I say we bring it to their attention and demand they fire him, right here on the spot, for being a pervert in slutty little glasses."

"Yeah, we should," I say, looking around to find someone official.

"You know, as much as I feel like Slutty Little Glasses should be fired,

I don't think we have the evidence for him to be fired for being a pervert," Bennett says.

"Yeah, we do. Just look at his face," I say irrationally. "Pervert."

"Could not agree more," OC says, making me like him more and more.

"Although justified, I don't think it will stand. And the last thing you want is word to get around that you're crying out 'pervert' without substantial evidence. None of us need that kind of press."

"Who needs evidence when we can smell it on him?" OC asks, wafting his hand toward his face. "Smells like retch with perv juice."

Okay, now he's going a little far.

"You didn't even get close to him," Bennett counters.

"Close enough to recognize the vibes he has going on. I demand he's fired."

"Okay, lower your voice," I say, my anger knotting together as people around us start paying attention to our conversation. "We shouldn't talk about this here."

"No, we need to reconvene the Gladdy—" OC stops himself as I glare at him. "I mean, we need to reconvene later. Charge your phones, boys, because we have some work to do."

---

"You done for the day?" I ask as I push off the wall of the flamingo building, catching Maple walking out with her bag and water bottle.

"I am. How was your media day?"

"Shit," I answer as I take her bag from her and hoist it over my shoulder. She smiles softly up at me, and I have the distinct urge to take her hand in mine, but I hold back, because Jesus, man. Not going there.

"Hey, Maple," Slutty Little Glasses calls out, causing the hairs on the back of my neck to stand on end. "You forgot this."

She turns, and he hands her a piece of paper. "Oh, thanks."

He keeps his eyes on her as he asks, "Do you need a ride home?"

"I got it," I cut in before she can even answer.

Slutty Little Glasses looks up at me. "Are you sure? I'm not that far from where she lives."

How the fuck does he know where she lives?

"I'm four blocks," I say.

"Really?" Maple asks. "I didn't know that."

"You live in her area?" he asks. "Not quite the kind of upscale living I'm sure you're used to."

I rub my lips together, trying not to shove his glasses through his skull. "Why don't you mind your own fucking business?"

His eyes widen, and Maple quickly moves in close to me, placing her hand on my chest. "It's fine, Hank. I have things to discuss with Graydon."

He eyes us, and I dare him to challenge me.

Fucking dare him.

After a few seconds, he nods and then takes a step back. "I'll catch you tomorrow."

"Yup, see you tomorrow," she says and then nudges me in the direction of the parking lot, but I give him one more glare before I take off with Maple at my side.

We make our way in silence until we reach my truck. I move to the passenger side and open the door for her, then offer my hand to help her up into the truck, not expecting her to take it, but when she does, there's a sense of relief that pushes down the anger in my chest.

I set her bag down next to her feet and then shut her door as she buckles up.

When I get settled on my side, I start the truck and pull out of the parking lot.

"You know, he's a good guy," Maple says, making me want to twist the steering wheel in half.

"I'm sure," I say through a clenched jaw because he's the last person I want to talk about.

"He was one of the reasons why I was able to adjust so easily when I was in Peru," she continues, ramping up the jealousy that I didn't even know I possessed until this fucking woman came into my life.

But I swallow it back because I know for certain that it won't help the situation. I'm not even sure what I want to get from this, from her, but what I do know is that showing jealousy and telling her how I want to rip that fuck's nuts off won't help me in any way.

So I decide to go for a different tactic that is way out of my wheelhouse.

"You've never told me about Peru."

I can feel her eyes flash to me in surprise, because yeah, I guess we haven't really talked about anything too personal. We've just been barking at each other.

"Oh, what do you want to know?"

I shrug. "Why did you go in the first place?"

"It was the opportunity of a lifetime," she says in a dreamy voice. "When I was studying in college, the dream was always to get out in the wild and study the animals in their natural habitat, so when the opportunity came about, I was beside myself, hoping I would get picked."

"How long were you there, again?"

"Three years. Life was so different. Slower, less chaotic. It made me see how...cluttered my life was here. Hence why my apartment was *sparse* in your eyes." *Colorless* and *empty* would be my chosen descriptors, which simply don't match this woman. "There were many days when I would just sit and observe, feeling nature surrounding me in the best way possible. Of course, there were days when I missed home, missed my family and friends, and that's where Hank filled in and kept me comfortable." Don't like the sound of that. "So yeah, we have a bond because we went through such a unique experience together."

I nod, not really wanting to talk about him at all.

"He's protective," she continues. "He was in Peru, and he is here now."

"I can see that," I say, keeping my eyes on the road.

"I told him that you were a good guy." That causes my brow to raise. "Because he was asking about you. Wondering what I saw in you."

"He asked that?" I shoot my eyes toward her. "Did you tell him it was a PR relationship?"

She shakes her head. "No, I signed an NDA, so I didn't tell him. But he was confused because he didn't understand what we had in common."

"That's none of his fucking business. Did you tell him that?"

"No," she answers. "But I told him I saw a kindness in you that you don't always show to everyone. That you're protective as well, and even though there might be a preconceived notion of the person you are from your appearance alone, you're not who you seem."

I shift my jaw, letting her words sink in.

"And I believe that," she says as I pull in closer to our neighborhood. "I believe you're so much more than the facade you try to hide behind."

"It's not a facade," I say. "This is who I am."

"Maybe, but there's another side of you that I'm sure you don't show many people."

"What side would that be?" I ask while I pull up to the front of her apartment. I put the truck in park and turn toward her.

She smiles softly, her goddamn face so beautiful despite the cut above her eye surrounded by bruising. She undoes her seat belt and scoots closer toward me, tilting her head as her gaze matches mine.

"The side that will pick me up by the waist, put me on a counter, and touch the side of my face to make sure I'm okay when he sees my bruised eye." She moves in even closer. "And the guy who makes sure I have medical attention when he knows how expensive it is. The guy who makes sure my apartment is comfortable and stocked full of food." She moves in the last few inches, sitting right beside me now, stealing the air from my lungs as she brings her hand to my face. "And the guy who makes sure that I have a ride, no matter where I'm going, and makes it his personal mission to drive me himself when he can. That's who you don't show to everyone."

She smiles one more time, then leans in, placing a very gentle kiss on the side of my face. "Thank you, Graydon. For everything."

I'm so stunned.

So goddamn out of my own body that I don't move an inch as my heart beats in my chest rapidly, pounding, thrumming with excitement as she moves away, picks up her bag, and then exits my truck.

Before she shuts the door, she looks me in the eyes and says, "See you tomorrow, Graydon."

Then she winks and shuts the truck door before taking off up the stairs to her apartment, my eyes fixed on her ass the entire time.

Fuck.

Me.

# CHAPTER 21
# GRAYDON

**OC:** So are we going to talk about it?

**Bennett:** Thank fuck you texted because I didn't want to be the first one.

**OC:** You know I will always be the first. I have no shame about it.

**Bennett:** You don't have any shame about anything, hence why you told the entire Bay Area about sitting in giraffe dung.

**OC:** Hey, Gretchen said it was relatable and that it would help people like the team more.

**Bennett:** That or she was just trying to humiliate you.

**OC:** Whatever, if it helps me with jersey sales then I'll wipe my embarrassed tears with my money.

**Graydon:** You didn't have to describe the smell.

**Bennett:** The smell part wasn't necessary.

**OC:** Might have pushed the envelope with the smell, but not ashamed of sharing the story.

**Graydon:** Clearly.

**OC:** Glad to see you're texting back and not in prison, because the way you were snarling at Slutty Little Glasses had me concerned with your whereabouts tonight.

**Bennett:** I fear for Slutty Little Glasses.

**OC:** I know, I saw steam come out of Gray Gray's nose.

**Graydon:** Do not fucking call me that.

**Bennett:** Why, man? Why would you try out a nickname?

**OC:** Just testing how close we are.

**Graydon:** We will never be close enough to have nicknames for each other.

**OC:** Shame, I kind of like Gray Gray. Anyway, what happened after you left us?

**Bennett:** I hate myself for wanting to know as well.

**Graydon:** I took her home after SLG tried to take her home himself. Don't know what the fuck he was thinking. And then she said some things to me and kissed me on the cheek before she exited my truck.

**OC:** UHHH WHAT? Hold on. You're just going to casually tell us that she kissed you?

**Graydon:** On the cheek. Don't make a big deal about it.

**OC:** This is a HUGE deal.

**Bennett:** I mean, I wouldn't say huge, but it's something. Has she kissed you before?

**Graydon:** No.

**OC:** What did you do after she kissed you? Did you kiss her back? Pull her on your lap? Tell her that you have secret feelings for her?

**Graydon:** No, you idiot. I just…I don't know. I was so stunned I really didn't do anything.

**OC:** Stunned, our big fella was stunned. That's kind of cute.

**Graydon:** It's not cute.

**Bennett:** It's a little cute.

**Graydon:** Bennett!

**Bennett:** I'm sorry but it is.

**OC:** Just admit, it was cute.

**Graydon:** Not admitting anything.

**OC:** At least tell us this: Did you like it?

**Graydon:** Would have liked it better if it was on my mouth.

**OC:** My nipples just got hard.

**Bennett:** Gross.

**Graydon:** And I'm done.

---

"You're getting really good at that," Maple says as she brushes up against me while I finish cleaning some more fucking dishes.

I glance at her, my brow raised, causing her to laugh. "The pink gloves were unnecessary." I hold up the rubber gloves she made me wear in a picture for Flock and Tackle.

"Um, according to the one hundred comments so far, I think they were absolutely necessary."

"Already?" I grumble, still hating this social media thing.

"Yeah. If you haven't noticed, we're kind of popular."

"Great." I offer her an eye roll.

She leans against the counter, watching me, arms folded over her chest. "How would you rate your first week of training camp?"

"Why are you asking me? I should ask you." I finish scrubbing the last dish, rinse it, and then set it to the side to dry.

She skipped out on today, and I told her that I'd come to the zoo after I was done so I could take her home...like I've done every day this week. Luckily, Coach Keenan has been generous in allowing me to leave training camp in the evening as long as I keep up my video training.

Do I think it's him being a nice guy? Absolutely not. I think it's Welcott telling Keenan to ease up on me because, according to public opinion, I've been growing excitement around the season starting...apparently by washing dishes.

"It was...interesting." She smiles up at me. Over the past few days, it seems as though we've found a bit of ease between the two of us. Not as much fighting, just the occasional temperature rise. "I'm really sore, but hopefully that will wear off at some point."

"The eye is looking better."

"Yeah, doesn't hurt as much either."

"Good," I say awkwardly, because I don't do this bullshit small-talk thing. I would keep it quiet if it was my choice, but she hasn't let me. She keeps engaging me in conversation, whether it's here, in the car, or at training camp, for fuck's sake. It's everywhere, and I feel myself getting sucked into it without any escape.

"So what are you doing this weekend?"

"Camp," I say. "Six days a week."

Her cute nose crinkles. "Ugh, that's not fun. At least you have Sunday. Are you going to do anything?"

My mind goes to my mom and my standing date with her during the off-season. Once the season starts, my schedule is more erratic, but I try to get in as many visits as I can. It's not that she would really notice if I didn't show up, but the thought of that makes my heart break.

"Uh, yeah." I pull on the back of my neck, not elaborating.

"That wasn't evasive at all." She smirks and pokes my side. "You know you can't go on any dates, right? You're kind of attached to me right now."

"Yeah, I'm aware," I say.

"Okay, so what is it? Ooh, are you taking knitting classes on Sundays and you feel like it would be embarrassing to admit? Listen, Graydon, I'm here to tell you that if Tom Daley, the Olympic diver, can knit during the Olympics, you can knit during a game." She leans closer and whispers, "And I think the fans would find it endearing."

"They wouldn't," I counter. "They'd be throwing beers at me and telling me to get my ass behind the line."

"Well, I'd cheer you on to knit."

"You coming to a game?" I ask, changing the subject from what I'm doing on Sundays.

"We've all talked about coming to a game," Slutty Little Glasses says as he walks right into our conversation.

*No one was talking to you, prick.*

"Thought we could make a zoo thing out of it, right, Maple?" He stands next to her, far too close for my fucking liking.

"Yeah, we did. Thought it could be fun to cheer you on."

The only person I want there is her.

And I want her wearing my jersey.

And I want her front row on the fifty-yard line.

"Not that we really know anything about football," he jokes, making Maple laugh.

"No, we don't." She laughs some more. "We were joking earlier about how we just hope we cheer for the right team."

They chuckle together and isn't that just fucking adorable?

It's not.

I hate him.

I hate that I have to see his stupid fucking face more often than I want.

I hate that he works here with her and they have inside jokes.

And I hate how close he feels he needs to be to her whenever I'm around. I'm surprised he doesn't have his hand down her pants, claiming Peru rights.

"Anyway, something to look forward to," Maple adds, clearly sensing my tension.

I push off the counter. "Ready to go?"

"Oh, right. Yup. Let me grab my bag real quick."

She takes off, leaving me with Slutty Little Glasses, and he has the audacity to try to have a conversation with me.

"You like her, huh?"

"Great observation," I say. "And good thing since she's my girlfriend."

He studies me for a moment, almost as if he's attempting to intimidate me.

Pathetic.

And then after a few seconds, he says, "She might be your girlfriend...for now..."

Then with that, he takes off.

The fuck did he just say?

Did he just threaten me?

Me?

Does he know what I'm capable of? That I could easily snap his thigh clean off his body, grill it up, and eat it for a fucking appetizer?

"Ready?" Maple says, coming back into the room and preventing me from moving in on the dangerous thoughts brewing in my mind.

Lucky for him.

I turn away from where he exited, grab her bag from her like I've done every day this week, then lead her out to the parking lot toward my truck, irritation nearly eating me alive the entire walk.

*For now*...as if it's even a competition. Like he has anything over me.

I open the door for her, help her in, and set her bag down on the floorboard. But this time, instead of leaving right away, I grab her seat belt and lean across her lap, buckling her in, letting my body invade her space, and soaking in the fact that I'm the one doing this, not her.

"Oh." She chuckles nervously. "Full service, how...different."

I remain where I am, inches away from her face. Her eyes search mine for answers, her tongue peeking out and wetting her lips.

"Are you not okay with that?" I ask.

"Um, no, it's...it's fine. You know, do what you want to do," she rambles. "If you like buckling me up, by all means, buckle away. I know you're all about protection. You know, helmets and...pads...and...probably condoms, right?" Her eyes widen. "No, not condoms, I mean...I don't know why I said that." She waves her hand cutely in front of her face. "Is it hot in here?"

Any other time, I might actually smile at that, but thanks to my annoyed state, her rambling rolls right off me as I lift away from her and shut her door, not saying a damn thing, and get in on my side.

"Want me to buckle you up?" she asks. I eye her sharply, basically telling her no with one unamused glare. "Yeah, didn't think so."

I start the truck, back out, then head out onto the road, Slutty Little Glasses on my mind.

*For now.*

He really fucking said "for now" as if he has some mastermind plan brewing that will magically make Maple dump me and go running into his arms.

Not that Maple and I are in a true relationship, but he doesn't know that.

"Um, you seem tense," Maple says.

"I'm fine."

"You don't seem fine."

"I am," I snap.

Jesus, man. Don't take your anger out on her. Then again, didn't she put us in this situation? A situation where now I think about her all the time? Where all I want to do is claim her in front of every goddamn man that even looks at her?

How the fuck did I even get here?

It feels like it happened in seconds.

She gets hit by a cop car, hurts her wrist, and then I'm the knight in shining armor, protecting her every chance I get, every chance I'm granted.

And I hate it.

I hate this overwhelming, consuming, out-of-control feeling I have whenever I'm around her. It's...it's fucking debilitating.

"You know...you don't have to be rude to me."

She's right about that. Then again, I don't know how to handle these feelings. Do I really like her?

I glance over at her, her long lashes blinking up at me. Jesus Christ, why is she so beautiful?

"I wasn't...I wasn't trying to be rude. It just came across that way."

"Well, it was rude to me, and I don't appreciate it."

Grinding my teeth together, I mutter, "Sorry."

"Ooh, so heartfelt."

"I'll send you a card in the mail tomorrow."

"Now that's the kind of apology I'm looking for. If you could tack another potted plant onto that, I'd love it. No flowers, though, because they just end up dying, and I think that's sad. But another potted plant—I'd keep that thing alive and become friends with it."

The way she just allows my grumpiness to roll right off her makes me like her that much more, because I know I don't have to pretend. I don't have to be someone that I'm not around her, and she'll still talk to me.

She'll regret it; I know she fucking will.

I'm not the type of person that you can put up with for a long time. The grumpiness won't wear off, but the acceptance of it will.

Seeming confused, she glances around and then asks, "Um, are we going in the right direction?"

"I want tacos," I say.

"Oh, the big man is hungry, okay."

"Do you want tacos?"

"Are they vegetarian?"

"They do have a vegetarian option, or else I wouldn't go there." When she told me she was a vegetarian, I made sure to plug that nugget of info away.

"Well, thank you. Then I'll definitely have some tacos. Love tacos."

So do I. Fucking love them, but I keep that to myself, remaining guarded as I sift through this bullshit running rampant in my head.

Instead of engaging in conversation, I remain quiet for the rest of the drive, mulling over all the ways I could bend and break Slutty Little Glasses in half.

By the time I park, I'm buzzing with energy, wishing the douche was standing right in front of me so I could try out some of the ideas that I conjured up.

But I'm pulled from my reverie when Maple reaches for the door.

"Don't."

She looks over her shoulder. "Don't, what?"

"I'll open the door for you."

I can see that she wants to argue with me, but she holds back because she knows I won't concede to certain things.

She stays in the car while I exit and round the front of the truck. When I open her door, I hold my hand out and she takes it as I help her down, but when we usually would let go, I don't this time. I keep her palm connected with mine as I shut her door.

She glances up at me, questions running through her mind judging by her expression, but I just lead her toward the food trucks lined up along the back of the parking lot. Every Friday, without fail, my favorite taco truck is parked here, as well as a Cuban-inspired sandwich truck, a wood-fired pizza truck, and a chili truck all ready to serve people looking to get outside after a long week at work. Hutton told me about them. His wife, Scarlett, stumbled across them on social media, and they dragged me with them one night.

Now, when I get a craving, I know when and where I have to go.

I bring Maple up to the side of the truck to look at the menu, still holding her hand. Leaning in close, I point at the two vegetarian options. "There's a veggie option, grilled fajita veggies, avocado, and cheese. And then there is just a bean and cheese taco. If those options aren't good enough, I can—"

"Excuse me. Are you Graydon St. John?" a little voice says from behind me.

I turn around to find a little boy, maybe six, with wide eyes and a toothless smile plastered across his cute little face.

On instinct, I drop Maple's hand and squat down so that I'm somewhat eye level with him. "Hey, little man," I say, clapping him on the shoulder. "I sure am. What's your name?"

"Carlton, but my friends call me CT."

"Can I call you CT?"

His eyes widen as he nods. "Yeah."

"Does that mean we're friends?"

His smile grows even wider. "Yeah. Yeah."

"Good. Do you play football?"

He nods. "With my mom, in the yard." I look up to see his mom, tears in her eyes as she holds her phone in front of her. She's not recording but just enjoying the moment herself.

"What position do you play?"

"Quarterback. I throw the ball to my mom."

"Ooh, I bet you're really good at it. I probably wouldn't have a chance at tackling you."

"I'm too quick."

I chuckle. "I can tell you are."

His mom leans forward and says, "Would you mind if we got a picture, and then we'll leave you alone?"

"Of course," I say, turning CT around to face his mom. I place my arm around him and turn my hat backward so you can see my face better, and she snaps the picture.

"Thank you so much."

I offer his mom a wink, then turn CT back around. "Listen, little man, keep working on those passes and be sure to thank your mom for practicing with you. You're a very lucky guy to have her in your life. I'll be sure to look for you one day when you're playing professionally."

"Okay." He throws himself into my arms, and I give him a big hug before letting go and standing back up. I offer him a fist bump, and then he takes off, his mom thanking me one more time before I bring my attention back to Maple.

"Sorry about that."

"Please don't apologize." Her watery eyes meet mine. "That was really sweet. You just made that mom's year, and that little boy will cherish that moment forever."

Feeling uncomfortable because I don't like the praise, I just nod and clear my throat. "Uh, did you decide on the tacos you want?"

I can feel her studying me, those devastatingly beautiful eyes attempting to find answers that I'm just not willing to give. Finally, she says, "I'll have one of each."

"Okay," I answer, then step up to the window and order four steak tacos for myself, two vegetarian for Maple, and three Topo Chicos—one for Maple, two for me.

It doesn't take long for our order to come up, and I grab it for us and bring her back to the truck. I set our food down before picking her up by the waist and setting her on the tailgate.

I look her in the eyes, my hands still on her waist, my thumbs pressing into her sides as I ask, "Comfortable?"

I watch her slowly swallow as she lets out a very breathy, "Yes."

I pause for a moment, letting my thumbs caress her sides, our eyes still matched up, my mind swirling with ideas of what I could do right here, in this position. How I could drag my hands farther up her body, to her neck...

*Jesus, what am I doing?*

I quickly release her, clear my throat, and hop up onto my side. I pick up the tacos and dish them out. She hands me a napkin, and I open her drink for her.

Once we're settled, she takes a bite of her taco, then lets out a long, satisfied moan that makes the hairs on my forearms stand at attention, alluding to something else that will be standing to attention if she keeps that up.

"Oh my God, this is so good." She examines the taco. "How did they make a flour tortilla so crispy?"

I finish chewing, swallow, and then say, "They grill and press them. And don't worry, they use a separate grill for the vegetarian tacos."

She looks over at me, a smirk on her lips. "You know, when you say things like that, it almost seems like you care about me or something."

I grumble under my breath, because maybe I do, but I don't want her to know that, then take another bite of my taco, finishing it in two bites.

I wipe my mouth and glance at her to find her staring at me, still just one bite gone from her taco. I'm going to be done with two before she's even done with one at this pace.

"What?" I ask.

"Nothing." She smiles and takes another bite of her taco. This time, I watch her eyes roll into the back of her head.

Jesus Christ.

This was a bad idea.

I just wanted tacos. I didn't want a front-row seat to Maple eating tacos like she's experiencing the best orgasm of her life.

"How did you find this place?" she asks.

"Hutton," I answer.

"Who is Hutton?"

"Hutton Marshall. Wide receiver for the Foghorns. He and his wife dragged me out one night and brought me here."

"Dragged you out? I would have loved to see that." She bumps her shoulder with mine. "Were you kicking and screaming?"

"Practically," I answer, then take another bite of my taco.

"I'm guessing that you don't get out much."

"Not so much." I wipe my mouth with a napkin.

"So how do you meet people?"

"I don't need to meet people."

"I mean...ladies."

I cock a brow as I turn toward her. "I have a girl. Don't need to look for another one."

She rolls her eyes. "Come on, I'm being serious. You have to have the ladies hanging all over you."

"Never put myself in a position where I would have them hanging all over me."

She pauses, and then asks, "Really? Like no bars or clubs or online dating?"

"No."

"So, what, you're just...celibate?"

"Don't you think this is a little personal?" I ask as she finishes the bite she just took.

"Probably," she says with a shrug. "Just curious. I've been celibate for quite some time now, but that's because I was in Peru. I'm just surprised if that's the case for you. Or if it's something that I have to work around, you know. Just trying to see if there is anything I have to deal with on my end if you have...ladies you call upon."

That gathers my attention as I wipe my mouth again. "You don't have to worry about that when we're together. I made a commitment to you, and I wouldn't do something like that to embarrass you or jeopardize our setup."

"Okay, I mean, if you need to, that's fine—"

"I won't," I say, my voice firm.

"Are you sure?" She looks so uncertain.

"You have my word."

"And I appreciate that, but don't you have needs? Especially after games?"

I think about the four numbers I have in my phone that I keep in reserve if I do ever have to get rid of excess energy. Four women who have all signed NDAs, four women that I really don't know much about other than they fulfill a need when I have one because I haven't had time to date…or even the urge to. I don't have a life that I really want to share with anyone. I have baggage I don't want people seeing or carrying. I'm busy most of the time, and I'm set on autopilot so that I don't ever have to think of anything outside my day-to-day life. Hence why this whole "save the team" PR stunt has been way out of my comfort zone.

"My needs are nothing you have to worry about."

She takes a bite of her taco, silent for a moment. Does she have…needs? Is that what her questioning is about? She said she's been celibate since Peru, but does that mean…does that mean she could fulfill her "needs" with Slutty Little Glasses? There is no fucking way I'm asking her that, even though that idea will now eat me alive inside.

She pulls her phone out of her pocket before setting her taco down on the paper and pulling up the camera.

"Take a picture with me and our tacos?" She hands me her phone and smiles back at me, a pleading look in her eyes. But that smile, Jesus, it has so much power, the kind of power I've never experienced before. Because it has a hold on me.

The kind of hold that packs a powerful punch, like she could ask me anything with that smile attached, and I'd say yes.

To anything.

Phone in hand, I hold it out, then wrap my arm around her while she curls into my side and holds up her taco.

She fits so fucking perfectly.

Together, we smile at the camera, mine more of a smirk than a smile.

When I'm done, I hand the phone back to her and she says, "Look at you not rushing and taking your time."

"Because I know you'd lambaste me if I didn't."

"You're learning. I like that."

I shake my head and devour my third taco before unwrapping my next one. I drink half of a Topo Chico while she finishes her first taco. We sit there in silence, eating together, staring out at the parking lot and the other food trucks. A few people point our way, but for the most part, they keep to themselves…thankfully.

"Does it ever bother you? All the people watching you?"

"Barely notice it anymore," I say. "Once you get used to it, it's pretty easy to ignore."

"Besides the little ones, right?"

I nod. "They're my favorite, the young fans, because it almost seems like they have stars in their eyes, like talking to them will make their entire year. I do my best to try to make a lasting impression, something they can hold on to, because you never know what their childhood might be like. So that small interaction with me could mean the world to them. It could change the trajectory of their life, and if I can make a positive impact like that, then I will bend over backward to make sure those fans get what they need from me."

"Wow," she says, a little breathy. "That's…that's what I'm talking about."

"What do you mean?"

She turns to me and takes my large hand between her two petite ones. When I look her in the eyes, she says, "You put on such an indifferent…detached front, like you're this Big Bad Wolf and no one should ever talk to you, but then you go and say things like that, and do things that don't match that facade. I know you don't want it to happen, but I see right through you, Graydon St. John. I see the real man that you are." She rubs her thumb over my knuckles, the intimate touch making my stomach tie up in fucking knots. "And you're a good man, no matter how much you want me to think otherwise. You're a good man."

Then she sets my hand down and goes back to her taco, leaving me, well…speechless. Just like I was when she spouted off about the different *sides* she sees in me. The different man.

*"The guy who makes sure my apartment is comfortable and stocked full of food. And the guy who makes sure that I have a ride, no matter where I'm going, and makes it his personal mission to drive me himself when he can. That's who you don't show to everyone."*

I don't show that side of myself to anyone else because no one else inspires that.

But I'm not saying that. Ever.

---

"Thank you for the tacos and driving me home," Maple says as I pull up to her apartment. "It wasn't necessary, but you know that already. Glad we got a pic, though. We can use it tomorrow since we won't see each other. Keep the fans coming back for more."

I shake my head. "Such a weird fucking thing, but if it gets the front office to shoot rays of sunshine up my ass, then fine."

She chuckles. "Do you like that? Rays of sunshine up your ass, Graydon?"

"Doesn't hurt," I say as she moves in closer, just like she does every time I drop her off.

She doesn't want help out of the car when I drop her off, and I'll respect that. I'm also not sure what I would really do if I walked her to her apartment. My truck is a safe zone. Almost neutral, which doesn't allow much to happen, and with my mind whirling in confusion, it's a good thing.

"Well, I'll remember that if I ever find a way to harness the sun's rays. I'll be sure to shine them right up your ass."

"That's not…weird at all."

She laughs again, and it's such a sweet fucking sound. So innocent. And the way my body reacts to it, it's as if it's a sound I've always been meant to hear. It's beautiful.

She's beautiful.

"Anyway, thank you again." She leans forward and places a soft kiss on my cheek. "Have a good night, Graydon."

"You too," I say as she shuffles out of the truck. With a wink, she shuts the door and heads to her apartment building, leaving me gripping my steering wheel tightly and wondering what the hell I'm doing.

I make the drive back to my apartment, park the truck in my garage, and am heading to my place to start doing my video reviews when my phone dings with a text.

I unlock my place and walk up the stairs as I pull my phone from my pocket. It's a text from Maple.

I lean against the wall as I open it up and see a picture of her in a robe, with some sort of green cream on her face. I chuckle and read the text.

**Maple:** Just a little insight into my nighttime routine, you know, in case an interviewer ever asks. You know it gets wild here.

I make my way into my bedroom, where I strip down to my boxers, brush my teeth, and get ready for bed. I already took a shower after practice, so I don't bother with another before I slip into bed.

I take a picture of myself and send it to her.

**Graydon:** Here's mine. Then again, you've seen this before.

**Maple:** You know, it's not fair that you can just go to bed like that.

**Graydon:** And here I was jealous that you look like you crawled out of a swamp, like the Loch Ness Monster's distant cousin.

**Maple:** *GASP* How dare you.

**Graydon:** Tell me I'm wrong.

**Maple:** Not all of us can look picture-perfect, flashing our abs for the camera every night.

I smile to myself and text her back.

**Graydon:** Picture-perfect, huh?

**Maple:** Oh please, you know what you're doing with those thirst traps.

**Graydon:** Would you classify those as thirst traps? Should I ask Martha Stewart, the flamingo?

**Maple:** OMG you remembered?

**Graydon:** Don't make it weird.

**Maple:** LOL. Fine, no need to ask her. I can tell you, they're the definition of a thirst trap.

**Graydon:** Nah, just a simple picture.

**Maple:** Graydon, if I know one thing for sure, not a single thing about you is simple.

# CHAPTER 22
# MAPLE

"PERFECT, JUST LIKE THAT," GRETCHEN says as I stand in front of Graydon in my football gear while he towers over me in his. "Got it."

She finishes taking the picture and then nods for us to follow her. We're between sessions at training camp, after a grueling morning of more freaking cones. If I never see another cone after this, I'll be the happiest woman alive.

We follow her to the side of the field and take off our helmets.

French braiding my hair on training camp days is the best way to go, because it keeps my hair from getting crazy under the helmet and prevents any sort of tangle situation. But God, does it hurt, even if my wrist is getting stronger.

"The popularity of Flock and Tackle has surged. All major sports media are picking it up and sharing it all over their socials. Everyone is talking about it. The team has seen an uptick in ticket sales and especially merch. They're thrilled. And since we're closing out our second week of training camp with a fundraiser tonight for the zoo, we thought it would be a great opportunity to possibly...allude to more than just a friendship between the two of you. I don't want to fully hard-launch a relationship, but I think giving the media just a little more intrigue will be good."

Graydon tenses behind me. "What exactly does that entail?"

"Well, we've pretty much edged everyone about the relationship between the two of you, and we thought it would be a great chance for you to be seen holding hands at the event, giving everyone a little more than what we've been showing them."

I mean, that shouldn't be too hard. He held my hand last week when we went to get tacos.

"No interviews," Graydon snaps behind me.

"No interviews," Gretchen confirms. "This is just a photo opportunity. We'll have a few inside shots, nothing staged, almost like the paparazzi took them, and then we'll have them leaked."

I turn to look up at Graydon because this is way out of my wheelhouse. His jaw is tight as he mulls it over. "Leaked to who?"

"Sports outlets only," Gretchen answers.

"What will be the narrative?"

"We're still working on the copy, but once we have it, we'll send it to you for approval."

What the heck are they even talking about?

"And the protocol for any backlash," he asks.

"There won't be any backlash."

"Gretchen," Graydon snaps and leans forward, his chest pressing to my back. "You and I both know there will be backlash, so don't tell me there won't be. I want a protocol for how to protect her if that happens."

Gretchen mulls it over. I can see in her eyes that she won't care about any backlash because her top priority isn't protecting me but rather protecting the goal—to make the Foghorns shine. And as much as that sucks, I accept it, because I knew that going into this.

"It's fine," I say. "I can handle whatever backlash there is. Just make sure everything works out for Graydon."

"Have you lost your mind?" he asks, turning toward me. "Absolutely not."

"She has a point," Gretchen says, and I knew it. I could see her hesitation when he asked for a protocol to protect me.

"She does not have a fucking point," he seethes. "There is no way I'm going to let her just drown if this goes bad."

"It won't," I say with conviction. "We have people eating out of our hands with Flock and Tackle. It will be fine."

"Yeah, and once we confirm what people are thinking, the trolls are going to surface from the dark parts of the internet and tear you apart."

"Let them," I say casually. "I have nothing to worry about. I know who I am, and I'm good with who I am. If people have a problem with that, then that's their issue, not mine."

"Then it's settled." Gretchen smiles. "I'll have hair and makeup meet you at your place again. And we're sending over a dress as well. You can get out of work a few hours early, right?"

"Yes."

"Wonderful." She looks at her watch. "Well, I should be going—"

"Hold on, we're not done here," Graydon says. "I want a protocol, Gretchen, or I'm not fucking going."

She sighs heavily. "Graydon, this isn't—"

"I'm not fucking around." He sticks his helmet on his head and points at her. "I want a protocol sent to me before the event or I'm not going." He latches his chin strap and is about to take off before turning toward me. "There should be a link waiting for you to get a ride to the zoo."

"Okay, thanks," I say, and then he takes off, making powerful strides toward the defense.

"I've never met someone more stubborn in my entire life," Gretchen mutters while shaking her head and staring down at her phone. When she looks up, she says, "Looks like I'll be putting together a protocol, just what I want to do on a freaking Friday." She then looks me up and down and asks, "How are you with wearing yellow?"

"Fine," I answer.

"Okay, I'll let the girls know."

Then, with that, she takes off.

Well, looks like we're going public. Better get ready, because even though I said I could handle the heat, I need to mentally prepare. I know just how critical the internet can be.

Time to put on the armor and prepare for battle.

---

"Thank you," I say as I pat down the slinky yellow dress that the makeup artist helped me slip on. It's a halter-top dress with no back whatsoever, the material sliding around just above my ass, exposing my entire back, which was something I was not expecting.

And there were no other options. This was it. There is one single thin strap that extends from one end to the other near my bra line that helps hug the top to my chest with its built-in bra. But the silky material is not forgiving in the slightest, leaving me completely bare under the garment.

"This is gorgeous on you," the makeup artist says as I turn and look in the full-length mirror, taking in the mermaid silhouette, the buttery color, and the way it hugs every single one of my curves. I turn to the side, checking out the back and how the fabric rests against my butt, curving along it until the fabric loosely hangs.

Okay, yeah, this dress is something else. Nothing I would ever have picked out for myself, but now that it's on, it makes me feel...special.

Beautiful.

They styled my hair loosely today by pulling it to the side to show off the slope of my neck. And they went minimal on my makeup once again, just using a heavy dose of mascara to make my eyes pop.

"Are you good? Do you need anything else?" she asks as she moves toward my door.

"No, I think I'm good. Thank you again for everything."

"Of course." She winks. "Have fun."

She grabs all of her things and heads out the front door. I go back to the full-length mirror and check myself out one more time. If they wanted to make an impact for the "unveiling" today, then they sure did it with this dress.

I move to the bathroom, where I swirl some mouthwash in my mouth one more time, adjust my lipstick, and then turn toward the living room, picking up my clutch just as there's a knock on my door.

Butterflies erupt in my stomach at the thought of Graydon seeing me in this dress. Not that I should care, but the last week has been...different.

He hasn't been as moody.

We've texted almost every night, just simple texts, nothing that lasted until the wee hours of the morning, but just a quick joke here and there. Or a picture from him. And when we have been at the zoo and training camp, everything has felt seamless, like we're finally finding a rhythm.

It's made my attachment toward him grow, and I can't tell if that's a good thing or a bad thing.

From the way my stomach's tying up in knots with nerves, I'm going to guess maybe a bad thing because I can't...God, I can't be developing feelings for him, right?

That would be insane.

He's...he's way out of my league.

He's closed off.

He doesn't date. He's made that very clear.

And he's almost an impenetrable wall, never letting his facade slip, never letting anyone in.

He's not the type of person I should gravitate toward.

Not even close.

Shaking off my thoughts, I take a deep breath and then move to the front door, where I open it to a foreboding and serious-looking man. His hair is styled in his classic fauxhawk, the light scruff on his jaw emphasizing the sharp angles of his face, while the black-on-black three-piece suit he's wearing just adds to the mystery and darkness this man carries in his soul.

"Hello," I say, feeling shy as his eyes rake over me, making my nipples hard from his blatant perusal. His brow angles down and his tongue quickly wets his lips like he just spotted his prey and he's about to attack. It's a heady feeling, and I can't recall ever having someone look at me the way he is right now.

He doesn't say anything as silence falls between us, his eyes moving over my chest, where my nipples are pressing against the thin fabric, then up to my neck, and right into my blue gaze.

"Um, you look nice," I offer, trying not to fidget under his examination. "They, uh, they provided me with this dress. A little more revealing than I would have picked, but you know, here we are." I turn to the side to show him the back, and I watch as his eyes grow even darker from the sight of my bare skin. "Yeah, I think any lower and my ass would be showing." I nervously laugh and then turn back around. "So yeah, yay for fundraisers." I swallow hard. "And, uh, and unveiling our relationship. That's, that's going to be fun—Oh hey, did you get the protocol? Well, I guess since you're here, you did, and that you approved it, so that's good." I twist my lips to the side, my upper lip starting to sweat from the pressure of his gaze. "God, please say something? Do you want me to change? I'm sorry my nipples are hard. I can just…I can rub them in the car to—"

"Stop talking," he grunts.

"Right, yup. I can see how I'm making it worse." I gesture to the hall. "Shall we go?"

His tongue runs over his teeth before he steps aside, making room for me to shut the door and lock up.

And I do just that, my hand shaky as I try to fit the key in the lock.

What I wouldn't give to know exactly what he's thinking at this moment.

Does he hate the dress?

Does he think I look ridiculous?

Is he dreading tonight?

Ashamed to have me on his arm?

All the worst-case scenarios are running through my head as I struggle to get the key in the lock. I'm seconds from just throwing the key down the hall and calling it quits when he moves in behind me, his chest to my bare back, and smooths his hand over mine, helping me with the key. I gulp as he assists in twisting the lock, then pulls the key out. He takes my clutch from my hand and deposits the key inside before closing it and holding it, as if it's his own. Then he takes my hand in his and guides me down the hallway, my mouth slightly agape in shock while I trail him out the front door to...not his truck.

I pause and ask, "What's that?"

"Gretchen didn't want me pulling up to the event in my truck, so she made me rent this."

A black Range Rover is parked on the street, making my lip curl up.

"That is so not you."

"Tell me about it," he mutters. After moving to the passenger side of the SUV, he opens the door and helps me inside. He doesn't buckle me in this time, but then again, I think it's because he can't really fit inside without bumping around. The man is a giant. But he waits for me to buckle up before handing me my clutch and shutting my door.

When he gets in on his side of the car, he slides in the best that he can and adjusts to make the most of the space.

I smirk, holding back my chuckle because he looks so freaking uncomfortable.

He glances in my direction. "Don't fucking say a thing."

"I wasn't going to."

"I could see it all over your face."

"I wasn't going to say anything," I say, chuckling now.

"Sure," he answers with an eye roll, then pulls out onto the road.

He heads down the street, his eyes fixed on the road in front of us as the faint sound of the Lumineers plays in the background. His body seems to relax, and then, to my utter surprise, his hand moves over the console and smooths over my leg.

A twinge of shock makes a bolt of lust fly up my leg as I stare down at his massive hand curving around the shape of my leg, the telltale sign of being claimed.

But is he claiming me?

No, he can't be.

He's just...he's practicing. That's what it is. He's practicing because it has to be like this when we're together now. More affection.

So because it's a moment I can't let pass me by, I take my phone from my clutch and snap a picture of his hand on my thigh.

Something I can post a little later, once everything is announced.

Until then, the picture will just burn a hole in my phone, and his hand will burn a lustful hole in my soul. It has been a *long* time since I had sex, and most days, I don't really think about it.

But Graydon's hand on my leg? Yep. Now I'm thinking about it. *Dear God.*

# CHAPTER 23
# GRAYDON

"THANK YOU, SIR," THE VALET says as I hand him the keys to the unnecessary rental Gretchen made me get.

Don't see why it fucking matters what I drive. There's no one out here taking pictures of our arrival.

I move to Maple's side of the car and open the door for her, holding out my hand. Her delicate hand slips into mine, the perfect fit in my large palm.

"Hand me your clutch," I say.

"Huh?"

"So you don't have to hold it with your bad hand."

"You're going to hold my clutch all night?"

"Yeah, you have a problem with that?"

"No," she says, her eyes wide as she hands it over. My eyes slide over that goddamn dress again, making my mouth water just like it did when I first caught sight of her at her apartment.

I can't even explain how much my brain short-circuited and begged me to push her back inside her apartment to peel the damn thing off her. Because the fabric didn't leave anything to the imagination.

Nope, I felt like the damn thing was painted on her as I took in every mouth-watering curve of her body. It molded over her breasts and tight, pebbled nipples, and the fabric clung to her waist and fitted perfectly over her hips. And that back? Jesus fuck, the back.

Her ass is the goddamn highlight as the fabric rests just above the slope, showing off two dimples that I want to run my fingers over. And from the way her ass bounced when she turned to show me the back, I knew immediately she wasn't wearing underwear. *That* made me break out in a full goddamn sweat and rendered me speechless.

She's so stunning.

So beautiful.

So effortlessly gorgeous that I couldn't stop myself from placing my hand on her thigh in the car, nor could I stop myself from stealing glances in her direction while driving. And I know for a fact that this entire evening will be spent making sure no other dickwad thinks he can even get near her.

Nope. She's fucking mine.

*Mine.*

"Are you okay?" she asks as we make our way through the door and down a hallway to a ballroom where the event festivities are being held.

"Fine," I answer, keeping her close.

These events are always so counterintuitive because the money they spend on the lavish event space, the food, and the decorations could simply be donated rather than forcing us to walk around, make small talk, and try to get people to care about the goddamn zoo animals we're here to promote.

When we reach the ballroom, I spot the bar and turn toward her. "Do you want a drink?"

"Sure," she answers, so I guide her through the crowd, hearing a few murmurs as we walk by. I ignore them, as I have one thing on my mind—getting a drink. Only one because I won't drive if I drink more than that, but Christ, I just need something to loosen the choke hold this woman has on me right now.

From her questions about changing dresses, she must have no fucking idea how stunning she is. She never seeks my approval, and yet she's tried to lift me up with her comments and encouragement, even if I don't resemble the man she's talking about. But the words to tell this beauty how stunning she is simply won't pass my lips. *I'm not good with words.* She's smart, somehow timid yet so strong too. She's loyal, a minimalist with a sassy sense of humor. And yes, I've even smiled around her. *She's so...real.*

*What am I supposed to do with a woman like this?*

When we pull up to the bar, I release her hand but then place my hand on her lower back, her soft skin making my palm feel like it's burning on the spot, but the kind of burn I want to suffer in.

"What do you want?" I ask, my mouth close to her head.

She glances up at me, that beautiful smile of hers practically making me weak in the goddamn knees. "Honestly, just some white wine."

I turn toward the bartender and say, "White wine for her, a whiskey for me."

He nods, and I set her clutch on the bar to reach for my wallet and pull out a tip.

"This is way fancier than the last event." She moves even closer, and I catch a hint of her minty breath as she whispers, "Did you see the size of the chandeliers? Yowza."

I don't know why that makes me smirk, but it does. "That's how you can tell how fancy the event is? By the size of the chandeliers?"

She leans into me, letting my hand curl over her bare skin as she plays with the lapel of my suit jacket. "You just smirked. Does that mean you might actually let loose a little? Because by the way you greeted me, I felt like I did something wrong."

"You did nothing wrong," I say as I let my thumb rub over her skin, causing her eyes to flutter.

"Then why were you so angry?"

"Not angry," I say. "Just..." I trail off, not sure how to explain it.

"Just what?" she presses, sliding her fingers over my lapel.

Her inquisitive, soulful eyes stare up at me, looking for answers. Answers that I want to keep close to my chest, but as she leans in closer, enveloping me in her sweet, flowery scent, I find the firm grasp I have on these…feelings slip for a moment.

"Just…awestruck," I finally answer, then allow my other hand to tug ever so slightly on her bottom lip. "You look fucking beautiful, Maple."

"Oh," she says in surprise, as if she didn't expect me to admit such a thing. "Um, thank you."

Silence falls between us. She's leaning into me, and I'm inching her closer with my hand as I curl my fingers over her ribs, wanting my fingertips to imprint on her velvet skin.

"Here you are," the bartender says, snapping us out of our moment.

Clearing my throat, I release my hold on her back and offer her drink to her before picking up mine and quickly taking a larger gulp than anticipated.

I snag her clutch and maneuver her through the crowd until we're standing at a high-top table in the middle of the room. The large chandeliers hang over us, the live band gently plays instrumentals, and occasional laughter spreads through the room—all signs of a stuffy event well on its way into the evening.

"So what should we do?" she asks, looking around and sipping her wine.

"Nothing," I say.

"What do you mean? Shouldn't we talk to people?"

"They'll come to us," I say as I set my whiskey down and move in closer to her. "They always do. And you want the people to come to you."

"Why?" she asks. I place my hand on her back again, this time inching it lower, just above the curve of her ass. Her smirk tells me she realizes just how close I am to what I've wanted since the first day I met her.

"Because the people who seek us out want our attention. The people who want our attention will want to donate because they'll want to impress us."

Her smile grows. "That's actually really smart."

"Not my first time, Baker." I turn toward her, keeping her close so I can keep my hold on her. She has to tilt her head back to look at me, but she doesn't seem to mind.

"Think they'll approach us with you holding me this tightly?"

"Yes," I answer, my thumb stroking her skin, causing her to gulp her wine, then set her almost empty glass down.

"You're, uh, you're really good at the whole deception thing."

"What do you mean?" I ask.

"Well, you know, playing up the intimacy like Gretchen said."

She thinks this is me playing a part?

Yeah, not so much.

This is me wanting to keep her close.

Wanting to touch her.

Hold her.

Feel her.

This is me being a jealous asshole, making sure everyone in this room knows to back the fuck off when it comes to Maple Baker.

"Not hard to do," I say, meeting her gaze.

She wets her lips as she lifts her hand to my lapel again, those eyes of hers looking hungry.

"St. John," a voice sounds from the right, breaking the spell between us one more time. I turn to see some old dude I know I've seen before, but I can't remember his name to save my life. He must notice because he says, "Gerry Gardner."

Oh right...some rich asshole in pharmaceuticals.

"Gerry, great to see you," I say, putting on the best fake smile I can muster and shaking his hand. "How are you?"

"Good. Good." He looks between us, seeming interested, so I take that moment to introduce Maple.

"This is Maple Baker, my girlfriend." The term rolls so easily off my tongue that I don't even flinch while saying it, something I probably would have done with someone else. "Maple, Gerry, he works in pharmaceuticals. Maple works for the zoo as a keeper for the flamingos."

Gerry smiles brightly. "Oh, I'm aware. My wife will be so upset because she's been obsessed with updating me on your social media profile. She was supposed to be here tonight but ended up having to work late."

"Ah, that's such a shame," Maple says. "It would have been lovely to meet her."

Gerry looks between us again. "You know, she thought something was going on between you two but couldn't confirm, but you just called her your girlfriend."

I nod. "I did." Then I pull her in tighter, my hand sliding around her side, my fingers slipping to the front of her ribs, under the fabric of her dress. I feel her take a sharp breath before she leans into the touch.

Gerry smiles brightly. "Do you think I could possibly take a picture with you two...for my wife?"

"Of course," I say. "But you have to listen to Maple tell you about the flamingos first."

Gerry smirks. "Why don't I do you one better and write you a check?"

I glance down at Maple, her eyes wide.

"That will work just fine," I say before finishing my whiskey.

---

"Yeah, they have a whole fridge full of krill, smells like rotten seafood, but the flamingos can't get enough of it," I say while a group of three sisters crowds around us. "And when they start padding their feet against the water to stir up their food, it's fucking cute. And that's coming from me."

The three sisters, best known in the fundraising circuit as the Gilded

Girls, all clutch their hands to their chests as they eat up every word I'm throwing at them.

"But yeah, Maple, my girl, spent three years in Peru, studying them and their habitat." I shake my head. "A habitat they're slowly losing. Flamingos are actually getting close to becoming threatened."

"No," one of them says, looking downright ready to cry.

"Yeah, that's why we're here, to bring more awareness to them and highlight such a beautiful animal that I think sometimes gets overlooked."

"Well, not by us," one of them says as she pulls out a checkbook. I grab a glass of water from a server walking by, smirk over the rim, and then take a sip of the cool liquid.

---

"Big Hermy," I answer for Maple. "She loves him. And how could she not? The dude is the proudest flamingo in the flamboyance." I say this with confidence to a really nice gay couple who are easily the best dressed in the room.

Jacob is a huge Foghorns fan, while his husband, Tony, is a fan of Flock and Tackle, so the moment they spotted us, they beelined to our table.

"Flamboyance?" Tony asks.

I nod. "Yeah, that's what a flock of flamingos is formally known as."

"Ooh, I like that," Tony says, giving his husband a little shimmy.

"Of course you would," Jacob says with a playful shake of his head. "So would Big Hermy be your favorite as well?"

"Martha Stewart comes in a close second, but yeah, Big Hermy is the man. He actually only has one eye."

"Really?" Tony asks, a frown pulling at his brow. "What happened?"

I slide my hand farther across Maple's ribs, my fingers now touching her stomach, causing her to gasp as I lightly dig my fingertips into her soft-as-fuck skin. *And fuck, do I want to rip this goddamn dress off her so I can lick every inch of her.* "Jackal attack," I say, shocked that I've been able to retain everything Maple has told me. And from the way she keeps glancing up at me in surprise, she's just as shocked as I am.

"Oh, that's terrible," Tony says, turning to Jacob. "We need to help them out."

"I saw that coming," Jacob says as he places a soft kiss on his husband's lips and then pulls a checkbook out of his breast pocket.

I smile to myself as Maple leans in even closer.

---

I get in the car and shut the door, and Maple quickly turns toward me, her eyes wide, her smile brighter than I've ever seen it.

"Oh my God, Graydon, that was…that was insane."

I pull out onto the road, trying to hold back the smile that wants to pull at my lips as well, because holy shit, that was insane.

I think I blacked out at one point, just on autopilot, talking about the flamingos, not letting Maple get one word in as I charmed the fuck out of nearly everyone in that room.

She ended up with six donations and some promises to invest in the zoo.

I've never done anything like it before. I know that if I were with anyone else, I probably wouldn't have pushed as hard as I did, but it felt so…easy with Maple at my side.

It felt like I was meant to be talking up the goddamn flamingos.

And it came so naturally, which is slightly concerning because…do I actually care about the fucking pink dodo birds?

No, I wouldn't go that far.

I do think I care about their zookeeper, though, and with every fact I dazzled the donors with, I felt her appreciation for me grow, which of course lent me the opportunity to pull her closer and closer. And I never wanted to fucking let go. I wanted to stay there, my palm under her dress, pressed against the warm skin of her waistline. I wanted to live there, but once she yawned, I knew it was time to give up the fantasy and take her home.

She pushes at my shoulder. "Are you really going to act like that was nothing? Graydon, you knew all the things about flamingos."

"Yeah, because you jabber on about them enough," I tease.

She chuckles. "Well, my jabbering paid off. Seriously, I don't think I've ever seen that many donations in such a short amount of time. It was amazing." She rests her hand on my arm. "Thank you."

"No thanks needed," I say as I maneuver through the traffic.

"Can't you just say, 'You're welcome'?" She sighs.

"Nah, this is better."

She shakes her head, then turns to face straight, but I don't let her put distance between us as I slide my hand onto her thigh again. I have an addiction, and it's unlikely it will ever be satiated.

Thankfully, to my surprise, she slides her hand on top of mine, where her thumb strokes my knuckles. The soft swipe sends chills up my arm, bringing awareness to how long it's been since I've been… touched.

My mom always offered me snuggles, hugs, and kisses—she doled out her love with physical touch—and when I lost her, that touch that I loved as a young boy just disappeared. *I had craved it.*

And as time went on, I became more jaded, hardened, and closed off, not letting a woman get remotely close to me, even when it came to something as simple as holding hands.

That is, until Maple came along.

She's different.

She makes me feel safe.

Comforted.

Like I can almost—and I mean almost—be myself around her.

Time passes as we make our way back to our neighborhood, not saying anything, just enjoying the silence between us, something else I can appreciate about her. She doesn't drown me with conversation anymore, and sitting in silence is just as comfortable as talking.

When I pull up to her apartment, I go to get out, but she stops me, keeping me in place.

"I can get out myself, and don't argue with me," she says, feigning a stern expression.

Letting her take the win on this, I settle in my seat as she turns toward me.

"Fine, but I don't like it."

She offers me a soft smile before growing serious. "Thank you, Graydon. Thank you for everything tonight. I can't tell you how much I appreciate how you spoke about the flamingos, the zoo…me. Not sure you will ever know just how grateful I am."

"No need to tell me; I can see it in your eyes."

"Can you?"

I wet my lips. "I can."

Her eyes fall to my mouth for a brief moment before they pick back up to meet my gaze. "Well, if you can see how grateful I am, then I should probably get going."

I clear my throat, my skin breaking out in a wave of goose bumps as she leans in closer to me. Her proximity always excites me, but tonight…tonight has been different. Tonight I've been yearning, begging, pleading, needing her to be close, and now that we're not in the public eye, and we're just alone, me and her, I want her to want this.

To want to feel my touch.

To want to be near me.

Fuck, I just…I want her.

Leaning in more, she cups my cheek, and like every other time I've dropped her off at her apartment lately, she very lightly presses her lips to my jaw.

It's almost unbearable after the night I've had with her.

A goddamn tease to what I actually want.

But instead of exiting right away, she stays close, her breath caressing my stubble. On a whisper, she says, "Thank you."

A shiver runs down my spine from the hitch in her throat while her fingers slide off my cheek and down my chest.

I don't want her to pull away. I don't want her to leave this car.

I want…fuck, I want so much goddamn more, and that's terrifying.

Because I don't know if I've ever felt this desperate for another person before.

I wet my lips again, my gaze set on hers. She's close, so fucking close, like she's expecting something more. Expecting me to make a move.

And that's dangerous, because desperation is crawling up my spine, pushing me to do more.

Ask for more.

When her eyes drop to my mouth, my stomach plummets in a fury of flutters.

She wants this too.

She has to.

So, before I can stop myself, I say, "If you're really appreciative, Maple, then thank me properly."

I hold my breath as the smallest of smirks tugs on the corner of her lips. Her hand slides up my jaw, where she cups my cheek and pauses. Her eyes search mine while the air stills, only to turn electric as she leans in the last few inches.

Her mouth is a whisper away.

So close I can practically taste her.

*Please do it.*

*Kiss me.*

And when I think she's not going to finish what she started, her mouth presses against mine in the most delicious fucking kiss of my goddamn life.

And I fucking melt.

I melt right there, in the seat of this stupid rental car.

Jesus Christ.

Her lips are so soft.

She kisses me, barely applying any pressure. And just as I'm about to loop my hand behind her head, she pulls away, her scent lingering around me, making me feel dazed, like I was just thrown into a whirlwind of lust and I'm expected to land on my feet.

*Fuck, I want her.*

I've wanted her for a while now. From her empathetic heart to her joyous demeanor, to that goddamn smile, to those sultry eyes. She's captivated me.

And after seeing so much of her gorgeous skin for the last few hours, after touching her softness, hearing her small gasps, I'm desperate for her.

Fucking desperate.

*I want to take you in this car. Then take you again against your front door inside your apartment. Then, once I've ripped this distracting dress off your body, fuck you so hard against every surface I can find that you'll never be able to look at another man again. My tongue wants to learn your taste and—*

"Night, Graydon," she says smoothly. *What?* She opens her car door, snags her clutch, and gives me one more smile before she shuts the door and works her way up the stairs to her apartment. My eyes are on her ass the entire fucking time.

I drag my hand over my mouth and let out a large sigh.

Christ, what the hell am I doing?

Pursuing her.

I think I'm fucking pursuing her, and that should terrify me, but right now, when I can still feel the imprint of her lips on mine, I know for a damn fact that I'm not terrified.

No, I'm fucking burning to take her off the market…to make her mine.

# CHAPTER 24
# MAPLE

"THIS LOOKS AMAZING," I SAY as I take a seat at Everly's table and look over the stuffed French toast she spent the morning making while Hardy spent half an hour squeezing oranges.

It was fun watching them prepare the brunch they invited me to. They worked seamlessly in the kitchen, predicting each other's moves, lending a hand without having to be asked, and occasionally running a hand over each other's backs or subtly kissing the other's head. It's really sweet seeing them together.

"Thank you," Everly says. "I saw the recipe on Instagram, and I had to try it. I just hope it's good."

"Smells amazing, babe," Hardy says, leaning over and placing a kiss on her cheek.

Everly smirks at him, then pours us some orange juice. "And the orange juice looks great, Hardy."

Hardy puffs his chest out as if he just got done making a Michelin Star–worthy meal. "Takes a steady hand to create a nearly pulp-free fresh orange juice."

If they weren't so cute, I'd roll my eyes.

"You're really impressive," Everly says.

"I think you said the same thing last night as well." He wiggles his brows, and now it's time for me to cut in.

"Okay, can you not with that? I know we're all friends, but that's pushing it."

Hardy chuckles. "Sorry." But then he glances at Everly, who's blushing.

Ugh, these two.

We fill our plates up with fruit salad and French toast and syrup, and then dig in.

"So," Everly says, a smile playing on her lips. "I happened to stumble across some pictures this morning. Seems like you and Graydon were getting cozy."

I pause in the middle of cutting my French toast and look up at her. "Where did you see those?"

"One of the gossip accounts I follow. They picked it up from a sports account, of all things."

"Let me see," I say, my heart racing as I think about last night.

From the way Graydon's eyes roamed over me to the feel of his warm palm against my skin to how he slipped his hand under the fabric of my dress, holding me close with the subtle press of his thumb. And then there was the short but intoxicating kiss at the end of the night. I went to bed with my heart fluttering, my body buzzing, and my mind whirling because I never would have expected that.

Ever.

Yet I wish it had happened sooner.

I wish it had happened more.

I wish I hadn't left that car without him.

Everly flashes her phone at me, and I let out a small gasp as I stare at the screen.

It's a picture of me and Graydon, taken from the side. You can clearly see his hand slipped beneath the side of my dress, his posture holding me protectively as I stare up at him.

I swipe to find another picture, us at the bar and me holding on to his lapel, smiling up at him.

And the third picture is of us leaving, his hand holding mine, him clutching my bag and us both smiling as we make our way to the car.

Holy shit. *We look stunning together. We look... seriously into each other.* Then I think about his gruff—yet insanely sexy—demand.

*"If you're really appreciative,* Maple, *then thank me properly."*

If this is what Gretchen wanted from last night, to unveil the PR romance, these photos would do it.

My cheeks blush as I look at Everly and Hardy smiling like fools.

"Care to share what's going on?" Everly asks. "Because that looks like a lot more than just a PR relationship."

Hardy leans forward and whisper-shouts, "His hand is practically cupping your breast!"

"Oh my God, it was not cupping my breast." Trust me, I would have known.

"Looked pretty damn close."

Not close enough.

"Soooo..." Everly presses. *Think, Maple.*

Except I'm struggling to think up anything because his every stroke tantalized me. Short-circuited my brain. *I loved every moment he touched me.* I'd wanted more. I'd wanted him to remove the dress...

"That was, uh...that was just for the cameras. We knew they were going to be there. Gretchen wanted to have the relationship leak last night."

"Uh-huh." Everly plops a piece of French toast in her mouth while Hardy sips his orange juice. "I understand the leaking of the photos, but there is no way you're just pretending in those pictures. So spill."

God, nothing gets past her.

I drag a piece of French toast around some syrup. "Well, I don't really know what's going on." I look up at both of them. "But I did kiss him on the lips last night."

"What?" Everly shouts, her eyes bugging out.

"Oh shit, really?" Hardy says, a smile playing on his mouth.

"You kissed him? How much? How long? How was it? Did he cop a feel? I need all the details."

She takes my fork away from me, sets it down on my plate, and then pushes the plate away. She then props her chin on her hands and waits intently for my answers.

So I guess we won't be eating right now.

"It was in his car, after the event. The kiss was maybe like five seconds, no longer than that. Nothing else occurred, and there was no tongue, just lips. But it was..." I let out a dreamy sigh. "It made my stomach flutter."

Everly claps her hands together excitedly.

"Who initiated it?" Hardy asks.

"Um, I guess maybe both of us?"

"So you attacked each other together?"

I shake my head. "No, I've been thanking him when he drops me off at my apartment every day with a kiss on his cheek. And yesterday, he was, God, he was so amazing at the event, getting donation after donation, relating countless facts about flamingos that I'd shared with him but hadn't thought he was paying attention to. And it was just..." My smile stretches across my face as my skin tingles with the memory of how engaged he was, how sweet and protective.

"Is that what it looks like to have hearts in your eyes?" Hardy asks.

Everly chuckles and nods. "It sure does."

I bring my attention back to them and clear my throat. "Anyway, I kissed him on the cheek and thanked him and then he barely let me pull away before he said, 'If you're really appreciative, Maple, then thank me properly.'"

Everly's hand goes to her chest as she whispers, "Oh my God."

"I know."

"I mean, I'm a straight man and even I got a bit sweaty on the upper lip," Hardy says as he dabs his napkin over his face, causing us both to laugh.

"So then you kissed him?" Everly asks.

"Yes, it was brief, but oh my God, it felt like...like all the other kisses I've experienced in my life meant nothing."

"Hey," Hardy says, a pinch in his brow. "I resent that. We had some good kisses."

"Not like the one I had last night." I smirk at him, causing Everly to burst out in laughter and Hardy to grow more irritated.

"You're saying that the smallest whisper of a kiss from Graydon was better than all the times I had my tongue all over your mouth?"

"Yup."

Everly laughs even harder, and he pokes her in the arm. "Everly, don't laugh at that. Tell her your husband is a very good kisser."

Everly lifts her hand and shakes it in a "so-so" manner. "Eh."

Flames erupt in his eyes as his anger shoots to the roof. "You take that back or...or...divorce." His hand playfully slaps the table.

Chuckling some more, Everly leans in close to Hardy and places her palm on his chest. "You're the best kisser to have ever kissed my lips." That satisfies him as he leans in and pecks her mouth. "Then again, I've never had a whisper of a kiss from Graydon St. John."

"That's it." Hardy pushes away from the table as Everly and I dissolve into a fit of giggles. "I don't have to put up with this kind of abuse." He picks up his plate and his orange juice and huffs. "I'm going to eat out on the balcony where the pigeons will appreciate me."

"Okay, JP," Everly scoffs, but then she stops him with her hand on his stomach and beckons him down to her. He leans in and she kisses him lightly, then shivers. "Ooh, nothing will beat that."

He rolls his eyes but says, "Better remember that, baby."

When he shuts the screen door to the balcony, Everly brings her attention back to me and says, "He's actually a really good kisser."

"When I kissed him, I was impressed."

"I heard that, you assholes," Hardy says through a crack in the sliding glass door.

We both chuckle and then attack our French toast.

Of course he heard that.

---

Comfortable in a pair of pink pajama pants and a white shirt that says Single and Ready to Flamingo, I bring my knees up to my chest and press play on my movie before snagging my popcorn bowl from the table.

After brunch with Hardy and Everly, I ran some errands, took a long walk around Golden Gate Park, and then came back here. I showered and promised myself an unhealthy dinner of popcorn and Butterfinger Bites.

Sometimes you just need one of those nights, and I did, because I needed the distraction.

All day, my mind has been on Graydon.

I've been tempted to text him, to ask him how training camp was today, to ask him to come over and watch a movie with me, but I've held back. I've kept my hand away from my phone and focused on things I needed to take care of because…frankly, I have no idea where I stand with him.

He wanted that kiss, I know he did.

He held me close last night, and he wasn't faking it.

He has been every bit attentive and protective, and it's made it seem like…like there's something special between us, but I'm too scared to ask.

I'm too nervous to even venture into the idea of there being more because is that something I even want? I've been out of the dating circuit for so long now that I don't even know how it works. And does he even want to date?

Ugh…I have no idea.

But, God, last night…it really didn't feel like it was all for show. It felt like so much more than that.

Sighing, I pick up my phone as *How to Lose a Guy in 10 Days* starts to play. I click on Instagram and take in all the notifications already waiting for me. We turned off the DM option because that became insane, and instead we just take the time to look at the comments.

Since we sort of announced our "relationship" last night, I decided to post the picture I took of us in the car, with his hand on my thigh. My caption was simple: "Best date ever. Save the Flamingos."

I left it at that, and from the looks of it, that's all it took. There are already over two thousand comments.

Good Lord.

I shake my head and bring my attention back to the movie just as my phone buzzes with a text.

When Graydon's name appears, I can't hold back my smile or ignore how seeing his name feels like a bunch of tiny fireflies just lit up in my stomach.

**Graydon:** Best date ever, huh?

Ignoring the movie completely, I sit cross-legged, drag a pillow on top of my lap, and text him back.

**Maple:** You checking up on our social media?

**Graydon:** Just making sure you're not posting anything embarrassing.

**Maple:** I thought you said you didn't have any embarrassing pictures.

**Graydon:** Who knows what you're doing when I'm washing dishes.

**Maple:** It's not taking embarrassing pictures of you, that's for sure.

**Graydon:** And what exactly is it that you do?

Stare at your ass.

Your back muscles.

Allow myself to wonder what it would be like to be one of those dishes that you're rubbing…

**Maple:** Considering all the ways I can save flamingos.

**Graydon:** Uh-huh, that's not what your eyes on my ass were saying the other day.

I gasp and then chuckle.

When he's like this, flirty and not so intense, he really is so much fun to be around. Kind of addictive.

**Maple:** Like you're one to speak. I've caught you a few times.

**Graydon:** I've been staring at your ass since day one. You thought I was making fun of your pants when I was just covering up for being caught looking at you.

Umm…what?

**Maple:** Wait, seriously?

**Graydon:** Yup.

**Maple:** I thought…I thought you assumed I was some kind of loser with high-water pants.

**Graydon:** Not even close.

**Maple:** Wow, okay. This is news to me.

**Graydon:** Shouldn't be. Looking at some of the pics Gretchen released. Seems like I haven't stopped staring either.

**Maple:** I didn't see any of you staring at my ass.

**Graydon:** [Link] Second photo.

I pull up the link he sent me and scroll to the second picture. It's of me shaking the hand of someone, and sure enough, he's there, staring down at my ass.

**Graydon:** That dress was unreal last night. I couldn't keep my eyes off you.

Oh God.

Oh God…that's…he's…oh God, he's flirting, and I just don't know if I'm equipped for this.

**Graydon:** This is where you say my suit was unreal as well.

I chuckle, grateful that he can so effortlessly ease the nerves I'm feeling.

**Maple:** Maybe I didn't think it was.
**Graydon:** Liar.
**Maple:** Perhaps.
**Graydon:** What are you doing tonight?
**Maple:** Cashing in on a promise I made myself.
**Graydon:** And what kind of promise is that?
**Maple:** Movie date with myself that includes popcorn and Butterfinger Bites (don't judge me) as dinner.
**Graydon:** Why would I judge you?
**Maple:** Because you're all about the protein intake.
**Graydon:** I like sweets.
**Maple:** Yeah, okay. What kind?
**Graydon:** I like chocolate.
**Maple:** Really?
**Graydon:** Do you find that surprising?

**Maple:** A little. I just assumed you ate broccoli for dessert.

**Graydon:** Love the opinions you have of me.

**Maple:** LOL. Sorry. Just for someone with that much muscle mass, I wouldn't think you'd eat chocolate.

**Graydon:** It's not every day, but when I indulge, I go for something like a chocolate lava cake.

**Maple:** That's…that's actually kind of cute.

**Graydon:** Nothing about me is cute.

**Maple:** Your chocolate lava cake is.

**Graydon:** Okay, maybe one thing. The rest of me is not cute.

**Maple:** Sooooo next time I see you, you don't want me saying how cute you look in your little football helmet?

**Graydon:** You're fucking with me.

**Maple:** LOL. Sorry, forgot you're supposed to look intimidating.

**Graydon:** I am intimidating. I've made grown men cry.

**Maple:** Grown men or just OC?

**Graydon:** Both.

**Maple:** Not that I like to boost your ego, but I honestly believe you've made grown men cry. I've seen the way your teeth snap when you're at practice, like you're ready to bite into someone's leg.

**Graydon:** If I didn't have a mouth guard, I probably would do some biting.

**Maple:** Have you always been this…violent?

**Graydon:** No.

**Maple:** What changed?

**Graydon:** Nothing you need to worry about.

**Maple:** Is that your nice way of saying you don't want to talk about it?

**Graydon:** Precisely.

**Maple:** I guess you'll always remain a mystery to me.

**Graydon:** Nah, you know what you need to know.

**Maple:** You think I know enough?

**Graydon:** Yeah.

**Maple:** Okay, well…here is what I do know. You enjoy wearing pink cleaning gloves because they make your hands look dainty.

**Graydon:** Nothing can make my hands look dainty.

**Maple:** You squeal in excitement when you tackle someone. Hands shaking, ass twerking…high-pitched squeals.

**Graydon:** Are you sure you're talking about me?

**Maple:** And in the mornings, when you pick me up, you pretend to be drinking coffee but it's really a Shirley Temple. Don't even deny it, I've seen you sipping that cherry.

**Graydon:** Trust me, if you saw me "sipping" on a cherry, you would know it.

My cheeks flame as I stare down at his innuendo, unsure how to really respond.

I can be flirty, but…dirty? That's a whole different level.

**Maple:** Oh, um, that's nice. I like cherries.

**Graydon:** Baker, could you be more awkward?

**Maple:** I wasn't ready for you to talk about sipping on cherries.

**Graydon:** You brought it up.

**Maple:** I was talking about Shirley Temples, not…you know.

**Graydon:** Can't even say it, can you?

**Maple:** I don't know what you're referring to.

**Graydon:** Liar.

God, dare I say it? No, I can't.

Can I?

My cheeks hurt from smiling so much.

My stomach is twisted in all kinds of knots.

And for the first time in a long time, maybe even in forever, I feel giddy…talking to a man.

---

**Graydon:** I can still smell the bird on me, even after a shower.

**Maple:** You are such a liar.

**Graydon:** It's never leaving my nose.

**Maple:** You were around them for maybe five minutes.

**Graydon:** Five minutes too long. They were eyeing my watch.

**Maple:** I told you not to wear anything shiny.

**Graydon:** Didn't think they were going to try to rob me!

**Maple:** LOL. That's very dramatic of you, seems like you've been hanging out with OC for too long.

**Graydon:** You're right. He's dead to me now.

**Maple:** He'll be crushed.

**Graydon:** Not my problem.

**Maple:** You put on such a front, but I know you secretly like him. Just admit it.

**Graydon:** Never.

**Maple:** Stubborn.

**Graydon:** Maybe. So…what are you doing?

**Maple:** Eating some homemade lasagna.

**Graydon:** And you didn't offer me any?

**Maple:** Didn't cross my mind.

**Graydon:** Ouch, Baker. That stings.

**Maple:** What stings worse, the bird smell in your nose, or the lasagna?

**Graydon:** Lasagna, because that means I could have seen you again…

---

**Graydon:** Did you really think you were going to beat me in a twenty-yard dash today?

**Maple:** *Currently in an Epsom salt bath* Wouldn't have hurt you to lay off the pedal for your PR girlfriend.

**Graydon:** And get shit from everyone, including my dad? I'm good.

**Maple:** You didn't even give me a chance.

**Graydon:** Exactly.

**Maple:** Just cruel.

**Graydon:** Did you really think a zookeeper could outrun a professional football player?

**Maple:** A girl can dream.

**Graydon:** Pick a different dream.

**Maple:** What do you suggest?

**Graydon:** Maybe more tacos on the back of a pickup truck?

**Maple:** Why would I dream about that when it already happened?

**Graydon:** Assumed you would want it to happen again.

**Maple:** Bold assumption.

**Graydon:** Nah, accurate one. I know you're looking for more time with me.

**Maple:** How do you figure?

**Graydon:** The way you licked your lips when I came to pick you up this morning.

---

**Graydon:** After a long day at the zoo, what do you do to unwind?

**Maple:** Wow, it almost seems like you care about my day.

**Graydon:** Maybe I do.

**Maple:** Is that you admitting it?

**Graydon:** In a roundabout way.

**Maple:** Should I answer in a roundabout way?

**Graydon:** Not recommended.

**Maple:** Usually shower and figure out what I'm going to eat. Nothing too exciting.

**Graydon:** The shower seems exciting.

**Maple:** Because of getting the smell off me?

**Graydon:** Not what I was thinking, but sure.

**Maple:** And what were you thinking?

**Graydon:** Too much to text.

**Maple:** Voice message it.

**Graydon:** Pining to hear my voice, Baker?

**Maple:** No.

**Graydon:** Liar.

**Maple:** Please, don't be insufferable tonight like every other night you've texted me.

**Graydon:** Insufferable, huh? And here I thought I was flirting…

---

**Graydon:** What are you doing, Baker?

**Maple:** Haven't you already used that as an opening line this week?

**Graydon:** Never claimed to be creative.

**Maple:** LOL. So, what am I doing? Well, I'm enjoying a girl dinner that consists of popcorn and candy once again and I'm gearing up to watch a movie. What are you doing right now?

**Graydon:** Talking to you.

**Maple:** You don't have anything else going on?

**Graydon:** Not really. Tired from practice. Just ate a steak, now watching the Bombers game.

**Maple:** Aw, you watch Bennett?

**Graydon:** Yeah, figured I might as well.

**Maple:** Is he good?

**Graydon:** Really fucking good. What movie are you watching?

**Maple:** *The Wedding Singer.* One of my all-time favorites.

**Graydon:** Never seen it.

**Maple:** Why did I know you were going to say that?

**Graydon:** Guess I'm predictable.

**Maple:** You're not in the slightest, actually. You're very unpredictable.

**Graydon:** How so?

**Maple:** Well, for one, never in my life would I have thought that you'd send me thirst traps.

**Graydon:** Is that you fishing for one? Because all you have to do is ask.

My phone buzzes again, and a picture of him lights up my screen.

Sigh.

Wet and rumpled, his hair is unstyled and falling every which way, including a few strands over his forehead. Chest on full display, he's sitting on his couch in a pair of sweatpants with the TV remote next to him while he casually smirks.

Despite my eyes roaming over his impressively cut chest, I take a moment to study his beautiful eyes. Dark, mysterious, but also with a hint of kindness. *He's so handsome.* The sharp angles of his face may be intimidating to an opponent, but they intrigue me. They make me want to run my fingers over them and create a softness along the hard edges.

**Graydon:** Your turn.

**Maple:** You don't want a pic.

**Graydon:** Then why the hell did I ask?

I press my lips together, nerves jumbling inside me.

Should I send him one?

Why the hell not?

I sit taller, angle the phone, and show off my shirt so he can see what it says. When I'm satisfied, I snap the pic, then examine it quickly to decide whether I should send it.

Hair looks good, face looks good. Shirt looks...oh God, my nipples are hard and pressing against the fabric.

I nibble on the corner of my lip, wondering if I should send it or not, but then I just say "fuck it" in my head and press send as insecurity laces my insides.

I wait for a response.

And wait.

And after what feels like ten minutes but is really more like ten seconds, he texts back.

**Graydon:** Um, pretty sure I was topless in mine.

My cheeks flame with heat as I scoot down lower on the couch, attempting to...hide? I don't know what I'm trying to do. This entire week, he's been doing a whole lot to my body without actually doing anything. Just using his words.

**Graydon:** Also...single and ready to flamingo? Last time I checked, you aren't single.

God, I hate that I'm smiling like a fool.

**Maple:** Fictitiously, I'm not single. Also, do you really think I'm going to send you a topless photo?

**Graydon:** A man can dream.

My teeth roll over my bottom lip, and my courage starts to ramp up because from the kiss the night of the fundraiser, to the touching and all the flirty texts he's sent, there's clearly something here. There's interest on his end, and I'd be lying if I said there wasn't interest on mine. Because there is.

And it's been a really long time since I've been on a date or have even thought about dating someone. I mean, there was a time when I was in Peru and had a bad crush on Hank, but I realized that since we were working together with no end in sight, it would be a bad idea.

But Graydon's different.

I've never met someone like him before.

Broody, but sweet.

Introverted, yet flirty.

Standoffish, yet so attentive.

He's a mystery that I want to solve.

And after the night of the fundraiser, the kiss, the way he pressed his hand into my skin, this week's nighttime text messages, I think I've found an opening, and...I'm going to take it.

**Maple:** What are you doing tomorrow? Maybe we can get brunch or something.

After I hit send, I toss my phone to the side and cover my eyes. Oh my God, I can't believe I just asked him out on a date.

What if...what if he says no?

What if I'm reading him all wrong?

I don't think I'll ever recover from the embarrassment.

My phone buzzes, making my nerves scream with dread.

*Please don't be a no.*

*Please don't be a no...*

I pick up my phone and go to his text.

**Graydon:** I have plans, but I'll pick you up Monday for training camp.

My heart sinks as my imagination considers every possible scenario for what he'd be doing on a Sunday. I'm trying to convince myself that it has nothing to do with me. That he's probably going to hang out with friends or something, given that it's his only day off. Why would he want to hang out with me when he sees me every day of the week? But it doesn't change the fact that I feel like an idiot for even asking.

Willing the embarrassment and tears not to take over, I let out a deep breath and text him back.

**Maple:** Cool, yeah, I was thinking about doing my own brunch anyway. Got some fresh strawberries that I need to cut up.

Fresh strawberries? Why?

That's such a stupid thing to say.

And he must think it too because he doesn't text back right away. Every second that ticks by, I feel more and more embarrassed.

He jokes around about a topless pic, and I take that as free rein to ask him out? What is wrong with me?

I set my phone down and stare blankly at the TV, Adam Sandler's voice barely registering as tears spring to my eyes from humiliation. After a few more minutes, my phone finally buzzes, and I hate that I'm so quick to pick it up.

**Graydon:** Bennett just hit a two-run home run.

Okay, we're just going to skirt right around the awkward situation of me asking him out and him rejecting me. That's cool. I'm good with that.

**Maple:** Cool. Adam Sandler just helped an underage drinker puke into a dumpster.

**Graydon:** Umm...okay.

I groan and then toss my phone again.

Yup, I'm done for the night.

# CHAPTER 25
# GRAYDON

"PLEASE, JUST...JUST LEAVE ME alone," Mom says as her eyes glaze over. Her words slice me in two, tearing at the scars that have barely healed from the last time she didn't recognize me.

Sitting next to her, attempting to share space while painting like I've done in the past, there is something different about this visit, as if there isn't an ounce of clarity in her eyes.

And like every other time she doesn't recognize me, it feels like life is driving a goddamn dagger right into my soul, carving out a piece of it that will never grow back.

My hopes were too high after last week's visit. I thought if we replayed everything that we did last time, we'd get the same result, but I was so wrong. My mom's brain just doesn't work like that. And even when you get through to her, it doesn't mean the next time will be the same. It's devastating. And it reminds me of how much I lost all those years ago. How alone I feel.

I glance toward Rhonda, begging for any sort of help, but she just offers me a sad smile, because we know where this is going. We know we can't do anything to stop it.

When she didn't recognize me and didn't connect the dots of who I was, I decided to just sit next to her and paint. At least I could be in her presence, which was better than nothing, but with every stroke I made on the canvas I've been working on for weeks every Sunday, she scooted her chair farther and farther away while moving her easel, as if I were a complete and total stranger.

Not just a stranger, but someone who scared her.

"Mom," I say quietly, forgetting to call her by her first name.

"Don't call me that!" she shouts and then stands from her chair as she clutches at her cardigan. "You're not my son." She picks up her paintbrush and throws it at me in horror. "You're not him."

The paintbrush splatters across my shirt, coating me in dark green paint as she backs up, tears forming in her eyes. My heart crumbles, shattering into a thousand pieces. *She's so scared of me.*

I want to reach out to her, take her hand, soothe her.

Hell, I want her to pull me into *her* arms, rub *my* back, kiss *my* cheek, and soothe me like she used to so many years ago.

I want all of this to be different. I want my fucking mom back. I don't want to be grieving the loss of her as she stands, breathing, with a goddamn heartbeat right in front of me.

But with a cruel twist of fate, not only was my mom taken away from me but she's still on this earth in her full form. It's the worst kind of torture, knowing I could still embrace her after her accident, but also knowing that the chances of being held tightly by her are slipping further and further away as her memory grows worse and I grow older.

A shaky hand covers her mouth as she says, "I want him gone. I want this sick man gone. How cruel of you to try to act like my son."

*Please don't say that. I am your son.*

I press my lips together to stop them from quivering as pain ricochets through me, battering me from the inside out.

*Please don't do this, Mom.*

*Please.*

"Graydon, you should probably go," Rhonda says, causing my mom to whirl around on her.

"Do not call him that. That is not my son!" she shouts, thrashing her arm around and knocking her painting over. "He's not…wh-what? Where am I?" She looks around frantically, her terrified expression threatening to break me. "Why am I here? Get me out of here. I want my family. I want my baby boy. Where is he? Why are you keeping him from me?"

I beg the universe for her to see me, for her to look me in the eyes, to recognize me as the boy I once was, and as I stand, with just a smidge of hope hanging on, I take a step forward, keeping my voice quiet. "Mom, it's me."

Her eyes snap to mine, and I hold still, waiting, praying.

*Please recognize me, Mom.*

*Please.*

Her shaky hand releases from her mouth, and a flash of hope races through me as I keep my gaze on hers, begging for her to notice her eyes in mine. Begging for her to have some clarity. I'm so fixated on letting her see me as the boy she once knew that I don't notice her pick up her water glass and, with a flick of her wrist, chuck it at me, hitting me directly in the corner of my right eye, sending me backward.

The glass crashes to the floor, and she screams before running off.

She doesn't get far, though, as nurses surround her and pin her to the ground.

Blood drips down my face as I call out, "Don't hurt her. Please don't fucking hurt her."

I watch as my mom struggles against the nurses, screaming for me, screaming for *her boy*, but not for the man standing a few feet away from her.

And as I stand there, blood dripping down my face, tears falling, my mom yells, writhes, and does everything in her power to be released before they sedate her.

Her body becomes lifeless, her head pressed into the floor, her cardigan hanging off her shoulder as the faint stains of tears still mar her cheeks. And that empty feeling that constantly takes up space in my chest grows. It grows and fills with sorrow and anger.

Hatred.

A distinct disdain for every circumstance that has brought my mother to this moment.

Rhonda comes up to me, presses her hand to my back, and whispers, "I'm so sorry, Graydon."

I wipe at my eyes and just nod, because what the hell am I supposed to say?

There's nothing to say other than…I'm fucking gutted.

---

"Fuck," I grumble as I lock my door, exhaustion overcoming me from a rough night and having to wake up early for another week of training camp. Even though this week won't be as harsh as the first three, it's still the drain of the day taking its toll on a body that's already goddamn weak.

I didn't sleep at all last night. Maybe half an hour if I'm lucky, because every time I shut my eyes, all I could see was my mom on the ground screaming for help…help that I couldn't give her.

And it haunts me.

The terror in her eyes.

The tears staining her cheeks.

Her cries were so harsh that her voice broke.

I just…fuck, I can't.

I scrub my hand over my face and get in my truck, pain blanketing me like a dark cloud, tempting me to do something stupid, tempting me to lessen the anguish gripping my heart and squeezing it so goddamn tight that it feels like I can't breathe.

Fuck, I can't do this.

I lower my head to the steering wheel, my anxiety lacing through me like a disease, spreading rapidly through every vein, taking control of my ability to function.

My breath becomes shorter and shorter.

My vision starts to fade, and I can feel it, the anxiety attack attempting to take hold of me.

*Breathe, Graydon. Fucking breathe.*

But it's so goddamn hard, because all I see is her…hurt…begging for help.

Help I couldn't give her.

*Breathe…*

I let out a shaky breath and right my mind, try to block out the horror of what I witnessed this weekend, what I felt. *Come the fuck on, man.*

On another deep breath, I pull out of my garage and head the few blocks to Maple's apartment. She's waiting for me at the curb. I glance at the clock, confused, and realize I'm running about five minutes late.

Shit.

I must have gotten lost in my thoughts.

She opens the door, and with a fucking gorgeous smile, she says, "Good morning—oh my God, what happened to your eye?"

Right.

I forgot about that.

"Nothing," I grumble and wait for her to buckle up before I pull out onto the road.

"Graydon," she says softly. "That's a really bad cut."

Yeah, I know.

Rhonda put some butterfly strips over it for me yesterday, encouraging me to go get it looked at, but I didn't give a shit. I wanted to be alone, so that was what I did.

And the throbbing above my eye last night was nothing compared to the agony in my heart. I welcomed the eye pain, anything to keep the anguish balanced.

Instead of answering her, I turn up the music in the truck, some bullshit top hit playing, so I don't have to talk to her. Explain to her what happened yesterday. Because she'd press. That's the kind of person she is—she'd want to help fix it. And there's nothing to fix.

I've tried.

I've spoken to every doctor.

I've met with every specialist money could buy.

And nothing.

We drive to the facility, not speaking a word to each other, just the way I wanted it. I'm not up for chatting, not with my mom's screams plaguing me. Not with the image of her cheek pressed against the floor branded in my brain. I just need to get out some aggression to calm my racing pulse. And practice will do that for me.

Once I park, I hop out, and Maple does the same, meeting me at the back of the truck. I can feel her eyes on me and sense the questions on the tip of her tongue.

*Don't do it, Maple.*

*Please don't fucking press me.*

*I can't... I can't expose you to this. Please, please don't ask.*

"Graydon," she says softly as we reach the door to the training facility.

My eyes squeeze shut, my anxiety ramping up once more. I can't tell her.

I won't.

I just need to get out on the field. Get out my aggression. Get lost.

She walks under my outstretched arm that's holding the door open, but instead of moving forward, she pauses at the door.

"Graydon." She tugs on my shirt as I try to move by her.

*No, Maple. Please.*

"Don't, Maple." I walk down the hall with one thing on my mind. *Get the hell away from her.* Not because I don't want to be around her, but because I fear what I might do if I'm near her.

I'm a ticking time bomb, wrapped up in an explosive ball of anger and anxiety, and with one wrong move, I'm bound to explode.

"Wait, Graydon." She tugs on my arm and moves in front of me. "What is going on? Why...why aren't you talking to me?"

"Maple..." I growl, running my hand over my face. "Just...leave me alone."

"If this is about this past weekend—"

My eyes snap to hers, my heart stuttering in my chest. This past weekend?

What the fuck did she hear?

The care facility has a strict NDA, but that doesn't mean some opportunist looking to earn some extra money didn't take the opening to bring the news about my mom to the media.

My skin prickles with fear as I stare down at her, waiting for her to continue.

"I didn't...I, um...I didn't want to make you upset. I was just, I don't know, you seemed open to it, and if I crossed a boundary, I'm sorry."

My jaw clenches, my fists opening and closing at my sides, my stomach so fucking nauseous from the onslaught of emotion that I actually feel like I might throw up.

"Sorry?"

"Yes, sorry. Just...let me in and accept my apology so—"

"I told you to stay out of my fucking business," I snarl, and her eyes widen.

"What?" Her head shakes as she takes a step back. "I didn't, I mean, I did. I...I just wanted to see if you're okay. I thought you were mad at me from our texts."

Our texts?

Fuck, does she not know about yesterday? She doesn't know about my mom?

What about our texts? I can't even fucking remember what we texted each other.

Concern laces her expression as her hand presses against my chest, but I push her away because this is all too overstimulating and overwhelming.

And too damn much for my mental state.

"Don't touch me."

My mind keeps flashing back to my mom.

The look.

The screams.

My agonizing inability to take care of her.

Maple's eyes well up with tears.

The thought of her knowing the truth.

It's too fucking much.

I need...I need a goddamn second.

"Graydon," she says, taking another step forward, her eyes searching mine, her hand once again against my chest, and that's all it takes.

I snap.

"I said don't fucking touch me!" I yell, moving her hand off me. "Jesus, what don't you understand about that? Don't fucking touch me."

Just then, three of my teammates, including Hutton, turn the corner, taking in the scene in front of them.

Maple looks over her shoulder at them, then turns toward me again, her eyes brimming with tears, embarrassment etched in her expression.

Her lip quivers.

And then before I can say anything, she pushes past me and hurries down the hallway, right out of the facility.

Fuck.

"Head to the field," Hutton says to the other two guys and then steps forward. When his eyes meet mine, he just nods and slips his hand around my shoulder, guiding me toward the locker room.

He knows.

He might be the only one who knows.

He knows Sundays are my visiting days.

He knows about my mom.

And he's very much aware of the toll a bad visit takes on me.

Because of that, he says nothing, just makes sure I get strapped into my gear so I can do some damage.

And that's exactly what I do.

---

I stare at Gate B, willing myself to get out of my truck to take Maple home like I've done every day since her car accident. I checked at the shop the other day on the progress of her car, wanting to try to give her some good news, but they were waiting on a part, so it's taking much longer than expected for things to get fixed.

And after this morning, I don't know what to say to her.

I know I embarrassed her.

I know that I was out of line, and I realized that by the first water break after getting some aggression out and somewhat clearing my head. Fear drove me to snap at her. Fear of her finding out the truth. The truth I don't want her to know because I don't want her pitying me like everyone else in this goddamn world.

I can't stand the look people offer me when they know my situation.

And I can't get that from her.

I fucking can't.

Blowing out a heavy breath, knowing I need to apologize, I get out of my truck and head toward Gate B just as it opens, Maple standing on the other side.

I pause, stunned to see her already leaving without waiting for me, but then the gate opens even more, revealing Slutty Little Glasses right behind her.

That.

Mother.

Fucker.

"What are you doing here?" Maple asks, looking sullen, like someone just told her flamingos are dumb.

"I came to take you home, like every day," I answer.

She shakes her head. "Hank is taking me home."

Hank is a fucking wank and saw a moment of weakness. He's trying to get fucking in with her. What a goddamn douche.

Ignoring him, I ask, "Can I talk to you, Maple?"

She shakes her head. "No."

She starts to walk by, but I pause her, my hand sliding into hers.

"Hey, she said she didn't want to talk to you," Hank says, getting all fucking huffy.

I tower over him and, through clenched teeth, say, "This does not concern you, so fucking scurry away like the sniveling squirrel you are."

Then, with my hand in hers, I bring Maple over to the side of the fence, far away from Hank the Wank so I can talk to her in private.

"He's not a sniveling squirrel," Maple says as she takes her hand away and folds her arms across her chest.

"The asshole is crawling all over you."

"He's being a friend," she snaps. "He saw how destroyed I was this morning when I came into work, and he comforted me."

"I'm sure he did."

Maple's eyes narrow as her anger grows. "Is there a point to this conversation?"

"Yes, I'm here to take you home, so why don't you—"

"You have lost your mind, Graydon, if you think that I'm going to get in your truck with you after that disgusting display in front of your teammates this morning." Moving in closer, she whispers, "That was humiliating. I've never been so embarrassed in my entire life, not to mention hurt. I understand that I crossed the line when I asked you to brunch, but correct me if I'm wrong, you were very misleading."

"What are you talking about?" I ask, confused.

"Our texts. Me asking you out to brunch, and you going silent after that."

"I didn't go silent."

"Pretty much. It was like I scared you away."

"I told you I had plans," I say. "I can't do things on Sundays. Did you think I was upset about that?"

"Isn't that what it was? I was coming on too strong for you, and you decided to start backing away rather than talking to me like a real man?"

My eyes narrow. "I'm talking to you now, aren't I?"

"After snapping at me in front of your teammates."

I drag my hand over my face. "I told you not to touch me. I was…I was going through some shit, Maple."

"That does not give you the right to treat me the way you did. Just because you're angry or feeling something awful inside doesn't give you the right to humiliate me in public."

"No one cared," I say.

"I did!" she shouts, pointing at her chest. "I cared. I cared about the way you spoke to me. I cared about the way you made me feel at that moment. You treated me like I was just someone you could toss to the side, reprimand like I didn't matter. And maybe that's how you really feel, but excuse me for thinking that maybe there was a little more between us. Clearly, I was wrong, though." She starts to move away but then says, "I have quite a few pictures stocked up on my phone to post, so don't worry about coming in right now."

"I have to," I say.

"Then you can work with someone else." Her eyes meet mine. "Because I can't do this temperamental side of you anymore. I can't work with the growly asshole who will snap at me at any given point. I don't want to deal with that, and I don't deserve to deal with that. I'll go through with the rest of the planned events because I will keep my word, but everything else, I'm done, Graydon."

Done?

She can't be done. Right?

She wets her lips and then quietly says, "Please don't text me. Don't pick me up for *anything*. Don't send me pictures, and...stop messing with my head."

Then she takes off, leaving me struck with...with a sense of loss. Like with every step she takes, putting distance between us, she's walking off with something I truly care about.

Hank slips his arm around her shoulders while staring at me the entire time, almost tauntingly, as he leads her to his worn-down tan Jeep.

My teeth grind together as I watch him help her into the passenger side. That's my fucking job. She's supposed to go home with me. I'm supposed to tuck her safely into my vehicle.

Not him.

Steam billows out of my ears as he rounds the back of his Jeep, his eyes on me, as if to say he just won.

Guess what, you fuck, you didn't. Because this is far from over.

*Even if I couldn't tell Maple about my mom.*

*Even if I'm a coward, and this morning...a bully...*

Maple's mine. *Or maybe...was.*

*Until I screwed up.*

*But I'm not going to give up that easily.*

# CHAPTER 26
# GRAYDON

SITTING ON MY COUCH, I stare down at my phone, a rage warring inside me.

A part of me wants to find out where Hank the Wank lives, tear his door off the hinges, and teach him a goddamn lesson about moving in on someone when they have no right to.

A part of me wants to go to Maple's apartment and sit outside it until she lets me in to talk to her. Because her words...her words sliced right through my brittle heart.

*"I cared about the way you made me feel at that moment. You treated me like I was just someone you could toss to the side, reprimand like I didn't matter. And maybe that's how you really feel, but excuse me for thinking that maybe there was a little more between us. Clearly, I was wrong, though."*

She isn't wrong. She...she means a lot to me. I might not say much, but I listen. I listen when she speaks.

But the other part of me, the part that actually wants to kick my coffee table over, stares at this inane text thread.

A text thread I don't want to be a part of.

But a text thread that I think I need.

Grumbling to myself, I type out a text.

**Graydon:** I need help. I think I fucked up big time.

I lean back on the couch, hating myself, because I swore up and down that I wasn't going to fall for this bullshit camaraderie thing that OC was pushing upon us, but after the way Maple looked at me earlier, I don't know if I have a choice in the matter.

My phone buzzes with a response.

**OC:** Are you saying that you need the Gladdy Daddies to assemble?

And this is exactly why I didn't want to text.

This reason, right here.

**Bennett:** Off night for me, I'm free.

**OC:** Free as well...I think we just need someone to say Gladdy Daddies Assemble.

**Graydon:** I'm not saying that.

**Bennett:** Kind of wishing you would.

**OC:** You know I can only help if you say it.

**Graydon:** That's fucked.

I stare out the window, the rain pelting the pane, adding to the mood in my place. A dark, foreboding mood that's screaming that if I stay here and wallow in my own faults, things are only going to get worse.

And I don't want it to get worse.

I don't like the way she looked at me.

I don't like the way she tore away from me.

And I don't like Slutty Little Glasses thinking he fucking won.

Tamping down my pride, I text the boys back.

**Graydon:** Gladdy Daddies Assemble.

**Bennett:** Holy shit, he said it. He must really need help.

**OC:** We're on our WAY! Send us your address, I'll bring beer. Bennett, you bring the snacks.

**Bennett:** What sort of snacks?

**OC:** Doesn't matter, just bring them.

**Bennett:** I have dried seaweed wraps.

**OC:** For fuck's sake, stop at the store, you asshat.

---

OC opens three beers and then hands them out as Bennett takes a half-eaten bag of Pirate's Booty out of his bag, along with the seaweed wraps he spoke of, and two regular Hershey's chocolate bars.

"What the fuck is that?" OC asks, pointing to the snacks.

Bennett shrugs. "Didn't feel like going to the store and I leave for a long away trip tomorrow, so figured that you could take some of the left-over things in my cabinet."

"No one wants that trash." OC leans down and snags a Hershey's bar. "But if anything, I'm a team player, so I'll take care of this for you."

I toe the seaweed wraps toward Bennett. "You can get those out of my fucking sight."

"They're really good."

He goes to open it, but I say, "Don't even think about it. Put those back in your bag. I don't want that smell in here."

He rolls his eyes but puts the seaweed wraps back in his bag, then sits back in his chair, spreads his legs, and takes a sip of his beer.

"So," OC asks, popping a rectangle of chocolate in his mouth. "What's going on?"

I spend the next five minutes recounting what happened, from the event, to the kiss, to Monday morning, skipping over what happened Sunday and just saying that I had a rough day. When I told them what happened in the training facility hallway, both of them winced in horror.

I already knew I was in the wrong, but to see their reaction to my fuckup, yeah, that didn't help ease my guilt or my worry.

"Wow." OC scrubs his hand over his head and drops the chocolate wrapper on the coffee table. "Uh, that's quite the pickle you got yourself in."

"Yeah, not great," Bennett says.

"Yeah, I'm well aware. That's why I'm asking you fucks for help."

"You know, being that we're friends now, I think you should reserve the term 'fucks' for people you don't like, like Hank the Wank, which by the way, great fucking name, man," OC says.

"So do I," Bennett adds, looking more loose than when I first met him. He's either dropping the shy-guy facade or something has changed in his life, like...like a girl has entered the chat. Not that I care, though... "Although, I miss using 'Slutty Little Glasses.' It was catchy."

"I think we can alternate between the two," OC says. "No need to completely bury the nickname. The art of a great insult is having many options to choose from when in the moment. If we really wanted to master the takedown of the obvious villain of this storyline, we would come up with one more name for him, something...to really dig at his character."

"Like, maybe calling him by the wrong name?" Bennett asks. "Like instead of Hank, we call him Henry?"

OC shakes his head. "No, it needs to be better than that. Using the wrong name is a slight at him, but he's after our friend's girl, so we need something bigger, better." OC turns to me. "What are the size of his nipples? Any chance we can come up with an insult involving his milkers?"

Jesus.

Fucking.

Christ.

"Can we please bring it back to the problem?" I growl.

"Why did you have to call them 'milkers'?" Bennett asks, disgust all over his face. "Fuck, that makes me feel dead inside."

OC dismisses Bennett with a wave of his hand. "Bennett, please, we're trying to solve a problem here." OC then turns to me, folds his hands together, and says in a very serious tone, "The problem is, you fucked up big time."

"Wow, I invited you to my place to point out the obvious, glad I had you come over." I shake my head and down half my beer. Going to need the alcohol to get through this.

"Listen, we have to state the obvious so we know exactly what we're dealing with here. From the sound of it, Maple does not want to be anywhere near you, and by the desperation in your voice, we're at the grand gesture phase."

For fuck's sake, I should never have invited them over.

"Oh yeah, I'd agree with that," Bennett says. "I don't think a talk with Maple is going to solve this."

Christ, now the sane one is jumping in on it too.

OC shakes his head. "No, we need a grand gesture. Something that is going to blow her hair right off her head."

And because he's right, I'm really that desperate—and want them out of my house as quickly as possible—I ask, "What do you mean?"

"Well, let me ask you this," OC counters. "What do you want your end result to be? When all is said and done and she's talking to you again, is this a pissing match with Slutty Little Glasses?" OC winks at Bennett, who nods. "Or do you actually want to be with her? Make something of this more than just a PR relationship?"

I work my jaw to the side as I scratch the scruff on my cheek, the question rolling around in my mind. There's only one reason why I care so much and it's because over the past few weeks, Maple has made an impact on me. Don't know how or when it happened, but all I know is that when she's around, I feel...lighter.

Happier.

*Wanted.*

And I want to hold on to the feeling she gives me whenever she's around.

I meant it when I said I wanted to pursue her, and that hasn't changed.

I take down the rest of my beer, then I set the bottle on the coffee table. "I want to make her mine."

"Oh shit." OC gasps and then holds his arm out and points at it. "Chills. He just gave me chills."

"Can you not make a spectacle?" I ask.

"I mean, hard not to when you make a strong statement like that," Bennett says. "That's some good shit you'd find in a romance novel."

Both OC and I turn to him, questions in our arched brows.

"I'll take this one," OC says to me. "Umm, romance novel?"

"Yeah." Bennett casually shrugs.

"Yeah, what? Do you read them?"

"What if I do?" Bennett asks. "You have a problem with that?"

"Just...didn't think that was something you'd read," OC says, looking Bennett over. "You don't seem like the kind of guy who would read, let alone read a romance book."

"Of course I fucking read."

"Clearly. Just didn't think it would be romance novels."

"What do I look like I read?" he asks.

Both OC and I take a second to study him and then I say, "Something like...hidden ballpark mysteries."

OC snaps and points at me. "Yes, that's exactly what he'd read."

Bennett shrugs. "I've been dabbling in romance because my sister's friend sent me some recommendations."

OC's eyes widen and I can see the whirl of questions he wants to ask, but I stop him before he can get going. "Don't," I say sharply. "We're focusing on my situation. Deal with him later on your own time. Don't waste mine."

"Jesus," OC says. "You know, Gladdy Daddies isn't just about you."

"Gladdy Daddies is about to be nonexistent."

Sighing, OC says, "Fine, but we're coming back to the sister's friend thing. I think that's the second time you've mentioned her, and I'm not about to just let it go."

Bennett just shrugs casually.

"Okay." OC takes a deep breath. "Graydon wants to make Maple his, and he's clearly put an obstacle in the way of that by humiliating her this morning. Dug us quite a hole, my man, but I think we can work with it. My boys on the Agitators have offered up some great advice before, and there's no doubt in my mind that they'd agree a grand gesture is the way to go. So, big guy, what kind of secret talents can we use to our advantage?"

"Secret talents not in the bedroom," Bennett adds.

"Yes, because you can't just try to attack her with your dick, especially since she's not even talking to you. Imagine going into her apartment and wielding your penis with an apology note hanging off it."

Bennett snorts as I look at OC, expressionless.

I really hate him most of the time.

"Say something else stupid, see where it gets you," I threaten.

OC leans toward Bennett and whispers, "Think I should see what he would do?"

Bennett glances at me and shakes his head. "Remember, don't poke the bear."

"Right." OC straightens. "Okay, so hidden talents? Anything you want to share with us, something like...I don't know, do you write poems?"

"Poems?" I lift a brow.

"Yeah, you don't seem like the intellectual type," he says, making me growl. "I meant the Shakespeare type."

"What about singing? Can you sing?" Bennett asks.

"Do you think I'm about to sing to a girl so she will talk to me? You had a higher chance with a poem."

"Yeah, Bennett, what a stupid suggestion." OC shakes his head. "Who brought that guy?" He clears his throat and continues, "We clearly can't have you ask her out because she won't even talk to you."

"What about doing something with the flamingos?" Bennett asks. "That would probably make her really happy."

"Ooh, like donate money to her cause," OC says, but I shake my head.

"No, that won't impress her. I think that would only piss her off more because it would be like paying to win back her affection."

"Right. See, another dumb suggestion, Bennett. Come on, think," OC says while tapping his chin.

"That was your idea, numb nuts," Bennett shoots back.

"You sure?"

"Yeah."

"Huh." OC chuckles and scratches his cheek. He's such a fucking idiot. "Okay, how do we like the flamingo thing, at least?"

"Has potential," I say. "But there isn't much that we could really do. You've seen the exhibit. It's kind of shit with that wall and the chicken wire..." An idea perks up in my head.

"Fuck, look at his mind at work. You can actually see the gears turn," OC says, leaning in close.

"If he punches you, I'm just going to stand over you and nod. Because with comments like that, you had it coming," Bennett says.

"I could handle a punch from him," OC says. He sizes me up. "Eh, it would hurt like a bitch, but I wouldn't be flattened."

"Want to see?" I ask.

He shakes his head. "Have a photo shoot with the giraffes tomorrow. I'm good."

"What's your idea?" Bennett asks.

I tug on my hair, thinking it over. "Well, there is this wall the zoo put up during the bird flu to help keep the birds safe. It's really haphazard, and they put windows in it, but covered them with chicken wire, so it's hard to see the flamingos sometimes. I'm not sure they would let me replace it because that would take time and permits, but I know how to paint. So what if I painted the wall to be something that would draw attention, something people would want to take pictures in front of? Then I can paint the chicken wire black because it takes the glare off the wire and you can see through it easier."

OC glances at Bennett and back at me. Then, like a fool, he starts to slow clap. "Look who just became president of the Gladdy Daddies because, dude, that's genius."

I chuck a pillow at him, skidding it right across his face.

"Hey, I gave you a compliment." He touches his jaw.

"You also called me 'dude' and made a spectacle."

"Facts," Bennett says as he reaches into his bag and pulls the seaweed out.

"You want a pillow to the fucking head too?" I ask.

Bennett slowly lowers the seaweed back into his bag.

"Whipped," OC says.

"Shut the fuck up. You'd do the same thing."

OC rubs his face and nods. "Yeah...you're right."

---

"Do you have everything you need?" Phil asks, looking over my supplies and the lights I have aimed at the wall.

It's after zoo hours, and I plan on spending as much time here tonight as I can to try to make a big dent on this mural I have mapped out in my head.

It's going to be simple, nothing too serious, something with a lot of color, abstract objects, minimal shading to make the objects pop, flamingos, and of course, a lot of pink. When I took the idea to Phil, he was actually pretty excited about it. He started talking about how it would be great visibility, especially with the way social media works, and the wall being a great place to pose in front of. Whatever the fuck that means, but it did make me think that I should probably record myself painting for Flock and Tackle.

"I have everything."

"Good. If you need anything or when you're ready to leave, the walkie-talkie is here for you to reach security. They'll help."

"Thanks," I say.

"How many nights do you plan on working on this?"

"Hopefully just one. If I have to finish up tomorrow after training camp, I will."

He nods. "And you don't want me saying anything to the zookeepers?"

I shake my head. "No, please keep this between us."

"Okay." He smiles tightly. "Have a good night."

"You too."

He takes off, and I set my phone up against a bucket of paint and turn the camera to face me so I make sure I have the right angle. When I'm satisfied, I press record on the time-lapse and get to work.

First things first, prime the wall.

I let the sounds of the zoo fill in as background noise while I pour paint and start rolling it out on the plain wood.

I hope it's worth it. Not having Maple to chat to, even if it's only been a day, has felt so...unnatural. *Wrong.* I've...missed her. Truly missed her. We've only known each other for a matter of weeks, but she's brightened my life, even if I haven't contributed the same light to hers. And I want her to know that she's special. *Seen.* And appreciated. I want her to know that *I* appreciate her...and that I don't want our relationship to only be part of a PR stunt. *I want...more.* And if painting something for her is what makes that happen, then, that's what I'll be doing.

It's going to be a long fucking night.

# CHAPTER 27
# MAPLE

I STARE AT THE LINK for a ride that Graydon sent me to get me to work this morning and swipe out of his text thread.

I couldn't possibly click on it. Not after yesterday. I don't want him thinking I need him in my life.

So instead, I order my own car and head outside when the app says the car is one minute away.

I feel exhausted.

I didn't sleep well last night, constantly tossing and turning, thinking about Graydon even though I didn't want to. I wonder what got into him on Monday if it wasn't about the texts I sent. He almost seemed confused when I was talking to him about it, like he couldn't quite understand why I brought it up.

Was I overthinking what happened on Saturday? Probably, but insecurity runs deep inside me when it comes to this man. Our entire "relationship" started off with him making fun of my pants, followed by him acting practically insulted at the thought of having to be attached to me, solidifying the thought in my head that I was not good enough for him. Not that I was looking to start anything at that time.

And yes, Friday night, at our event, it changed things. We kissed, for crying out loud, and now...God, now I feel like if I even look at him, I might start crying...or jump in his arms and beg him to talk to me, to tell me what's going on in that head of his.

And I hate it.

Because I don't want to be that person.

I don't want to be the cliché who gets hurt, then goes crawling back to the person who hurt them. I'm stronger than that.

Yet there is a voice in the back of my head saying, *What if he was hurting?*

It doesn't matter.

Even if he was hurting, he didn't need to take it out on me.

I will not be treated like that.

My car pulls to the curb, and I get in and buckle up before pulling up my text thread with Everly.

**Maple:** He sent me a link this morning for a ride.

The car takes off down the road as she texts me back.

**Everly:** Well, if anything, he's consistent. How are you feeling?

**Maple:** Like total shit.

**Everly:** That's to be expected. I'm sorry he was a dick to you.

**Maple:** I'd like to say he's always been a dick to me, but that's not true at all. He's showed me genuine kindness and thoughtfulness, and I think that's what makes this hurt even more. It's so stupid. It's not as if we're a real couple.

**Everly:** You don't have to be a couple to develop feelings, Maple.

**Maple:** Yeah, I guess so. Ugh. I wonder if he'll come to the zoo today. I told him not to, but who knows what he'll do. Hank will probably freak out on him.

**Everly:** I'd love to see Hank try to tell Graydon what to do. Nice guy, but he doesn't have a chance against him.

**Maple:** He tried yesterday, but it fell flat the moment Graydon barked at him.

**Everly:** I'm sure Hank had something to say afterward.

**Maple:** He started to talk about Graydon, but I cut him off. I told him I didn't want to get into it. He asked if I wanted to grab something to eat, and I told him no, that I just wanted to go back to my place.

**Everly:** You should have come here. Hardy made burgers on the grill.

**Maple:** As much as I would have loved to spend time with you and sulk on your couch, I can't intrude on you every time something goes to shit in my life.

**Everly:** I don't mind.

**Maple:** I know, and I love you for that, but you're a newlywed couple and deserve your time together.

**Everly:** But we'd drop anything for you. Even our pants if that's what you're into. *Wiggles eyebrows*

**Maple:** LOL! Needed that.

**Everly:** Try to have a good day today, and if anything, just immerse yourself in your flamingo friends.

**Maple:** Now that is something I can do.

I spend the rest of the trip trying to pick out a picture I can post today on Flock and Tackle to keep the momentum going, but I'm struggling with what shot to go with. Ugh, I'll figure it out at lunch.

When I arrive at the zoo, I thank my driver and head to the employee entrance, then straight back toward the flamingo exhibit. My head is down as I read an article about a new study on flamingos in captivity, so I don't even notice Phil when I run directly into him.

"Oh, goodness. I'm so sorry," I say as I try to right my balance. "I didn't mean to bump into you."

"Maple, just the person I was looking for. Wanted to get your reaction."

"My reaction to what?" I ask as he holds his phone up to me and acts like he's recording.

"Gretchen is going to love this. Go ahead, look."

He nods toward the right. Thoroughly confused, I turn toward the flamingo exhibit, then gasp as I take in the wall that has separated the guests from the flamingos for so many years.

The wall that's been an eyesore.

The wall that has hurt my heart every time I see people walk right by it as if they can't be bothered to catch a glimpse of the flamingos.

But now, the chicken wire doesn't even seem like it's there, and the wall is covered in bright, almost fluorescent colors, flamingos everywhere in multiple colors, not just pink, but green and blue and yellow. Text boxes pop out with cute statements like "I love flamingos" and "Save the flamingos" and...

Oh my God.

On the farthest end of the wall, where one of my fellow zookeepers is already taking a picture, is the phrase "Single and ready to flamingo."

There's no way.

No.

He didn't do this.

Did he?

Does he even know how to paint? Did he hire someone?

Wait, no, he wouldn't do this, right? He was...he was so rude, dismissive, would he really do something as kind...as wonderful as this?

"What do you think?" Phil asks as tears start to prick at my eyes.

"I...I love it so much," I say as I walk up to the wall and take in the simple yet fun design, my mind whirling with what this will do and how this will help. I can see it already. The families who'll want to take pictures in front of it, who will come to the flamingos just to see the mural once I post about it.

This is...this is a game changer.

"This is so incredible." I run my finger over the wall. "How? Who did this?"

"A friend to the flamingos," Phil says as he lowers his phone. "Glad you like it. I believe the person has to finish up the left side, but for the most part, it's done. And do you like how they made the chicken wire almost seem like it's disappeared?"

"Yes," I say as I run my fingers over the black-painted wire. "This is…this is so amazing." I turn to Phil and hand him my phone. "Can you take a picture of me in front of it?"

"Of course," he says with a smile.

I pose in front of the wall, and he snaps a few pictures before he hands me my phone back.

He takes off, talking about how great the wall is, all while I stand there and stare for a few moments, taking in every stroke, every little detail.

And that's when some things start to fall into place.

A flamingo in a yellow dress.

A flamingo eating tacos.

A flamingo wearing a football helmet.

A flamingo holding up a phone with his wing, taking a selfie.

It's subtle, but it seems like they're all hints.

Hints as to who did this.

I can't believe it. I really can't…

In shock, I send a text to Everly with a picture of me in front of the brilliant colors.

**Maple:** Showed up at work to find this. Oh God, Everly, I think he painted it.

She's quick to text back, thankfully, as I make my way into the flamingo building.

**Everly:** Oh my God! Why do you think that? Can he even paint?

**Maple:** No idea, but all these hints in the mural lead me to believe that it's him.

**Everly:** And if it is?

*And if it is? Such a good question.* If it is Graydon, I think he's using a way other than words to say he cares. That he has heard me. That he's sorry.

**Maple:** I don't know. I think he might have just stolen my battered heart.

But can I actually let him take it?

---

This has been the longest day ever.

It has dragged on.

I swear, anytime I check the clock, only five minutes have passed.

I take a long lunch, debating on texting Graydon, but every time I think about it, a piece of me pulls away because of how he hurt me.

I resign myself to work instead, and focus on talking to guests and watching in excitement as everyone is pulled toward the mural. They're forming big crowds, to the point that Phil set up a kiosk next to it with flamingo merchandise—which has sold out twice today.

I hate to admit that his merch idea works, but it does.

The whole thing has transformed an area that was once just walked by into a prominent attraction at the zoo.

All because of some paint.

"The wall's pretty cool," Hank says, coming up to me. "I wonder who Phil paid to do it. Smart idea."

"Was it his idea?" I ask.

Hank shrugs. "Seems like it, given the kiosk. Also heard him talking about getting some T-shirts made ASAP with the phrases on them. He's going all in."

"Doesn't surprise me," I say. If anything, Phil is an opportunist.

Phil walks up to us with the biggest smile on his face. "We ran out of flamingo stuffed animals. We put in an order for so many more. This is incredible."

"Great idea with the wall," Hank says, patting Phil on the shoulder.

"Oh, it wasn't my idea, but I'm certainly exploring how we can apply this to every exhibit moving forward."

Of course he is.

I roll my eyes and then step forward into the crowd, lingering in case anyone wants to ask questions.

"Go ahead," a mom says. "I think you can ask her."

A cute little girl with pigtails walks up to me and says, "Why are the flamingos pink?"

I squat down and start explaining to her in simple terms why they're pink just as a group of people start cheering, pulling my attention.

"Back up, please. Back up," a man with a deep voice says.

I stand up just in time to spot Graydon walk through the crowd and head on over to the left side of the mural.

My heart trips in my chest as he keeps his gaze down, then settles in front of the wall.

Whispers erupt all around, while I will my lungs to find air to breathe. When he lifts his hand with a paintbrush grasped in his fingers and starts painting, I can feel every single bone in my body start to melt.

I knew it.

It was him.

It had to be him.

But...how? How did he do all of this in one night?

Phil must catch me staring as he comes up to me. "I heard from security that he was out here painting until three in the morning."

My pulse rages in my veins, almost drowning out the noise around me.

"Three in the morning?" I ask.

"Yeah. Said he would have finished if he didn't have to go to training camp."

God, he must not have gotten any sleep by the time he cleaned up, drove home, and had to leave for training camp.

He stayed up all night?

"This was his idea?" Hank asks, walking up to us.

"It was," Phil says. "Genius. He took a time-lapse of himself painting it last night. I'm sure he'll share it with you to post. But this...this is exactly what we need to revive this zoo. Good work, Maple." Phil pats me on the back, then takes off as I stare at Graydon, watching him concentrate on finishing his work.

Oh my God, what am I supposed to do now?

# CHAPTER 28
# GRAYDON

I FINISH WASHING THE LAST brush and then set it on the drying rack before soaping up my hands and getting rid of the rest of the paint.

When I came to the zoo, I had one mission on my mind: to finish the mural. I didn't stop to talk to anyone. I didn't stop to take pictures. I focused on making sure that everything was done so Maple could enjoy the mural.

So she could soak it all in.

And from what Phil told me, she did.

He sent me a video of her seeing it for the first time, but I've yet to watch it.

The door to the flamingo building opens, and I can already feel her presence before I glance to my left.

She's standing there with a bucket in hand, looking hesitant, like she doesn't know what to say to me or how to approach me.

And that's fine. She doesn't need to say anything to me. I just want her to know that I'm sorry, that I care about her, and that I was a fucking idiot for treating her the way that I did.

"You ready?" Hank asks, walking into the room as well. "I grabbed your bag for you."

"Oh, yeah, thanks," Maple says as she diverts her eyes from me.

She's going home with him again?

*Looks like the boys were wrong.* This "grand gesture" sucked. Good for the zoo, but no change between Maple and me. *Fuck.*

"Hey, thanks for the mural, man," Hank says. "That was huge of you."

The urge to plow my fist through his skull is incredibly overwhelming, and the only reason I haven't is because I know Maple wouldn't approve. Punching Slutty Little Glasses might feel good in the moment, but it will get me nowhere with Maple, so instead, I take a calm approach and simply nod.

"Yeah," Maple says, surprising me. "It was…it was really nice." She smiles softly, her gaze falling on mine.

That smile.

Those eyes…

Fuck, there are so many things I want to say to her. So many things I want to do as a storm kicks up inside me, pushing me in her direction. But I hold still, because even though when she walks into a room, I feel my pulse kickstart, I'm not about to have a conversation with her with Hank present.

No goddamn way.

So I just nod as well.

"Here you go," Hank says, handing her bag to her. I feel her eyes on me one last time before they exit the building.

Sighing, I lean forward, pressing my head to the cabinet above the sink and wishing this was so much fucking easier.

I give them a second to leave and then pull my phone out and watch the video of Maple taking in the mural for the first time.

I watch as her expression morphs into awe.

As tears fill her beautiful eyes.

As she commits the wall to memory and speaks on how amazing it is.

It gives me a sliver of hope. Not much, because Slutty Little Glasses is still in the way, a fucking thorn in my side. Unsure how to handle him, I lean into the one source I wish I didn't have to use.

The Gladdy Daddies.

**Graydon:** She liked the mural. A lot.

I head out toward the parking lot while I wait for their response. Hopefully, Maple and Hank will be gone.

**OC:** Fuck yeah! So are you guys good?

**Graydon:** Not quite. Slutty Little Glasses is taking her home.

**OC:** What? Why?

**Bennett:** How did that happen?

**Graydon:** Because when I say I fucked up bad, I did. She could barely look at me. Not sure the grand gesture worked.

When I arrive at the parking lot, I'm happy to see that they're gone, so I hop into my truck and buckle up, but don't start it yet.

**OC:** Are you sure you did it right?

**Graydon:** There is only one way to do it, you fuck. There's just too much animosity there. I hurt her.

**Bennett:** You did, but this is the perfect opening.

**Graydon:** What do you mean?

**Bennett:** Did she talk to you at all?

**Graydon:** She did. She thanked me in person.

**OC:** How? With a hug?

**Graydon:** With her words and a slight smile.

**Bennett:** That's all we need. She opened the door. The grand gesture worked. Now you have to go apologize. Take it from me.

**OC:** Yeah, remember, he's reading those romance books. I think he might know what he's talking about.

**Graydon:** So I'm just supposed to apologize to her tomorrow?

**OC:** Maybe take her coffee and flowers or something.

**Graydon:** She hates flowers.

**Bennett:** No, you're not going to wait till morning. You're going to go to her place tonight. Strike while the iron is hot.

**Graydon:** What if Slutty Little Glasses is there?

**OC:** Ooh, a painful obstacle.

**Bennett:** Then you wait. Tell her you will wait because what you need to say is important.

**OC:** Authoritative but respectful. Nice approach.

**Graydon:** Will you shut the fuck up with your useless commentary?

**OC:** Respect the group. Everyone gets to shine in the Gladdy Daddies.

**Graydon:** I actually hate you, truly, truly hate you.

**OC:** If I knew you weren't so down on your luck right now, I might take offense to that, but I know you love me. Nice try.

**Graydon:** Christ.

**Bennett:** Focus. Graydon, go to her place and apologize, give her the biggest apology of your life, and while you're at it, end the mind games and tell her how you feel.

**Graydon:** I wasn't playing mind games.

**Bennett:** Maybe you didn't think you were, but she needs answers and deserves them. If you want to make her yours, then fucking do it. Now.

**OC:** Is it weird that while reading that, my nipples got hard?

**Bennett:** Seriously, dude, no one is going to want to talk to you anymore.

**Graydon:** I second that.

---

I glance around the street, looking for that piece-of-shit Jeep, and when I don't see it, relief floods me because I don't know what I would have done if he was here, in her apartment, doing fuck knows what with her.

I find a parking spot down the block because parking is a bitch sometimes, and I walk up to her apartment, my nerves tumbling inside me as I try to figure out the words I want to use.

Unfortunately, nothing eloquent comes to mind.

I make it up her stairs and then down the hallway to her apartment, where I take a deep breath and then knock on her door. I stuff my hands in my pockets and wait, steeling myself, reminding myself to be calm and honest.

If I'm going to change the course of this "relationship," then this is the moment.

I rock on my heels, waiting for her to answer, but with every second that ticks by that she doesn't answer the door, my worry ratchets and my heart starts to sink further and further because…is she out with him?

When they left, did they leave together to go have dinner?

To go out on a date?

Would she move that goddamn fast? Did I totally misread her affirming words from Friday night? Did the thank-you kiss mean nothing? *Am I simply too fucking hard for her to deal with?*

I push my hand through my hair, messing with the style but not caring. I know I fucked up, and I shouldn't have yelled at her like that. I know I should have talked to her, but could that really have driven her away to fucking Slutty Little Glasses that quickly?

It makes me wonder what he has been doing and saying to her when I haven't been at the zoo. Has he been slowly sliding in with every second he had with her?

I grind my teeth together and turn around, knowing she's not home.

I glance out to the street, wondering what the hell I should do.

Do I leave and text her?

Who's to say she'd respond?

If I stay, does that make me seem desperate?

Hell, who am I kidding? I am desperate.

So, I lean against the wall next to her door, and I wait. I will wait as long as I need to in order to talk to her. I'm just hoping it's not all goddamn night.

---

The door opens to the street, and my eyes shoot up from my phone, where I've been distracting myself by studying videos of other teams. The minute Maple comes into view holding a bag of groceries, relief washes through me because she wasn't out with him, she had to get food.

Thank—

Oh fuck…

That bout of relief is quickly stolen from me as Hank the Wank walks in behind her, holding reusable grocery bags as well.

I fucking hate him.

He says something to her, she chuckles, they smile together, and I've never felt more like an outsider than in this moment. Insecurity grips my heart, my fight-or-flight kicks in, and for a brief second, I consider fleeing, but when her eyes lift to find me at her door, she comes to an abrupt stop.

"Graydon," she says, almost a whisper. "What…what are you doing here?"

*Here's your moment, your chance. I only wish the douche wasn't behind her.*

Hands in my pockets, I say, "I wanted to talk to you."

"Oh." She moves forward, Hank eyeing me like he's ready to strike at any minute. *Don't even fucking try, I will bury you.*

"Just for a moment," I nearly beg.

"I can stay with you," Hank reassures her as Maple opens her apartment door.

*She doesn't need you, fuckwad. Go back to Peru and leave my girl alone.*

"That's...that's okay," she says as she moves into her apartment. "Let me just put the cold stuff away."

Hank and Maple slip into her apartment together, and the door shuts on me, closing me out from what's happening between the two of them.

Normally, I'd fucking charge right through that door, pick the guy up by his shirt, and shove him out to the curb, letting him know exactly where he belongs, but I'm trying to rein in my anger. So instead, I scrub my hand over my face, and I wait, my skin prickling with irritation and my pulse thrumming with the need to destroy something.

After what feels like ten goddamn minutes, the door opens, and Slutty Little Glasses gives her a hug right fucking in front of me, then takes off without sparing me a glance. That's probably best because I might have unhinged my jaw and bitten his stupid head off.

I try to calm the anger in my chest and focus on the girl in front of me, who is standing in her doorway, arms crossed, as she looks up at me, waiting for whatever it is I have to say.

I glance behind me to make sure the douche has left, and when he's out of sight, I turn back to her, my words failing me now as I look into her beautiful, captivating eyes.

"You wanted to talk?" she asks in a soft voice.

I clear my throat. "Um, yeah." When she doesn't invite me in, I realize I'm going to have to do this in her apartment hallway. "I want to start by saying I'm really sorry for how I treated you yesterday. I was going through some tough shit, and instead of pushing it to the side, I took it out on you."

She nods, her gaze falling to the floor.

"You don't deserve that kind of treatment, Maple. You've been patient with me, you've cared about me and my well-being, and you've given me multiple chances to make up for my shit behavior. So I understand why this time...this time you've taken a step back. Not only was I an asshole to you, but I hurt you."

I wet my lips, my nerves making my skin crawl as I try to articulate what I'm feeling.

"I need you to know that, that...fuck." I let out a deep breath. "I like you, Maple, and these feelings I have for you, they're...they're out of my comfort zone, which doesn't give me an excuse to treat you the way that I did, to belittle you in front of my teammates. It's inexcusable, and I'm really fucking sorry." I tip her chin up so she can look at me, and fuck, there they are, the tears once again brimming in her eyes. "It was never my intention to hurt you, Maple. I don't want to hurt you. Ever."

She blinks, and a tear falls down her cheek.

Yet here I am, hurting her.

She's crying.

Because of me.

Because I'm a fuckup.

I quickly wipe her tears away with my thumb, and as the hot liquid melts into my skin, I question if I'm doing the right thing. If I should even be here.

If I can make her cry like this, then how the hell do I come off trying to tell her about my feelings?

Do I even have anything to offer her other than heartache?

I'm a man with so much baggage, so much heartache of my own, that all I would be doing is loading it onto her when she is too goddamn innocent for any of it.

She's sunshine and radiance.

She's joy and strength.

She's so much more than I could ever be, and standing here, witnessing the pain I can cause her, I realize just how much I don't deserve this.

I don't deserve her.

What the hell am I even doing?

I need...hell, I need to let her go.

I wet my lips and pull my hand away, knowing that at least I can offer her the reassurance that she did nothing wrong, that I truly regret how I acted.

I owe her that much.

I stick my hands back in my pockets and take a step away from her, attempting to keep my distance so I don't do something stupid, like push her into her apartment, up against her wall, and steal that innocence right from her mouth.

"I'm sorry, Maple. Really fucking sorry, and I hope that...that we can move forward from this and at least be friendly with each other." Friendly, Jesus, I hate everything about that. "And moving forward, you have my word that I won't ever put you in a situation like I did ever again because you deserve better treatment than what I bestowed upon you yesterday."

Her lashes flutter up as her eyes connect with mine, causing my heart to tumble out of my goddamn chest, right in front of us, on the dirty, scratched-up floor of her apartment hallway.

She's so beautiful that it takes my breath away, and I just wish there was an alternate reality where I could claim her. Make her mine.

Where I wasn't weighed down by my past, by my fucked-up future.

Where I could be a healthy contribution to her happiness rather than a troubled burden.

"Okay." I tug on the back of my neck, taking another step away from her. "Um, I guess I'll see you tomorrow unless you don't want to. Up to you." God, I sound like a rambling moron.

*Just leave.*

I offer her a sad smile, then turn and head through the hallway of her apartment and down the stairs to the street.

When the fresh air hits me, I let out a deep breath, the stress of that conversation constricting my chest.

I truly thought that was going to go so differently, but the minute I saw the pain I caused, I knew I didn't have a right to even consider asking her to give me a chance. She lives in a world of sunshine, where she takes care of birds and can bring joy to others while standing up for those who don't have a voice.

I live in a world of dark, foreboding clouds that are ready to strike me down any chance they get. Between the tumultuous, abusive relationship with my dad and the agonizing relationship with my mom…it's not something she needs to be a part of.

Not to mention, I'm not mentally capable of a relationship. I told myself that a long time ago, so I don't know what the hell I was thinking—other than that I feel lighter around her and I wanted to hang on to that.

I head down the street toward my truck, my brain a muddied mess of emotions that I'm having a hell of a time working through. My phone buzzes in my pocket, and needing the reprieve from my thoughts, I pull it out and find a text from Maple.

I pause, about to turn the corner to head toward my truck.

I swipe open the screen and read two simple words that steal my breath.

**Maple:** Come back.

I look over my shoulder at her apartment building, my body wanting to flee in that direction, my brain telling me I should leave her be.

The problem is, though, I've never made the smartest decisions, and before I can stop myself…I head back in the direction of her apartment building.

# CHAPTER 29
# MAPLE

MY HAND SHAKES AS I set my phone down, hoping that he gets the text, that he looks at it before he gets in his truck and leaves.

Seeing him here, waiting for me at my apartment, surprised me so much that it took a second for my brain to register what was going on. Then Hank had warned me when I was putting away my groceries, telling me to be careful, to not let him hurt me...as if Graydon has ever laid a hand on me.

I reassured Hank over and over that Graydon wasn't that kind of guy, but when he stands there, towering over you, hands flexing, I can understand where Hank gets that idea. But Graydon would never.

I know Hank is going to text me later to ask if I'm okay, and as I'm standing here, hoping Graydon comes back, I honestly don't know what I'm going to say because I'm so confused.

He painted a mural...for me.

He came and apologized.

And that hurt look in his eyes that he seems to carry more often than not, I looked straight into it as he apologized from the depths of his soul, and I felt, at that moment, my walls break and crumble. The walls I haphazardly put up after he embarrassed me. With one apology, they were torn down, and I was left with a raw, beating heart and the need to comfort this man, to reach out to him and...and...God, I don't know, but I need to see him.

I can also admit to myself that the only reason he had the capacity to hurt me so much...*is because I care about him so deeply.*

There's a quiet knock at my door, and my body freezes as I stare at it for a second.

Heart hammering.

Chest heaving.

I reach out and grab the door handle, opening it to find Graydon on the other side, his head bent down, his shoulders slumped and defeated.

"Maple," he says quietly.

"Don't say anything."

His eyes flash up to mine, sorrow so strong in his expression that I feel the threads that are holding me together unravel. That look, it's torture, and within seconds, it's my undoing.

Any last bit of anger I have toward him fades into a distant memory as I move in close, bringing my hands to his chest and slowly sliding them up to his face. When his dark, hurt eyes meet mine, I know there's nothing left that I could hold back.

This is it.

I'm handing my heart over.

I stand on my toes, bring him down closer to me, and press my lips to his.

He sucks in a sharp breath of surprise and then, as if the stars have aligned, his arms slide around my waist, and he deepens our kiss, bringing us both into the apartment and shutting the door behind him with his foot.

He gently presses me against the wall, where his hand moves to my cheek, and he angles my chin up with his thumb while his other hand grips my waist tightly, keeping me in place.

Keeping me close.

Shivers of need, of lust, spike up my spine as his kiss continues to deepen, continues to grow with more passion, and when he lifts me, I wrap my legs around his waist while he holds me against the wall, making the angle of our kisses so much more intense.

"Fuck," he breathes shallowly, his forehead pressing against mine. "I don't…I don't deserve this."

I nod. "You do."

He pulls back just enough for me to look him in the eyes. "I don't, Maple. I really fucking don't." His eyes search mine. "But, fuck, I'm just selfish enough to take it." And then his mouth is on mine again, his hand moving into my hair, his chest pressing against mine like he can't get close enough.

His lips, although exploratory, are urgent, like he can't believe this moment is happening, and he isn't going to let it slip through his fingers. And I feel that same urgency as I part my lips to catch his gasp, his lips parting as well.

Tendrils of desire pool in my stomach as I grip his face, my thumbs rubbing over his scruff while my tongue slips past his lips and strokes his.

The touch causes a groan to slip from him, and it's the sexiest sound I've ever heard. Given that he's such a dominant man, I wouldn't expect to be able to control him with a swipe of my tongue. But from the way he's pressing against me, I know that I have him in my grasp.

And I want so much more.

I pull away for a moment and look him in the eyes, my thumbs running over his cheeks. He expertly navigates my apartment and brings me to my bedroom, where he lays me down gently on the bed and kneels on the mattress as well, his arms caging me in as he stares down at me.

I reach around his back and tug up his shirt. He grabs the hem when I bring it close to his neck, and in one swift motion, he has it over his head and drops it to the floor.

My eyes immediately fall to his chest, the planes and curves carved out by his rock-hard muscle enticing my fingers. It's not the first time I'm seeing him shirtless, but it's the first time I get to feel his smooth, hot skin against mine, and I can't stop myself from letting my fingers explore every contour of his body.

Our eyes connect as he allows me to feel, allows my fingers to skim across him, over his pecs and across his abs.

He swallows thickly when I draw closer to his waistband and loop my fingers in his jeans, tugging him down so he's on top of me, his bare chest to my clothed one. His forearms cage my head, and his hand pushes some of my hair off my forehead in a very intimate act before he slows down our kisses and expertly lowers his mouth to mine, now taking his time, letting our tongues tangle and our heady attraction to each other mix.

One of his hands travels down to my waist, where he untucks my shirt from my pants, then slides his hand under the fabric, his palm connecting with my skin.

A bundle of nerves tightens in my stomach from his touch, and I wiggle beneath him, wanting to take off my shirt completely.

Thankfully, he lifts up for a moment to let me do just that and I move it to the side, lying beneath him in just my pink bra and pants.

He growls in my ear before kissing the skin just below it, then my jaw, then my neck, and as he works down to my collarbone, anticipation rips through me when he nips at the swell of my breast. He glances up at me, looking for me to stop him, but when I don't, he pulls down the cup of my bra, releasing my breast to the lustful air that surrounds us. He kisses it, his beard like a delicious sandpaper across my skin right before he kisses the tip of my nipple.

I suck in a harsh breath as he parts his mouth and brings the tip right between his lips and sucks, torturing me with the thought of so much more.

Like for him to take off the rest of my clothes, spread my legs, and remind me what it's like to be held, licked, sucked, and fucked by a man.

"More," I whisper, my nerves grabbing hold of me, but my hunger driving me to speak up.

But he doesn't listen. He lets go of my breast and drags his mouth, kissing the whole way up, to my neck, then my jaw and back to my lips, intoxicating me into a drunken state, his mouth in control.

*How did we get here so quickly?* I mean, I've been attracted to him since day one—*even if I've told myself I haven't been*—but here we are making out...a prelude to sex.

Sex. With. Graydon.

But I am so ready. He was so remorseful for hurting me, and right now, I don't feel anything but desire for this man. He could have kept his distance, but he sought me out. Made me hear him. *Showed me how he had heard me.* How could I not want him?

I run my hands down his ribs, his lungs sucking in a breath, tightening his muscles as I lower my hands even farther, to the waistband of his jeans. His mouth continues to take charge, his tongue luxuriously driving into mine, tangling, dancing, so I bring my hands to the front of his jeans, and I undo them, just enough to push them down over his ass.

He continues to make out with me, his mouth never leaving mine, so I slide my fingers under the waistband of his boxer briefs and run them along his firm ass.

"Fuck," he breathes against me, pausing for a moment, so I take advantage of it and slide my thumbs forward, over the V in his hips and right above his hard-on. "Maple," he says darkly, a warning on his tongue that I don't bother to acknowledge. I push down on his briefs, wanting them to fall off, but he doesn't give. He lifts up before I can make the move and stares down at me.

My eyes fall to the massive bulge in his briefs, my nerves getting the best of me as I come to terms with the fact that it's been a really long freaking time since I've done this, and I'm about to be with easily the hottest, most attractive, and probably most experienced man I've ever kissed.

"Don't," he says, probably noticing the worry in my brow.

"It's...it's been a long time," I say, embarrassment staining my cheeks.

He leans down again, kissing my forehead, then my cheeks, my nose, and my lips, keeping it a light kiss before he presses his forehead to mine and quietly says, "If it makes you feel better, this is the first time I've ever been with someone I care about, that I have feelings for." His nose lightly rubs against mine. "I'm just as nervous."

And if I wasn't sure how much I liked this man, I'm pretty aware now, because the way he so easily just soothed my nerves, with a simple confession, I know that I want this. That I want him, and no amount of time will stop me from wanting him.

I wrap my arms around his neck, bring him closer, and then hungrily lock his lips with mine, devouring him while he works his hands to my pants, undoing them and tugging on them. He lifts just enough to pull them all the way off, leaving me in just my underwear and bra.

He pauses for a moment, staring down at me, his eyes feasting.

"You're fucking beautiful," he says in awe, his gaze roaming. "Fuck, I'm so lucky."

The worth he makes me feel, like I'm the most precious thing he's ever laid his eyes on, does me in.

I sit up on my knees and his arms automatically wrap around my waist, one of his hands traveling down to cup my ass right before his lips find my neck, his teeth nibbling at the column, heightening the thrill inside me.

Wanting him to lose his clothes as well, I push down on his jeans, and he pauses on sucking my neck for a second so he can take off his shoes, socks, and jeans, only to cup my ass again, pick me up, and turn so he's sitting on the bed, my center rubbing over his erection. He leans back on my pillow, and I straddle his lap as I drag my hands up the planes of his pecs, memorizing every contour while I slowly move my hips over him, making his eyes fill with lust.

He rubs his teeth over the corner of his mouth as he fists the strap of my thong with one hand and then moves his other hand up to the clasp of my bra. He pauses for a second, waiting for me to stop him.

But there is no way I'm stopping this, so he undoes the clasp. His eyes immediately go to my chest, but instead of taking my bra off right away, I let it hang loosely, barely covering me. That seems to drive him nuts as he grips my thong tighter, the feel of the fabric cutting into my skin, turning me on even more as he restrains himself from ripping it off completely.

I lean down, grip his jaw, and tilt his head up to meet mine, letting my tongue slide over his lips while my bra slowly slides down my arms until it's completely off. Keeping my mouth on his and dancing our tongues together, I slide my bra off and let my hardened nipples lightly drag over his chest.

He groans into my mouth and brings his hand up to cup my breast, his thumb instantly swiping over my nipple, the heat in my body turning into an inferno from the touch of another human, something I didn't realize I missed until this moment—now I feel crazed for more.

I release his mouth and kiss down his neck to his collarbone as he releases me and lets me slide down his body. I run my tongue along his pecs, over his nipple, and then down his stomach, my nipples grazing across his skin while my mouth glides over every single one of his abs until I reach the waistband of his briefs.

I glance up at him, his chest rising and falling rapidly as I slip my fingers along the waistband and drag the fabric down, letting his erection spring up his stomach, the heat in my body prickling all over my skin as I take in just how large he is.

Jesus.

I remove his boxer briefs completely and then grip his thighs, letting my thumbs slide inward. I watch in fascination as his cock twitches over his stomach, seeking out any kind of touch.

Insecurity tries to take over my thoughts, but I push it aside because he would not be that hard if he wasn't interested, nor would he be looking at me the way that he is if he didn't want this. So I start kissing up his thigh, over the V in his hips and his stomach, letting my cheek graze across his length.

He lets out a deep groan as I slide my mouth just over the top, never touching, so I can kiss the other side of his stomach.

"Fuck," he breathes, his legs spreading. "I want that mouth, beautiful," he says encouragingly, and it spurs me on.

I wet my lips and then run my palm over his length, only to angle him up and press my lips to his tip, where I gently suck him into my mouth.

"Jesus...Christ," he growls, his hand falling to my cheek as he watches me with an adoring look in his eyes.

His rapture only heightens my arousal. I can feel a thrumming sensation between my legs, pulsing up into my stomach as I bring him deeper into my mouth, my good hand that's not braced gripping his length and pumping.

"Shit," he says breathlessly as he shifts beneath me.

I lift and swirl my tongue around the head, flicking it on the underside and taking him to the back of my throat, the motion bringing a long moan from his lips as I repeat the process, over and over, sucking harder every time I pull him farther into my mouth until he's hissing and pulling me up his body.

"Not coming in your mouth," he says as my center falls over his length.

I press my hands to his chest and start rocking over him.

"Why not?"

"Because I want to come inside you," he whispers. His eyes find my breasts, his hands squeezing and making my head fall back as I ride him, letting the friction between us drive my arousal higher and higher.

"God, you're huge." My hips shoot forward faster, my stomach starting to tighten, my orgasm building to the feel of my clit rubbing over his length. "Fu-uck," I grunt, my eyes slamming shut. I can't stop.

I'm so close.

And I know he wants to come inside me, but this feels too good.

"Graydon," I whisper. "I'm. . . I'm so close."

"Then ride me, beautiful. Come all over my cock."

My eyes fall to his, and I dig my fingers into his chest, anchoring down as I let my hips fly, my clit throbbing, tightening. A bolt of pleasure shoots up my spine, and my orgasm pulses through me as his name falls off my lips, and I start coming on his length.

"Fuck," I rasp as my hips slow down, and my eyes open to look up at him, a bashful feeling setting in until I see the pure hunger in his expression.

"Jesus Christ, that was so hot," he says right before flipping me to my back.

He gets off my bed, his cock standing tall, and he pulls his wallet out of his jeans, snagging a condom. Eyes on me, he sheathes himself and then pulls my legs to the edge of the bed, flipping me to my stomach.

He leans over me, his cock rubbing against my ass cheek as he leans down, moves my hair to the side, and kisses my neck. Whispering in my ear, he says, "Face down, ass up, beautiful."

He drags his mouth over my shoulder, along my shoulder blade, and down my back until he reaches my ass. With his teeth, he grabs hold of my thong and drags it off my body. From the side, I see him toss it to the ground while I get up on my knees and stick my ass in the air like he wants.

With anyone else, I think this position would have made me feel self-conscious, but with him, it makes me feel sexy.

"This ass," he says, his hand smoothing over it. "Fuck, I've wanted it from the moment I set my eyes on you."

His fingers slide down my crack to my arousal, where he feels just how turned on I still am.

"Good girl," he says, sticking two fingers inside me and slowly pumping me while his thumb rubs along my clit.

I let out a silent breath as I feel my nerves pull inwardly again, amazed at how quickly my body can react once again. And I know it has everything to do with him.

His palm glides over my ass, then pulls back and spanks me gently.

"Oh God," I yelp, not prepared for that, but then surprisingly liking it. He must notice because his fingers are still inside me where I'm clenched.

"Shit, beautiful."

He removes his fingers and then positions his length at my entrance. He angles my hips up more as he stands behind me, his height lining up with me perfectly as he eases inside me, stretching me in the best way possible.

Halfway in, he asks, "You good?"

"Yes," I answer in a raspy tone.

He keeps pushing until he's bottomed out, my ass pressing against him.

"Fuck," he breathes heavily. "You feel too damn good."

Then he spanks me again, and I tremor around him, squeezing him involuntarily as I ride out the feeling of being so full.

"Shit," he whispers, spanking me again.

And again.

And again.

He smooths his hand over the red mark every time, then does it again until I'm panting, my body shaking as I can feel myself ready to break into a full-out sweat from how turned on I am, how full. I need friction in order to finish off but he's not giving me that.

"Fuck me," I groan. "Fuck me, Graydon. I need more."

He pulls out all the way, causing me to feel such a great loss as he rubs his cock along the crack of my ass, giving himself some friction but leaving me hanging.

"Graydon, please."

He leans forward over my body, bringing one of his hands to my chest, and starts playing with my nipple. He kisses my shoulder and neck, then yanks my head to the side, where he finds my lips. He makes out with me for a moment before moving back to the curve of my shoulder and neck. His teeth bite down on me while he sucks, and I know it's going to leave a mark. It's something I will have to cover up tomorrow, but I don't care because I want him marking me.

Claiming me.

His mouth trails back down my body again. His lips press against the curve of my ass while he pinches my nipple until I'm panting, about to come just from the torture he's putting me through.

When he finally pulls back, lines up with my center, and pushes into me, I cry out his name before he starts pounding into me, his hips flying at a rapid pace while he grips my waist, hoisting me up higher for a better angle. My forearms rest against the mattress, anchoring me as they're the only part of me touching the bed now that he's holding me captive, taking charge and fucking me to the point that I can practically feel him in my throat from how deep he's going.

"Fuck, Graydon. Oh my God, so deep."

"So goddamn tight," he groans, his pace picking up as he feels me starting to tighten.

"Oh God, yes, yes, Graydon...oh, I'm...I'm going to come." My body tightens, my pussy clenches around him, and with a few more thrusts, I'm moaning so loud that I know every single one of my neighbors can hear me. But I don't care because it's the most delicious, mind-bending feeling.

"Fucking shit!" He pulses a few more times, then stills as he yells, "Fuck," and comes inside me, his fingers digging into my skin. "Jesus...Christ." He lightly pulses a few more times, then lowers me to the bed before kissing between my shoulder blades for a few seconds.

When he lifts away, he goes to the bathroom, where I assume he's taking care of his condom.

When he comes back into the room, he flips me to my back, picks me up, and brings me to the head of the bed. He lies down with me, his back to the mattress and my chest to his, and I rest my head in the crook of his neck.

His hand lazily drags up and down my back as we both catch our breath, my mind still trying to comprehend what I have just experienced.

With Hardy, it was always good, but it felt like something was missing.

With Graydon, I know what that something was—this deep pull I feel whenever he's around. It's like we were bound to be connected from the moment we first met, and now that we've finally given in, the missing puzzle piece in my life has finally connected.

He kisses the top of my head and lets out a deep breath.

After a few seconds, he says, "I really like you, Maple."

I chuckle because, yeah, I could tell. "I like you too."

He lifts my chin so I have to look him in the eyes. "And I'm so fucking sorry I hurt you. I promise that will never happen again. You are mine to protect, mine to keep, and I'm not going to fuck that up."

His words, a whisper of a promise coming off his tongue, cover me like a warm blanket because I believe him.

"Thank you," I say as I lean forward and kiss him.

He sighs into the connection, his hand sliding down to my ass before I pull away and rest my head back on his chest, completely and utterly content.

# CHAPTER 30
# GRAYDON

SO THIS IS WHAT HAPPINESS feels like.

It's been so goddamn long that I've forgotten the way it feels to have my mouth keep tugging into a smile, the burdens I bear taking a break from pressing down on my chest, and the world seeming to fade away as joy seeps into my soul.

And she's the reason.

Maple.

My beautiful Maple.

Did not see that coming.

She walks into the kitchen, wearing my shirt that swallows her whole, and it's so goddamn cute that it makes me want to take it off and worship her all over again. But given that I only had one condom, I'm going to have to practice some self-control.

When she catches me staring at her, her cheeks pinken. So fucking adorable.

"Is this okay?" She tugs on the hem of her shirt.

"More than okay," I say as I take her by the hand and pull her closer. I grip her cheek, angle her chin up, and kiss her lips, letting my tongue explore her all over again.

Supple.

Responsive.

Addictive.

Her hands move over my pecs, digging into my skin, branding me with her touch, something I reveled in just moments ago, trying to commit the way she touched me to memory because it felt so damn good.

I want to bottle up the feeling and live on it.

And as her mouth works over mine, her fingers imprinting into my muscles, excitement pulses through me at the thought of getting lost in her all over again.

I've fucked my share of women. It's not something I'm proud of, but it's something that has kept the edge off all these years, and I can honestly say, without a shadow of a doubt, that no one has ever felt like anything even close to Maple.

The moment her pussy started clenching around me when I was spanking her, I knew I was gone.

Fucking endgame.

There was no holding me back, and I took exactly what I wanted until I blacked out, curse words falling from my lips while I came.

She groans into my mouth, and I pull away, trying to give myself a fighting chance before I start getting hard again.

Her eyes flutter open, and she looks up at me, the most beautiful smile pulling on her lips.

My thumb slides over her cheek, her soft skin imprinting with the touch of my thumb. "You truly are breathtaking."

Her smile grows wider before she starts shaking her head.

"What?" I ask.

"It's just so crazy, all of this."

"What do you mean?" I ask before I lift her, spin her around, and put her up on the counter so we're more at eye level to have this conversation.

Her legs pull me in as she wraps them around my waist. "Being here, with you, like this. I don't know. I just…I never really thought you and I would ever get to a place like this even though I knew I was developing feelings."

"Maple," I say, my hands sliding across her sides. "How could you not see it? The number of times I stole glances at you, wanted to be near you, the way I would touch you for no reason, how I would stare at your ass, desperately send you thirst traps..."

She chuckles, and her hands fall to my shoulders. "The thirst traps were surprising, but I didn't always catch you looking at me, and I don't know, you weren't giving off the vibe of 'Oh, I think she's pretty.' I guess I just thought it was all for show."

"Not pretty," I correct her. "Beautiful, Maple. You're fucking gorgeous. You're so smart. And your heart is, fuck, it's one of a kind with the way you care for everything and everyone around you." I press my hand to her chest. "I've never met someone with a heart like yours."

"I could say the same about you."

Now it's my turn to shake my head. "No, it's all darkness and shadows inside this hollow chest."

Her brow creases. "How can you possibly say that after everything you've done for me?"

"I did those things because I liked you. If you recall, I was a dick at the beginning."

"Yes, but there was always a heart inside your chest. You took care of me when you didn't need to. You've spent your little free time driving me around, making my apartment more comfortable, and helping me spread awareness about the flamingos. You have a brilliantly beautiful heart."

"Once again, I did those things because it was brought upon me and because I liked you."

"I don't believe it. What about that boy who came up to you when we got tacos? You made his year." Her hands slide up to my neck, locking me in place. "Please don't say you're dark and hollow inside because I see so much more than that."

I rub my lips together, her eyes boring into me, making me feel this overbearing need to share. To open up. But such a concept is so foreign to me. I don't talk about my feelings. Never have since the moment my mom had her accident. I did what my dad told me to do. I bottled them up, pushed them down, and forgot about them.

And with every day that passed, I grew more and more angry and less and less vulnerable, and before I knew it, I was going through the motions of life, moving toward one goal and one goal only: playing football.

And now that I'm here, several years in, I've become completely numb to the world.

At least I thought I was until Maple came into my life.

She started calling me out on my bullshit and challenging me. She made me care for something again, something new in my life, and she opened my eyes to see the moving world around me, rather than the stagnant rut I've been living in.

"Are you listening to me?"

I nod, my head tilting down.

"Tell me you believe me."

"Hard to when I know the person I've been for over fourteen years. When I know the person I grew up with tainted me."

She pauses and then softly says, "Are you talking about your dad?"

"Yeah. It was a lot, growing up with him as my dad, with him consistently damaging what little positivity I had left in me. I know the darkness he's put inside me. I know the shadows I possess, Maple. And it only gets worse when he's around."

"But you are not that person. I've seen the man you truly are, Graydon."

"You see someone different from who I'm used to being, and I think it's because you brought it out of me, not because it's the person I actually am."

"You wouldn't just change like that," she says. "You were always this person. You were just hiding it." She lightly presses her lips to mine, and I groan as I deepen the kiss.

I might not be the person she perceives me to be, but if being that person means I get to indulge in her, get lost in the feel of her arms and her mouth, then I will do everything to try to be that person.

Because I don't want to lose this.

Not when I've finally found an ounce of joy in my pain-ridden life.

I'm going to be a selfish fuck and cling to this for as long as I can.

---

"Here, add what you need." Maple hands me her phone as she makes herself comfortable on my lap, where I'm sitting on the couch.

I glance at the DoorDash order on her phone and scowl. "What the hell is this?"

"An order from a store. Figured you'd need a toothbrush since I've claimed you for the night. Oh, and you might want to add a shirt in there because I'm keeping this one."

I shake my head and set her phone down before picking up mine.

"What are you doing? Do you not want to stay here?"

I give her a *get real* look. "Try kicking me out," I scoff while pulling up DoorDash on my phone and then handing it to her. "Go ahead, put in an order for whatever you want."

"Um, this is the same thing that's on my phone."

"No, it's not, because it's my credit card being charged, not yours."

"Graydon, I can buy things."

"I'm aware, but you're not buying things when I'm around." When she goes to protest, I add, "Don't argue with the millions in my bank account. Okay?"

She sighs. "I don't like taking advantage of you."

"You're not. I'm forcing you to let me pay."

She chuckles. "Uh-huh, and what if I say no?"

"Don't test me," I say, my arm snagging around her waist, making her laugh.

"And here I thought I softened you up."

One single brow picks up as I look at her. "Maple, if you've accomplished anything tonight, you've hardened me."

Her eyes flash to mine in humor. "Oh, look at you being clever and carefree, just like in your texts." She leans forward and kisses my lips. "I like it."

Then she goes back to my phone and picks a store. "Now what sort of condoms do you use?" She gives me a mischievous expression, and it's so damn cute.

"Give me that." I take the phone from her, making her laugh, and I add condoms, a toothbrush, a shirt, and a few other things to the cart before I check out, making sure the delivery comes directly to me, because the quicker I can get those condoms, the better.

When I set my phone down, she turns to straddle my lap and pushes me up against the back of the couch.

I let my hands rest on her hips while her palms sear into my chest. "I've been meaning to say something to you, but I haven't really had a great chance."

"Hit me," I say, feeling so goddamn relaxed that it actually feels unnatural.

"The mural. I know I said thank you, but I really want you to know how special it is. I had no idea you knew how to paint, and then to do it so beautifully, with all the hidden meaning behind it. It means so much to me, Graydon. Thank you."

I smile softly at her, making her face light up. "You're welcome."

"Look at you smiling." She says it in a way that's more in awe rather than teasing. "You need to do that more often."

"I think I might," I say, smoothing my hands over her legs. "And I'm glad you like the mural."

"Where did you learn to paint like that?" she asks, her thumb rubbing over my chest.

I swallow thickly, the answer on the tip of my tongue. I've never really talked about this with anyone. Hutton knows a little bit of my past—because my family was in the public eye—but talking about the accident and my childhood is something I haven't done. But this is Maple. So warm, so welcoming. I feel myself loosening that tight grip I have on my past. I truly believe I can trust her.

Clearing my throat, I softly say, "My mom."

She pauses for a moment, her head tilting to the side as she studies me. "Your tone makes me think that maybe your mom isn't here with us anymore?" she asks. "And I'm sorry if that's overstepping."

I shake my head, my nerves getting the best of me as I try to find my voice. "She, uh, she's still here, but not technically with us," I say, the words rushing out of me, filling me with relief but also dread.

"Oh." Maple continues to rub my chest with her thumb. "I don't want to pressure you to talk, but if you want to share more, I'm here to listen."

I look into her eyes and feel the truth in those words. There's no judgment there. There's understanding. There's empathy.

And this is why I like her, because she offers me a sense of calm in the wake of the destruction blistering through my head. *If only I'd seen this on Monday, rather than lashing out at her. Fuck, I'm a dick.* I lift her hand to my lips and kiss her knuckles, so grateful that I made the decision to pursue her.

"I've never told anyone this or ever talked about it, really," I say to preface my next statement.

"You don't have to," she says soothingly.

I look in her eyes and say, "I want to." She nods, and I brace my hand against her hip, looking for warmth from her as I continue. "I was sixteen, and my mom was out riding horses with a friend. She loved horses and was taking riding lessons. She was always super cautious and took it seriously. But this one day, she decided to hop on a horse really quick without any gear—she got in a fight with my dad that day and was looking for some peace—and the horse bucked her off, throwing her into a fence.

She slammed her head against a pole, giving her a serious head injury, among other things."

"Oh my God," Maple whispers softly, only to lean into me, pressing her head into the crook of my neck while she grips me tightly, bringing me into a deep embrace, one I haven't felt in years. I wrap my arm around her, holding on to her as well and welcoming the feel of her pressing into me.

Clearing my throat again, I continue, "She was in a coma for a few days, and when she came back to us, there was something off. Something different. We realized she wasn't remembering why she was hurt or what happened. After a gauntlet of tests and examinations, she was diagnosed with anterograde amnesia."

"What's that?"

"It's when your brain can't form new memories, so basically all she's ever known up to the point of her accident is all she will remember. Meaning, when I go to visit her, she doesn't know who I am anymore, because to her, I'm supposed to be sixteen, not thirty."

Maple sits up. "Oh my God, Graydon. That's...that's heartbreaking. I'm so sorry." Her hand caresses my cheek. "Do you see her often?"

I wet my lips. "Every Sunday during the off-season."

Realization sinks in as she thinks about my answer. "That's why you couldn't go to brunch."

I nod. "I reserve Sundays for her and for...well, for me because..." I push my hand through my hair, hating this part the most but knowing it will help to get it off my chest. "When I visit her, there's a high probability of her not believing who I am and not wanting to even be near me."

Tears of empathy fill Maple's eyes as she experiences my pain as hers. "I'm so, so sorry." She presses her forehead against mine. "I can't imagine what that must feel like." *Devastating. Heartbreaking. Lonely.*

"It's...it's not easy. And it fluctuates; I never know what I'm going to get when I go to visit her. Her nurse, Rhonda, tries to help me out, showing her a binder we put together of me growing throughout the years, gradually showing her the man I am now. There are days when it works, when she pulls me into her arms and holds me, and those..." I let out a sigh. "Those are the happiest days. But the days she can't process the change, the days when she won't accept me even being near her, they cut deep. Sunday was one of those days." My throat tightens as I say, "They, uh, they had to sedate her as she was screaming, begging for me to be with her, but not thirty-year-old me. She was looking for sixteen-year-old me."

"That was this Sunday?"

I nod. "Yeah, and it broke me. Normally, I can handle it, but this time, it cut me deep, and I brought those feelings into the next day." I cup her chin, making sure I look her in the eyes when I say this. "That morning, I wasn't angry or upset with you or anything that you did. I was spiraling from what happened with my mom the day before and having a hard time getting her scream and the panic in her eyes out of my head. I didn't sleep much that night, and all I wanted to do was get out on the field and bury those feelings with aggression. Instead, I took them out on you, and I'm so fucking sorry."

Her eyes search mine, tears spilling over her cheeks. "That's why you were upset?"

"Yes, and I know I should have said something, but I just...I wasn't in the right frame of mind to divulge that sort of information."

"Oh my God," she whispers as she cups my face with both hands. "I...I'm so sorry, Graydon."

"For what?"

"For..." More tears. "For pushing you that morning and not just letting you be. I should have recognized your pain and listened to you."

"You didn't know."

"That still...it's no excuse." She shakes her head. "I have this annoying need to fix everything and fix it right then and there. And that's what I was trying to do, I was trying to help you, when in reality, you just needed space. I'm so sorry."

"Why are you the one who's apologizing, Maple?" I ask as I run my fingers over her bare skin.

"Because I shut you down that day and blocked you out of my life when you needed an understanding heart instead. That's so...that's so fucked up of me."

"Don't." I shake my head. "Don't do that. You didn't know."

"I know, but I should have noticed something was bothering you. Instead, I blamed it on my insecurities." She leans in close, her forehead rubbing against mine. "I'm so sorry I did that to you, and then you felt the need to make it up to me and paint that mural and—"

I cut her off, pressing my mouth to hers and slipping my hand to the back of her head. She parts her lips for mine, and I open my mouth to kiss her, letting myself fall into the comfort of her hold on me, letting all my worries and anger pour out of me as I cling to hope. To joy.

After a few seconds, I pull away and allow my racing heart to steady.

"I shouldn't have treated you like that," I say. "There's no excuse great enough to warrant that behavior, and I know it. Please don't offer me excuses."

Her teeth pull on her bottom lip as she nods. "I understand, but I still feel awful that you were going through something so traumatic and going through it alone, and I just...I missed it."

"It's not like I've been an open book, Maple."

"I know." She sighs and then tucks her head in the crook of my neck again, curling up on my lap and holding on to me tightly. "Maybe you can tell me a little bit about her if you want."

A small smile peeks past my lips because I honestly can't remember the last time I talked about her, and having this outlet, this person in my life who I can open up to about something that I've been holding in for so long, is amazing. It's like she broke the dam and I'm pouring everything out.

"She was, is...was, I guess, since she's not the same woman anymore."

I rest my hand on Maple's hip and drag my fingers leisurely over her warm skin. "She was the kind of mom involved in everything, and I know a lot of it was because my dad was so absent playing football that she overcompensated for it. But thinking back, it meant everything that she was there for me. I didn't have that person who showed up for me in my life after her accident. I was practically raised by a nanny."

"That's awful."

"It wasn't too terrible. It was better than dealing with my dad."

"Was he...was he abusive to you?" she asks, her voice shaky.

"Not physically. Mentally and emotionally, yeah. Fucked with my head a lot. By the time my mom had the accident, they were already divorced, and I was living with her, so I had to move in with him. I was a wet blanket to his single life."

"How did he fuck with your head?"

I feel myself tense before saying, "When I was in college, he had no problem pursuing the same girls I was. Would always flirt right in front of me when he was still with my mom when I was younger, just...a total and utter asshole. I don't...I don't really want to get into it, but the day that I punched him at training camp, it was because he was talking to you in a way that I did not appreciate one bit."

"Oh, that's terrible. I'm so sorry."

I shrug. "He's a dick, and I hate him. The only reason he's in my life right now is because he falsifies this father-son relationship to the press, especially at the beginning of the season. It's all for media and clout."

"That's so messed up."

I pause for a moment, taking a breath, because I can't remember the last time I actually talked this much. "There are times when I wish he was the one with the brain injury. The guy who played football—it just seems like it was supposed to be him, but instead, it was her. She was so vibrant, so full of life, would try anything and never shy away from a challenge.

She was resilient and believed in doing the right thing, even if it caused you hurt and pain."

"Is that why you visit her every week?" Her thumb strokes my pec.

"Yes," I answer. "That, and a piece of me hopes and prays that there will be a day when she recognizes me, that she will hold my hand and just let us live in the moment, where we can paint together. Those sessions are few and far between, but fuck, Maple, when they do happen, it feels like one of the greatest moments in my life. Seeing her smile, seeing how proud of me she is. It's...it's a feeling I will continue to chase, even as those moments grow fewer and fewer."

I can feel her tears on my chest as she lightly cries against me.

"Please don't cry."

"I'm sorry," she says as she lifts up to look at me again. "It's just...God, I can't imagine feeling such agony. I hate that for you."

I swipe at her cheeks, ridding her of tears. "Could be worse, she could be completely gone, and I wouldn't have any moments. And it's not all bad. There are days when she's apprehensive, but she will still paint with me, side by side. It just makes me sad that I can't hug her or hold her hand, but it's better than nothing."

Her lips meet mine in the faintest whisper of a kiss as she straddles me again, her hands smoothing over my shoulders. Her lips against my cheek now, she says, "You're a good man, Graydon."

"Could be better," I say honestly. "You don't know everything about me. I have anger issues. I have a fuck ton of baggage, and if I were a better man, I would stand up right now and walk out your door, sparing you the struggle." My hands slide under her shirt and run up and down her sides. "But I'm not a better man. I'm a selfish prick who set my eyes on something I shouldn't have, and I'm going to take it anyway."

"You deserve me, Graydon."

I shake my head. "I really fucking don't, but that doesn't mean I won't try to be the man you deserve, because I will."

She sighs, and then she brushes her lips against mine again, parting my mouth and delivering the sweetest open-mouthed kisses, allowing me to get lost in her.

Lost in the feel of her.

Lost in the moment of being able to cling to her after such a tough conversation.

My hands drag her shirt up and over her head, leaving her completely bare to me.

"Fuck," I rasp as I fill my palms with her breasts and gently squeeze while my thumbs stroke her nipples back and forth.

She groans into my mouth, her hips sinking down on my hardening length while her hands dig into my hair, holding me in place but also making my skin tingle with every scrape along my scalp and thrust of her hips.

I release one of her breasts and stroke her spine until I reach her perfect ass. My fingers glide along her crack and then over the round globe, completely and utterly obsessed with her body and her curves.

When she releases my mouth, I flick my tongue at her nipple, licking and then sucking, loving how she arches her back.

I then explore her spine, feeling the curve in it as she allows me to suck on her breast, flicking my tongue over the point. The strain in her back muscles is tantalizing, and I never would have thought that I'd become fascinated with such a thing, but here I am, getting turned on by the way she contorts her back.

"Fuck," she whispers softly as she reaches between us and pulls my cock out of my boxer briefs. In an instant, she's pushing her clit against the hard ridge, pumping herself over me again and again while I suck at her, switching to the other breast and reveling in her nails biting into my skin and the moans falling past her lips.

"Yes, Graydon. God…yes." Her hands fall to my shoulders now, her body moving faster as she holds on to keep herself steady.

She uses me.

Uses my cock.

Uses my strength to keep her on pace.

And I love every second of it.

"That's it, beautiful," I whisper. "Fuck me. Use me. Get off on me."

"Yes," she yells, her body growing stiffer, her muscles starting to strain. "Fuck, I'm right there, Graydon. I'm...oh fuck, I'm sorry."

Her head buries in my shoulder, and she moans loudly as she comes all over my cock, riding out her orgasm along my length until she's completely sated and falling into my body.

Jesus, that is the hottest thing I've ever experienced.

I kiss the side of her head. And then I lift her and place her face down on the couch. She turns her head to look up at me as I release my cock the rest of the way from my boxer briefs and then start pumping, using her arousal on my cock as well as the precum running down the side of my length as lube to assist in my stroking.

I stare down at her ass, and as she looks back up at me, she smiles, then sticks her ass farther in the air.

Fuck.

Me.

My hand strokes harder, my breaths growing shorter.

"Come on my ass, Graydon. Claim me."

"Fucking Christ," I grumble as I lean forward, the sound of her voice as she practically begs me to come all over her sapping my ability to hold back.

I pump feverishly, over and over again, groans pulling from my chest, my gaze fixed on her round ass.

"That's it, Graydon. Let me see you come."

"Fuck!" I roar as my balls tighten, my cock swells, and in an instant, I'm spilling all over her ass, the droplets marking her as mine as I watch every last spurt fall on top of her smooth, sexy skin.

"Jesus fuck," I groan, placing my hand on the back of the couch, steadying myself as my muscles ache with pleasure, my body so unsure of what the fuck is going on because I wasn't even inside her, and I almost blacked out again.

After a few seconds, I lean forward and lightly kiss her lips. When I start to pull away, she brings me back to her face by gripping the back of my neck.

She places a ghost of a kiss, tender and sweet, on my mouth before letting go. I stare down at her in awe, my heart swelling in my chest.

*How the fuck did I get this lucky?*

# CHAPTER 31
# MAPLE

I CURVE MY FINGER OVER the scruff on Graydon's jaw while I rest in his lap, the lock of his arm around me keeping me close. We haven't moved except to grab the groceries from the door.

He's been through so much.

It's all I keep thinking about.

I couldn't imagine living his life with his circumstances. Losing his mom, being raised by a nanny because his father really didn't want much to do with him. Only for the same father to turn around and stake a claim when Graydon finally made it in football.

Disgusting.

And don't get me started on how he spends his Sundays. To even think about it makes me feel ill, sad...hopeless.

"What are you thinking about?" he asks, his hand tightening on my thigh.

"You," I answer.

"What about me?"

"How the scruff on your jaw seems to be growing thicker by the hour," I answer, not wanting to bring up his past again because it was clear just how much it hurts him to talk about. And that's not what I want to do while I have this time with him.

"Curious how it feels between your legs?"

My entire body heats at the thought of it.

"I would be lying if I said I wasn't curious."

He chuckles, and it's such a beautiful sound. A low rumble in his chest tumbles through me, warming me up from the inside out. "Why don't you just ask, then?"

I continue to drag my finger over his jaw as I say, "You realize that I've never asked for something like that, right? Completely out of my comfort zone."

He nuzzles his nose against my neck as he whispers, "Says the girl who told me to come on her ass."

My cheeks flame while goose bumps spread over my skin at the feel of his mouth traveling over my neck.

"Are you sure I said that?"

He chuckles again. "Positive. It's been ingrained in my brain."

His hand coyly slides under my shirt. "Doesn't sound like me."

*Come on my ass, Graydon. Claim me.* I'm still in shock I said that, but I've simply never felt so turned on, so gloriously sexy, in my life.

"Trust me, beautiful, it was you."

With one finger, he turns my head toward his, and he kisses me, his lips parting casually, not a sense of urgency anywhere as he explores my mouth all over again.

And I sink into his touch, into the way he claims me with such a possessive hold on me. I turn toward him, straddling his lap, letting my body sink over his just as my phone starts to ring.

I pause, glancing over at the phone on the coffee table, and when I see Hank's name flash over the screen, I know I have to answer.

"It's Hank," I say.

Graydon's expression grows dark. "So?"

"So I should answer it, or he'll keep calling."

"Okay, so answer it and tell him he needs to get a life."

"Graydon..."

"Fine, I can." He reaches for the phone, but I stop him and pick up the phone myself. I climb off his lap and move toward the center of the living room with Graydon's dark gaze on me the entire time.

"Hello?"

"Hey," Hank says. "Didn't hear back from you when I texted, so I thought I would just give you a quick call. Is everything okay?"

"Yeah, everything is fine," I answer.

Graydon leans his forearms on his legs, staring at me, the calm from a few moments ago completely erased. Now he looks like he's ready to rip someone's head off with the way he's flexing his hands and the deadly expression in his eyes.

"Are you sure?"

"Yeah. We, um, we worked things out."

There's silence for a moment.

"Is he still there?"

My eyes move to Graydon, and I say, "Yes."

More silence.

"Okay, did he pressure you? Say...say, 'The flamingos need food,' if you need me to come over there and help you."

I sigh. "It's not like that, Hank."

Graydon runs his tongue over his teeth, clearly ready to do some damage.

"Are you sure? Because you can tell me. You can talk to me, Maple."

"And I appreciate that. But I promise you, everything is good."

He lets out a long breath, and I can see him in my mind, pushing up his glasses, something he tends to do when he's thinking. "Okay, but text me or call me if anything changes. I don't...I don't like the anger he holds. And I don't ever want to see that anger pushed onto you."

"You don't need to worry about that."

"I hope not." He clears his throat. "Okay, I'll see you tomorrow."

"See you tomorrow."

We both hang up, and I can practically taste the tension that has rolled into my apartment from one simple phone call. It's no secret that Graydon doesn't like Hank. I noticed that the first moment they met. And it's also not a secret that Hank doesn't like Graydon. He hasn't been quiet about it. And right now, I feel like I'm stuck in a tough spot, trying to navigate a world where my friend believes the man who…is interested in me is not the person I should be with. And the man who is interested in me would pay good money to be alone in a room with my friend…with no cameras.

After a stretch of silence, Graydon asks, "What does he not have to worry about?"

"Huh?" I ask.

"You told him he doesn't need to worry about that. What were you referring to?"

"Graydon, it doesn't matter—"

"It matters to me." He stands. "Because that asshole is trying to move in where he doesn't belong and plaguing you with his negative thoughts about me."

"Really?" I ask, setting my phone down and then crossing my arms. "You truly believe that I don't have a mind of my own and I'm letting some man taint my thoughts about you? If that's the case, then why are you here, in my apartment, freshly fucked, while I wear your T-shirt?"

He scrubs his hand over his face, his muscles tense as he brings his attention to me. "That's not what I meant."

"That's exactly what you meant, Graydon, and it's insulting. I make my own choices, and not a single person will convince me to do anything I don't want to do."

"He made it a point that he was going to try to steal you away from me."

"Okay, so what if he did? Does that mean he gets me?"

"No," he says, the tension rolling through his shoulders easing.

"Then give me the benefit of the doubt and understand that I have a mind of my own, and I go after what I want without being swayed by other people."

He tugs on his hair. "And what do you want?"

Seeing the vulnerability in his eyes, I move in toward him and place my hand on his chest, looking up at him. "You, Graydon. I want you."

His hand slides down my back, and he pulls the hem of my shirt up and then palms my bare ass, bringing me in an inch closer.

"Yeah?"

"Yeah," I answer.

His other hand cups my cheek. "I don't fucking like him."

"I know, and I'm not asking you to like him, but I'm asking you to at least trust me. Do you trust me?"

He nods. "I just don't trust him."

"You don't need to trust him. You just need to trust me."

His thumb passes over my cheek. "He wants you."

"And I want you, so him wanting me means nothing."

"Are you sure?" he asks, his voice more insecure than anything I've heard from him before. "You two have more in common, more history."

"Are you trying to make a case for me to be with him?" I press my palm into his chest.

"No, but I don't want you to regret this when someone clearly wants to make a case for himself to be the man at your side. A man who, I hate to fucking admit, you have so much more in common with."

"And that's what makes him a good friend," I say. "What I see in him and what I see in you is so different. Yes, I might have history with Hank, and we might be able to talk to each other about flamingos until we're blue in the face, but that's the extent of it. With you, it's different. Because we don't have things in common, it pushes us out of our comfort zones to learn new things. And what I do know about you, I like." I pat his chest. "I like your heart, I like your loyalty, I like…" I smile. "Your cock."

That makes him smile as well, the last of the tension finally extinguishing. "So this isn't just a PR thing for you?"

I shake my head. "I think after the first thirst trap you sent, this was never going to end up being just a PR thing."

The corner of his lips tilts up. "Still unsure why I sent that."

"Yeah, right." I roll my eyes. "You knew exactly what you were doing."

"Really, I didn't. That's not me. Never sent one before."

"You've never sent a thirst trap before me? I find that hard to believe."

"Believe it," he answers, his hand dragging the back of my shirt up even higher.

"Okay, and I might not like the answer to this, but then how would you contact your lady lovers to come over and play with your willy?"

"There are so many things wrong with that question."

I chuckle. "Just answer me."

With a growl, he bends and scoops me over his shoulder, causing a gasp to pop out of my mouth as he brings me back to the bedroom and deposits me on the bed, flinging me down. I stare up at him as he crawls on the bed, hovering over me and dragging my shirt up and over my head, leaving me completely naked.

He takes my knees and spreads them, then pushes them down on the mattress, leaving me exposed and turned on all at the same time.

Wetting his lips, he leans close to my face and says, "I would text them."

My breath hitches in my chest as he brings his mouth to my jaw, then down my neck, his scruff scraping against my skin, only for his lips to soothe the tender spots with kisses. "What would you say?"

His mouth skims across my skin, up to just below my ear, causing a wave of goose bumps to spread across my skin just before he says, "Let's fuck."

Oh God.

His hands trail over my breasts as he moves down my chest with his mouth to my stomach, then right above my pubic bone, where he swirls his tongue, teasing me.

"So...do you want to?" he asks.

"Do...do I want to...what?" I ask, my arousal thrumming with anticipation, my nipples harder than stone as he plays with them, and the heat in my body blistering into an inferno.

"Fuck," he answers.

"Yes," I whisper just before he kisses his way down my slit. "Graydon," I groan as he spreads me and his tongue presses against my clit.

"Shit," he grumbles. "You taste fucking amazing."

Heat swarms me as I gain the courage to spread my legs even wider. One of his hands continues to play with my breast while the other moves between my legs and spreads me for his tongue.

I sink into the mattress as pure euphoria fills me, Graydon knowing exactly what to do and how to do it. His tongue drags slowly over my clit, driving up my need for him with every stroke.

My hands fall to his head, where I play with the short strands of his hair, my fingers pressing into his scalp, creating a moan, which vibrates against me. It's such a delicious feeling that I moan as well.

"Graydon, more."

But he doesn't listen. Instead he continues the slow, laborious torture of dragging his tongue over my clit, pulling the focus of my body's nerve endings to one point, but never really getting me where I need to be.

And when he pulls away and starts kissing my inner thighs, I want to scream.

"No, Graydon, please."

I can practically feel his smile against my leg as he kisses up my abdomen, bypassing my clit and moving up my taut stomach to my breasts, where he starts feasting on them, sucking them into his mouth, lapping at my nipples, driving me mad with need.

A prickling sensation bolts through me as he shifts beneath me so I can feel how hard he is.

Wanting to urge him on, I reach between us, press my hand into his boxer briefs, and take his length into my palm. He groans against me but doesn't stop, so I use my feet to help me push his boxer briefs down until he's completely naked with me. I thrust up into him, trying to feel much-needed friction, but he pulls away from me, making it impossible to get what I need to fall over the edge.

"Graydon," I complain, driving my hands into his hair and trying to lift him up to look me in the eyes. When he gives in to my tug, his eyes are heady, and the expression on his face is downright sinful.

"Problem?"

"You're edging me."

"And you have a problem with that?"

"I want you to make me come."

He smirks, then leans in close and kisses me, his mouth parting and his tongue darting out, wrapping around mine for a few seconds before he pulls away and drags it down my body, past my breasts, over my stomach again, and straight between my legs, where he spreads me one more time. Instead of long, flat strokes, he flicks his tongue this time, hard and fast against my clit while keeping my legs spread.

"Oh fuck," I say, my chest rising as I move up to my elbows, staring down at what he's doing. "Oh my God, right there, Graydon. Please don't…oh God, please don't stop."

But with those words uttered, he pauses his strokes, then lays a gentle kiss against my clit before moving to my legs, across my thighs, up my stomach, sucking, nipping, kissing, doing everything in his power to make me crazy.

"Graydon, stop. Please, I need…I need to come," I pant, my chest rising and falling, the spot between my legs throbbing uncontrollably.

"You'll come when I'm ready," he says before sitting up on his knees and gripping his cock. His large hand starts pumping over his incredible length while I lie here, unable to do anything but stare at him, at the way he not only commands me but commands his own body.

The finely honed muscles flex across his chest, abdomen, and arms.

The tension in his neck.

The sinful stare he has in his eyes, which are transfixed on me.

It makes me so incredibly hot, so incredibly on edge, that I know the minute he lets me come, I'll lose all semblance of control.

Lowering, he brings the tip of his cock to my pussy and gently runs it along my slit.

"Jesus," I say as I squirm, looking for more friction, but he doesn't give it to me. He just keeps edging and edging.

He lets me pulse and throb, every bitter, beautiful feeling inside me pulling to the center of my body, where they swirl and swirl, waiting to be released.

"Graydon, fuck...please."

The sexiest smirk pulls at his lips before he leans down between my legs again, hooks them over his wide shoulders, and presses his tongue to my clit, where he flicks rapidly again.

Harder.

Faster.

I'm so overwhelmed, I forget to breathe as my body climbs and climbs.

Higher and higher.

Every muscle tensing.

My legs numbing.

My stomach hollowing as my clit throbs against his tongue, pushing me so fucking close.

So close.

And when he lifts up again, I scream.

"Graydon, stop. Please make me come. Please let me."

Satisfied with my begging, he brings his mouth back down again and sucks my clit between his lips. In seconds, he has me sweating, panting, and, with one final suck, falling over the edge and straight into white-hot bliss as my orgasm rockets through me.

"Fuck, fuck!" I scream, my chest convulsing, my pussy contracting, everything in me feeling the onslaught of what he just did to me.

He lets me ride out my orgasm on his tongue until I'm completely sated.

That's when he moves away, and I can hear him breaking into the condoms. He tosses one on the bed while I take a few seconds to catch my breath because I know he's about to rattle my world again. He lies on the bed, and then I hear, "Come here, beautiful."

I part my eyes open, and feeling weak and spent, I climb up his body, straddle him, and then lean my chest against his as I rest my head on his shoulder.

"Give me…a second."

He chuckles and drags the tips of his fingers over my back as he slowly pumps his length with his other hand.

I push his hand away and grip his cock myself, pulling on his length slowly, attempting to give him the same torture, knowing I'll never match it. Ever. But I can at least try.

As I continue to pump, my strength starts to come back and I sit up to find him with his eyes closed, enjoying my hand. It's such a hot thing to witness, that I can control his pleasure like this.

I move on top of him, straddling his legs, and then I lower myself down so my mouth is a whisper from his cock.

He lazily looks at me and runs his teeth over his bottom lip while his gaze roams over me, promises held in his expression, promises of control but also a hint of submission as he lets me take over and tease him.

I lower down some more, sucking the tip of his cock past my lips while I grip the base, squeezing tightly while I swirl my tongue around the head, soaking up the saltiness of his precum and loving every second of it.

He sighs heavily, his chest now rising and falling faster as I tease him, tempt him, try to torture him the way that he did to me, but the only indication that I'm repaying the favor is the slight flex in his legs and the rise and fall of his chest.

I decide to push him further and bring him deeper into my mouth, all the way to the back of my throat, where I swallow.

"Jesus," he whispers.

So I do it again.

And again.

And every time I pull off, I let my teeth drag over his length. When I lower down, I suck as hard as I can until he hits the back of my throat.

"Fuck," he says, his body shifting, his energy buzzing now.

I glance up at him, and he has his bulky arm draped over his eyes, his hand curling into my hair while he lets out a hiss as I suck him into my mouth one more time.

"Maple...fucking amazing. Too damn good."

The compliment spurs me on, and I pump harder on his length, bringing my attention back to the tip of his cock, where I flick my tongue against the sensitive spot under the tip, loving how he reacts with a slight twist of his body and his fingers tangling in my hair.

"Fuck yes, beautiful," he breathes. My heart's pounding in my chest, my body thrumming with the chance of pleasure all over again. "Don't make me come, though. Edge me."

Why on earth would he want that?

It doesn't matter. He asked for it, so I'll give him what he wants.

I spend what feels like the next minute or two gagging on his cock, pumping it hard, sucking, and then flicking my tongue over every inch until he's panting and pulling me away.

He hands me the condom he pulled from the box and, in a sexy-as-sin voice, says, "Put it on."

I wet my lips and undo the wrapper before sliding the condom down his length, causing him to hiss when my fingers trail over his balls.

"I want you riding me," he says. "Are you wet?"

I pull on my lip and nod.

"Let me see." He moves his fingers between my legs and feels exactly how much turning him on turned me on. "Fuck, you're so goddamn perfect."

Then, to my surprise, his abs flex right before he picks me up and turns me around so I'm facing away from him. I'm about to protest, but he spanks my ass so hard that I cry out before he soothes his hand over the spot.

"Oh my God, Graydon." A rush of arousal swarms over me. My stomach hollows from the pleasure of his dominance.

"Lift up," he demands.

I lift on my knees, and he positions his length at my entrance before gripping my hips and bringing me down on top of him. I cry out as he fills me, bottoming out and not leaving an ounce of room inside me.

"Fuck," I whisper as my hands fall to his shins.

But he doesn't give me much time to adjust as he spanks me again and then thrusts up when I contract around him from the contact of his hand.

"That's it, beautiful," he encourages. "Let me feel that tight pussy."

I grind my teeth together as he slaps my ass again and again, thrusting up every freaking time, creating a deathly dangerous friction that's building fast in the pit of my stomach.

"I'm already too close," I say, embarrassment washing over me.

"Me...too..." he grunts as he spanks me again, and I convulse over his cock.

"Fuck, I'm sorry." My body betrays me; it's all too much. Between how thick he is, the friction of my clit against him, and the spanking, it's sending me, and with one more slap of his hand to my ass, I call out his name. My orgasm takes me into another realm while I ride him hard, my hips flying up and down over his length, taking everything I can to hold on to this perfect, addictive feeling.

"Jesus Christ," Graydon says as he pumps harder and harder until he lets out a long, sexy moan. "Fuck...me." He stills, and then he comes, his fingers digging into my hips and his cursing biting into the air as he fights to gain control of his body.

After a few seconds, I lift off him, and I'm about to go to the bathroom when he tugs my hand and brings me on top of his body, where he gently kisses my forehead.

"You okay?" He strokes my back again. My eyes are growing heavy from how late it is and the exhaustion of pleasuring each other.

"Perfect," I answer as I snuggle in close. "What about you?"

He kisses the top of my head and quietly says, "Honestly, I can't remember the last time I was this happy."

I smile against his chest and allow myself to be in this moment. To feel our sweat-soaked skin pressed together, to listen to the beat of his heart against my ear. And to revel in the fact that something so surprising, so perfect, so overwhelmingly special came from a PR stunt.

I never expected anything like this when I first met Graydon, but now that I'm here, in his arms, I never want this to end.

# CHAPTER 32
# GRAYDON

"YOU TOUCH HER AND YOU fucking die, got it?" I say, helmet off, staring down each and every one of my teammates, murder pulsing through my veins.

It was Keenan's idea to have Maple do a run route and try to score a touchdown. I said absolutely not, but Keenan wasn't letting up, especially when Gretchen got into the mix.

My teammates, on both offense and defense, all nod and break the huddle before taking their positions, leaving me with just Maple, who looks so goddamn tiny in her gear.

"Don't you think that was a little much?" she asks as she adjusts her helmet on her head, attempting to look up at me but struggling with the weight of it.

"No."

Gretchen is off to the side, phone in her hand, snapping pictures. She's pretty much frothing at the mouth from the amount of attention we've been getting from the media lately. Not that I've been paying attention too much, but according to my agent, my jersey sales have spiked, my followers on my social media account that I have and don't pay attention to have grown, and more and more tickets have been sold for upcoming games.

I just can't fathom how a relationship, fake or not, could garner so much support for the Foghorns.

"You know I can handle myself, right?" Maple asks, playing her defiant side once again.

Leaning in close, I say, "Trust me when I say these men could take you out with just their pinky finger. They're not to fucking touch you. If they do, they answer to me."

"If I wasn't so irritated with this macho-man attitude, I might allow myself to be slightly turned on from your possessiveness. But your protective instincts are irritating me this morning."

My brows shoot up in surprise. "Irritating you?"

"Uh, yeah. Just because we..." She leans in closer and whispers, "Fucked last night—"

"And this morning." Don't want her to forget about this morning.

And she apparently doesn't, as her cheeks redden under the shadow of her helmet. "Just because we did those things doesn't mean you can threaten other men."

"From the way you were screaming my name while I was nine inches deep inside you, yeah, beautiful, it gives me all the goddamn right."

Her mouth parts in shock, but I don't let her counter with her snark.

"Do you remember the stiff arm I taught you?"

"Of course," she says on a huff.

"Show me."

She rolls her eyes but then sticks out her noodle arm and presses her palm to my chest.

"Good. Now use that if anyone even comes near you."

"What if you come near me?" she asks.

"I'm not dumb enough to mess with the likes of you."

That puts a stunning smile on her face as her chest puffs with pride. "Glad you see it that way."

With that, she heads off to her position behind the quarterback, and I shake my head in mirth as I line up as well.

The ball is hiked, and the team barely moves as the ball is pitched to Maple and she catches it.

Rather than cradling the ball like any other running back, though, she holds it out in front of her as if it's a bomb ready to explode, and she high-knees it toward the right-hand side of the field, screaming bloody murder.

Jesus Christ.

This coming from the woman who was annoyed by my protective instincts just seconds ago.

The field stops, besides one rookie who looks like he wants to prove himself as he chases after her, tucking his shoulder, looking for a hit.

That motherfucker.

I run in his direction, ready to bury his head in the grass, when Maple looks to her side, spotting him.

She lets out a feral scream, a scream so loud I am surprised I heard it because it felt like a pitch only dogs could hear, and she starts running at the guy who is running at her.

What the hell is she doing?

Everyone on the field stops while we all watch in horror as Maple lifts her foot in the air and presses the bottom of her sneaker right into the rookie's junk.

"Hi-ya!" she yells, connecting her foot solidly to his dick, crumpling the rookie over in an instant. When he's on the ground, writhing, she says, "That's what I call Maple's stiff leg, but to you, it's just Daddy." Then she jogs toward the end zone, where she spikes the ball and starts turning and jumping with her nonbraced hand above her head.

Jesus.

Christ.

My teammates pick her up and place her on their shoulders as they parade her around while I just stand in my spot, glancing at the rookie and then back at her. Gretchen takes pictures like crazy. Maple removes her helmet and lifts it above her head like she's fucking Rudy while they all cheer for her.

Even the people on the sidelines.

The media.

The onlookers.

The staff.

When they put her back on the ground, she jogs over to me, a huge smile on her face.

Tapping my chest, she says, "I match your stiff arm with my stiff leg." She winks. "Told you I could take care of myself."

Yeah, apparently.

I spare the rookie one more look as he continues to lie curled up on the ground. Serves the fuck right.

I drape my arm over Maple and pull her in close, kissing her on top of her head. "Proud of you, beautiful."

"Are you?"

I nod. "Yeah, really proud because if you didn't stiff-leg that rookie, my foot would have found his ass if he even touched a finger to you."

"Good thing I can take care of myself."

"Yeah, good thing."

---

OC: So are we going to get an update? From what I gathered online and through social media, it seems like you two are getting along swimmingly, but then again, it could be all show because I can't fathom a time when the Gladdy Daddies would help you and you wouldn't update us.

I stare down at the text from OC, slightly wincing, because, yeah, I didn't update them. I was kind of busy.

Well, really busy.

Too busy to be bothered with simple gossip.

"You look different," Hutton says as he takes a seat next to me at my locker.

I lean back in my chair and rest my phone on my lap. "Yeah, in what way?"

He studies me for a moment, making a show of really observing me. I'm about to swat him away when he says, "Less…growly."

"Is that the technical term?"

He smirks. "I think it is." Then he pushes at my shoulder. "Seriously, man. What's going on?"

I shrug and grab a pair of socks from my locker. I'm going to need to replenish my spare clothes since I'm using them up today after staying the night with Maple. "Nothing is going on."

"You're such a goddamn liar. I saw the way you were eyeing that rookie. You were about to murder him for even chasing Maple down."

"That immature nimrod doesn't know how to listen. I said don't fucking touch her. He's lucky Maple was the one who took him down and not me."

"Is he lucky, though? He had to be carted off the field."

"Am I supposed to feel bad for him?"

"Maybe a little."

I shake my head. "I don't."

"Okay, what about after the play, when the guys were celebrating with Maple, and you were just standing off to the side with heart eyes, watching her the whole time?"

"I didn't have heart eyes."

"Dude, the cameras all around the field were snapping shots of you looking at her. I'll be shocked if there aren't memes already out there that say something like 'Find a person who looks at you the way Graydon looks at Maple.' Hashtag Flock and Tackle."

I roll my eyes. "Seriously, man, you're—"

Hutton presses his hand to my chest, pausing me and looking me dead in the eyes. "Just fucking tell me."

He knows me too well at this point not to see when I'm about to bullshit my way out of a conversation.

I sigh and lean in closer, closing off the conversation to just us. "I spent the night with her last night and basically confessed my feelings."

"Jesus," he whispers. "Does she feel the same way?"

The lightest of smiles tugs on the corner of my lips, and I'm unable to hold it back. "She does."

"Wow." Hutton smirks. "So what does this mean?"

I shrug. "I guess I'm in a relationship."

"Well, fuck." He tugs on the short strands of his hair. "Never thought you would say those words. Honestly thought you were just going to be alone forever."

"Same." I drag my hand over my face and stare down at the ground, still in disbelief. "She's different." Then I look up at him, concern filling me. "I just worry about how this is going to play out."

"What do you mean?"

"The whole public thing. I know we are already public, but the more steam this picks up and the more we are seen in the public eye, being affectionate, intimate, the more people are going to have an opinion. You know, you went through it with Scarlett."

"Still go through it," he answers. "And that's just something you'll have to navigate together. It's not easy, but as long as you two stick together, it will be okay."

"Yeah, I don't know," I say, leaning back in my chair and taking my phone in my hand as it buzzes with another text. "I want to say she's strong enough to handle it. I know she claims she is, but I don't know if she understands the severity of being under the microscope."

"I think you need to trust her on the fact that she knows what she's getting into. Give her the benefit of the doubt, man." Hutton stands and pats me on the back. "Happy for you. Carve out some time for a double date. I want to get to know her better."

I nod, then look down at my phone, where there's a text from Bennett and one from Maple.

I click on the one from Maple first.

It's a picture of her hefted up on my teammates' shoulders, the biggest smile on her face, her helmet thrust in the air. I immediately save the picture, because Jesus, she's fucking adorable in it.

**Maple:** Look at me winning the big game.

I snort and shake my head as I text her back.

**Graydon:** You look good.

The rookie hobbles back into the locker room, ice held to his crotch. I'm not sure how hard Maple hit him, but I will say he's lucky it was her and not me because he wouldn't be walking if I took care of him.

**Maple:** I've never felt so invigorated. I showed Big Hermy the picture, and he didn't seem as impressed.
**Graydon:** Did you show it to his good eye?
**Maple:** Of course. Do you take me for a fool?
**Graydon:** Never.
**Maple:** I feel kind of bad for stiff-legging that one guy. Is he okay?
**Graydon:** Don't feel bad, he deserved it. He just walked back into the locker room with an ice pack pressed against his dick.
**Maple:** Oof, really? Now I really feel bad.
**Graydon:** Don't. Be happy it was you who did it, not me.
**Maple:** So possessive.
**Graydon:** Only where you're concerned.

**Maple:** Oddly, I find that very appealing.

**Graydon:** Oddly?

**Maple:** I've been taught to take care of myself, so having someone like you wanting to do that for me feels unnatural. But...I don't know...I kind of like it. And I kind of like you.

**Graydon:** Kind of?

**Maple:** Can't give away all my cards too quickly.

**Graydon:** Pretty sure you gave them away the moment I buried myself between your legs.

**Maple:** OMG Graydon. Don't make me blush at work.

**Graydon:** I can say a hell of a lot more.

**Maple:** Don't. People will know I'm turned on.

**Graydon:** That doesn't seem like a bad thing to me. Let people know.

**Maple:** What is wrong with you? I will not be turned on around the flamingos.

**Graydon:** And here I thought they were your friends and they didn't judge.

**Maple:** You're reading them wrong. They're extremely judgmental.

**Graydon:** Maybe I need to spend more time around them then, stop washing their dishes all the time.

**Maple:** But you're so good at it. 😊

**Graydon:** Pretty sure I'm average, and you just don't want to do it yourself.

**Maple:** That's neither here nor there. Anyway, will I see you later?

**Graydon:** Plan on picking you up and taking you out.

**Maple:** Oh? Really? To where?

**Graydon:** That's for me to figure out.

**Maple:** Okay, well, I look forward to it. I have to get to medications. I'll see you later.

**Graydon:** See you later, beautiful.

I set my phone down and pull on my shoes before sticking my dirty laundry on my laundry line, grabbing my bag, and then heading out, phone in hand.

I dump my laundry into the laundry bin and then open up the text from Bennett in the thread with OC.

**Bennett:** I don't want to be nearly as annoying as OC, but yeah, an update might be good.

Shaking my head, I glance at the time and then text back.

**Graydon:** Meet me at Roads in an hour.

**OC:** You act like I don't have a life and can just drop everything to meet you.

**Graydon:** Don't bullshit, you don't have a life.

**OC:** Uh, I'm training.

**Graydon:** Then don't come. It's fine. I'll just meet with Bennett.

**Bennett:** I'll be there. Day off means I'm rotting and doing nothing.

**Graydon:** Great, see you in an hour.

**OC:** Wait…I'm coming too.

**Graydon:** I thought you had a life.

**OC:** You know I just put up a front. Don't exclude me. The Gladdy Daddies are all I have going for me right now that brings me joy.

**Graydon:** You're pathetic.

**OC:** Well aware.

# CHAPTER 33
# GRAYDON

I BRING MY COFFEE TO the back corner of Roads where I like to sit and take the seat that's up against the wall so I can watch people walk in.

I grabbed an egg burrito with chorizo and beans as well, my stomach growling from the workout and the lack of food I consumed because I was busy last night…consuming Maple.

The door opens and Bennett walks in, spotting me immediately. He nods his head in my direction and then goes to the counter, just as OC walks in as well, looking disheveled. He's wearing a pair of royal blue sweatpants, one of the pants legs pulled up, the other cinched around his ankle. His shirt is stained with what looks like pizza sauce, and his hair is sticking out in every direction.

Jesus…

One hundred dollars says he didn't even shower yet.

I watch him tap Bennett on the shoulder, and when Bennett turns around, OC claps him in a hug, burying his head against Bennett's shoulder and clinging to him like he's a lifeline.

Okay, all I can say is he's lucky he's doing that to Bennett and not me because there's no way in fuck I would be as giving as Bennett is being right now.

Why do I have a feeling this meetup is going to quickly turn in a different direction?

They grab their orders, Bennett coming over with a coffee and OC holding a bottle of cranberry juice and…Jesus, five blueberry crumble muffins.

"Hey," OC says as he takes a seat and sets his plate down.

I eye the muffins the size of my fist and then look up at him. "Uh…hey."

Without even removing the muffin wrapper, OC picks one up from the plate and takes a bite from the very center like a goddamn psychopath. Then, to my horror, he tilts his head back, bringing the muffin with him, and starts lapping up the center with his tongue.

What the actual fuck?

I glance at Bennett, who looks just as concerned.

"Uh, are you sharing those muffins?" Bennett asks.

OC snaps his head forward and his brows turn down. "No. If you want a muffin, get your own."

"Five muffins?" I ask in a judgmental tone. "Not a good way to prepare for the season."

"Oh, fuck off, as if you've never eaten your feelings before." He takes another bite, burying his mouth in the center of the muffin, leaving the sides untouched just like the wrapper.

Never in my life have I seen someone eat a muffin like that.

Bennett and I exchange glances before Bennett carefully says, "Do you want to talk about it?"

"No." OC sets a ring of a muffin back on his plate as he picks up another and buries his mouth in the middle again.

"Fuck, I can't watch you eat muffins like that. What the hell are you doing?" I ask.

"Practicing," he says. "I haven't eaten a muffin in a long goddamn time and I don't want to forget how to do it."

Bennett and I both pause—his drink halfway to his mouth and my burrito in my hands.

"Wait, what?" I ask.

"Dude, are you talking about eating a woman?" Bennett asks, the thought that was clearly on both of our minds.

OC's eyes look between us as he says, "Of course. What else would I be referring to?" Then he takes another bite, this time leading with his tongue.

Oh, fuck no.

He lowers the muffin just as I smack it out of his hand, sending it flying against the wall.

"Hey!" he yells. "What the hell?"

"You're not about to eat that goddamn muffin like you're eating a pussy in front of me. Have you lost your fucking mind?"

"Yeah, I'm with Graydon on this. Gross, dude."

OC turns to Bennett. "Hey, Young Buck, if you think eating pussy is gross, then you're going to have a hard time scoring that friend of your sister's."

Bennett's expression falls flat. "I don't think eating pussy is gross. I think it's gross that you're pretending the muffins you bought at a coffeehouse are pussy, and you're using your tongue to eat it out in front of us."

"It's the same thing."

"It's not." I shake my head.

He hefts a heavy sigh, then leans back in his chair. "Fine. I'll eat it normal."

"As if that's the biggest hardship you've ever encountered," I say.

"It is, because I like eating muffins. Both from the bakery and the ones between legs."

"Jesus," I mutter as I drag my hand over my face. "I knew this was going to be a mistake."

"Yeah, I felt it the moment I agreed to come," Bennett adds.

OC's eyes dart between us, a disgusted expression scrunching his nose. "I'm sorry, but are you expecting me to apologize for having feelings?"

"We're expecting you to act fucking normal, which is not what you're doing," I say.

"Ever wonder why?"

"I'm sure you'll inform us," Bennett replies.

"Not with that kind of nonempathetic attitude." He crosses his arms over his chest, and I'm seconds away from getting up and leaving. The only thing that is keeping me from doing that is the realization that he helped me when I needed some advice, so I can at least see whatever this is through.

"What's going on, man?" I ask, mentally preparing myself for whatever nonsense is about to come out of his mouth.

"I'm glad you asked," he says, slouching some more in his seat. Staring off at his half-mutilated muffin, he says, "There's a girl who I'm in love with and have been for a long time. Her name is Grace." Okay, so girl problems. At least it's not anything else...weird. Never know with this guy. "We have history, and when I was sent to the Agitators, she also got a job as an athletic trainer there. The boys and I were working on a plan to rekindle our love, but I was traded to the Rogue before we could put it into action."

"Ouch," Bennett says, looking more interested in this than the muffin eating.

"Yeah, well, I just found out that she is now dating someone, and it seems pretty serious. The guys told me."

"Shit," Bennett says. "I'm sorry, dude."

"Yeah, I'm sorry," I say because, in reality, that does suck, despite how annoying he is.

"Thanks." He lets out a sigh. "And I'm trying to decide if I just...go up there and tell her I love her and figure out a way to make this work, or if I, I don't know, move on because clearly she has moved on as well."

Bennett glances in my direction before he asks, "How happy is she?"

OC's lips press tightly together. "Pretty damn happy."

"Then maybe...let her just live her life," Bennett says. "Because isn't that what is most important, that she's happy?"

OC lets out a long, dragged-out breath. "Fuck. Yes, you're right, but what about my happiness?"

"To be fair," I say, "she lives far away, man. Did you really think it was going to work out?"

He shrugs and then twists one of the muffins on his plate, staring down at it. "I don't know. I thought it might work out." He sighs again and then sits back in his chair and crosses his arms. "I don't want to talk about it anymore, or I'll start tonguing the muffin again."

Jesus.

Why is that how he deals with his feelings?

"What happened with Maple?" he asks.

"Are you sure you want to talk about it?" I ask, because chances are, he's going to be jealous.

"Yeah, I do. Please tell me at least one of us is happy."

Bennett raises his hand. "I'm pretty happy."

We glance at him, a small smirk tugging on his lips.

"Why are you happy?" OC asks.

Bennett just shrugs. "You know, patience is paying off."

OC's brows shoot up. "The sister's friend?"

"Maybe, but I don't want to get into it because I don't want to jinx it."

"Understandable." OC turns back to me. "What's going on with you and Maple?"

I sip my drink, set it on the table, and then say, "I went to see her at her place and tell her how I felt, like we talked about, but she showed up with Slutty Little Glasses."

OC's mouth falls open. "No she fucking didn't."

"She did. He took her grocery shopping, which I fucking hated because my goddamn job is to take care of her."

"Please tell me you didn't dent his face," Bennett says.

I shake my head, then explain how it all went down, including my confession and her text telling me to come back. When I'm done reliving the moment of the kiss that nearly brought me to my knees, I look between them, a smirk pulling at my lips.

"Holy shit," OC says. "He's smiling."

"I see it," Bennett agrees. "Like, actually smiling."

OC sits a little taller. "Did you two…fuck?"

"Don't demean it like that," I say.

"Uh, do you want me to say, 'make love'?"

"'Copulate,' maybe?" Bennett suggests.

"We were…intimate," I say, not liking the sound of that either.

OC turns to Bennett and takes his hand in his. Wistfully, he says, "They were intimate."

"That's…sweet," Bennett adds.

"And from the way you're radiating with light and happiness, I'm going to assume it was the kind of night that you will remember for the rest of your life."

It was, but they don't need to know that.

"Don't make it weird," I say.

"Well…" OC crosses his ankle over his knee and loops his hands behind his head. "Looks like the Gladdy Daddies did their work."

Even though I hate to admit it, he's right, and given that he's having a weak moment, I decide to throw him a bone.

"You did."

His head whips around fast to meet my gaze. "Do you mean that?"

Jesus Christ.

"I do."

"Wow, I never expected you to make such an admission. I don't…I don't know what to do." He frantically looks around and then picks up one of his half-mutilated muffins. "Tongued muffin?"

I glance down at the muffin and then back at him before I swat the muffin out of his hand, shooting it against the wall once again.

His eyes land on the baked good smashed across the floor, and after a few seconds, he nods and says, "That's fair."

Fucking moron.

# CHAPTER 34
# MAPLE

VOICES OUTSIDE RISE, AND THERE seems to be a commotion as I finish logging some observations into the diaries we keep on each flamingo. The door opens, and Hank walks in, looking…tense.

"What's going on out there?" I ask as I shut the diary.

"Your *friend* arrived."

The emphasis on "friend" is laced with discontent.

"Do you mean Graydon?" I ask.

"Yeah. He's taking pics with some kids outside in front of the mural." Hank shakes his head. "He's making a spectacle of it all."

"Is he?" I ask, not believing that. I stand from my chair, push it in, and then lean against the counter where Hank is. "Or is he using his name to bring awareness?"

"Right now? A spectacle. No one is even looking at the flamingos. They're all worried about getting a picture with him."

"In front of the mural, though."

He shakes his head. "Never mind."

He starts to walk away, but I stop him by the arm. "He's not a bad guy, Hank."

"As you've told me before."

"So then why won't you give him a chance?"

"Because he's not good enough for you," Hank replies without even having to think about it. "You're better than that, Maple. You're better than this...this PR stunt that you two are attempting to pull off, and I can see you getting wrapped up in it."

"What PR stunt?" I ask, my breath coming out heavier, because how does he know?

"Please." He rolls his eyes. "Graydon isn't a guy you would go for unless you had some sort of ulterior motive. He's bringing awareness to your cause, and you're making him look better by letting him."

I mean...sure, that's how it started, but he's cheapening what we have, at least what I think we have. There's more to it than that. I feel a connection with Graydon, something driving me toward him as if I was meant to be brought into his life, not just to promote the Foghorns and flamingos, but because I'm the person who fills that empty space in his heart.

At least that's what it seems like.

"I can tell by your expression that you don't agree with me," Hank says and takes my hand. "Listen, Maple. I just don't want you to get hurt, okay? I've known you for a really long time, and I know the person you are. This spotlight thing, with him, it's not you—"

"Everything okay in here?" Graydon asks as he walks into the building, spotting me and Hank...holding hands.

I take my hand away and nod, putting on a smile. "Everything is good. Did you, uh, did you take pictures with some fans?"

Graydon looks between Hank and me, and I prepare for him to put Hank into a choke hold, but then his eyes settle on me again, ignoring Hank completely. "I did. A group of kids spotted me and made the most of it." He nods in my direction. "Ready to go?"

"Yeah, I'm ready."

He walks past Hank, and I'm surprised he doesn't bump into him, possibly elbow him in the nose, or all-out bite his ear off. Instead, Graydon remains decently calm, lifting up my hand and kissing my knuckles. "Let's go."

Okay, going the mature route; I can get on board with that.

Then he guides me away from Hank and helps me gather my things, and we head out of the building. His hand clamps around mine, and he keeps me close while we make our way out to his truck, where he opens the door for me like always and helps me in. But this time, instead of shutting the door and moving to his side, he stays put.

"You good?"

I nod. "Yeah, I'm fine." Why am I so nervous?

Maybe because I've seen him lose his mind over Hank, and him walking in on Hank holding my hand could have very well ended Hank's young life.

He studies me, those dark eyes eating me up. "Doesn't seem like you're fine. Seems like that dick back there said something to you."

"Graydon, it's nothing."

"It's fucking something if he's making your brow crease like that." He presses his thumb between my eyes, trying to get me to relax. "Talk to me."

Talk to him.

How easily he's willing to do that now—not that I'd chastise him, not even a little. I'm truly honored and fascinated that he has offered me such trust, that he's opened himself up to me and is not so guarded anymore. He's not just protective but also caring.

I turn toward him, and he moves between my legs and rests his hands on my sides as he leans in, ready to listen. I run my finger over his jaw as I tell him the truth.

"He was just saying things about our relationship and how it doesn't make sense. How you're not someone I would normally go for." His brow creases, but he continues to listen. "How he thinks it's just a PR stunt and I'm not someone looking for the spotlight."

"You're not, and that's not what you're doing."

"I know," I answer.

"Then why are you looking like what he said has some truth to it?"

"I don't know. I guess I didn't like what he said. I feel like there's more to us than what he claims, but then again, we don't know a lot about each other yet, and I don't know, I might be getting in my head or I might be jumping the gun, but I feel...connected—"

"We are connected," he says softly, then cups my cheek. "Trust me when I say, if I didn't feel that pull toward you, I never would have told you about my mom. I wouldn't have even pursued you. I don't take my decisions on the people I place in my life very lightly. I learned that quickly when even my own father turned his back on me." His thumb rubs my cheek. "Don't let other people make you feel a certain way about what we have going on. Remember what you told me? That you have your own mind and you don't let people sway you? Where did that girl go?"

"Momentarily taking a break."

"She can't." He shakes his head. "You have to stay strong for me, Maple, because the dickhead saying that to you, that's just a drop in the goddamn bucket. I don't want to scare you, but it can get way worse, and it will get way worse."

"You're right." I place my hands on his shoulders. "I'm sorry. I shouldn't have let him get to me."

"You're human, beautiful, it's going to happen, but just keep talking to me about it, and don't hold it in, okay?"

"Okay."

"Now..." He moves in closer. "Pretty sure you owe me something."

I smirk and lean forward, wrapping my arms around his neck. One of my hands shifts into his styled hair as I brush my lips against his. "Is this what you're talking about?"

"Yeah."

I allow myself the moment to sink into this man, let our mouths get lost in each other as our lips part and I kiss him.

I kiss him like no one is watching.

I kiss him with such demand that I can feel the lust I have for him blossom and sprint all throughout my veins.

He grunts against me, his grip on me tightening. I could stay like this forever, just blocking out the world around us and letting myself feel him. Join him in a world where there is no reality, no one is watching, and it's just me and him and this infatuation that keeps growing between us.

"Fuck," he says as he pulls away, his heady eyes staring me down. "You can't...Jesus, you can't kiss me like that in public."

"Why not?" I ask as my fingers sift through his hair.

"Because I was seconds away from tearing your shirt off. And this body"—his hands smooth over my sides—"it's only meant for my eyes."

"Oh, is that so?"

"Yeah, it fucking is."

"And what about yours?" I ask. "It seems as though your body is up for grabs all over the internet."

"That means nothing."

"People still get to see you. Maybe I'll pose in a bikini for some zookeeper calendar."

"The fuck you will."

I chuckle. "You are far too possessive."

"Only where you're concerned."

He kisses me one more time and then turns me in my seat.

"Can we stop by my place before our date?" I ask. "I really want to take a shower before we go out and change into something that's not my work outfit. I promise I'll be quick."

"Sure, but I can't promise I'll stay out of the shower."

I point my finger at him. "No, you are not allowed in."

"Okay." He rolls his eyes as if he doesn't believe me.

He better believe me, because I have no intention of letting him in that bathroom.

---

"Stop pouting," I say, poking Graydon's arm as he drives through the streets of San Francisco.

"I'm not pouting."

"Yes, you are. You're pouting because I locked you out of the bathroom."

"Because you were naked and wet, and you didn't let me play."

I chuckle because this big, bad man with the energy of a dragon and the expression of a villain looks like a hurt puppy who just got their toy taken away.

"Because I wanted to go on a date with you, and if I let you play, we wouldn't be out right now."

"You underestimate me."

"No, I estimate you appropriately. I know how long it will take you to make me come. You like to torture me."

The corner of his lip tilts up.

"See?" I point at his mouth. "You even know it."

"I would have been quick."

"Liar."

He lightly chuckles and then places his hand on my thigh, the feel of his warm palm against my skin sending my pulse racing with promises of what's to come tonight.

This intense connection I feel with Graydon is completely different from anything I've felt before. With Hardy, there was comfort there, the kind of comfort I've come to find as friendship. It took me a while to figure that out, but now that I look back at it, I see it. We were together for a long time, but examining that relationship now, it was almost like we were really good friends…with benefits. The love, the lust, the palpable need I feel with Graydon was not there.

And when I was in Peru, around Hank all the time, yes, I had a crush.

I thought about him often. Even after I came back to the States, a piece of me felt like I left something behind in Peru. But being around Hank now, it feels like that piece I left behind was friendship again. Because when Graydon is around, it feels like everything and everyone else fades to black, and he's what is helping me pump air into my lungs.

I want his attention on me.

I want him touching me, keeping me close.

And it did not start out that way. It did not start with friendship. It started with pure hatred, but that hatred built into so much more…yearning.

The "friend" label is something I would never slap on Graydon because if this thing between us ever ended, I know I wouldn't be able to be around him afterward. Especially if he started dating someone else. I'd be gutted.

Devastated.

I wouldn't want to continue some sort of friendship. No, it would have to be a clean break, never to see him again, never watch a Foghorns game, never once look at social media out of fear of seeing his handsomely carved face.

I wouldn't be able to sustain any contact with him.

And that right there is the difference.

I place my hand on top of his as he navigates the roads, and ask, "So when do games start?"

"We have preseason games next week, and then the season starts."

"Really?" I ask. "Wow, that's quicker than I expected."

"Training camp can't go on for that long. We would be dead by the time the season starts."

"What are you talking about? Training camp is not that hard."

He side-eyes me, making me chuckle. "Says the girl who cut her eye open just from putting her helmet on."

"Excuse me for being inexperienced with helmets."

"Beautiful, it's putting something on your head. It doesn't take experience."

"I beg to differ."

He chuckles and squeezes my thigh as we pull up to the pier and right into a private parking spot.

When he puts the car in park, I glance over at him with a question in my brow. "What do you have planned, mister?"

He winks, and I nearly melt right there on his truck seat as he says, "You'll see."

With that, he gets out of the truck and moves around to my side, where he opens the door and helps me out. I chose a simple pair of white jean shorts, brown strappy sandals, and a navy blue off-the-shoulder sweater. I didn't want to get too dressed up, given what he was wearing, but I also wanted to look nice for our first official date. I kept my hair in a high ponytail, but redid it just to fluff it a little bit more.

Good thing I kept it in a ponytail because it seems like we're going to be going out to sea.

He takes my hand in his and guides me out to the docks, where a decently sized yacht—nothing too obnoxious—is floating, three crew workers wearing white shirts and shorts waiting for us.

"Graydon, what is all of this?"

"A private evening," he answers just as one of the crew members, wearing a hat, steps up.

"Good evening, Mr. St. John, Miss Baker. I'm Captain Rodger. We are very excited to have you join us this evening."

Graydon shakes his hand firmly. "Thank you for making accommodations for us."

"Of course. Let me introduce my crew to you." He gestures to a man next to him. "This is Lionel, my first mate. And next to him is Sam. He will be taking care of all your needs tonight. Please do not hesitate to ask him for anything."

Graydon nods toward them, and I wave while I lean into Graydon.

"Shall we get you on board?" Captain Rodger asks.

"That would be great," Graydon says.

Captain Rodger leads us onto the boat and gives us a brief tour. It's really not a big yacht at all, which I like. Anything too big would have been obnoxious. There is a back sitting area where I can foresee spending most of the night, an indoor dining space if it gets cold or rains, and the front of the boat, also known as the bow—just learned that—has space to lie down but it feels more exposed to me. I'd rather sit in the back.

"Get comfortable. We will bring out drinks soon."

Graydon thanks the crew and then turns toward me. "Where do you want to sit?"

"Can we sit in the back?" I ask.

"Don't you mean 'stern'?"

I roll my eyes. "Whatever. It just feels more private back there."

"I agree." He lifts my knuckles to his lips and kisses them softly before walking me out to the back of the boat where there is bench seating, a table, and two chairs that face out toward the ocean. I choose one of those to sit in.

"What are you doing?" he asks, staring down at me while I get comfortable in my chair.

I look around as if I'm missing something and then say, "Uh, sitting down."

"Yeah, in a chair."

"Isn't that what they're made for?"

"You need to sit on the bench."

I glance at the bench and back at him. "But then I have a view of the boat when I want a view of the ocean."

"But with you sitting on the chair, I can't hold you like I want. On the bench, you can sit in my lap."

I chuckle. "Umm, didn't know you were so needy."

"Not needy, that's just how I fucking like it."

I nod. "Okay, I hear you, but how about this? We sit in the chairs for a little bit and then we can move to the bench, but only if we sit in the corner so we have a view of the ocean too."

He seems to mull that over for a moment before grumbling under his breath and taking a seat in the chair next to mine.

"Let me know how you really feel," I say on a laugh.

"Unpleased." Then he scoots his chair as close to mine as it will go and places his hand on my thigh.

"Are you…throwing a tantrum?"

He stares out toward the dock. "No."

I chuckle and lean in toward him. "Oh my God, you are." I run my finger over his chest and then up to his jaw, where I turn his head so he's looking at me.

"You are so throwing a tantrum."

"Throwing a tantrum would be me lifting you out of that chair and chucking it across the bay before pulling you down on my lap. Now, if you would like to see that, I would be more than happy to oblige you."

"As tempting as that is, I think we should keep all chairs on the boat."

"I can chuck it and keep it on the boat too."

I chuckle. "Not necessary." I turn toward him and lean in close as the boat starts up and we pull away from the dock. "Is this what I'm going to have to get used to? You needing to be close as much as possible?"

"Yes," he answers.

"Just like that. Just a yes."

He nods. "You have a problem with that?"

"No, you just don't seem like the type of guy who needs to be touching his girl at all times."

"I wasn't…until you."

Well, if that doesn't make my cheeks blush…

And my body heat.

I was right about how different this relationship is compared with every other one I've had.

"Your cheeks are flushed," he says, turning toward me as well and cupping my face.

"That's what happens when you say things like that."

"It also happens when I'm buried between your legs."

My face heats up even more from the brazen comment.

"Graydon." I chuckle.

"What?" He looks at me as if genuinely curious and unsure why I just said his name.

"You can't say things like that in public."

"Sure as hell can."

I laugh. "God, do you ever care what anyone thinks about you?"

"The answer would be no unless it has something to do with my mom and my family...well, and now you."

"I thought we weren't supposed to care what people think about us."

"We aren't, but that doesn't mean I'm not going to get pissed about it when someone tries to fuck with us."

"But people love us."

"For now," he says. "The true trolls haven't sunk their teeth into our situation yet. Trust me, everyone will have an opinion, and the internet will make it easy for those opinions to be voiced."

"Then we just stay off the internet."

"Solid plan." He takes my hand in his and links our fingers together. "By the way, I was thinking about our upcoming games and was hoping that you would be at the first one. Not just because of our PR thing we got going on." He looks me in the eyes. "But as my girlfriend."

Oh God, why is he so adorable, asking like that?

The insecurity in his voice, the uncertainty in his eyes, as if I would say no.

"I would love to," I answer. "I don't think I could miss it. Maybe I can even suit up for you." I wiggle my eyebrows, and he chuckles.

"Not happening, but if you happen to wear my name on your back, I wouldn't mind that."

"Like a jersey?"

"Yeah, a jersey. I can grab one for you. One that actually fits."

"I would love that. Should I put your number on my cheeks too? Paint it on there? Oh wait, is that what the other girlfriends do?" I wince. "Oh God, I'm not going to fit in with them, am I? Aren't they all fancy with how they dress?" I glance down at my simple outfit and think about how Gretchen had to find me a dress for one of the fundraising events. "I might need to style—"

"You don't need to do anything."

"Graydon. Not that I'm full of myself, but you know people will be looking at me and taking pictures. I don't want to embarrass you."

His brow creases. "You're not going to embarrass me."

"Maybe I should at least get my nails done or something. I don't really like fake nails, though, because of what I have to do for work—"

"Hey." He grips my jaw, forcing me to look him in the eyes. "Don't change a goddamn thing. I like you the way you are. I don't want you to be like the other wives and girlfriends. If I wanted you to be like them, I would have dated the girls who flung themselves at me a while ago. I like you because you're different, because you don't care about things like nails and makeup. I like you for your heart, for your smile, for the way you can so easily understand me without judgment. So I want that woman at my games. Got it?"

"Are you sure?"

"Positive. If she doesn't show up, I'm going to be pissed."

"Well, won't you being pissed only help you in the long run because then you're more likely to plow through more men?"

"Making me angry will get me in trouble."

"How so?"

"I've been known to lose my temper. And as much as it might seem so, we're not allowed to punch in football."

"Ah, I see. Well, we can't have you losing your temper because then I wouldn't be able to see you play."

"Exactly. So just show up as you, and I'll be sure to have Hutton introduce you to his wife, Scarlett. You can hang with her. She's cool."

"You'd do that?" I ask, leaning in closer and lightly pressing my lips across his.

He sighs and nods as his arm loops around me, his hand landing on my backside. "Yeah, beautiful, I'd do pretty much anything to make sure you're taken care of."

"Oh yeah?" I smirk. "Would you…become friends with Big Hermy and sit and let him come close to you?"

"How would that take care of you?" he asks.

"It would take care of my heart. My best guy…being friends with my other newly best guy."

"Not sure you can have two best guys."

"If you think for a second that I'll be giving up Big Hermy, then you are sorely mistaken. Never going to happen, so I think it'd be best if you come to grips with it now and understand that he will always be one of my best guys whether you like it or not."

"And if I don't like it?"

"Then it looks like me and that flamingo will be walking off into the sunset, hand in feathers."

His brows rise. "Wow, just going to ditch me like that?"

"Don't mess with my one true love."

His lips twist to the side. "I know this is going to sound really fucking ridiculous, but do you know how jealous that makes me feel?"

A laugh overtakes me that I can't seem to pull back because it is ridiculous, but I can also see it being so true.

"Do you really want to laugh at me?" he asks. "I have no problem throwing that chair of yours."

I cling to it, gripping the armrests. "Don't you dare."

"Don't tempt me." He gives me a pointed look, and I chuckle some more.

---

"I didn't know you liked tofu," I say as I fill my fork with more mango rice and a slice of tofu.

"I don't," he says, his body shivering after taking a bite.

"Wait, you don't?"

He shakes his head.

"Then why are you eating it?"

"Because I wasn't about to eat a huge slab of meat in front of you when I could choose something that would make you less uncomfortable."

I set my fork down in awe as I turn toward him. We are now out in the bay, far away from the city, so we can only hear the subtle sound of the waves lapping around us. The sun is setting, and it's one of the most beautiful nights I've ever experienced here in San Francisco, with the orange and pink hues hugging the sky.

"Graydon, you can eat meat in front of me. You have before."

"I wasn't dating you then."

"I understand that, but you can still eat meat in front of me. Don't torture yourself with something you don't like just because I don't eat meat."

"What am I going to do, gnaw at a dead carcass in front of you?" He shakes his head. "Doesn't feel right."

I place my hand on his forearm. "Well, you don't gnaw on dead carcasses, first of all, and second of all, that's really considerate, Graydon. Seriously. But please, I'll feel guilty if you stop eating meat just because of me. This is a personal choice, not something I push upon others."

"Are you sure?"

"Positive."

He lets out a sigh and leans back in his chair. "Thank fuck, because the texture of this tofu will live with me forever."

I chuckle. "Really? I think it's delicious."

He shakes his head. "Like curdled cheese."

"Oh my God, it so isn't."

"It is," he counters just as Sam walks up to our table.

"How is everything?"

Before Graydon can answer, I step in and say, "Do you happen to have any sort of real meat on board for Graydon? He tried to be sweet and eat the tofu for me, but he's not feeling it."

Sam smiles. "Of course. We have a few filets. Shall we cook one up for you?"

Graydon glances at me, and I nod. "Yeah, that would be great."

"How would you like it cooked?"

"Medium," he answers.

"Right away."

Sam takes off, and Graydon drapes his arm over my chair. "You didn't have to do that."

"Yeah, well, you didn't have to plan this entire night, and you did, so it's the least I can do." I lean over and kiss his cheek. "By the way, thank you for this. The best date I've ever been on, and not just because of the scenery, but because of the person I'm on the date with."

His brow cutely rises. "You flirting with me, beautiful?"

"I am. Is it charming you?"

He smirks. "I think it is."

"From the way your lips are tilting up—a very unusual thing for you—I would say it is."

"Seems like you're the only one who knows how to make me smile."

"That can't be true. What about OC and Bennett? Don't you joke around with them?"

Graydon lets out a long sigh. "Don't get me started on those two fools."

"Wait, what?"

"Don't get me wrong, they're nice, but Jesus Christ, I met them for some coffee, and OC purchased five muffins and stuck his tongue in the middle of each of them, lapping them up. It was vile to watch."

"Ew, why would he do that?"

"You don't want to know."

"Maybe I don't." I scoop up more rice. "Do you three get together often?"

"Not really." His hand caresses my back as he waits for his meat. "Recently, we've sort of, I don't know, gotten together and talked."

"Why do you say that with such pain in your voice?"

"Because it is painful most of the time. I'm not a social kind of guy."

"Really?" I say sarcastically. "Could have fooled me."

He gently tugs my hair, making me laugh. "Smart-ass."

"So what goes on in these painful conversations you have?"

"Why do you want to know?"

I shrug. "Just curious to know more about you."

He slowly nods and draws circles over my bare shoulder. I love how affectionate he is. Never would have pegged him as such, but I do love it. "It's usually OC leading the conversation, being ridiculous about something. Bennett will join in on occasion, getting caught up in OC's antics."

"And let me guess, you just sit there like a grump."

"Pretty much."

I chuckle, actually able to see that play out in my head.

"Although, they're part of the reason we're hanging out on this boat right now."

"What do you mean?"

"Well, hate to admit it, but they've been a sounding board in helping me sort out my feelings for you."

I can't help the smile that pulls at my lips as I slowly turn toward Graydon, because how freaking cute is that.

"They helped you with your feelings?"

"Unfortunately."

"Why 'unfortunately'?"

He links our fingers together and says, "Because OC turned it into this whole thing, gave us a group name, and now—"

"Wait, I'm sorry, a group name? Please, you have to tell me what it is."

"No fucking way." He shakes his head.

"Graydon, you can't just mention that you have a group name and not tell me what it is."

"Sure as hell can."

"Why won't you tell me?"

"Because it's really fucking stupid."

I laugh. "How stupid? Is it something like...Lads Helping Lads?"

"Although not the best, I would take that over what OC calls us."

"Stop, I need to know." He shakes his head, so I tug on his hand. "Please, Graydon, you can't leave me hanging like this. I must know."

"Why?"

"I don't know, I just need to. How about, if you tell me, I'll spend the night at your place tonight?"

"Maple, there is an overnight bag in my truck right now that says you already planned on doing that."

Dammit.

"Fine, if you don't tell me, then I won't spend the night."

"Nice try, but I have the keys. Therefore, I will drive you wherever I damn well please."

"Fine, then...if you tell me, I'll be sure to put on the lingerie I packed."

His interest piques. "You brought lingerie?"

"I did, and I've been nervous about putting it on, convincing myself that you won't like it, but if you tell me, I'll muster the courage to wear it for you."

His brow turns down. "You never have to be self-conscious around me. I think you're fucking stunning, Maple."

"Thank you," I say softly. "Do we have a deal?"

He twists his lips in irritation while also looking curious at the same time. "Fine, deal."

"Yay. Okay, what do you call yourselves?"

He sighs heavily. "I need to preface this by saying I've been against the name from the very beginning."

"I have no doubt in my mind that you have been."

"Okay...OC calls us the Gladdy Daddies."

"The Gladdy Daddies?" I roar and then let out a burst of laughter. "Oh my God, why?"

"Because, as he put it, we're glad to be together, and we're daddies—as in hot men."

"Oh Jesus." I laugh some more, my stomach and cheeks hurting from the humor roaring through me. "That is...amazing. So freaking good." I wipe at my eyes and then chuckle again.

"You done?"

"Almost." I let out a few more laughs and then take a sip of my drink. "Okay, sorry." I laugh. "I'm done."

"Are you?"

I laugh some more and shake my head. "Nope, that will sit with me for a while." After I settle down, which takes a second, I bring my drink to my lips again, sip, and then set it on the table. "For the record, I planned on wearing the lingerie no matter what and can't wait to show you."

He purses his lips. "You're evil."

# CHAPTER 35
# GRAYDON

"I COULD NOT EAT ANOTHER piece of food," Maple says as she snuggles into my chest on the bench seat. I have my feet propped up along the long stretch of the bench while my back leans against the L part. She is lying on top of me, her head tucked into my chest while I drape a blanket over the both of us.

Bulbed lights hang above us and the night sky is dark, almost black, with no other lights nearby.

This evening could not have been more perfect—well, minus the tofu.

"Thank you for tonight." Her lips find my neck, then my jaw, and I fucking settle in as I let her just love on me because I can't get enough of it.

It's like I've been depleted of all physical and intimate touch, and now that I have it, I need to fill up, but only from her.

I want nothing but her.

"You don't need to thank me."

"You always say that, but you need to realize I like to show how grateful I am."

"Show me in another way," I say as my hand skims up and down her back.

"Are you asking for sexual favors, Graydon St. John?"

A rumble of a laugh comes out of me. "When it comes to you, I'll ask for anything."

"Clearly." Her fingers dance along my chest. "What will the upcoming season entail? Do I need to prepare for anything? Like am I going to miss seeing you a lot? Is there going to have to be a long-distance thing where we do phone sex?"

"I'm not going to deny you phone sex if you're interested, but our schedule isn't like other sports teams since we only play one game a week."

"So you're around a lot?"

"Typically, yeah. I'm usually just gone on Saturdays and Sundays if it's an away game, but back home late Sunday night. During the week, it's practices, game review, and treatment, but I'll still be able to see you at night like we do now."

"Oh." She lifts up to look at me. "Why did I think that some hellish travel time was going to start for you?"

"Not sure, but you can't get rid of me that easily."

"I would never. I need you to wash the dishes for the flamingos."

"Funny," I say. "I might have to cut out on that responsibility and focus more on the media stuff like Flock and Tackle and taking pictures that boast about the zoo."

"Oh no, you don't. Just because the season started doesn't mean you can cut out on your responsibilities."

"I'm beyond washing dishes, Baker."

"Yeah, but the one time I brought you into the exhibit, you wouldn't get close to the flamingos."

"Because their beady eyes were looking at me weird."

"Oh my God." She laughs. "You're ridiculous."

"No, I'm cautious."

"You really think a flamingo could hurt you?"

"Yeah, and I'm not taking the risk."

She shakes with laughter on top of me. "Fine, I'll find some pretty pose you can stand in and take pictures with the flamingos...with something between you."

"Whatever you think is best." I kiss the top of her head.

"I want you to know that I didn't fear the giant men out on the field."

"It's because you're braver than me."

"Clearly." She nuzzles against my chest for a second. "I don't have to worry about you traveling for extended periods of time during the season. I get to go to games and wear your name on the back of my shirt...What about postgame activities?"

"What about them?" I ask.

"What kind of postgame activities are there? For instance, is it mandatory for me to go home with you?"

"Yeah, it's part of the contract."

"What contract?" she asks.

"The contract that you signed to be in the PR relationship. There was fine print that said if we become real, then you must go home with me, especially after games."

"Fine print, huh?"

"Yeah, that's why you should always read it."

"You know, you're a lot more easygoing when relaxed."

"Isn't everyone?"

"Possibly." She kisses my neck again. "I like you like this. I like the snarly side of you too, but I also like hearing your voice, and when you're relaxed, you talk more."

"You like my voice?"

"Oh my God, yes. It's so smooth. Sometimes dark, a lot of the time gruff. I remember when you first opened your mouth and you said mean things about flamingos, I thought, 'That was rude,' but also, 'He has a sexy voice.'"

"Don't think I've ever been told that."

"I feel like if this football thing doesn't pan out—"

"Feels like it is panning out."

"But if it doesn't...you could possibly read for one of those nighttime apps where you help put people to sleep or, better yet, one of those erotic ones where you say naughty things and turn people on."

"And how do you know of such a thing?"

I can practically feel her eye roll as she says, "Social media, of course."

"Uh-huh." I continue to run my hand up and down her back. "Are you into some dirty stuff, and I don't know about it?"

"I mean, I don't know much, which feels embarrassing to say in front of you, someone who practically held me upside down while pounding into me, but I'm open to things."

"Hey," I say softly. "You never have to be embarrassed around me, okay?"

"I know, but I can't help it at times." She lifts up and looks me in the eyes. "You know when I was blowing you last night?"

I nearly choke on my saliva, because where did that come from? "Uh, yeah, hard to forget."

"Was I doing it right? I always worry that I'm not doing enough."

"Maple, you did plenty, more than enough. In fact, I hate that you mentioned it because just thinking about your mouth on my cock is going to make me hard."

"Do you not want to be hard while floating on a boat in the ocean?"

"Preferably not."

"You know, they showed us a bedroom..."

"Don't even think about it," I say.

"Really?" she asks, surprised. "I would have for sure thought you would be someone who would take advantage of the opportunity to do something like that."

"Not with you," I answer. "Maybe with a random, just to get off, but you're more sacred, and I'm not about to fuck you and have the staff here on the yacht listen to you moan. That's for my ears."

"Oh. That's...kind of sweet."

"It's the goddamn truth. You're mine. Your moans are mine. This body is mine. Those lips are mine. Everything about you is mine, and I don't plan on sharing one single bit of you. Not even for a quick fuck out on the ocean."

"Well." She leans in and lightly kisses my lips. "Oddly, that might be the most romantic thing I've ever heard."

---

"Will you show me how to paint something one day?" Maple asks as we head back to shore, our yacht currently traveling under the Golden Gate Bridge. It's massive, a feat of engineering that I don't think I will ever be able to wrap my head around.

"What do you want to paint?"

"What do you think I want to paint?"

I chuckle. "A flamingo."

"How did you know?"

"Lucky guess." I kiss the top of her head. "How about this? We have a naked painting night."

"If we're naked, we won't actually get anything done."

"Not true. I know a lot of things we can get done."

"Graydon."

"What?"

She lifts up to look me in the eyes. "You know if we're naked, the only thing that will happen is you on top of me."

"That's not entirely true. I prefer you on top of me sometimes as well."

She rolls her eyes and then snuggles back into my chest. "How about we compromise: with every five minutes that tick by as you teach me, I will take off an article of clothing."

"How many articles of clothing do you plan on wearing? Just a towel? Then I'm in."

"Oh my God, Graydon, seriously, why are you so...horny?"

"Not horny, just obsessed with you." I drag my fingers over her back, absorbing my words.

Because, yeah, I'm pretty obsessed, and it feels like it hit me out of nowhere.

Well, maybe that's not the case. It's been building, and I've been ignoring the feelings. But now that I've accepted them, I'm all in.

I kiss the top of her head again. "Is an obsession such a bad thing?"

"No," she says softly. "As long as it's okay for me to be obsessed as well. I don't want to come off too needy."

"Did you hear the tantrum I threw when you sat in a chair that wasn't my lap?"

She laughs. "You said you weren't throwing a fit."

"It could have been worse. Not sure you're aware how much of a fit I can really throw."

"Something I would treasure seeing."

"And yet you stopped me from chucking a chair."

"It's close quarters here, and throwing a chair is never safe. But if we were in an open field where no one could be harmed, and you decided to start stomping your foot and huffing in displeasure, then that's something I for sure would want to see."

"Why do I feel like you find pleasure in my discomfort?"

"I don't know. You're this big, grumpy guy, so seeing you act like a child is kind of funny."

I tickle her side, causing her to laugh. "I see where your head's at, Baker."

"Hey, no tickling." She squirms on top of me.

"You ticklish?"

"Yes, and unless you want a knee to your junk, I would refrain from tickling me."

"Ouch. Noted."

We pull into the harbor, the boat slowing and our time out on the sea coming to an end.

"I'm sad. I don't want to leave."

"Want me to ask them to go back out? I can."

She shakes her head. "No, I know we need to get back. I'm just so comfortable."

"So am I."

"This has been such a wonderful date. Thank you, Graydon. You spoiled me. I've never been on a date like this."

"Then clearly you haven't been with the right people."

"I've come to figure that out," she says softly. After a few moments of silence, she asks, "Now that you're going to be playing games on Sundays, when are you going to visit your mom?" She pauses for a second and then says, "And if that is too much of a personal question, I'm really sorry."

"I'm an open book to you now," I say. "You don't need to apologize."

"I just never want to push you too far."

"You won't," I say. "And I'll visit her on Mondays."

"Well, if you ever need me to go with you, I can wait in the car while you visit and then hold your hand after. You just let me know. I hate that you have to go through that alone."

I feel my breath constrict in my chest because…shit, I've never had anyone go with me. Not even when Mom was first admitted to her living facility. My nanny would drop me off, and I would go in by myself, so this…this is different. Do I want her there? Do I want her to see the devastation that sinks into me when my mom doesn't recognize me?

"I'm sorry, I don't know why I said that. Don't feel like you need to answer," she says before I can respond. She lifts up to look me in the eyes. "I'm just…I like helping and—"

I press my thumb to her lips as I cup her jaw. "Don't apologize."

"But I overstepped."

"You didn't." I shake my head. "I was just surprised is all. No one has ever visited with me, ever."

"No one?" she asks as she straddles my lap now, my hands falling to her waist, keeping her in place. "Not even your dad?"

"Especially not my dad. Not sure he's even aware what the facility looks like."

"That's terrible."

"That's him, though, a terrible human being."

"I'm sorry you have to deal with that. You deserve so much better."

"Maybe that's why you're here," I say, looking her in the eyes. "Maybe the universe decided to grace me with someone beautiful in my life to make up for all of the ugly."

Her expression softens. "Well, I'm here for as long as you want me, need me."

"That's going to be a long time. I'm having a hard time getting in my fill. Not sure it will ever be topped off."

"Good." She leans forward and kisses me, letting our lips mingle for a few moments before she pulls away. "Are we headed to your apartment after this?"

"What the hell do you think?"

She chuckles. "I think you're wishing this boat would dock a whole lot quicker."

"That's exactly what I'm thinking."

# CHAPTER 36
# GRAYDON

MAPLE SITS RIGHT NEXT TO me, curled into my side. My arm is wrapped around her, and my other hand is gripping the steering wheel. Alex Warren is playing in the background, and we are rounding the corner, about to turn onto my street.

After we got off the boat, it took a second for Maple to balance herself, but then we thanked the staff, and I brought her to the back of my truck, where I lowered the tailgate and parted her legs just enough for my body. She wrapped herself around me, and we made out. I know it was risky because it was in the middle of a parking lot and anyone could take a picture of us, but I didn't care. I needed her mouth on mine.

I needed to taste her.

I needed to let her know that this was only the beginning of the night.

And now that we're closing in on my apartment, anticipation is clawing up my spine as her hand moves over my thigh, making me grow hard in my goddamn pants just from the placement of her palm against my leg.

Pathetic.

That's me.

I'm fucking pathetic.

I allowed myself to give in, to open up to her, to let her see the man I really am, and now I feel like I have to cling to her. I have to hold her, make her mine, because by telling her about my life, I let her take me as hers.

"You know, you're the first woman I've brought back to my place."

"Really?" she asks.

I glance at her quickly. "Yeah. Haven't trusted anyone enough to bring them here."

Her thumb smooths over my thigh. "Well, I'm honored."

"It's not much but—" My brow creases as I catch a human sitting on the steps of my place, dressed in a sweatsuit, their hood pulled up, hiding their face.

"What's wrong?" she asks.

I pull into the short driveway but don't open my garage door just yet as the figure stands.

"Wait here."

She grabs my hand before I can leave.

"Who is that?"

"I don't know, but lock the doors when I leave."

"Graydon, no. You have no idea if they're armed or if they're high. It's not safe. Just go back to my place."

"No, I don't want this fuck on my steps. I can handle it."

"Graydon—"

"Lock the doors."

I slip from her grasp and shut the door, her worried expression nearly making me stop, but I'm not going to let some asshole scare me from my place. He needs to know not to fuck with this house.

"Hey," I say, their head snapping in my direction. "Get the fuck off—"

"You're home!" The person's hood is lowered, and OC's face comes into view. "Dude, I didn't think you would ever come home."

I pause midstride to blast my fist through this stranger's face, as I take in OC's disheveled appearance.

"Don't call me 'dude,' and what the hell are you doing here?"

"I need a hug."

My shoulders drop, the tension in them sagging as I say, "Are you fucking kidding me?"

"Du—uh, I mean...Graydon, I'm having a rough night, and Bennett isn't available. My teammates don't know me. My former teammates are in Vancouver. My family is nowhere near me. You're my only other friend, and I'm in need of some TLC."

"No," I say as I roll my eyes and head back to the truck, where I open my door and get in.

"Is everything okay?" Maple asks.

"Yeah, it was fucking—"

*Bang.*

OC splatters himself against the passenger-side window, causing Maple to scream bloody murder as he yells, "Wait!"

"Jesus fucking Christ!"

Hand on her heart, Maple takes in OC and says, "Oh my God, is that OC?" She rolls down the window, but I stop her when it's a few inches from the top.

"Do not roll down your window for him."

"Maple, please," OC pleads. "I'm sorry, I didn't know you were in here, and I didn't mean to scare you. I'm in dire need of some help, and Graydon is the only one I know who I can talk to about this."

"He needs your help," Maple says, her empathy shining through.

"Listen to her, Graydon. I need your help."

This motherfucker is about to learn what my kind of help delivers—a steady kick up the ass.

"Please," he pleads. And here I thought I was the pathetic one. "It won't be long, I just need to talk something out."

I don't care if it's five minutes. The moment I walk into my house, I have plans of taking Maple up against every fucking surface I can, and having an audience is out of the question.

"Of course we can spare some time for you," Maple says, brightening the stupid look on OC's face. "Can't we, Graydon?"

"No."

"Graydon," Maple chastises. "Don't be rude."

"He's the one being rude. He came over uninvited without any indication he needed help in a text before he headed over, and he's ruining my plans for us."

"Oof, were you planning on having the sex?" OC asks.

"Don't fucking phrase it like that."

"Well, I don't want to step on toes."

"It's okay," Maple says. "We're more than happy to help you. Graydon is going to park his truck, and then we can sit down and have a chat."

"Thank you," OC says, and then Maple rolls up the window and turns toward me.

"Let him get whatever he needs off his chest, and then we can have our night."

"You don't know him the way I do. This is not going to be simple. Why can't I just talk to him next week?"

"Next week? Graydon, are you really that heartless?"

"No, I'm really that horny."

That pulls a smile from her. "Okay, but I promise you, the moment he leaves, I'm all yours, and you can do whatever you want to me."

"Whatever I want?" I raise a brow.

"I'm yours."

"And what if I say no?"

"Then I'll take him back to my place where we can chat."

Fury rages through me. "The fuck you will."

She chuckles. "Then make this easy on everyone and just get it over with. Then spend the rest of the night making me come."

I wet my lips. The prospect of what's to happen after he leaves helps me put the stupid truck in drive, open my garage door, and pull into the tight space. OC meets us in the garage, and together we head up into my place.

This is not how I envisioned Maple seeing my house for the first time, with a sullen teenager walking behind us with his hood up, sulking the entire time.

"Doesn't he have a nice place?" OC asks.

Maple glances around, a smile tugging on her lips as she nods. "He does, and it smells like him."

OC lifts his head and sniffs the air. "You know, I don't smell him enough to recognize his signature scent, but if this is what he smells like, you are one lucky girl."

"Can we get on with whatever insane shit you came here to talk to me about?" I flop onto the couch and line my arm across the back of it, irritation pumping through me as my eyes fall on Maple and those shorts she's wearing.

"I can really feel your compassion. Thanks for making this easy, man," OC says as he takes a seat across from me in one of my chairs.

I'm shocked he didn't come over here and snuggle into my chest.

I wouldn't put it past him.

"I'll, uh, I'll give you guys some space," Maple says.

"No, stay," OC calls out. "You might be able to help as well."

"Are you sure?"

"He is," I say and then pat my lap.

She rolls her eyes and takes the seat next to me, causing me to grumble in disapproval.

"I'm not going to sit on your lap in front of your friend."

"For one, he's not my friend—"

"That hurts," OC scoffs, his hand to his heart.

"And two, I don't care about who is with us, I want you on my lap."

"Now, now, demanding will get you nowhere, just like the Beast," OC says.

"Who the fuck is the Beast?"

"From *Beauty and the Beast*?" OC rolls his eyes. "Come on, man, do you not pay attention to anything? The snarly monster tried to force Belle to do his will, but she wouldn't budge. It was only once he started being nice that she started to bend."

"Jesus...Christ." I carve my hand over my face, begging the universe to let this end.

Maple smooths her palm over my thigh and leans into me, temporarily easing some of my irritation as I lower my arm around her and rest my hand on her side as her legs curl up on the couch.

"Why don't you just tell us what's bothering you, OC?"

He dramatically flops back in his chair, arms draped over each armrest, legs spread. "It's Grace."

"Who's Grace?" Maple asks.

"The girl he likes," I answer.

"You remember?" OC asks, looking like I just patted him on the head and told him he was a good boy.

"I will never forget what you did in that coffeehouse while talking about her."

The tonguing of the muffins. It will never, ever leave me.

A core memory developed, one I wish I could shake off.

"What happened with Grace?" Maple asks.

"Long story short. We were once a thing, I thought she was the love of my life, then we parted ways—my fault, don't need to get into it—and I was traded to the Agitators, where she was also working. I thought the stars were aligning and we were going to be able to rekindle what we had, but then I was sent down here and she stayed up in Vancouver. I never got a chance to fix things, so I started planning on doing so, coming up with a scenario where I could show her how much she means to me, only to find out she's with someone else now."

"Oh gosh, I'm so sorry."

"How is this different from what you said at the coffeehouse?"

"I was just catching your girl up," he says, and I appreciate that he called Maple my girl. Maybe I'll give him a little bit of a break for that.

"Okay, so what happened now?" Maple asks.

OC lets out a pain-filled sigh. "My boy Posey just called. Grace is engaged."

Oh shit.

Maple lightly gasps next to me as if she's watching a storyline from a soap opera unfold. "Oh no, that's...that's terrible."

"I know." He throws up his arms. "It's really fucking terrible, because what am I supposed to do with that?"

"Nothing," I answer.

"What?" OC asks. "What do you mean, 'nothing'? I know we're all in shock here and we need to catch our breath and face the facts that she is engaged, but that doesn't mean we just throw the towel in immediately."

"OC," I say, letting my voice carry a hint of softness. "If she's engaged, that means she said yes, and the only way she would say yes is if she's in love with this person. And if she's in love, that means it's really serious. Do you really want to be that person who comes back into her life and muddies her reality?"

I can feel Maple's eyes on me, her hand warming over my thigh.

Yes, I'm an asshole most of the time, but there are points when I'm not a complete and total dick, when I can offer some solid advice and give a fuck about you. It's a small amount of time and the quota runs low often, but he caught me in a moment when Maple was pushing her energy into me.

Lucky him.

"I don't want to be that person," OC says, looking deflated. "Fuck, do you really think it's over?"

"Yeah."

"But what if...what if she still has feelings for me and doesn't know it?" OC asks, hope hitting him in the chest. "What if she's just saying yes to this guy because she doesn't know how I feel? Don't you think I should give her the chance to know how I feel and then she can make an informed decision?"

"You have a point," Maple says. "But let me ask this: When you were there with her, was there tension between the two of you? Did it seem like she wanted to work things out? How were the vibes?"

Check out my girl hammering out the details.

He rolls his teeth over his bottom lip as he looks away. "The vibes weren't great."

"Then that should be your answer," I say.

"But I never got the chance to woo her. I was helping all the other fools with their girl problems, like I helped you, and now look at me, alone and sad and heartbroken."

"Aw, he helped you," Maple says, leaning in and kissing my cheek.

"A lot," OC says. "Like the reason you two are sitting there all snuggly, making me jealous, is because of me."

"Don't fucking exaggerate," I say. Sure, he helped, but also, I had a lot to do with this, thank you very fucking much.

OC just shrugs. "Anyway, don't you think she deserves to find out how I feel?"

"No," I answer. "She deserves happiness, and she found it."

"Yeah, don't be a Rachel."

"A what?" OC asks.

"Rachel," Maple says again. "Rachel Green from *Friends*. She has feelings for Ross and goes to London to tell him how she feels before he gets married, only to mess with his head, and he goes and says the wrong name at the altar."

"That's because Ross is unstable at best." OC sits taller. "How on earth can someone who once owned a monkey as a pet function properly in society? There's a screw loose up there."

"Uh, Ross is the glue that holds that show together."

"Preposterous!" OC shouts. "It's Chandler, and everyone knows it."

"Chandler is the easy answer."

"You're the one who's easy," OC shoots back.

"Hey," I snap at him. "Don't fucking call my girl easy."

OC winces. "Sorry, that...that just flew out of me. Apologies. I'm a bit stressed at the moment, so forgive me for anything stupid that I might say."

"It's okay," Maple says, even though I want to tell her that it's not. "Back to the problem at hand. I know this is not what you want to hear, but I think you just need to let her go."

He sighs heavily. "Why did I know you were going to say that?"

"Because you know what's right, and that's what you should do. If she's happy, let her be. Let her live her life. Don't complicate it for her."

OC brushes his hand through his hair, pushing his hood back.

"Fuck," he says, and I can see that cocky yet goofy demeanor he wears all the time slip as he lets us see him in a raw, vulnerable moment, realization setting in that this is what his life is going to be.

A life without Grace.

And as much as he annoys me, I feel bad because I feel very attached to Maple right now. Not that I have the kind of history that OC and Grace had, but if she were to just walk away right now, I would feel pretty sick about it.

I wouldn't be able to stop thinking about her.

And I know deep down inside that if it were her who just got engaged, I would probably have something to say about it. And I wouldn't just let her go live her life.

Then again, I don't usually fall under the line of morally correct decisions.

"I'm sorry, OC," Maple says, her expression turning into deep sympathy. "If you want, you can hang out with us for a while."

Uh...what?

"Really?" he asks. "That would mean a lot to me."

And before I can even protest, he stands from the chair, takes the two steps he needs to make it to the couch, and sits down, grabbing the remote to the TV with him before turning it on.

"Ooh, *Pretty Woman,* love this movie."

He grabs one of my throw pillows, hugs it to his chest, and stares off at the TV as I slowly turn to look Maple in the eyes.

She gives me an apologetic expression, and I know she can feel my displeasure.

Because this is the last fucking thing I had in mind when we were driving back to my place.

OC on my couch, watching *Pretty Woman,* was not how I planned on ending this evening.

---

"He's kind of precious when he sleeps," Maple whispers as she stares down at OC, who is now sprawled across the couch, mouth hanging open, gripping my throw pillow like it's his personal little spoon, covered in a blanket that Maple insisted on me draping over him.

"Not the adjective I was looking for," I say, already in my boxer briefs, ready for bed. I got ready once the dickhead started drifting off to sleep.

Maple did too once I brought her bag up to my room.

She asked if maybe she should go home since it was so late, and I told her absolutely not.

If anything, I was going to at least sleep with her in my arms.

She changed into a cute pair of pink shorts and a flamingo shirt that I'm sure is one of many in her wardrobe. She took her hair out of the tight ponytail it was in and has opted for more of a messy bun now. Her face is freshly washed, and she looks so damn good that it's going to take a very huge effort not to strip her down right here in the middle of my living room like I had planned.

Maple pats my chest. "You are very grumpy."

I gesture to the lovesick nimrod on my couch. "I wonder why."

"It was nice that you helped him and offered him a place to crash while he's hurting. That's being a good friend."

"We're not friends."

"I don't know." She takes my hand in hers. "It seems like you might be."

"Trust me, I would never be friends with someone like him. He's too…annoying."

She chuckles, and I tug her upstairs to my room, catching that it's past midnight already. Everything I had planned for us is completely ruined.

Yeah, thanks for the cock block…*friend.*

When we get to my room, Maple takes off toward the bathroom, and I go to the bed, where I draw down the covers. Our phones are already plugged in, so I turn on my nightstand light and turn off the others, casting the room in a soft glow. I lie down on the bed and prop one hand behind my head as I wait for Maple. Irritation creeps through me, but I try to tamp it down because the last thing I want is for Maple to see it.

The bathroom light turns off, and the door opens. My eyes fall to the silhouette in the doorframe just as she takes another step forward, revealing Maple in nothing but a black see-through bra and matching thong.

Jesus.

Fuck.

Her dusty-rose-colored nipples poke up against the fabric, nothing concealed from my sight, while the strings of her thong run incredibly high on her hips.

I wet my lips as she moves forward, climbs onto the bed, and starts crawling toward me.

Immediately, I'm hard.

That's all it takes, her…in lingerie, making her way toward me.

"Fuck," I whisper as she crawls up my body and straddles my lap, where she lowers herself down.

"Mmm…you're hard."

"Of course I'm fucking hard," I say, my voice raspy as I take her in. "Jesus, you're so fucking beautiful." I glide my hands up her sides to her bra, where I let my thumbs run over the see-through fabric.

"Have you been wearing this the whole night?"

"No, I changed when I got ready for bed."

"You mean you've been sitting in this while that asswipe has been falling asleep on my couch?"

"Give him a break," she says softly as she lets her hands travel up my chest. "He's lovesick and hurt."

"I don't give a fuck about anything other than you, right here, in my arms, wearing this." I let my eyes roam, my heart rate picking up the more I take in.

The subtle curve of her hips.

The hard nub of her nipples.

The goose bumps along her skin.

Fuck, I want this woman, and bad.

And she must see it in my eyes because she lifts off my lap and pushes the blankets down. She grabs my boxer briefs and pulls them down as well, letting my length stretch up my stomach.

Her eyes find mine, and they slowly travel down my body until they reach my cock. She wets her lips, straddles me, and gradually lowers her center over me.

"Jesus," I grumble right before her hips start rotating over my length.

"God, I love your cock, Graydon. I love how big you are, how ready you are. How you allow me to take control when I want to use you."

"Use me all you want, beautiful," I say as my hands land on her hips, guiding her movements. "Fuck me however you want. I'm yours."

Her eyes fall to mine, and with a smile that could kill, she turns around, her ass facing me now. She bends forward just enough to give me a perfect view and starts humping my cock, her arousal moving fast over me, creating enough friction to drive me wild as I stare at her two perfect globes.

She knows me too well now.

She knows my goddamn weakness.

I spank her loud enough for the sound to echo through the room. She holds her moan in, only letting the smallest of sounds fall past her lips.

That's not good enough.

"Let me hear you."

"Not with OC in your living room."

"Fuck him."

"No, I'd rather fuck you," she says, looking over her shoulder, her expression so sinister that I forget what we were just arguing about, and I spank her again.

I watch as her teeth pull over her lip, and she lets out a tiny moan for me.

"Fuck. Again, beautiful."

I spank her once more...and another...and another, her pace increasing with every slap to her ass until we're both panting and she has me forgetting what the hell I'm supposed to be doing as my pleasure climbs and climbs.

"Shit, stop, Maple. I'm going to...fuck, I'll come."

"Then come," she says and continues driving over me. It only takes three more strokes before I'm coming early, exploding all over my stomach like a fucking rookie.

"Fuck..." I groan, hating myself. "Shit, I'm sorry."

She turns around, a smile playing on her lips as she takes in my stomach.

"What are you sorry for?" she asks as she leans forward and starts licking the cum off my stomach. "Seems to me like you're doing just what I want."

Jesus...Christ...

# CHAPTER 37
# MAPLE

GRAYDON'S EYES GLAZE OVER AS I finish licking his stomach clean, not missing one drop. I could sense his tension all night from the moment we got back here and OC popped out of nowhere. I know he had plans for us, and as time ticked by, he was getting more and more frustrated, but in the back of my mind, all I could think about was how it could be two in the morning and I would still want to have a piece of this man.

I didn't care what time it was.

He was mine.

When I'm done, I lift back up and drag my fingers over his abs, loving how I was able to make him come early. Something is so hot about him losing all control and not being able to hold back because of what I'm doing.

It's powerful.

Makes me feel desired.

Wanted.

Needed.

"Your turn," he says, wetting his lips.

"Or we can just go to bed."

His expression flattens.

"Not fucking happening."

I chuckle as he flips me to my back, then tears off my thong in one quick stroke, snapping the fabric apart.

"Hey, I liked those."

"I'll buy a whole goddamn lingerie store for you, just so I can rip your underwear off like that every time."

He spreads my legs and smiles down at me while he takes in my arousal.

"I'm wet," I say as if he can't see it.

"Yeah, and it's fucking killing me knowing that I already blew my goddamn load."

"I like it," I say, fire blazing in my eyes at the thought.

"Well, it will be the only time it happens." He then reaches into his nightstand and pulls out a simple vibrator.

My eyes widen. "I thought you didn't bring women here."

"I don't."

"Then why do you have that?"

"Why do you think?" he asks, a wicked gleam in his eyes.

"Oh my God," I whisper. "Do you...do you use it on yourself?"

"Sometimes." He moves back between my legs and turns it on, letting the vibration sound fill the air. "If you wake up OC with your screams, I'll buy you all the goddamn lingerie you want."

"I thought you were going to do that anyway. Maybe you could never rip them."

"No goddamn chance." He drags the vibrator over my chest and across my pebbled nipples. "This bra is dangerous."

"Mmm? How so?"

"It will get you in a lot of trouble." He drags the vibrator down to my stomach as he leans forward and sucks my nipple into his mouth through the sheer fabric of my bra.

My hand shifts into his hair, my back arching from the ache I feel for him. "If this is the kind of trouble you're referring to, then I want it."

"Then be a good girl and spread your legs wider for me," he whispers before bringing his mouth to mine and dipping his tongue past my lips and up against mine. I moan into him, letting him swirl his tongue as he drives into the inferno that is building inside me.

When he pulls away, I feel lost until he maneuvers his mouth down my body, past my chest, my stomach, and right above where I ache for him.

His expression turns wicked as he turns off the vibrator and slowly slides it inside me.

"Oh…that's…" He switches on the vibrator, and my pelvis lifts off the bed. "Oh fuck, Graydon."

His gorgeous smile stretches across his lips right before he lowers his head, parts me with two fingers, and flicks his tongue over my clit.

"Fuck," I hiss, my hand falling to his hair immediately. "Fuck, Graydon."

The sensation of the vibrator matched with the light flicking of his tongue has me spinning immediately. Within seconds, my pleasure starts to climb, my legs trembling as every nerve ending pulls tight, right to the center of my body.

"Graydon…fuck." My back arches off the mattress, my chest heaving, the throbbing in my clit so intense that I know I'll only be able to hold on for seconds.

And he must sense it because he pulls away and turns off the vibrator. He rests right between my legs, letting the shock of what he did settle deep in my bones, spurring me on and making me beg.

"Don't." I shake my head, my arm draped over my eyes. "Don't torture me. I'm so close."

"How close?"

"Embarrassingly close…Please," I moan. "Please make me come, Graydon." My pussy throbs, pounding for release.

Little contractions start to erupt all over me, not giving me what I need.

"Please," I beg one more time in a last-ditch effort before I fall over the edge without the pressure I need from him.

And thankfully he listens, because he turns the vibrator back on just as he sucks my clit between his lips.

"Fuck!" I scream as my body unravels and my orgasm hits me square in the chest. My body writhes under him, my moans growing louder and louder as I float up into the abyss where nothing exists but this unbelievable pleasure.

I don't even realize what's happening until Graydon is positioned above me, the vibrator now at my slit while his cock sinks into me.

"Oh God," I moan from how full I feel. "Oh fuck, Graydon."

"Jesus...Christ," he groans as he starts thrusting into me, hard, hitting me in the G-spot, where only he has ever touched.

I continue to spasm around him while he drives me toward another release, building me up when I didn't think it was possible.

"Fuck, this cunt," he whispers as his hand loops behind my back, and he picks me up off the bed. He swings me around to the wall in the bedroom and starts moving me up and down on his cock so fast that I can't do anything other than hold on to his shoulders and revel in the way he makes me feel.

"You're so big. God, fill me."

He growls and then lowers my feet to the ground, turns me around, and bends me forward before entering me again. I spread my legs, and he reaches to grab the vibrator, pressing it to my clit again.

It's all I need.

"Fuck me," I cry as I find my release for the second time tonight, squeezing around him to the point that he smacks my ass and then groans so loud that I can feel the rumble of his chest from where I'm bent over.

"Fuck!" he yells as I can feel him spill into me...every...last...drop.

Once he stills and takes a second to breathe, I can feel him stiffen behind me as he slowly pulls out.

"Oh shit, Maple." I turn to find panic in his eyes. "I didn't use a condom." His hand goes to his hair. "Fuck, I'm sorry."

"It's okay. Remember, I'm on birth control."

He swallows and then nods. "I'm clean, I promise. I just got checked a little bit ago."

"I trust you," I say, my hand on his racing heart. "It's okay."

His hand smooths over my back and right to my ass as he presses his forehead to mine and pins me against the wall. "I'm sorry, beautiful. I just, fuck, I lost my mind when you started coming apart on my tongue."

I smile up at him and cup his cheek, letting my thumb scrape along his scruff. "Don't apologize. I really liked it."

"I know, but I should have been more careful."

"It's okay, Graydon. Seriously." I stand on my toes and press my chest against his as I grip the back of his neck and kiss him wildly, letting him know just how much I don't care.

He groans into my mouth and lifts me into his arms, where he presses me against the wall again, pinning me in place. "I've never felt this fucking out of control with someone before." His nose rubs against mine. "It's like I'm desperate for my fill of you, and I can't get enough. Even when I'm inside you and your sexy fucking cunt is squeezing me, it's not enough. It will never be enough."

I kiss him softly. "I feel the same."

"So I'm not crazy? I'm not the only one who feels like this?"

I shake my head. "No. Even right now, two orgasms in, I'm not satisfied, Graydon. I want more."

He sighs heavily, and I can feel him harden against me...again.

"Fuck, so do I."

"Then take me, Graydon. Make me come all night."

His eyes search mine for a second, then his mouth is on mine again, his kisses bruising me with desperation.

Just the way I like it.

Just the way I want it.

---

Graydon's alarm goes off, and he groans in disapproval as he rolls over to turn it off.

"Fuck," he whispers and turns back toward me, pulling me into his large, warm chest. "I don't want to leave this bed."

"Me either," I say as I hold on to him.

I think we probably got two hours of sleep.

And maybe that's being generous.

There were small breaks between, but like he said, it just felt like we couldn't get enough. And even now, being sore from everything we did last night, I could still have this man.

I still want him.

His hand slides up to my breast, and his fingers play with my nipple.

"Mmm, don't start something you can't finish," I say just as there's a loud crash downstairs.

Graydon sits straight up and pulls the covers over me.

"Stay here," he demands as his protective nature kicks in.

"It's probably OC," I say, causing him to relax ever so slightly.

"Fuck, I forgot he was here." He hops out of bed, and I watch his beautifully tight rear end head into the bathroom, where he shuts the door. After a few seconds, he comes out wearing boxer briefs and a pair of athletic shorts while he brushes his teeth.

There goes morning sex. Then again, I doubt Graydon would want to make me scream when OC is actually awake. He doesn't seem like the kind of guy who wants to share the sound of me coming, despite him teasing me about it last night.

I step out of bed and immediately feel his eyes on me as I strut naked through the bedroom and right past him to his closet, where I grab one of his hanging shirts. I slip it on and then fill my toothbrush with toothpaste before turning toward him and leaning against the counter. My eyes are on him the entire time.

He takes in my plain gray shirt, or his plain gray shirt, his eyes blazing with what he wants to do with me. He walks toward me, still brushing his teeth, and lifts the hem of the shirt until his hand is resting on my bare hip. He leans over me, spits in the sink behind me, then rinses his toothbrush before wiping his face.

I do the same and turn back toward him.

He stares down at me, indecision written all over his face, temptation knocking at the door.

"Come over again later?" His hand shifts higher until he reaches my breast, and he gently squeezes it, tugging on my nipple.

"Are you asking for another sleepover?" I slide my fingers just inside the waistband of his shorts.

His jaw clenches.

"Yeah, I am."

"Would it be like the one we just had?"

"Yes, but without the cretin sleeping on the couch."

I chuckle and slide my fingers farther, just above his pubic bone.

"Jesus," he whispers as his thumb rubs over my nipple, making me so wet.

"I don't know, it's kind of nice having someone as an audience. It makes it more...naughty, don't you think?" I slide my hand farther into his shorts until they connect with his growing length.

His eyes grow dark, he wets his lips, and then he yanks my shirt up and over my head and turns me to face the mirror. He pushes his shorts and briefs down before lining himself up behind me.

"Yes," I whisper, spreading my legs as I look at our reflection. My cheeks are flushed, his muscles contracting as his hands grip my sides.

"You want this cock?"

"Yes, fill me, Graydon."

He groans, then positions himself at my entrance. "Stare at me in the reflection when I enter you. I want to see the moment I bottom out."

My eyes fall onto him as he slowly enters me, stretching me out to the point of almost pain, and with one final thrust, he fills me to the hilt, causing my mouth to fall open in surprise.

"That's it, beautiful. Show me how you take my cock."

"I love it," I say, looking him in the eyes. "I love when you make me come."

"Mmm...good girl," he says right before slapping my ass.

"Oh God," I moan. My words are louder than I want them to be, but I'm unable to control my volume.

Fingers digging into my hips, eyes on me in the mirror, he pumps into me, slowly at first, drawing out the pleasure and creating a heat between us that ignites the moment I purposefully squeeze around him when he pushes in.

His eyes light up as his mouth falls open, and oh my God, it's the sexiest thing I think I've ever seen.

His chest tightens, his muscles flexing in a way that I've never seen before, and when he pushes in again, I squeeze once more.

"Fuuuuck," he drags out and pauses, eyes still on me, taking a few deep breaths. "You'll make me come early again."

"Good," I say as I squeeze one more time as he enters me.

"Jesus...fuck," he grumbles, and then his eyes fall to my ass, his pace picking up, his body slamming into mine, the sound of slapping skin filling the bathroom.

But I watch him the entire time. I watch how the muscles in his neck tighten.

I watch the way his teeth bear down on the corner of his lip.

I watch the flex of his abs, which turn into impossibly carved stones as he moves in and out of me.

"Shit, beautiful, you're so goddamn tight. So perfect."

His voice is gruff, like he's about to slip any second.

"Fuck," he groans as I clench around him, my orgasm climbing, tightening, pulling all my attention to that one sacred spot driving my pleasure.

But I don't shut my eyes. I don't let my gaze slip because I want to watch him. I want to see him when he comes.

He pumps faster.

Harder.

Sweat builds between us.

Our moans mix.

The feeling of ecstasy spirals up my spine as the friction builds and builds until…

"Motherfucker!" he yells as he stills inside me.

And the view of him coming, his entire body freezing as pleasure rips through him, is the sexiest, most erotic thing I've ever experienced.

His hand falls between my legs and rubs against my clit, finishing me off so I find my release as well, my body shaking with my orgasm as I try to catch my breath.

He leans forward, his lips brushing along my shoulder blades and then to the back of my neck. "Will never have enough of you. Never."

He turns my face and kisses me on the lips just as he removes himself from me and helps me stand tall.

He spends the next few minutes cleaning us both up, making sure I'm properly dressed in a pair of shorts and his shirt, then he takes me downstairs, where we find OC in the kitchen with a display of pastries on the counter and orange juice in some glasses.

Smiling brightly, he says, "That might have been your most entertaining sex session yet."

Oh, dear God.

He did hear us.

Graydon tenses next to me, pulling me closer to him. "Talk about it again, and be prepared for my fist to meet your face."

OC quickly holds up his hands in defense. "Sorry, just...wow." He looks Graydon up and down. "Impressive, man."

"Shut the fuck up."

"It's fine," I say, trying to calm Graydon before he really does punch OC, because I could see it happening. "He's right, Graydon. You're very impressive."

His eyes land on mine, and the scowl in his brow lessens as he leans down and lightly kisses my lips.

OC clears his throat and says, "Uh, anyone want to compliment my spread? I woke up early to grab it from the corner café, along with some orange juice and coffee. Thoughtful, right?"

"Are you really looking for a compliment?" Graydon asks.

"Dude, I gave you one."

"Don't call me 'dude,'" Graydon snarls.

Tugging on his arm, I say, "The spread is very impressive. Thank you, OC."

He lifts a chocolate croissant and takes a large bite from it. "I know it's not the most nutritious, but when dealing with a broken heart, I find that I work best when filled with buttery, flakey goodness." He lifts the plate. "Pastry?"

Graydon moves past him and grabs the milk from the fridge, then pulls a tub of protein powder from up top. "I'm good."

OC's face falls, so while Graydon makes his protein shake that I know he likes to have every morning, I take a seat at the kitchen island and pick up one of the Danishes with cherries in the middle.

"Don't mind if I do." OC lights up like a puppy dog when his owner returns home, and tosses me a napkin, then hands me a cup of orange juice.

"Are you a pastry girl?"

"Pretty much love anything with carbs."

"Same." He leans against the counter right next to me, ignoring

Graydon completely. "I really like it when they have something inside. Like a plain croissant is not my jam, but stick some chocolate in there, and I'm game."

"Same. I really like a sugary fruit mixture or an almond croissant."

"Oh shit." OC grips my shoulder. "The ones with that almond paste in the middle? Those are so fucking good."

Graydon appears out of nowhere and removes OC's hand from my shoulder, nearly butting chests with him. "Don't touch her."

"Du-uh, I mean, Graydon, it's not like I was hitting on her."

"I don't care. She's not yours to touch."

"Graydon," I quietly warn, but he just turns to me, presses a kiss to my lips, then goes back to his protein shake.

OC glances back at him and then at me. "A little possessive, huh?"

"I don't think you should say that in front of him," I whisper. "He might hurt you."

"You think so?"

"I think so." I nod.

"I don't know. I think he likes to act tough around me, but I'm not sure he would actually hurt me."

"I would hurt you," Graydon says and pops his bottle open to take down some of his shake.

And I believe it. I don't think Graydon would care who took the impact of his fist if it was because they were messing with me. He wouldn't put up with it.

"Maybe if you ate more pastries, you wouldn't be so hostile."

"But then he wouldn't have those abs," I say with a sigh, staring at him.

"Not true." OC takes that moment to lift his hoodie and flash me his stomach. "A pastry a day didn't take these abs away."

I glance over at his stomach and...oh my God, he's...he's right.

"Put your fucking sweatshirt down," Graydon growls, causing OC to cover himself up quickly.

"Please, there's no way she's going to have eyes for anyone but you," OC says, taking me in. "Girl is infatuated."

I feel my cheeks flush as my gaze falls on Graydon's. His eyes darken, his jaw clenching as his lips roll together. My heart nearly explodes in my chest from that one look, a look full of sin and promises I know he can keep.

"Jesus," OC says, tugging on the collar of his hoodie. "The temperature in this room just skyrocketed. No wonder you did it six times last night and this morning."

Graydon turns toward him, a furious look on his face. "You counted?"

OC shrugs. "After the third time, I was truly invested in what kind of record you were planning on setting. Got to say, man, your stamina is remarkable."

"It was," I say as I take a sip of my orange juice. "Then again, Graydon is quite a remarkable man."

The smallest smile lights up his handsome face as he walks over to me again, grips my neck possessively, and brings his mouth to mine. "Don't forget it, beautiful."

---

Things at work are...awkward, to say the least.

After a long debate about who would take me to work, OC won out because he said he was better than a stranger in an Uber. Graydon argued, but I said goodbye to my man and hitched a ride with OC.

Graydon told me that my car should be ready anytime now. They're just finishing up the paint job. It will be nice to have my car back so I won't have to rely on anyone for a ride anymore.

But now that I'm here and all of the early chores are done, we have some downtime, and Hank is doing everything he can to avoid me. I don't blame him, though. Things have gotten uncomfortable, and he doesn't believe in the relationship I have with Graydon. Not that I need him to believe, but it would be nice if I didn't have to stand next to him, knowing he's judging me.

"Ah, there you are," Gretchen says as she walks into the room in her no-nonsense power suit and with her hair perfectly styled into coiffed waves. "Let's talk."

Not *Do you have a moment?*

Or *Do you think we can chat?*

Just . . . *Let's talk.*

She gestures toward the office of the flamingo building, which we use more for storage than anything else.

"You want to talk in there?"

"Unless you have a better option."

I nod and push off the counter. "Follow me."

I take her out back toward the event space where we usually meet. I bring her into the kitchen for a more intimate setting, then lean against the Sub-Zero fridge.

"I wasn't expecting to see you today," I say, feeling slightly nervous because a meeting with Gretchen never means anything good.

"Well, I wasn't expecting to wake up to these photos," she says as she flashes her phone to me, revealing a picture of me sitting on the back of Graydon's truck, his mouth and hands all over me.

Yup, just as I expected. Nothing good can come from Gretchen.

I swallow and attempt a smile. "Oh, that—"

"I'm going to ask you to be honest with me, Maple." Her take-no-prisoners gaze cracks through whatever strength I just mustered. "Is there something more to your relationship with Graydon than I know of?"

"And if there was?"

"Then that's something I need to know because if there are feelings in the mix, it makes it hard for me to control the narrative to Graydon's benefit."

Notice how she just said "Graydon"?

I knew she never really cared about me and the zoo.

Then again, she's being paid by the Foghorns, so why would she put any care into the zoo?

"So tell me the truth about you two so I can best prepare for all worst-case scenarios."

"Worst-case scenarios?" I ask. "What is that supposed to mean?"

She sighs heavily and folds her arms over her chest. "Maple, as someone in public relations, it is my job to *not* live in a land where nothing bad happens and a zookeeper can make out with a football star in the back of his truck without consequences."

Wow, she's spicy today.

"I have to think about what happens to the public perception of Graydon if or when you two decide to break things off."

"When? What makes you think we're going to break things off?"

"Like I said," she answers in her no-nonsense tone that lacks any ounce of bedside manner, "I have to be realistic, and the probability of a multimillion-dollar star football player living a long, happy life with a zookeeper is very slim. Not to mention the high-stakes pressure that you are already receiving from the public and the investment they've shown in your relationship. The direction this can go is bad and bad quick, which is why I need to know everything about you and Graydon. I need to make sure a breakup does not sully the hard work we've put into this relationship."

"The hard work we've put into it? Not to be rude, Gretchen, but it was my idea to start Flock and Tackle."

"Yes, and I commend the idea. It was the jump-off point for the PR relationship that was created and curated by me, the true commander of gathering the public's attention. And need I remind you, the idea of the PR relationship was to keep it just that: PR? There was no mention of turning anything between the two of you into something real. Now that you have, I have to work overtime to make sure we don't have any more mishaps like this." She flashes me the screen of her phone again, where I see Graydon's hand very close to my breast.

My throat grows tight as I bring my attention back to her. "I doubt anyone is going to be mad about seeing us kissing. If anything, it might spur on the excitement and love for Graydon."

"Yes, you are right about that, but what I'm worried about is that you were completely unaware of this. These photos have been leaked everywhere and picked up by every major media source, meaning the relationship you thought you had with Graydon just became exponentially more difficult."

"This doesn't make sense. We were already...sort of public."

"Public in a curated way," Gretchen corrects me. "There is nothing curated about these photos other than a raw horniness that has been captured for the world to see. The public will become feral for more, which means the paparazzi will look for more opportunities. You're not just a zookeeper dating a professional football player, Maple. You're one of the most talked about, up-and-coming stories in pop culture right now."

"Oh my God, don't you think that's a little—"

She flashes me her phone again, and sitting at number two on trending topics is "Graydon St. John and girlfriend."

"By tonight, you will be number one. And it won't die down, not with the season starting right around the corner. This changes everything, which means I need you to cooperate."

My nerves tickle the back of my neck as I think through everything Graydon warned me about before I entered into the PR relationship with him. His promises that the public would tear me apart.

Break me.

I look at Gretchen and ask, "When have I not cooperated?"

"You have, but like I said, this is going to become a whole lot more difficult to maneuver." She opens her notes app and starts typing away. "Now, who knows about your relationship with Graydon?"

"Uh...everyone, apparently."

Her brow lifts as she looks up at me through her lashes, unamused. "In your inner circle. Who knows about the personal details?"

"Oh, um...my friend Everly and her husband, Hardy."

"Full names."

"Everly and Hardy Hopper."

She looks up at me. "Hopper as in the Hopper brothers, heirs to Hopper Industries?"

"Well, technically, they're not heirs anymore since they separated their business from their dad's, but yes, that Hardy Hopper."

"How do you know them?"

"Hardy and I used to date back in college. But we're just friends now."

"How close of friends?"

"Seriously?"

She sighs. "I told you, I need to know everything, Maple. Everything."

Well, this meeting is about to get a lot more complicated than I thought.

# CHAPTER 38
# GRAYDON

**Graydon:** Leaving the practice facility now. Will pick you up soon.

**Maple:** Already left. Hank is dropping me off at my place.

I CLENCH MY JAW AND take a deep breath as I try not to get angry at Slutty Little Glasses still sticking his fucking sniveling body where it doesn't belong.

**Graydon:** Be there shortly.

I pocket my phone, sling my bag over my shoulder, and head out of the locker room just as I come face-to-face with my father.

He's leaning against the wall opposite the locker room entrance, wearing a pair of worn jeans, a gray Foghorns shirt, and a matching hat. He looks like a goddamn idiot trying to relive his glory days. *Get a fucking life, go somewhere else, you piece of shit.* Preferably far away from Mom and me.

Not sparing him any of my time, I start to turn away, but he pushes off the wall and grips me by the shoulder. "Graydon, a word."

From his tone, I know I don't have an option in the matter, so I let him direct me away from the locker room and toward my coach's office.

Great.

Can't wait to see what they have planned for me this time.

We enter Coach Keenan's office, where he's sitting at his desk. Gretchen is perched on a chair as well.

"Take a seat," Dad says, pushing me down into a chair but having a hard time doing it, given that I'm bigger and stronger than him.

Wanting to get the hell out of here and to Maple as quickly as possible, I don't put up a fight.

"Did you have a good night last night?" Coach Keenan asks, and immediately, the hairs on the back of my neck stand at attention. "Because from the pictures I've seen, you had one hell of a night."

Fuck.

My mind reels back to my room, where I fucked Maple on every surface. Were the curtains shut? I think they were. Pretty sure they were. It's rare that I actually open them. But on the off chance, were they open?

Did OC say something? I don't think he would, but he also is an idiot and could have said something without thinking.

"From the panicked expression on your face, I'm going to guess that you did," Coach Keenan says as he turns his computer screen toward me and shows me a picture of Maple sitting on the tailgate of my truck, me standing between her legs, my hand obviously gripping her breast while we make out.

Shit.

But at least it's not my bedroom.

"Gretchen went to visit Maple today at the zoo." My eyes fall to Gretchen.

"What the fuck did you say to her?"

Is that why she went home with Hank? Gretchen better not have scared Maple away. There will be fucking consequences if she did.

"Your tone," my father says.

I shoot a look at him and say, "This does not concern you. Why the fuck are you even here?"

"Because you're my son, and even though you don't believe it to be true, what you do in your everyday life affects me as well."

"Right, forgot your reputation is far more important to you than any other real-life situation."

"We're getting off-topic." Gretchen steps in, clearly not wanting to be part of another father-son fight. "I spoke with Maple today about your relationship and how your moving from a PR relationship to a real one would have been information we needed to know. I don't like waking up to surprises like this, Graydon."

"We're kissing. It's not that big of a deal."

"Your hand placement is a big deal," Dad says.

"Oh, fuck off. As if you've been innocent throughout your entire career. You paid millions to get rid of a sex tape you made with some whore on a road trip."

Dad's eyes narrow. "This is not about me."

"Exactly, it's about me and my private relationship with Maple."

"That's where you're wrong," Coach Keenan says. "The moment you signed to be in a PR relationship with the zookeeper is the moment you gave up all rights to keeping this private."

Eyeing my coach, I ask, "Shouldn't you be talking to your offensive coordinator and figuring out why it's so difficult for your O-line to stay up on their goddamn feet for more than three seconds? Seems like that might be a more productive use of your time."

"You're about to cost yourself a starting position," Coach Keenan says, throwing around an empty threat. There's no way they'd start without me. I'm one of the reasons our opponents aren't able to run the score up as our offense struggles to reach a first down.

"You know, I think I should just talk to Graydon alone," Gretchen says.

"I would prefer to hear what he has to say and how he plans on handling this breakup."

"Breakup?" I shout, looking at my dad, who had the audacity to even mention such a stupid thing. "Where the fuck did you come up with that?"

"Graydon, you can have your fun with her, but we all know where this is headed and it's why we're getting in front of the crisis beforehand, coming up with an action plan. Gretchen already secured a breakup relationship NDA with Maple today—"

"What?" I stand, my heart pounding. "What the hell did you have her sign?"

Did she say she would break up with me?

Panic ensues because I know Maple. I know that she would just give in to make things easier. And I'll be damned if she just signed away her rights to be with me.

I slam my fist on the desk. "What the fuck did you make her sign?"

Gretchen calmly says, "Just a document that says she will not comment on your relationship when it inevitably falls apart."

"Inevitably?" I ask.

"We have to cover our bases, Graydon. And you haven't had a serious relationship since, well...since you've been in the public eye."

"Did it ever occur to you it's because I haven't found the right person?" I tug on my hair. "Jesus, fuck, what did you do? Just go to her work, corner her, and scare the shit out of her so she'd sign some bullshit NDA?" My eyes fall on Gretchen. "I would expect that from them, but you, Gretchen? I expected a little more from you."

I need to get the hell out of here and go see Maple.

Turning away from them, I head toward the door, but my dad steps in the way, blocking my exit.

"Move," I say through clenched teeth.

"Graydon, it's important to hear them out. You've made a lot of progress and have brought the team forward in popularity. We don't want to see that all go to waste."

A sneer on my face, I look my dad in the eyes and say, "Because that's all that matters, right? The public perception? That's all you've ever cared about. You never even thought about visiting Mom in her care facility because it didn't fit the image you were trying to create for yourself."

His eyes widen just as I push him to the side.

"Get the fuck out of my way."

I open the door and take off, fury firing off my shoulders as I make my way down the hallway. Heels clack against the cement floor behind me, but I don't bother to pause. I have one thing on my mind, and that's getting to Maple and making sure everything is okay. Making sure she's okay.

I can't believe they—

"Graydon, wait," Gretchen says, pulling on my shoulder.

I turn to face her, blistering her with the anger in my eyes. "What?" I shout.

And for the first time since I've met this woman, I actually see a hint of fear crossing her features before she adjusts and straightens. "This is all to protect you."

"I don't give a fuck about protecting myself. I care about protecting Maple. She didn't ask for this, for any of this, and yet…"

"She did when she signed onto the PR relationship."

"Out of force. Out of the hope of bringing awareness to an animal she loves. Her motives were selfless, yet the Foghorns keep asking so much of her. And now this, a fucking breakup NDA? Jesus Christ, Gretchen, you're not even giving this relationship a chance to succeed before you're calling it dead."

"We have to be prepared, Graydon."

"If you want to be prepared, then figure out a way my girl can come to the games and be safe. Find her a seat up front with Scarlett, Hutton's wife. Get her a goddamn jersey of mine, treat her like a queen, and give her a positive experience that she can lock away about the Foghorns rather than making her sign some disgusting contract about us breaking up." I move close to Gretchen, and in a threatening tone, I add, "Because I can tell you right now, I have no intentions of breaking up with Maple. In fact, I see her as the endgame, so figure out how to deal with that and protect her. Not me. Got it?"

She swallows and then nods. "Of course."

"Good."

Then I take off and head to the parking lot.

---

I jog up the steps to Maple's apartment, a nauseous feeling in my stomach as I grow closer and closer to her. The entire drive over here, all I kept thinking about was what would happen if Gretchen scared her. What if she put negative thoughts in her head? What if Maple's waiting in her apartment right now, trying to find the right words to end this?

End it when it just started.

When I reach her door, I give it a knock and then stick my hands in my pockets as I wait for her to open it.

It takes a few seconds, but when she does, my breath catches in my throat as I take in her fluffy pink robe, makeup-free face, and wet hair that is now braided.

"Hey," I say, feeling awkward.

Then, to my surprise, she takes my hand in hers, tugs me into her apartment, and shuts the door. She stands on her toes, loops her arms around my neck, and pulls me down, crushing her mouth to mine.

The worries all fade away as I lift her by her ass, right into my arms, and walk her over to her couch, our mouths molding the entire time while I take a seat, situating her so she's straddling my lap. My hands slide along her legs, up to her hips, where I find that she's not wearing anything under this robe, at least on her bottom half.

She moans into my mouth, the sound so sweet, so goddamn perfect that I almost get lost in it. . . almost.

I pull away and attempt to catch my breath before saying, "We need to talk."

As if I just slapped her, she pulls back, fear replacing the lust in her eyes.

"Shit, that came out wrong," I backtrack, trying to gather my wits. "Sorry, I just…I was expecting a different greeting, and you kind of short-circuited my brain for a second."

"What kind of greeting were you expecting?" she asks.

I run my palm over the back of my neck as I say, "Honestly, I thought that maybe you came back here, to your place, because of the conversation you had with Gretchen. And had Hank drive you because you were upset."

"Oh…no. Not to make things gross, but I got into a situation at the exhibit today. I'll spare you the details, but I was in desperate need of a shower and wanted to take one before I saw you. And I didn't have Hank take me to your place because I don't want him knowing where you live." Her hands run up my chest. "Did Gretchen tell you about the conversation we had?"

I nod. "She did. She cornered me with my dad and coach as well. She told me what she made you sign." I shake my head. "I need you to know, I knew nothing about that and—"

She places her finger over my lips, silencing me. "I know what Gretchen talked to me about today has nothing to do with you and everything to do with what she's paid to do."

Relief starts pushing through me. "You sure? I don't want you doubting this…doubting us. We just got started. I would be…fuck, beautiful, I would be gutted if you backed away because of something they said."

She leans in close to my ear and whispers, "It's going to take a lot more than some stupid NDA to break me." Then her lips kiss along my jaw, to the spot below my ear, and then to my neck, where she slides down my body and between my legs, kneeling on the floor.

Her hands find the waistband of my jeans, but before she can undo them, I say, "I need to make sure you're okay, Maple."

"I'm okay." She offers up that soft smile of hers.

"Promise? You're not second-guessing anything?"

She shakes her head. "Of course not. It's you and me, right? Any outside noise doesn't matter."

God, she's so fucking perfect.

So strong.

Everything I need in life, wrapped up into this beautiful human.

"Right," I answer, rubbing my thumb over her cheek. "You and me. As long as we're communicating, then everything will be okay."

She nods, her eyes darting to my pants, but I grip her chin, forcing her to look at me. "Communication, Maple."

She nods again and then undoes my pants, pulling them down along with my boxer briefs, taking my shoes and socks off at the same time. I reach behind my head and pull my shirt off as well while she drags her hands up my thighs, leading with her nails, scraping along my skin and turning me on faster than any other goddamn woman I've ever been with.

I lean my head back as her hand finds my length, and she starts pumping me.

Perfect.

She's so perfect.

*"Of course not. It's you and me, right? Any outside noise doesn't matter."*

Fuck, I hope that stays true. Because I know there will be a shit ton of outside noise.

I won't deny that it stung when neither Coach, nor Gretchen, nor my dad—not that he surprised me—believed I was capable of having a lasting relationship. *But I will prove them wrong.*

Maple Baker is the best thing to ever happen to me.

# CHAPTER 39
# MAPLE

"I'LL TEXT YOU," GRAYDON SAYS, his mouth inches from mine before he lets his lips linger for a few more seconds. "Bye, beautiful."

I smile. "Bye."

One more kiss, then he takes off down the hallway before I shut the door, lean against it, and slide down to the floor, where I let all the pent-up tears I've been holding back for the past fifteen hours spill over my cheeks.

I cover my face with my hands and allow my sobs to rip through my body.

For the anger and frustration to take over.

For the fear and worry to consume me.

And for every last word Gretchen said yesterday to seep in.

After she cornered me into signing an NDA about my future breakup with Graydon, Gretchen put me through a crash course in what to expect when Graydon "does end things." There was no doubt in her mind that the breakup was inevitable, and I felt like absolute shit. *You're just a zoo-keeper. What draw could you possibly have?*

I was shown examples of the narrative we'd follow, of how I'd have to take the blame, which would then mean I'd be followed and pursued by the media for explanations and statements.

It was...unlike anything I've ever seen before, like witnessing your funeral before it even occurs. Then I was thrust back into work, where I had to act like my heart wasn't being torn apart, one word at a time. It took everything in me to hold back, to not crash and burn in front of all the visitors, but as the day went on, my heart weighed heavier and heavier, and when I didn't think I could do it anymore, I slipped and fell into the flamingos' water. Hank thankfully brought me home so I could shower, and I blamed my tears on embarrassment.

Then I cried in the shower, sobbed actually, letting the hot water sluice over me. When I got out and saw Graydon's text, I knew I was going to have to pull it together before he got to my apartment. So I thought of his handsome face and pushed away the idea of having to say goodbye to it.

By the time he came around, I'd had enough time to put on a happy face and push the day to the back of my mind. I'm glad that I did because I saw the worry etched all over his brow, and I didn't want him worrying about me. He has enough going on in his life, and I've learned that he's not great at processing stuff when he's overwhelmed, so I took the burden of what happened and let it rest on my shoulders while I eased his anxiety.

But now that he's gone, I let all of that bottled-up anxiety and fear pour out of me.

I don't know how long I stay there, sorrow racking my body, but I stay there until I don't have one more tear to shed. On a shaky breath, I stand from the ground and move over to the kitchen, where a mug of cold coffee waits for me.

Graydon made it.

My lip trembles.

Of course he made it.

He's sweet and considerate and cares about me.

My lip trembles some more from the thought of losing that, losing him.

No, not again. Keep it together.

My phone rings from the other room and I hurry to go answer it. When I see Graydon's name appear, my heart races with excitement. I take a second to steady my voice before answering.

"Hello?"

"Hey, beautiful," he says, his husky voice instantly calming me. "I forgot to mention that we have a team dinner Friday night. I meant to ask you if you wanted to go but forgot, given everything that happened. Would you do me the honor of being my date?"

My smile stretches from ear to ear. "You sure you don't want to take someone else?" I sit on my bed, pulling my knees up to my chest as I pick up the pillow he slept on and hug it close.

It smells like him.

"Who the hell else would I take?"

"OC," I tease.

"Fuck...no."

I let out a low chuckle. "You two would look cute together."

"Would rather eat rusty razor blades than take that annoying puke anywhere."

"He's not that bad," I reply, making Graydon grumble.

"He counted how many times we had sex the other night."

"As if you weren't counting."

"I was counting, but that's because I was the man fucking you, not him."

God, the way he says "fucking," it's like he's purring in my ear. Such a turn-on.

"I don't know. Maybe you should give him a chance. He would be the sunshine to your grumpy."

"Keep joking about it and see what kind of spanking you'll get next time I see you."

"Is that supposed to be a threat? Because to me, it sounds more like a good time."

"Maple," he says in a gruff tone.

"Yes?" I ask, a smile on my face that I can't seem to hold back.

"You can't turn me on before I head into training."

I laugh. "Is it really that easy?"

"With you? Always."

How can he say something so simple like that, yet make my cheeks blush like he's right here in the room, staring me down?

"Well, we can't have you hard while touching your teammates."

"Yeah, I want to try to avoid that."

"Then let's change the subject. About this party..."

"Right. Are you going to say yes?"

"I would prefer to keep you on the edge of your seat about my attendance, but given your possible hardening situation, I think I'll be nice and let you know that I'll be there."

"Good."

"Is there anything special I need to wear? Like, is this a fancy event?"

"No, really casual. Some of the guys who have kids bring them. It's really relaxed, just a kickoff before the season starts."

"Oh, okay. And are you sure it's okay that I go?"

"Why wouldn't it be okay?"

I drag my hand over my comforter. "Because I'm new. We're new. I don't want to make anyone uncomfortable."

"How would you make anyone uncomfortable?"

"I don't know, Graydon. I just want to make sure it's okay."

"I'm saying it's okay. Therefore, it's okay."

"Am I on the approved list?"

"I'm not sure you understand how this works. I tell them you're going with me, and it's done. That's it. Are you hesitant because you don't want to go?"

"No."

There's silence for a moment, and then he asks, "Are you hesitant because of what happened yesterday?"

*Yes.*

And terrified.

"I just don't want to step on anyone's toes."

"The only toes you would be stepping on would be if I was dating someone else, and that's not the case here. It's you and you alone. Maple..." He sighs. "Please tell me everything is going to be okay."

Tears spring to my eyes. *God, I thought I was out of tears.*

I swallow back the emotions, though, not wanting to cause him any concern.

"Everything is great," I say, but it doesn't sound as cheery as I want it to.

"I'm turning around."

"No," I say. "Don't, you're going to be late. I'm fine, I promise. There's nothing you need to worry about."

"Yeah, but you're questioning if you should go to this party, and you don't sound like yourself. Yesterday, I needed you to know where I stand, and it's anywhere where you're by my side."

My heart clenches as I nod even though he can't see me. "I know."

"Do you?"

"I do."

"Promise?"

"Promise," I answer, hating myself for being so weak.

"Okay. Can I come over later?"

"I hope you do," I answer, hugging his pillow closer. "I can make us dinner."

"Maybe we can make it together."

"I would like that."

"Okay." He lets out another sigh. "Are you good?"

"I am."

"You're not going to hide anything from me? Your feelings or anything like that?"

"No," I answer, swallowing the lump in my throat.

"Because we're in this together. I don't care what anyone else around us says. This is between you and me and no one else, got it?"

"Yes," I answer.

"Good. Okay, I'll talk to you later."

"Okay, bye."

"Bye, beautiful."

We both hang up as the tears I've been holding back fall down my cheeks.

God, what the hell is wrong with me?

I need help, and I need it quick. I shoot Everly an emergency text. If anyone can help me, it's going to be her.

---

"Wow," Everly says, shaking her head after I finish explaining how Gretchen came to the zoo yesterday and basically uprooted my entire life. "You know, I was kind of into the whole badass female PR person, but that was...that was uncalled for."

"I know. She scares me, but also, I approve of the strength she has, something I'm jealous of at the moment." I sip my coffee, grateful Everly could meet me at the zoo. We pulled up seats at the Lemur Café, grabbed some subpar coffee, and are sharing a muffin—one we are not licking from the center because I'm not sure anyone does that besides OC.

"You have strength," Everly says. "Think about how you handled Graydon this entire time. Anyone weaker would have thrown in the towel, but you stood your ground and now look where you're at. You have the strength. You're just a little shaken right now. And rightfully so." She leans in closer. "Here you are, having the time of your life, fucking a mammoth of a man in front of a mirror, and then bam, you're signing a contract about your breakup. I mean, if it were me, I would be rocking back and forth in the corner asking for my mommy."

I let out a snort. "Well, you're not my mommy, but you were my first call, that's for sure."

She presses her hand to her chest. "I'm honored, but this means I need to give you much-needed advice, right?"

"Yeah, that would be the requirement of being my first call."

"Well." She places her hand on top of mine. "My advice to you is to block out the noise and enjoy that man's penis."

"Everly." I let out a boisterous laugh as I look around.

She casually shrugs. "What? It's the truth. That's exactly what I would do. Who cares what Gretchen says? Who cares what his coach or his pill of a father says or the fans? You like him, right?"

"I do," I answer. "A lot. No offense to Hardy, but I don't think I've ever felt this enamored with a man before."

She chuckles. "Hardy will be fine. Trust me." She winks. "And if this man has captured you this much, then stop worrying about everything around you and start worrying about what kind of lingerie you plan on wearing for him tonight. Seriously, Maple, take it from someone who worried a lot when it came to pursuing a relationship—it's a waste of time. Take what you want and enjoy it. Fuck everyone else around you."

I nod. "It's just...he's so high-profile."

"You knew that going into this, though."

"I know, but feelings weren't involved then."

She nods. "Ah, I see. Well, if feelings are involved now, then all the more reason to tell everyone to fuck off and serve yourself. I think as women, specifically empathetic women, we tend to want to please everyone around us and make sure people approve of our decisions, but for what? To make others happy? Screw that. We need to start taking care of ourselves, start caring about what the reflection in the mirror wants, not everyone else."

She's right.

I'm always trying to please.

Always trying to be selfless, to be the good girl, the person who appeases everyone else around her, because I don't want to come off as a bitch or difficult. But why?

Am I living this life for others or for me?

"I can see by the way you're sitting taller that you're possibly giving yourself a mental pep talk. Please, invite me into it."

I laugh.

How many times have I acquiesced to Phil's demands of me at the zoo? Even if it's taken extra time in my day. If I'm honest with myself, I only stayed together with Hardy for as long as I did because I didn't want to make waves or disappoint him. *We were never the right fit.* If I went down the proverbial rabbit hole, I'm certain I could revisit many situations where I've stayed quiet in my life and not demanded what I wanted.

"I was just thinking that I've spent my entire life appeasing others, even my beloved flamingos, and that maybe it's time that I appease myself. I want him, Everly, so why don't I just take him?"

"That's what I'm talking about." She smacks the table. "You take what you want and do it unapologetically. If anything, the Foghorns should be grateful for the relationship you've developed with Graydon. I saw the other day that season ticket sales have increased, and the social media for the Foghorns is on fire. Their social media team is running on content of you two."

"What? Really?"

"Uh, have you not been paying attention?" she asks as she picks up her phone and taps away on the screen.

She shows me the feed for the Foghorns, and there are a few videos of me watching Graydon. One of Graydon pushing my hair out of my face. Another of him smiling down at me. And the views on the videos are insane.

"Oh my God."

"Yeah, they're going crazy, so I understand why they're worried about the breakup and how it might play out."

"But to preplan a breakup? That just seems so...ominous."

"I could not agree more, but they are seeing your relationship as a business. Not that I'm sticking up for them by any means. They can rot in hell for all I care, but what you need to do is block out that noise and focus on the way Graydon looks at you, because girl, that look he's giving you...It's the same look Hardy gives me. It's the same look I see Brody give Maggie. Hudson practically devours Sloane every time he sees her, and don't get me started on those Cane brothers. Uteruses weep whenever they look at their soulmates. This is very much real for Graydon, and I think you need to hold on to that and not overthink it. Just feel and enjoy."

I attempt to hold back my smile. "He really does look at me in a special way, doesn't he?"

"Uh...yeah. If I wasn't so massively in love with my husband, I might have watched that video ten times while weeping instead of three times."

I laugh and then click on the video, watching his eyes light up as I jog toward him. God, she's so right. It's all there, the evidence. And this wasn't for the cameras, this wasn't for some PR idea, this was him just watching me, taking me in, and someone catching it secretly.

I wet my lips. "This whole relationship was so unexpected. I truly did not like him at first, but then, something just switched. I started seeing past the grumpy facade and started noticing the little things. And all those little things have added up to something so much bigger. I really like him, Everly."

"Good, because clearly he really likes you."

I nod. "He's told me several times."

"Then hold on to that, live off that, and the rest of it, the rest...it can just fade into black. Because you have everything you need."

"I do." I smile and stare down at the video again. "I have Graydon."

# CHAPTER 40
# GRAYDON

**OC:** Bennett, did you start a book club?

**Bennett:** I did.

**OC:** Uh, did you not think that it would be a good idea to run that by us first?

**Bennett:** Why the hell would I run that by you?

**OC:** Uh, because I heard that you were pulling out of the zoo PR, and you're now into this whole book club thing. Is this your subtle way of telling us you're leaving the Gladdy Daddies?

**Graydon:** I hope so. Maybe we can disband the whole damn thing.

**OC:** Says the guy who leaned on the Gladdy Daddies when he was in desperate need of help. I would consider how you profited from such a group before attempting a disbandment.

**Bennett:** I'm not leaving the Gladdy Daddies.

**Graydon:** Not the correct thing to say.

**OC:** *Exhales loudly* Thank God.

**Bennett:** I felt the exhale from here.

**Graydon:** Yeah, someone forgot to brush his teeth.

**OC:** First of all, I have excellent oral hygiene, I'm constantly cleaning the silverware…if you know what I mean. Second, my nipples got a little hard from you making a joke, Graydon. We are wearing you down.

**Graydon:** I'm about to block you.

**OC:** But you won't.

**Bennett:** Can we get back to the silverware thing? Are you talking about your tongue?

**OC:** Yeah, because that's how I eat…you know…a woman.

**Graydon:** If I was a dick, I would say no wonder Grace is engaged to someone else, but I won't go there today.

**OC:** Uh…you just did. You still said it without saying it.

**Graydon:** But technically, I didn't say it.

**OC:** Doesn't mean it doesn't still hurt. You owe me a hug.

**Graydon:** Over my dead body.

**Bennett:** I mean, I think he deserves a hug.

**Graydon:** Did he tell you how he forced himself upon me, slept on my couch, and then counted the number of times I had sex with Maple that night?

**Bennett:** Dude…

**OC:** In my defense, I got them pastries for breakfast the next morning.

**Bennett:** Doesn't matter. No hug, but the comment evens the playing field now.

**OC:** I'll take it. BTW…it was six times.

**Graydon:** I will rip your goddamn head off.

**OC:** Which head? I have two.

**Graydon:** Blocking.

**OC:** Wait, we have yet to find out about the book club. Don't you want to hear what Bennett is up to?

**Graydon:** I'll text him separately.

**Bennett:** Now, now, let's not get too hasty. OC is going through a crisis and is extra annoying. I think we can all agree upon that.

**OC:** I'm even annoying myself, if that helps.

**Bennett:** See, it's not just us. He's suffering too.

**Graydon:** Why are you so adamant about keeping the Gladdy Daddies?

**Bennett:** Well, it's nice to have friends. And you never know when one of us might need help.

**OC:** *Gasp* It's the sister's friend, isn't it?

**Graydon:** Why are you so dramatic?

**OC:** Someone needs to bring the fun, or else this chat would just be full of grunts and growls, and that's only sustainable for so long. Now, please don't interrupt our fellow daddy while he tells us about the sister's friend.

**Bennett:** Not ready to really talk about anything, but you know, if there was something to say, it would be great to know that the Gladdy Daddies are here to talk.

**OC:** Are you starting the book club for her?

**Bennett:** Sort of. I was talking to Gretchen about the zoo and how it hasn't had much of an impact. We had a brainstorming session, and she was asking what I like. I said romance novels, and well...she ran with that. It was the first thing that came to mind because well...Bower is always on my mind.

**OC:** Is that her name? Bower? I think I forgot that nugget.

**Bennett:** It is.

**OC:** Bennett and Bower, wow, has a great ring to it.

**Graydon:** I'm not into the dramatics, but yeah, it does.

**Bennett:** I might have written our names in a heart a few times.

**OC:** Well, that just got my dick hard.

**Graydon:** And then you go and fucking ruin it. Jesus Christ. I'm out.

---

"Are you going to be okay?" I ask Maple as I turn to her in my truck.

I picked her up from the zoo and brought her back to her place, where she took a shower and got ready for the team party. She made me stay in her living room while I waited and she grumbled about things not fitting right, mentioned possibly not going because her hair was doing "a thing," and even lay on the bed, staring up at the ceiling for a whole two minutes reciting all the different breeds of flamingos.

If I wasn't so goddamn terrified that she might not go, I might have thought it was funny. But I was on bated breath the entire time, hoping she wasn't going to change her mind.

"I'm fine." She straightens the hem of the sundress she chose to wear. It's red with white flowers, and she paired it with a jean jacket and white sneakers. She braided her hair into two loose French braids because it wasn't doing what she wanted and then put on a little bit of makeup, going for a more natural look. When she walked out of her bedroom, I felt my heart hammer against my chest from the sight of her. Like a fucking nineties heartthrob.

I kept it simple with a pair of worn jeans, white sneakers, and a black shirt.

"Are you sure? You're a little jittery."

"Yeah, fine." She nervously laughs. "I'm just…I'm nervous to meet everyone."

"Maple, you already know everyone. You've been training with them."

"This is different. This is their families, and we're not in football gear. This is more personal."

"You're going to do great. Just stick with me."

"As if I would wander off by myself," she scoffs. "If I'm not glued to your side the entire night, someone stole me."

I chuckle. "Good to know. Stay there."

I hop out of my truck and move to her side, where I open the door. Before I let her out, I twist her toward me and move between her legs. I gently cup her cheek and say, "You look beautiful, by the way."

"So you've said." A genuine smile falls across her lips.

"Just need you to know since you were fretting over it."

"I just don't understand why out of all nights, my hair decided to be rude and not work with me."

I tug on her braid. "I like the braids. I even like the little pieces that frame your face."

"Thank you." She places her hands on my shoulders. "Okay, take me to the party before I try to hide away in the glove box of your truck."

"I would love to see you attempt that, but maybe another time."

I take her hand and help her out of the truck. When I shut the door, I pinch her chin with my forefinger and thumb and tilt her mouth up before stealing another kiss from her.

When her lips mold around mine, I take a second to just sink into her, taste her, revel in the way she fits so perfectly against me. Jesus, why did it take me so long to give in to the temptation? I could have been doing this for much longer.

Fucking fool.

When I pull away, I smile down at her and then kiss the tip of her nose. "Ready?"

She nods. "Ready."

"Then let's go."

Her hand in mine, I lead her into the training facility, where they've transformed the practice field into a giant event space. On the far end are jump houses, obstacle courses, and tables full of family-friendly craft projects. I've never ventured down toward the end because I've never needed to.

On the closest end, a DJ hangs out on a stage and there are rows and rows of tables and high-tops. They've strung bunting from pole to pole, celebrating the Foghorns' new season, and a photo booth, a dance floor, and a bar are nearby.

That's where we will be headed.

"Wow, it looks amazing in here and smells good too. Not the usual dirty-sneaker smell."

I chuckle. "Yeah, they must have cleaned everything, knowing families were coming."

I nod to a few guys in passing, some of them giving fist bumps to Maple as we make our way to the bar.

I lean down to her ear and say, "And you were worried that no one was going to want you here."

"An 'I told you so'? Really, Graydon?"

I chuckle and kiss the side of her head. "Not sure I'll get many, so I have to claim them when I can."

"For your benefit, I wouldn't." She pats my cheek, and I smirk because I love the confidence.

The past few days have been different. Like there's been something missing from her eyes and whatever it is has been replaced with worry. And I know it has everything to do with the contract Gretchen had her sign, even though Maple kept telling me over and over again that she was fine. That she wasn't upset. I knew she was hiding her true feelings from me.

But night after night, we've made dinner together, we've spent time just talking about everything and anything, and when it's time for bed, I've shown her just how much she means to me, how much I need her.

So seeing that sass come out? I fucking love it.

"What do you want to drink?"

She presses her lips together as she gives her answer some thought. "Umm, I don't know. Are we doing alcohol?"

"We're at a bar, at a team function, where my dad will be making an appearance. Yes, we are doing alcohol."

"Your dad will be here?" she asks, her eyes going wide.

"Yes, he's at every Foghorns event because he doesn't have a life of his own and attempts to live his glory days through me despite thinking I'm a waste of human space."

She frowns. "Well, he's rude, and I hope he stubs his toe today."

"Yeah, I hope for a lot more than that," I say, and then turn to the bartender. "Can we get a Guinness and…does a wine work for you?"

"White," she says.

"And a white wine."

The bartender nods and gets to work while Maple loops her arm around my waist. "Is he going to try to talk to you?"

"If he's smart, he won't."

"And if he's dumb?"

"More than likely, yes. I'll be pleasant because there are children here, and I'm not about to get into a fight with him, but if he says anything about you, I can't promise to hold back."

She smooths her hand up my chest. "Don't cause a scene because of me. If he says something, we can just send a glitter bomb to his house later on."

I raise a brow. "A glitter bomb?"

"Yes," she says with a smile. "It comes in the mail and looks like a package, but when they open it up, it sprays glitter all over their home."

A smile tugs on my lips. "Why haven't you mentioned this before? Can I get a weekly subscription sent to him?"

She laughs. "We'll set it up when we get back to…well, your place, I'm assuming?"

"Yeah, I just got some toys that I want to try out on you."

"Toys?" she asks just as our drinks are placed on the bar. I stick a twenty in the tip jar and hand Maple her drink.

"Yeah, you nervous?"

"With you? Never."

"Good answer," I say as I take her lips with mine, leaving it as a simple kiss but letting everyone in the room know she belongs to me.

"Aw, it's about time." I pull away just enough to see Scarlett, Hutton's wife, walk up to us wearing a pair of skinny jeans, white sneakers, and a white tank top that shows off her toned midriff. Hutton is right behind her in a matching outfit, which makes me smile. "I've been asking Hutton to set up a dinner so I could meet Maple, and I can't believe it's taken a team dinner to make it happen."

Scarlett pauses and then studies Maple for a second. "Holy shit." She laughs. "Oh my God, why am I so stupid?"

"Do you know each other?" I ask, feeling confused.

Scarlett pulls Maple into a hug and holds her tight.

"Girl, why am I so dumb?" Scarlett asks as she pulls away.

Maple chuckles. "Uh, no, why am I so dumb?"

"Kind of feeling dumb as well," Hutton says, raising a hand.

"Babe, this is Maple."

"Yes, I know," Hutton says. "She's been at training camp all week."

"No, this is Maple, one of Everly's bridesmaids from her wedding."

Hutton pauses, scratches his head, and then laughs. "Oh fuck, you're right."

"I can't believe I didn't put it together. I even follow Flock and Tackle." Scarlett shakes her head. "Babe, I might be losing it."

"I want to say you're not, but…this is pretty damning."

"You know what? I blame Everly," Maple says. "I don't know why she didn't say anything. You work with her, and I've gone to her several times about—ehhhh." She glances at me, and I question her with a look.

"What have you gone to her several times about?"

"Oh, you know." She smiles cutely. "How to handle a broody defensive end who used to scowl more than smile."

"You know, he is smiling a little bit more. It's a little freaky," Hutton says. "Don't know what to do when he's flashing his teeth all the time."

I glare at my friend, who laughs.

"Ah, there it is, the murderous expression I've come to love."

Ignoring him, I say, "So you two know each other?"

"We do," Maple says. She turns to Scarlett. "I guess I kind of forgot that you were married to a football player. You don't really talk about it."

"Oof, can't hear that enough," Hutton says, hand to chest. "My wife not talking about me feels really good."

Scarlett rolls her eyes. "Please, you get enough attention."

"Not from the right person." He snags his arm around her waist and kisses her neck. She leans into him for a moment before pulling away but keeps close as she slides her arm around his waist as well.

"Okay, so we are both dense, didn't put everything together, and are now here with someone we know. Looks like it all worked out."

"You know the other wives," Hutton says.

Scarlett scoffs. "I know them, but that doesn't mean I like them." She winks. "I like Maple. She takes care of flamingos, and now that she's here, we can get to know each other better. I've only ever really seen her in passing, so this is exciting. I can hear all about the flamingo keeper who has put a smile on our nasty friend's face."

"Nasty?" I ask.

"Well, you know...you don't have the best bedside manner."

"She's right." Hutton claps me on the shoulder. "You're kind of a dick."

Maple kisses my shoulder and smiles up at me. "But he's my nasty dick."

"Can you not call me that?" I ask as everyone laughs.

"She's a keeper if she's claiming you as her nasty dick." Hutton chuckles. "Shit, I should have that put on a jersey for you. Instead of your last name, it will just say Nasty Dick with your number."

"Ooh, maybe that's the jersey I can wear at your first game," Maple says, looking far too excited about it.

"You're not wearing 'nasty dick' on your back."

"I don't know, has a bit of pizzazz to it," Scarlett says with a shake of her shoulders. "And the chants." She cups her hands over her mouth and says, "Bury their heads, nasty dick. Bury them."

"Okay." I take a step back. "If this is how it's going to be, I think I'm going to go talk to someone else."

"Great," Scarlett says, looping her arm through Maple's. "We will just take this little gem with us and get to know her better. Have fun."

Scarlett waves, and before I can stop her, she directs Maple toward a high-top table where they both take a seat.

"Well, that idea backfired," Hutton says as I keep my eyes on Maple and how she so effortlessly fits right in with Scarlett.

"Yeah…it did," I say absentmindedly as a lightness fills my chest.

I've been to several of these kickoff party dinners. I've stayed for no more than an hour and made an appearance just to make it seem like I'm a team player, but I've gone home alone, annoyed and irritated that I had to go in the first place.

But this year…it's different.

Because I have Maple.

And she brings light to the dark life I've been living. She makes the colors around me brighter, the heaviness in my chest weightless, and makes me think of a future rather than just the day-to-day grind.

"Oh shit," Hutton says, pulling my attention back to the present.

"What?"

"I know that look." He shakes his head. "Graydon, you're into her, really into her."

I slowly nod, my eyes trailing over my girl. "Yeah, I fucking am."

---

"Graydon, it would be great if you could come over to our house sometime and wash our dishes since you're so good at it," Scarlett says as she and Maple walk up to us, each of them holding a plate of food.

Hutton and I found a four-person table, but only with three seats, so

I take Maple's plate, set it down in front of us, then have her take a seat on my lap, where I circle my arm around her waist and hold on to her.

"And deprive you of watching Hutton slip on rubber gloves to clean them himself? I would never."

"Do you really wear rubber gloves?" Maple asks as she stabs her fork into some of her salad.

"My hands get pruney quick," Hutton says as he takes a bite of his cheeseburger.

The Foghorns have dinner catered by multiple local restaurants from a variety of cuisines. A dessert bar spans three tables, including a make-your-own sundae bar for the kids. The drinks are all free—the least they can do—and now that I have a date, it's honestly one of the best kickoff dinners I've ever had.

"How did you two become friends?" Maple asks, motioning between Hutton and me. "Because you're offense and defense and, frankly, don't seem like a likely pairing."

"We're not," I say as I slip my fingers under the hem of Maple's dress.

I already ate and am now just picking at my plate.

"It's really a stupid story," Scarlett says.

"Oh? I like stupid stories."

Hutton wipes his mouth and places his napkin on the table. "I was new to the team, was unaware that Graydon was—as we have established—a nasty dick, and started sitting next to him in the cafeteria because no one was sitting near him. Didn't think much of it and started talking to him."

"And he talked back?" Maple asks, surprised.

"No. But then I saw it as a challenge, so I kept sitting next to him and talking. Bonded over our favorite flavor of Gatorade. And when I say bonded, I mean I talked about how his choice of lemon-lime was the same choice as mine. He didn't start budging until one day on the airplane when he forgot his headphones, and I had a spare. I let him borrow them, and from then on, we were besties."

"Headphones, that's all it takes?" Maple asks.

"My dad was on the plane, and his voice was grating on my nerves. Hutton saved me."

"You heard it here first," Hutton says, sitting taller. "Graydon said I saved him."

Maple chuckles. "Why do I feel like he's going to make a T-shirt that says that?"

"And why do I feel like I'm the one who will have to make it?" Scarlett asks.

"Because you're so good at it," Hutton says while kissing Scarlett.

I press a kiss to Maple's shoulder and then lean my chin against it as Maple asks Scarlett and Hutton, "And how did you two meet?"

"College," Scarlett answers. "We went to Brentwood University in Chicago. He played football there."

"Yeah, and she played the field."

Scarlett scoffs, playfully swatting Hutton. "Oh my God, as if you have room to talk."

"Listen, I was ready to settle down with you. You were a hard one to catch."

Scarlett rolls her eyes dramatically. "That's not how it went."

"That's entirely how it went. I was desperate for your attention. You were not desperate at all, and it took a whole lot of convincing on my end to get you to commit."

Scarlett shrugs. "Can't blame a girl for wanting a man to prove that he actually wants her. Right, Maple? Did Graydon prove to you that he wanted you?"

Maple glances at me and smiles softly. Her thumb tugs on the corner of my lip. "He did. Although, before that, I thought he was toying with me because he would text me thirst traps."

"No way," Scarlett says, eyes wide. "Graydon St. John sent you thirst traps?"

"They were not thirst traps," I answer with a heavy sigh.

"Uh, you were shirtless, and you angled up so I could see your entire chest and abs."

"Really?" Hutton asks with humor.

"It was the angle that I found to be most flattering." I shrug, making the table laugh.

"Wow, thirst traps from Graydon St. John. Did you save them?" Scarlett asks.

"I might have."

"Really?" I ask.

Maple's cheeks blush. "How could I not? It was a thirst trap from the nasty dick."

"Jesus," I grumble while Scarlett laughs.

"Well, maybe you can show me later." She wiggles her brows, only for Hutton to playfully pinch her side.

"Hey, you can get thirst traps from me. You don't need to see his." He then looks at me and Maple. "See what I told you? A wandering eye, this one."

"Oh my God." Scarlett turns to Hutton and cups his face. "You really are annoying." Then she plants a big kiss on his lips, only for him to cup the back of her head and pull her in closer.

Yeah, it's doubtful Scarlett is going anywhere with that "wandering" eye.

# CHAPTER 41
# MAPLE

"WILL PEOPLE JUDGE ME IF I make my own sundae?" I ask as I eye the ice cream and toppings.

"If they do, they'll be eating my fucking fist for dessert."

"Is there ever a time when you don't have violent thoughts?"

"It's rare." He moves in behind me and places his hands on my hips, then kisses my neck.

I tilt my head just enough to give him better access even though I know I shouldn't. I know I should shrug him off since we're in public and technically at a work event, but I don't want to push him away. I don't want to stop him, not when he's so loving like this.

So affectionate.

And I know he's been missing that in his life. So, because he so freely gives it to me, I never want to make him stop or feel insecure about it.

"How about I just have you for dessert?" he whispers into my ear.

"I'm all for it. How about right here, on top of all the desserts, we give everyone who's been staring an actual show?"

"There've been people staring?" he asks, moving his mouth back up to right below my ear.

"All night," I whisper and then sigh. "God, Graydon, you're making my nipples hard."

He pauses and then clears his throat.

"Really?"

I turn to face him and show him exactly what he's done to me.

His eyes go dark, and I can feel his hands itching at his sides, wanting to do something about it.

"There are children present, Graydon," I warn.

"Then what the hell are you doing showing me your hard nipples?"

"Uh, just giving you evidence of what you do to me. If you don't want to see it, then don't—"

"Graydon," someone says from behind him. I glance over his shoulder and spot one of his coaches, a man in a baseball cap and goatee. For the life of me, I can't remember his name because from what it seems like, there are a hundred coaches on staff.

Graydon turns toward him. "What's up, Coach?"

"Can I have a word? I know we're not talking football tonight, but I had a quick question about a play I was just mapping out on a napkin, and I wanted to get your input on it."

He turns to me, and I just smile. "Go ahead. I'm going to load up on a sundae."

"You sure?"

"Positive."

He leans down and presses a kiss to my cheek before whispering, "We're not done here."

And then he takes off with his coach.

We're not done here...

Don't I know it.

I pick up a bowl from the stack and move to the soft-serve ice cream machine they brought in for the event. The moment I saw that it was soft serve, I knew exactly what I was getting for dessert. Not to mention, there's hot fudge and peanuts. And I know, I know, why put hot fudge on soft serve when it melts it immediately, but soft-serve soup tastes just as good.

I take my time, making a bowl for myself with twist soft serve, fudge, peanuts, and chocolate sprinkles for the hell of it. Then I grab a spoon and a napkin, and I move over to one of the couches up against a partition and take a seat.

I noticed not many adults were going for the soft serve but rather opting for the fancier treats, but that's their loss, because this...this is where it's at. I take a bite and get lost in the flavors as I lean back on the couch and cross one leg over the other.

Graydon hovers over a high-top with his coach, who is pointing out something on a napkin. He's listening intently, and it's cute to see him all focused on his sport.

Adorable.

"Who have you spoken to?" a voice says from behind, startling me. I glance over my shoulder, and when I spot the partition, I realize the person is not talking to me.

"Philly and Miami," the other voice says.

Why do they sound so...familiar?

"And what have they said?"

"That they're interested, but they're not willing to pay more than what he's worth."

"And this is his last year under contract?"

Wait...is that...is that Graydon's dad?

"Yes, then we go into negotiations again. It might be hard to get the GM on board given the favoritism he's found from the fans, especially with this dumb flamingo thing."

Oh God, are they...are they talking about trading Graydon?

"I'm not worried about it. He'll screw it up somehow, he always does. The boy has too much baggage to be able to hold on to a normal relationship. She will see that quickly and break it off. Not to mention, she's too soft to handle the fame. It will fall apart quicker than it started, especially if I can rope that PR girl into it."

"Gretchen? I don't think she would do anything to jeopardize the team."

"I don't care about the team. We can jeopardize the girl. Welcott was telling me he already made the donation to the zoo, so we can label her as a gold digger. And you know. . . a sordid breakup could possibly force his hand in wanting to trade to another team."

My heart nearly pounds out of my chest as I attempt to hold my breath so I don't miss one single damaging word.

"All this for some records?" the other man, who I'm assuming is Keenan, asks.

"He doesn't deserve the team records," Troy says in a low tone. "He doesn't care about this team. He doesn't even care about the goddamn sport. He's just playing out of spite for me, and he will continue to play until he owns those records. We need him out. And it's not like he's getting any younger. He will be useless to you next year."

"Yeah. . ." Keenan hums. "He had a great training camp, which I hate to admit, but then again, he was fueled by rage. Don't you think breaking him up with that girl will do the same thing?"

"No," Troy answers. "I see the way he looks at her, and I actually think he cares. Losing her will destroy him, and he'll end up playing like shit. This will be to our benefit."

"Okay, let me see what I can do."

And then they take off, leaving me in a state of worry, fear, and anger.

They want to get Graydon to move? To be traded? What kind of father would do that? Over some stupid football record? He really is terrible.

A horrible human being.

Doesn't he know Graydon is here for a reason, for his mom? He's just going to take that away from him. Not to mention, Graydon is happy and succeeding. He's not as angry as when I first met him, and his dad just wants to shove him right back into that hole?

There's so much to unpack.

I'm not even thinking about the stuff he said about me. I can deal with that on my own—no need to worry Graydon about that—but trading him? That's…that's something he needs to know.

"There you are," Graydon says as he takes a seat next to me and looks down at my bowl. "Uh, why is your ice cream all melted? I thought you were excited to eat it."

I startle out of my thoughts and slap on a smile. "I like when it's a little soupy."

He glances at my bowl again. "Well, that's exactly what it is." He studies me for a moment. "Everything okay?"

"Yeah, everything is great."

Clearly, it's not, but I'm not about to tell him what I heard at the kick-off dinner. I know Graydon well enough to know that he would lose his shit and confront his dad right away. That would lead to him making a scene, and that's the last thing he needs right now, especially after what his dad and coach were just talking about. I'm not sure how the trade system works, but I would hate for them to use it as fodder.

"Are you sure?" He eyes me, then glances around. "Did someone say something to you?"

"Nope, seriously, everything is great." I pick up my spoon and attempt to scoop some ice cream up. Sheesh, this really is soup. "How did your little meeting go? Is it a good play?"

"Has some merit," he says, still seeming skeptical. He places his hand on my thigh. "You would tell me if someone said something to you, right? If something was bothering you?"

"Yes," I answer. *I just might not tell you right away.* But I will find the right way to frame this. I know he has little respect for Coach Keenan, but finding out that even he would eagerly sabotage Graydon's happiness has me fighting back tears. It's no wonder he was so angry when I first met him. From what I can tell, he'd only had Hutton in his corner. He has just been so…alone for so many years. I hate that for him.

"Okay." He glances at my bowl again. "I can't watch you eat that. We need a new bowl."

I laugh as he takes my bowl from me.

"Come on."

---

The door shuts behind us, and Graydon turns on me, pushing me up against the wall and pulling my leg up around his waist before I can even take my next breath. His mouth descends on mine, and his fingers filter into my braids, ruining them for the night.

Thankfully, we're in his apartment for the rest of the evening.

His lips trail across my jaw, to the spot behind my ear, and I sink into the wall, letting this man own me, possess me…claim me.

"Why did we stay so long?" he asks as his hand tugs on the hem of my dress and pulls it up.

"Because you kept talking to Hutton," I answer as he attempts to take my clothes off, but I stop him. I want this to happen more than anything, but with the knowledge of what his dad said resting on my chest, I have to talk to Graydon first.

He gives us just enough distance to look me in the eyes and ask, "You okay?"

"Yeah, I just…I need to talk to you about something," I say, my mind feeling just clear enough from lust to stop this before we get started.

"Why does that not sound like a good thing?"

"It's just…something I overheard."

"At the party?" he asks, releasing my dress. "I thought you said everything was fine."

"It was, up until a point, but I didn't want to tell you at the dinner because I didn't want to start drama at the party."

He frowns, looking none too pleased.

"Maple, you said you wouldn't hold anything back from me."

"And I'm not, I'm telling you now. I just wanted to tell you in private is all."

His jaw clenches for a few moments, and then he lowers my leg and takes me by the hand. He leads me over to his couch, taking a seat, and then pulls me onto his lap, where I straddle him, his hands resting on my hips.

"Is this my permanent seat...your lap?" I ask, trying to lighten the mood.

"Yes. Get used to it."

The clench in his jaw and the tightness in his shoulders lead me to believe that my attempt to ease his tension did absolutely nothing.

I wanted to do this here because I know his anger and instinctive behavior to protect me. I've seen it firsthand, and sharing this information with him where he won't gather attention is exactly what I needed to do.

I place my hands on his chest and prepare for whatever wrath is going to be unleashed from him once I tell him what I heard. "Please don't be mad at me for waiting to tell you this. I just wanted to make sure we were in a place where you could express yourself without getting in trouble."

"Is what you're about to say going to piss me off?"

"Yes."

"Was someone mean to you? Because if so, I want to know who the fuck it was because I'll be dealing with them."

I rub my hand over his heart, the thumping of it going wild as he's ready to pounce and make right however I was wronged, and I love that about him.

"It was about you," I say softly. "I overheard your dad and coach talking about you."

His eyes narrow. "What were they saying?"

I try to keep him calm by rubbing his chest, but I can tell already that it's not going to work from the way his grip on me tightens and his breath hitches.

"They were devising some sort of plan to try to get you traded."

"Traded?" His brows shoot up. "They can't fucking do that. I have a no-trade clause."

"For next year," I say. "Something about your dad not wanting you to beat his records."

"Are you fucking kidding me?" Anger billows up in him, tension rolling through his muscles. He gently shifts me to the couch and then stands to start pacing. "That motherfucker is scared that I'm going to break his records? So he's going to try to upend my fucking life."

Yikes. His anger went from zero to sixty, and I'm honestly wondering if this is something I should have told him. Maybe he would have found out on his own, and if he did, who knows what he would have done if it wasn't in the privacy of his own home. I've seen him punch his dad at training camp. This…this might—

Graydon takes off toward the garage, grabbing his keys.

Oh shit.

"Graydon, stop, where are you going?"

"Going to talk to my dad."

I'm off the couch and running after him before I can take my next breath. Quickly, I put myself in front of the garage door and place my hand on his chest. "Please don't go over there, Graydon."

"Why the fuck not? He needs to realize that he has no right being a part of my goddamn business. And I have no problem teaching him that lesson."

"I know." I rub my hand against his chest. "But going over there, especially in this state, is not going to help."

"It'll help me. I've been wanting to bury his goddamn head with my fist for a long time now."

"And that's what I'm worried about."

"You don't need to worry about me." He shifts me to the side, but I hold his arm.

"Please, Graydon," I beg. "Please don't go over there. Stay here with me."

His eyes find mine, and I plead with him, hoping he can see my desperation.

"He's never going to learn if I don't tell him to mind his own damn business. He's going to keep interfering with my life. Over and over again, until...until he does something like take you away from me."

If Graydon only knew the full extent of the conversation I heard. But considering his reaction to the little news I gave him, there is no way I'm going to give him all the information. He would combust.

"That's not going to happen," I say softly, attempting to ease the tension rolling through him. "I'm not going anywhere, Graydon. This is where I want to be, with you, here, so don't worry about me."

"I am worried about you," he says, a small piece of him calming. "I have...I have too much baggage, beautiful." And my heart cracks from that statement because I know he sees that as a negative...a burden, but I don't see it that way.

"Everyone has baggage in their life, Graydon. Some more than others, but that doesn't make you any different."

"It does," he says, his eyes snapping to mine. "My own father abandoned my mother when she needed him the most. He abandoned me, left me to rot with a goddamn nanny while he was off fucking women and playing football. And now, while I'm older, living my own life, he's still trying to fuck with me. Attempting a trade for his benefit. Parents are not supposed to do that."

Neither are good coaches, to my knowledge. How could his coach support his jerkface father's plans?

"I know," I say softly. "And I'm so sorry that you have to have someone like him in your life. You don't deserve that—"

"No, I do." He shakes his head. "It's not like I'm a goddamn hero that goes around saving lives. I'm a selfish asshole who plays football."

"Selfish asshole? How on earth do you see yourself that way?"

His eyes land on mine, insecurity puncturing his pupils, and in a low, saddened voice, he says, "Claimed you as mine."

"Graydon," I whisper, my heart breaking. "That's not selfish."

"It's not?" he asks, taking a step back. "Look at the shit I've already put you through. From the moment I met you, I've been a burden. I've hurt you. I've asked you to do things I had no right asking you to do, and now you're subject to—"

"Stop," I say, gripping his cheeks. "You're spiraling."

"Of course I'm spiraling." He pushes his hand through his hair and steps away. "You realize how ridiculous this is, right? My dad wants to get me traded so I don't break his records because he's so damn full of himself that he can't possibly watch his son, that he couldn't care two shits about, rise above him. And you, the girl I fucking like, have to be the one who sits there and listens to it. It's embarrassing, Maple. You deserve better than this."

"Stop saying what I deserve because you don't get to have an opinion on that matter. This is my life, and I'm choosing what I want to do with it."

"You're choosing wrong," he snaps, causing me to falter in my confidence. He walks over to the kitchen and places his hands on the counter, where he takes a few deep breaths. "Maybe...maybe you should leave."

Absolutely not.

I see what he's doing, and I see where this is going.

He's attempting to push me away, and I'm not going to allow it.

"If you want me to leave, you'll have to physically remove me," I say, chin held high even though he's not looking at me. "You can push me away with your words, but I'm not going anywhere. So go ahead, do your best, Graydon. Say your worst, try to hurt me, because it's not going to work."

He turns to face me, his shoulders showing defeat, his expression twisted with pain.

"You don't want this."

"I do."

"You don't," he says, his voice growing harsher.

"Graydon, do not tell me what I want, what I deserve, or what my opinion should be." I stand with conviction, my voice unwavering. "That is not your choice."

He blows out a heavy breath and shakes his head. "Please just leave, Maple. This is not something you can fix."

"I'm not trying to fix anything. I'm just not letting you push me away because you're spiraling. You've had enough abandonment in your life; I refuse to be someone else who does that to you. So like I said, do your worst, but whatever you do or say is not going to make me leave you here alone. Not happening. We're in this together."

He pulls on the back of his neck, defeat evident in his body language as he pushes off the counter and approaches me. I hold my breath, preparing for him to escort me out the door. But when he reaches me, instead of forcefully taking me outside, he closes the space between us, wraps his arms around me, and buries his hand in my hair as he pulls me in close, hugging me.

The feel of him clinging on to me like a lifeline nearly breaks my heart.

"Fuck, I'm sorry," he whispers, all the pain I know he's feeling coming out in those three words. "I'm so fucking sorry, Maple."

I wrap my arms around him as well, and I rub my hand up and down his back, attempting to soothe him.

"Let me help you, Graydon. Please. I want to be here with you. If I didn't, I would have left already. Okay?"

He nods and then presses his lips to my neck. "I'm sorry." He pulls me in tighter, holding me as close to him as possible. I press my face to his chest, letting him use me to calm down.

We stay like that for a few minutes before he bends, brings his hands to my ass, and then scoops me up into his arms. I circle his waist with my legs and hold him as he brings me to his bedroom and lays me down on his bed.

Standing in front of me, he pulls his shirt up and over his head, then drops it to the ground. With his eyes set on me, he spreads my legs and kneels between them, hovering his massive body over mine before slowly lowering his head centimeters from mine. After a second of looking into my eyes, he closes the space between us and kisses me softly while his hand gently cups my cheek.

Our tongues mold together, his kisses like a drug, making me feel breathless and needy all at the same time. I could stay like this forever and be happy, getting lost in him and only him.

But there is a worry tapping at the back of my head, a gentle reminder of how the evening started. I kiss him once, twice, and then I pull away just enough to say, "Wait, we need to talk."

He lifts up so our gazes match. "Talk?"

I bring my hands around his neck, holding him in place and reassuring him that I want him here, this close…with me.

"Yes, I just want to close out the issue with your dad." My thumb strokes the back of his neck. "I need you to promise me that you're not going to leave this house tomorrow or the next day or the next and have words with your father that lead to using your fists."

His brow pulls together.

"I'm serious, Graydon. Please. I know what he has planned is wrong and could mess with your life, but taking action like I know you want to will mess with your life even more. There's a smart way to go about this, and it doesn't involve getting into a fight with your father."

"He's never going to stop if I don't handle it."

"And you can handle it without using your fists. Let's be smart about this and think how we can best him with your smarts and the popularity you've been able to obtain over the years." I play with the short strands of his hair. "We don't have to come up with a solution right now, but we can think on this together, okay? Please just don't try to go fix it yourself."

His jaw ticks, clearly not happy with my ask.

"Please, Graydon. Promise me."

He drops his head and lets out a heavy sigh. "Okay. I promise."

"Look at me and say it."

His eyes meet mine, and softly, he says, "I promise."

"Thank you."

He leans down, his body draping over me like a blanket as his forearms fall on either side of my head. "When did you start caring about me so much?"

I softly smile. "I think I started caring about you the moment you insulted my flamingos."

He shakes his head. "No way you started caring then."

"I did. I cared enough to get you to realize the error of your ways." I lightly press a kiss to his lips.

"And you did it by making me clean dishes."

"It was your penance."

"I would prefer another punishment."

"Yeah, well, at the time, we were not in a position where I could dole out that kind of punishment."

He chuckles, his hand dragging up my side. "Trust me, if you did, I would have accepted it."

"You're such a liar. You could barely stand to be around me when we first met."

"I didn't want to be around the zoo. You, on the other hand, that's a different story."

I shake my head. "Uh-huh, and why were you such an ass then?"

"Because I might have wanted to be around you, but I wasn't ready to admit how I was feeling."

"So you were acting like an elementary school kid."

"Exactly." He chuckles, the lightness in his expression finally appearing again.

"That's not very grown-up of you, Graydon."

"Never claimed to be mature." His thumb strokes my cheek before he sighs again. "You're so goddamn beautiful, Maple."

My cheeks heat from the compliment.

"That's what caught my eye first, your gorgeous face."

"And I thought it was my ass."

He laughs. "That was what got me to start sending thirst traps. Because if you could walk around with an ass like that, then I was at least going to show you what I had to offer."

"I didn't need a thirst trap to notice," I say, surprising him, which is so cute.

"Tell me more."

"How about I show you?" I ask, pushing at his chest so he lies flat on his back. I straddle his lap and then pull my sundress up and over my head, revealing my strapless bra and red lace underwear.

I reach behind me and undo my bra, his eyes going dark as they hungrily roam over my chest.

One of his hands cups my breast as his thumb caresses my nipple. "I don't know what I did to deserve this...deserve you, but I'm going to continue to be a selfish motherfucker and hold you as long as you will let me."

"It's not selfish when I want the same thing," I answer as my hands go to his jeans, and I start undoing them.

"Trust me, Maple, I'm getting the better end of the bargain."

I shake my head and then pull his pants and boxer briefs down, revealing his hard-on. I let my palm glide over his length before leaning down and letting my tongue circle the head.

"Mmm, no...I am."

And then I take him fully in my mouth while he lets out a satisfied moan, allowing his body to sink into the mattress as his hand pulls my hair to the side.

When I glance up at him and catch his gaze on me, all I can think is *Wow*. This man, who has faced so many obstacles throughout his life—including his father's jealousy and scorn—is looking at me as if I hung the moon. *Talk about undeserving.*

He's a man I could fall in love with. *If I'm not there already.*

Everly's words have gone through my mind several times since she pointed out how Graydon looks at me. I can understand if he can't find the words to tell me he loves me—*and I bet the last time he heard them was from his mom before her accident*—but the reverence he's showing me now? That suggests love.

*I'm the lucky one, Graydon. You are incredible, and I think I love you. Will always love you.*

# CHAPTER 42
# GRAYDON

**OC:** Does this shirt make me look fat? [Picture]

**Bennett:** No.

**Graydon:** Yes.

**OC:** Are you saying that just to be a dick?

**Graydon:** Yes, because why the fuck are you texting us that?

**OC:** It's called camaraderie.

**Graydon:** Don't you have another group thread with the hockey guys that you can ask?

**OC:** I did, and they all said I looked great. Maybe learn a lesson from them.

**Graydon:** If they said you look great, then why the hell are you asking us?

**OC:** To create a safe space where we feel comfortable asking each other these types of questions. Don't you ever feel like you look fat in shirts?

**Graydon:** Never.

**Bennett:** Feeling pretty good over here.

**OC:** Maybe it was the dozen donuts I ate that're making me feel fat.

**Bennett:** Fuck, man. That's...that's incredibly unhealthy.

**Graydon:** And pathetic.

**OC:** I know! I'm not proud of myself. Nor am I proud of myself for waking up this morning with my face in the box, chocolate smeared across my cheek, but here I am.

**Bennett:** You're a mess.

**Graydon:** I really don't know how to handle this.

**OC:** You think I do? I'm lost. Can I come over and talk?

**Graydon:** No.

**Bennett:** Out of town, sorry, man.

**OC:** Graydon...please.

**Graydon:** No. I have plans, and they don't involve you.

**OC:** Do you even like me?

**Graydon:** Barely.

**OC:** Ah! You said barely. That means there is a sliver of likeness.

**Bennett:** Don't push your luck. He'll take away the sliver.

**Graydon:** Listen to the young one.

"Who are you texting over there that has you smirking?"

Shit, am I smirking?

I set my phone down as Maple walks over to me. She's wearing one of my shirts and nothing else, holding a cup of coffee. The last two nights, she's stayed at my place, in my bed, under me, and yesterday, when she went to the zoo for a half shift, I went with her, and she took a few pics of me feeding the flamingos to post on Flock and Tackle. I harped on how brave I was for letting the flamingos get that close and she dramatically rolled her eyes. We then went to dinner at the food truck again and spent the night talking and, well...fucking.

I've never felt this relaxed before the start of a season.

Never.

I always dread the grueling schedule because it takes a second to get into the swing of things, but this year, I have someone by my side.

I like knowing that after a long day on the practice field, I have someone excited to see me, waiting there with open arms when I get home. I like that I can forget everything around me with her, that I'm not constantly battling the demons in my head but rather getting lost in another world where I feel safe and cared for.

I'm really fucking comfortable.

Relaxed.

And even though it's Sunday, a day where I usually grow tense and nauseous, I'm feeling loose, comforted.

And it's all because of her.

Maple.

My girl.

"Just some stupid thing OC was asking."

Maple takes a seat on my lap like the good fucking girl that she is and then blows on her coffee before taking a sip. I slide my hand over her bare leg, attempting to keep my composure and not maul her while she's drinking her coffee.

And it's a valiant effort because I would like nothing more on this earth right now than to be buried between Maple's legs. I'm addicted. Every time I see her, it's all I think about. My skin itches for the feel of her wrapped around me, for the sound of her sweet moans echoing through my ears, for the feel of her fingernails digging into my back.

Jesus...I fucking like her so much.

"And what was he asking?" She smirks over her coffee cup, looking so perfect with her makeup-free face.

"If he looked fat in a shirt."

She pauses. "Wait, seriously?"

"Yes, I told you he's exhausting. Then he went and told us that he ate a dozen donuts last night and woke up face-first in the box."

Maple quickly covers her mouth and chuckles. "Oh God, did he really?"

"That's what he said."

"Aw, I kind of feel bad for him. He's so heartbroken."

"Don't feel bad for him. He's being dramatic."

"Have you never been through heartache like that before?" she asks.

I shake my head. "Never cared about someone enough to experience that feeling."

"Never?"

"Never." I rub her thigh. "But I think I might be with someone right now who has the potential to bring me to my knees if she ever decided to walk away."

"Just to your knees?" she asks with a grin. "Not face-first in an empty box of a dozen donuts?"

"I would never eat that many donuts in one sitting. So no."

"Are you saying that I'm not worth a dozen donuts?"

"You're right." I squeeze her thigh. "It would be two dozen."

She chuckles and pats my cheek. "That's more like it." She sips her coffee again and then says, "I'm going to finish this coffee, and then I'll be out of your hair."

My brows draw together. "What do you mean you'll be out of my hair?"

"Well, it's Sunday. I know it's your private day, and I don't want to get in the way. Plus, I should probably do my laundry and prepare for the upcoming week."

I smooth my hand over her thigh as a bout of nerves erupts in my stomach because I've been thinking about something, something that feels out of character for me, but I can't seem to get the idea out of my head, especially since the season is about to start.

I want her by my side for all of it.

I want her immersed in my life.

I want to be able to share every aspect of my life with her, and there's really only one piece left that she's not a part of. And even though it's the most traumatic, heart-wrenching part, it's also the most beautiful part. The reason I am the man I am today. And I want her to know that side of me.

"What if you stayed?" I say, then clear my throat. "What if you...umm...came with me today?"

She stills, her coffee halfway to her mouth before she lowers it, and her eyes meet mine. "You want me to go visit your mom with you?"

"Only if you want to," I say, feeling insecure. "I don't want to pressure you. I just..." I push my hand through my hair. "I want you to see that side of my life. You've seen it all. That's the last piece, and I want you to be a part of it."

"Are you...are you sure?" she asks, trepidation in her voice. "Being with your mom is such a private moment for you. I don't want to impose."

"I wouldn't ask you if I thought you would be imposing. But if you're not comfortable with it, or if you think it's too soon, you won't offend me."

She shakes her head, then sets her mug down on the coffee table. "I would be honored to meet her, Graydon. Truly, it means so much to me that you trust me enough to take me with you. I just want to make sure you're comfortable with it. I can always just wait in the car for you."

"No, I want you there."

Her arm loops around my neck as she shifts and straddles me. "You're sure?"

"Positive."

She smiles softly. "Then I would love to go with you and meet your mom."

I let out a sigh of relief. "Thank you," I practically whisper.

She brings her lips inches from mine. "Thank you for trusting me enough to bring me."

And then her mouth is on mine, and I'm sinking into the couch, into the sense of relief this woman brings me.

---

Maple pats down her dress as I help her out of my truck. "Are you sure I look okay?"

I let my eyes roam over the baby-blue sundress she chose to wear. The sleeves cover her shoulders, but the square neckline offers an expansive view of her chest, without it being too much for my mom. And its simple frame hugs her torso but then lies loosely around her hips. She put her hair half up, half down, and she coated her eyelashes with minimal mascara and dotted her cheeks with some blush. She looks perfect.

"You look beautiful," I say and kiss the top of her head.

"Thank you," she says as she loops her arm around my waist and hugs me. I return the hug, holding her there tightly in the parking lot as I know her nerves start to get the best of her.

After agreeing to go with me, she slipped some clothes on, and I packed a bag before we headed to her place. We showered together, and I bent her over and fucked her while the water poured around us.

Then we got ready, and with every second that ticked closer to us leaving, I could see her growing more and more nervous.

"Are you okay?" I ask, rubbing her back.

"Yes, I'm just…I'm nervous. I want this to be a good day for you. I want…I want her to recognize you. I want it for you so badly."

"I do too," I say, kissing the top of her head again.

"I don't know how you do this every week. She's not even my mom, and I feel sick with worry." She tilts her head back to look at me. "I don't want to see you devastated and hurt. I don't think my heart will be able to take it."

"I spoke to Rhonda when you were getting ready. That's my mom's aide, and she said that it seemed like she was having a better day today. She, uh…she added some pictures to the album that she shows my mom on days that I come to visit. They're of you and me. I hope that's okay."

Her eyes widen. "Of course, that's...that's so special. You didn't have to do that."

"I wanted this to be as easy as possible." I take her hand in mine. "If this goes south, just know that I will be okay in time."

She nods. "You just tell me what you need and want from me. If you need space, don't be afraid to ask for it."

I shake my head. "If anything, I'll need you more than ever."

She squeezes my hand and leans into my shoulder. "Then I'm here for you, Graydon."

Like I said...she's perfect.

I press my index finger under her chin and lift her mouth to mine before lightly kissing her, soaking in her essence before I pull away and guide her to the front door of my mom's care facility.

We check in, and I show Maple the facility, pointing out different pieces of art my mom has painted as we make our way to the main living space.

"Wow," she whispers, taking it all in. "These windows, there's so much light."

"It's one of the reasons my mom's parents liked it here so much. They thought it would be a great place for her to soak in the sun and just live the best life she could." My eyes fall to the left, where the floor-to-ceiling windows look out toward the garden and giant willow tree. My mom is in front of her easel, wearing a set of pink silk pajamas. Rhonda told me it's what she likes to wear the most, so I stocked her dresser full of sets.

Her salt-and-pepper hair is held back with a clip, and instead of painting, she's looking out the window while the album we've made for her rests in her lap.

Clearing my throat, I say, "She's over there, by the window. Come on."

She tugs my hand one more time. "You're sure?"

"Positive, beautiful," I answer.

Together, hand in hand, we walk over to my mom. My stomach twists in knots the entire time, my heart hammering, my mind begging for this to go over okay. For her to at least recognize me.

To just give me this one moment to share Maple with my mom.

With my mom's back toward us, Rhonda spots me, offers me a nod, and then gently whispers in my mom's ear.

Her back stiffens, and fear creeps up my spine. I squeeze Maple's hand tightly, clinging on for strength. *She's not ready. It's not going to be a good day for Mom.*

I wait as Mom sets down the album on the stool next to her, where she usually keeps her paints, and then she turns around, her weary eyes confused as they connect with me.

*No, please, Mom. Please not today.*

Clearing my throat, I let go of Maple's hand, then squat in front of my mom, trying not to tower over her and scare her. I feel Maple take a step back, but not too far that I can't still feel her presence.

"Hey, Mom," I say softly. "It's me... Saint." I speak in a soft tone, trying to hide the timbre of my voice and the pain from her not recognizing me.

"It's Graydon," Rhonda says sweetly. "See how he's grown, like in the album?"

Mom's eyes flick to mine, confusion infused in them.

She shakes her head, and I can feel my heart plummet, crashing into my ribs and breaking off another piece of my soul that I'm not quite sure will ever heal.

"It's okay," I say softly. "I understand how this can be confusing. I'll let you get back to your—"

Her hand lifts and connects with my cheek, the warmth of her palm nearly bringing tears to my eyes as her head tilts to the side.

She studies me.

Confusion is still in her expression, but there is a hint of recognition. The smallest hint, so I don't move. I don't even fucking breathe. I just let her process.

*Please, Mom, please recognize me.*

*Please see me.*

*Please…*

"Saint?" she asks, and my legs almost give out on me.

"Hey, Mom," I answer quietly, tears springing to my eyes.

"Oh, my boy, you're so…you're so big."

I chuckle as my emotions fill me to the brim. My tears spill over my lids and to my cheeks. "Yeah, I kind of grew."

She slowly nods. "You're so handsome."

"Just a product of you, Mom."

A small smile presses against her lips as she wipes away my tears. She picks up the album and brings it to her lap. She flips to the pictures of me from high school. My football pictures are the first on the page, next to my senior pictures and graduation.

"I missed you graduating."

"You didn't. You were with me," I say. "Grandma sewed a picture of you into my gown, right over my heart, so you were with me."

Her eyes find mine. "Really?"

"Really," I answer.

She moves to the next pics of me in college, playing football, draft day, and some of the most important moments where she wasn't physically present.

"And here," I say. "You were sewn into my jacket when I was drafted, so you were there too. When I got the call, you were the first person I hugged."

Her eyes well up.

I turn the page. "And here, in my helmet, I keep a picture of you while I'm playing, so I always have you with me."

She stares down at the picture, her tears matching mine. "You play for the Foghorns, like your father."

As much as it kills me to acknowledge his presence, I nod. From the beginning, I've said that I wouldn't speak ill of my father, not because I owe him that, but because I don't want to snap my mom out of this dreamlike state where she knows who I am.

"I do. I've been playing for a while, but there isn't a day that goes by when you're not with me."

She turns the page and there's a new set of pictures, the ones of me and Maple. She takes a moment to look them over, her fingers swiping over a picture of me holding Maple closely.

"Is this...your girlfriend?"

"It is," I say. "That's Maple. She's right behind me, actually."

Mom's attention shifts to the figure behind me, and the smallest of smiles crosses her lips. Quietly, she says, "She's beautiful."

"I know. I'm really lucky she chose me. She's a zookeeper, Mom. Takes care of the flamingos. I've been helping out at the zoo. Do you know what she makes me do?"

"What?"

"Wash the dishes."

My mom clutches her chest and lets out the best sound to ever hit my ears...her laugh.

It brings back a flood of memories, hitting me all at once.

Sitting at the kitchen table, playing cards.

Attempting to have her run routes in the backyard but failing miserably.

Carving pumpkins the night before Halloween, getting slime and seeds all over us.

Making smoothies but forgetting to put the top on the blender so everything shoots up.

It's one memory right after the other, filling me with joy, happiness, and not a hint of heartache.

"Well, I need to meet this girl who makes you do dishes."

I stand and then offer my hand to Maple, who takes it and carefully walks up to my mom. She squats in front of her as well, mimicking my position, and places her hand on top of my mom's.

"Hi, Mrs. St. John. I'm Maple."

Mom's eyes light up, and her smile grows. "Maple, it's so nice to meet you. I hear you make my son clean bird dishes."

Maple chuckles. "I do, and between you and me, he's really good at it, hence why I keep having him do it."

I watch as Mom takes Maple's hand in hers and encourages her to stand and then move over to the stool next to her. Maple takes a seat, and my mom brings the album between the two of them.

"Tell me what you're doing in these pictures."

"I have something even better," Maple says and then pulls her phone out of her dress pocket. "Let me show you where this all started."

For the next few minutes, I watch Maple charm my mother, showing her picture after picture of us that we've posted on Flock and Tackle. Maple talks about how much she likes me and how I've helped her in her endeavor to save the flamingos, and she even shows her the mural I painted. My mom is completely infatuated as she takes her time, looking over every picture.

Occasionally, Maple looks in my direction, offering me a smile that nearly splits me in half.

And as my mom bumps shoulders with Maple, laughing and talking about the flamingos, I watch them, my eyes enraptured by the woman who has not only captured my attention but my mom's as well. I consider her words from the other night, when she grabbed me from the abyss of both self-loathing and anger at my dad.

*"You've had enough abandonment in your life; I refuse to be someone else who does that to you. So like I said, do your worst, but whatever you do or say is not going to make me leave you here alone. Not happening. We're in this together."*

Fuck, those words. Her heart. Her tenderness and kindness toward my mom.

I'm falling in love with this woman.

There's no question about it.

She's it.

She's the one.

And I will do everything in my power to hang on to her because I will never forget watching her sit with my mom and treat her as an equal, as if nothing is wrong with her.

This is a core memory unfolding right in front of me, and because I don't want to ever forget a moment of it, I take my phone out and take a picture of the two of them together, my mom holding her hand as they laugh together.

I stare down at the picture, my attention on Maple.

The love of my goddamn life...right there.

---

I had Maple pack a bag. Just in case things went south, that meant I could go back to my place with her and just sulk in my own space. The trip home has been silent.

But instead of sulking, I feel...full.

Emotionally and mentally full.

Like the clouds have parted and are being driven away by this sense of calm in my chest. And there's only one person to thank for it.

I put the truck in park and grab her overnight bag, then go to her side of the truck and help her out. I take her hand and lead her into the apartment, where I set her bag down, shut the door, and turn toward her.

I scoop her up by the ass, and she wraps her legs around me, then her arms around my neck. I carry her up to my bedroom.

"Is everything okay?" she asks when I set her down on my bed. "You've been quiet, and I'm worried that maybe I did something wrong."

I shake my head. "No, you did everything right."

I kneel in front of her and take her hands in mine. Looking up at her, I speak from the deepest part of my once aching soul and say, "You have no idea the impact you've made on my life today, Maple." I kiss her knuckles. "You had a choice today. You could have treated my mom like she was sick, or you could have been nervous, unsure of how to be around her, yet you weren't. You treated her like your equal, like a long-lost friend. You made her smile, laugh, and you brought a light to her eyes that I haven't seen in a while. I'm...I'm so grateful for you and don't know how to express that, other than showing you just how grateful."

I let go of her hands, then take the hem of her dress and push it up around her waist. Then I reach around her and undo the zipper before pulling her dress completely over her head.

She sits on my bed in a set of lavender lingerie. "You don't need to show me anything, Graydon." Her fingers drag across my scruff. "I know how you feel."

"I don't think you do," I say as I stand and pull my shirt off, then push my pants and boxer briefs down while taking off my shoes and socks. Her eyes fall to my cock, already straining between my legs.

I tug on her hand and have her stand, then I undo the clasp of her bra and let it fall to the floor before kneeling again and dragging her underwear off her. When I move back up her body, I allow my mouth to trail across her skin, my hands skimming her flesh as I go until I reach her face. I cup her cheeks and bring my mouth to hers, where I torturously kiss her, moving slowly, showing this woman how much she means to me.

She gasps when our tongues collide, and I gently wrap my arms around her and lower her to the bed, pulling her up along the mattress and resting her head on the pillow. I pepper her jaw and neck with kisses, moving over her collarbone, to her chest, and right to her breasts, where I bring her hardened nipple into my mouth while I cup her other breast at the same time.

"God," she whispers as her chest shifts beneath me.

Her legs spread, and my cock twitches from the movement, but this isn't about me. This is about her.

I switch to her other breast, where I let my tongue swirl around the hardened nub before sucking it between my lips.

"Yes, Graydon." Her hips lift off the bed and against me, looking for friction. And normally, I would torture her and not give her what she wants, but not today. I want my girl satisfied. I want her to know just how grateful I am for her in my life.

"You tell me what you want, beautiful. Anything, it's yours."

"You," she says, her hand playing in my hair. "All I want is you."

Same.

Forever, Maple.

I want you forever.

I kiss down her stomach and move between her legs, where I press my lips below her belly button, to her pelvic bone, and then right on top of her arousal.

She moans and spreads her legs farther, pulling her knees up and giving me better access.

I run my nose along her slit, taking in her essence, the scent of her like a goddamn drug. I spread her with my fingers and then drag my tongue over her clit on a long, languid stroke that has her relaxing into the mattress.

"Just like that," she whispers.

I listen, continuing the pace of my tongue while smoothing my hands over her inner thighs, letting my thumbs stroke just around her arousal, attempting to make her feel everything. From pleasure...to...love.

I want her to know she's cherished.

Important.

My woman.

"Fuck," she says as she tenses. "Faster, Graydon."

I do one more slow stroke, then I pick up my pace, flicking my tongue over her clit, creating a humming vibration with my mouth at the same time. It seems to kick up the lust pulsing through her because her breathing picks up and her hand starts to tug on my hair.

The tension coiling through her only drives me to work harder, bring her to the edge, and give her exactly what she needs.

"God…oh God, Graydon. Right there, baby. Please don't stop."

My skin tingles from the sound of her voice calling me 'baby.'

My tongue drives harder against her clit.

And my cock presses against the mattress, begging for friction, for her.

For her warmth.

But I keep my focus on her, driving my tongue against her, heightening her climax, bringing her to the edge, where I slow down for a moment, flattening my tongue and dragging out the pleasure.

"No," she says in a frustrated tone. "I'm right there. Please make me come."

As if she has to ask me twice.

I go back to intensely swiping against her clit in short, fast strokes as she tenses around me.

Her back arches.

Her mouth falls open.

And her hands grip the comforter beneath her as she rears her chest up, and a long, sexy moan falls out of her mouth as she clenches around me and climaxes.

"Oh fuck," she calls out, her hips flying against my tongue as she rides out her orgasm.

And I fucking love it. I love that she uses me like this and doesn't even think twice about it.

When she finally settles down and falls into a calming breath, I hover over her and rest my lips against her neck, kissing her softly. Then her jaw. Her cheek. Her forehead.

The tip of her nose.

Lightly against her lips.

And then as a smile peeks out over her lips, I bring my cock to her entrance, running the head over her slit and feeling just how much I satisfied her.

"I want to be inside you, beautiful. I need it."

"Then take me," she answers, her stunning eyes meeting mine.

Maintaining eye contact, I slide myself inside her warmth, taking it slow because even though I've been inside her several times, she still needs to adjust to me, and fuck, is it amazing. She's still pulsing from her orgasm, the slightest contractions barely squeezing my cock.

I lower to my forearms and gently push her hair back as I settle inside her.

"You take my goddamn breath away," I say, observing the swell of her lips and the headiness in her eyes. "Nothing will ever be better than this feeling I get when I'm with you. Inside you." I lightly thrust, listening to the addicting sigh that slips past her lips. "I want this to last forever."

Her eyes sparkle.

Her hands wrap around my neck.

And she pulls me down to her mouth, where she makes out with me, letting her tongue slide against mine and tangle with it.

I let my hands travel all over her body, feeling her soft, warm skin.

Dragging over her sides.

Her breasts.

Her thighs.

I commit her curves to memory. I revel in the feel of her beneath me. And I vow at this moment to always protect her. To keep her close to me. To make sure I never fuck this up and to be the man she deserves.

Because today, she showed me the kind of woman she is, the kind of woman I don't deserve. But I will steal her from the rest of the world because that's how damn selfish I am.

"Fuck," she says as she pulls away, her back arching. "I need... more."

"Anything you want," I whisper, then kiss down her neck, nibbling my way to her collarbone as I start to move in and out of her. The friction immediately pulls the muscles in my body to tense into my core.

I bite across her skin, marking her as mine.

I thrust into her powerfully, claiming her cunt.

And I whisper her name, reminding her who she belongs to.

"More," she says, her fingers digging into my shoulder.

But I want to keep it slow.

I want to make love to her.

I want her to fucking remember this day.

But from the tug on my hair and her fingernails biting into my skin, I know I have to give her what she wants because that's what I swore I would do. So I sit up on my knees, then take her legs, straighten them, and hold them in front of me in a V position. I nestle right up against her, garnering a deeper connection. I grip her legs, just above her ankles, and start thrusting my hips, driving farther inside her and hitting that glorious spot that makes her squeeze around me involuntarily.

"Oh...fuck!" she shouts, her hands falling to her breasts. "Yes, Graydon. Right there, oh my God, baby. Please...more."

I grunt from her response, my body starting to sweat as I drive into her. My skin tingles with awareness, and my legs start to go numb as my climax tugs on my spine.

"Fuck, beautiful. I'm...I'm close."

"Same." She bites down on her lower lip, her eyes squeeze shut, and she moans, her body right on the edge.

"Look at me," I say. "Eyes on me, beautiful, when you come."

Her eyes shoot open, her mouth parts, and her body tenses just as she shouts, "Graydon...fuck!"

And then she unravels, her gaze on me the entire time, and that's all it takes to put me over the edge.

My muscles still, then twitch…

My balls tighten.

My cock swells, and then I bust inside her with a roar that could probably be heard throughout San Francisco.

"Jesus fuck!" I cry out, my orgasm pulsing over and over again, up and down my spine as she contracts around my cock until we're both completely sated. "Shit," I whisper and then lower her legs and climb on top of her, my cock still very much inside her.

I twist us slightly to the side so my weight is not on her, and I kiss her forehead, cupping the back of her neck and holding her close.

She kisses me on my chest, holding me just as close, the embrace making me feel so safe, so comforted, like this is where I belong.

I'm falling in love, right here, with her in my arms.

I can feel the spiral of my heart.

The tumbling of my soul, trying to stitch together with hers.

This desperate, consuming need to never let her go hitches onto my subconscious.

I love her.

I fucking love this woman, and I want to scream it.

I want to whisper it.

I want her to know exactly how I feel.

How she completes me.

How she is the missing piece of my life that I didn't know I was searching for until she showed up.

But I can't. Not this soon. I don't want to scare her away.

I don't want her thinking I'm only feeling this because of what happened with my mom.

No, I've been feeling this for a while, but today solidified those feelings.

Today was the stark realization that no matter what I do in this life, the greatest accomplishment I will ever have is making sure I keep Maple happy.

Her happiness is all that matters to me.

Because if she's happy, then I'm swimming in goddamn joy.

And the feeling of joy, the consuming, elated feeling of it pulsing through my veins, attaching to my bones and making me feel light as a feather...it's a feeling I never want to let go of because it's what's been missing in my life ever since my mom's accident.

I don't want it to ever leave.

Which means I need to do everything in my power to protect her, keep her close, and bring her joy.

"Are you okay?" she asks, her hand caressing my chest.

"Fucking perfect," I say, kissing her forehead.

"Are you sure? You seem quiet."

"Just processing," I say as I slip out of her but then turn to my back and let her curl up next to me. I keep my arm protectively around her the entire time.

"Processing the day?"

"Yeah." I kiss her again, unable to rid myself of this need to claim her over and over again.

"Thank you for letting me be a part of it. I know it was meaningful for you, but you allowed me into a moment that is incredibly private to you, and that means so much to me, Graydon." She lifts up to look at me. "Truly, I will forever cherish the time and clarity I had with your mom."

Jesus Christ, how did I get so lucky?

She's thanking me?

When she's the one who flipped my entire world upside down today?

"You don't need to thank me, Maple. I'm forever in your debt after today. The way my mom looked at you..." I shake my head. "I'll never forget it."

Just thinking about my mom's smile, her laugh…once again, it brings tears to my eyes, and Maple notices them immediately.

"Like I said…it meant everything to me," I say as one single tear rolls down my cheek.

She kisses it away and then rubs her thumb over my scruff.

"It meant everything to me too, Graydon."

# CHAPTER 43
# MAPLE

I SWISH MY ICED COFFEE around, letting the contents mix as I lean forward and whisper to Everly, "I think he made love to me last night."

The green smoothie she chose at the Lemur Café pauses halfway up to her mouth before she sets it back on the table. Blinking, she asks, "Excuse me?"

I pull my chair closer, so glad that my friend could meet me at work for a little break today because I've been dying to talk to her.

"Graydon. I think he made love to me last night. Not just had sex, but actually made love."

"Okay, walk me through this, because...Graydon St. John made love? He didn't fuck you senseless? He was...sensual?"

I slowly nod. "Yup."

I tell her about how I went to visit Graydon's mom yesterday, how it went, how we were able to connect, and even though it wasn't very long, it was something special. I explain how he was after, his gratefulness, the words he said, the way he would stare into my eyes while thrusting...

And just reliving it now, I can feel goose bumps tickle my skin as I remember the feeling of him connected to me in all ways, including his beautiful soul. Last night was different from any other time I've been with him. There was a palpable emotion connected to it, a promise that felt like forever, and I'm still reeling from it...in a good way.

"Wow," Everly says as she sits back in her chair. "Did he say he loves you?"

I shake my head. "But it felt like he wanted to say it."

"Really? That's...wow, how do you feel about that?"

A smile spreads across my lips. "I think I would say the same thing."

"Oh my God, seriously?"

I nod. "Yeah, I think so. I mean, I think about him all the time, and it isn't just lust. I care about him, and I want him to succeed. I worry about him and the demons he battles. I crave him when he's not around. I want to be in his arms all the time, and when I can't be, I want to be texting him, calling him on the phone, just...being connected to him in some way. And not to bring Hardy into this, but I didn't feel that way with him. Sure, I cared about him, but this is so different. It's like Graydon has buried himself into the marrow of my bones, and I can't rid myself of him, and I don't want to."

"Yeah, Maple, that's love." She sips her green smoothie. "That is one hundred percent love."

"That's what I thought." I cross one leg over the other. "What am I supposed to do with that new information?"

"What do you mean?" She chuckles.

"I mean, do I tell him I love him? Do I wait for him to say it? Do I throw a surprise party for two, an invitation to express our feelings to each other?"

"For the love of God, please do not throw a party."

I laugh. "Then what do I do?"

"I don't know. How do you think he would take it if you said it first?"

I shrug. "I want to say well, but if he felt it last night, why didn't he say it? Do you think he's not ready?"

"Could be a possibility. He could also think that you're not ready. He could be holding back because of you. I mean, would it hurt to wait? You two did move pretty fast. It might be good to just live in these feelings for a moment, don't you think?"

"Probably," I answer. "And I know it's been a short amount of time, but it also feels like it's been forever, like we've been building up to this moment this entire time."

"Well, you've been flirting since the minute you met each other."

I snort. "I wouldn't consider our first or second or even third interaction flirting. There was no flirting involved at all. We kind of didn't like each other."

"Yeah, but all the hate banter, that's flirting. You might not think so, but it is. And if anything, it built the tension between the two of you so when you finally gave in, it was explosive."

"You can say that again. Very explosive."

"See. You two have been bound to get together from the moment he insulted your flamingos. You just had to travel down the path to get there first."

"So what do I do now?"

"Enjoy every second of it." She smiles. "Don't put pressure on the relationship, and allow things to happen naturally. The 'I love you's will come. Until then, just soak up every second."

"That I can do." I smirk, and Everly matches my grin.

Shaking her head, she says, "God, you're so freaking in love."

---

"Hey, beautiful," Graydon says as he stands from his chair and pulls me into a hug.

I sigh into him and wrap my arms around his waist as he kisses the top of my head.

"How was your day?"

"Great," I answer and look up at him. "How about you?"

"Better now." He tips his finger under my chin and leans down to press the softest of kisses to my lips. "Sorry you had to come all the way over here."

"It's fine. I was finally able to drive my car again, which was very exciting."

"Yeah, I liked it better when I was driving you around."

"I'm sure you did." I flash him my arm and smile. "And look, I got my brace off. I dropped by the training room before heading up here, and they said I was good to go. It's like I'm a brand-new person. Car, no brace, have the most handsome boyfriend ever. . . Look at me go."

He chuckles. "I like the last one the best."

"I'm sure you do."

"Well, aren't you two cozy?" Gretchen says, walking into the conference room with a bag and a folder. "Sorry I'm running behind." She checks her watch. "Well, technically right on time, but that doesn't settle well with me." She gestures to the chairs. "Please, take a seat."

When Graydon texted me that Gretchen wanted to meet with us tonight, a slight panic passed through me because it's rare that something good comes from Gretchen getting involved. Then again, she did bring me close to Graydon, so maybe that statement isn't entirely true.

Graydon takes a seat in a chair, and I take the one next to him despite him attempting to pull me onto his lap.

I don't mind that when we're anywhere else, but in a professional setting, I think it's better if we have our own seats. From the disgruntled look on his face, I can tell he doesn't agree with my decision.

He'll live.

And I'll for sure hear about it later. Who knows, maybe he'll punish me. . .

"Okay, this is for you." Gretchen hands me a Foghorns bag. "It should have everything you might want when it comes to dressing for the games, including cold gear."

I open the bag, and I'm surprised to see a plethora of jersey options, T-shirts, winter hats, baseball caps, and two jackets, all in my size. Man, she's right. That's everything I might need.

"The only requirement is that you wear at least one branded item. If you prefer to layer up on the branded clothes, that's up to you." She opens her folder and shuffles through some papers.

"Are they all her size?" Graydon asks.

"Yes, they should be. But if something doesn't fit, just let me know, and I will get it traded in for you."

"Are these for the games?" I ask, feeling like I'm missing something.

Gretchen lifts her gaze just enough to peek at me through her lashes. "Yes, I was told that you are to be outfitted for the games. If you want to wear them other times, that's fine too, but for the games specifically, this is what we prefer you to wear."

"I made the request," Graydon says.

"Oh, well…thank you. This was very kind of you. I could have gotten my own jersey, though."

Graydon scoffs. "No fucking way."

Yeah, should have known he was going to say that.

"Now, with the first game coming up next Sunday, I've been able to secure you field passes as well as seats on the wall, right at the fifty-yard line. I have two, so choose your plus-one wisely."

"On the wall?" I ask.

"Front row," Graydon helps.

"Oh, is that…is that necessary?"

Gretchen gives me an exhausted look. "It is if we want to capture the perfect after-game kiss between the two of you. Graydon, win or lose, we ask that you go up to her at the wall. Maple, you lean over and kiss. Social media will have a frenzy over it."

"So you're not still pushing for a breakup story."

"That's covered. But you were caught making out down by the docks."

*So…we're okay to be in a relationship now in Gretchen's mind?* Gretchen takes out a piece of paper and shoots it over to me.

"Here are the instructions for parking, who to talk to and how to get into the facility. There will be staff with badges for you, waiting for you in the parking lot—"

"I'll get a car service to drop her off."

"I can drive."

Graydon takes my hand in his. "I know you can drive, beautiful. But game days get crazy, and if someone spots you, I would rather have the knowledge that you're being taken care of by a professional driving service, so I don't worry about you trying to park your car. Okay?"

I can see the actual worry in his eyes, so I don't argue with him. "That works, then."

"Thank you," he says softly and kisses the back of my hand.

"I can set up the car service," Gretchen says, surprising me with her generosity. "As for after the game, you will be led by staff to the hall outside the locker room, where I'm sure you're going to want to wait for Graydon. I need you to be aware that you might run into press. Whatever you do, do not comment on your relationship. Even with fans you might be sitting next to during the game. If they want to take pictures with you, by all means, take pictures, but do not remark on anything personal. We don't want people taking a video and mishandling what you said." She presses her fingers to her temple as she sifts through papers. "The last thing I need to handle is another PR nightmare."

Man, does she look stressed. She's usually very cut-and-dried, but today seems different.

"Finally, Bennett and OC will be at the game as well." Gretchen looks up at Graydon. "They'll have field passes. Before the game, we would like to take pics of all of you together. We're also attempting to find a time to get you to one of Bennett's games before the season is over, and since his book club is picking up some speed, we thought it would be good to highlight you three together. OC, on the other hand..." She shakes her head and then rubs her temple again. "That man will be the death of me."

I wince because I can only imagine what he might be putting her through.

"Is he giving you grief?" Graydon asks.

"No, he's driving me up a wall with his need to be as popular as you two. I told him sulking around about an old girlfriend is not helping. I thought about putting him up for a dating show."

Graydon snorts next to me, then lets out a low chuckle. "I would pay good money to watch that."

"Not that my opinion matters, but I think that would be a total disaster. OC is too unhinged to be on a dating show," I say.

Gretchen leans back in her chair, showing a hint of a personality as she smirks. "Wouldn't that be the appeal, though?"

"It would make him a target on the ice," I say. "He could get hurt."

"Yeah, and if he's hurt, there's no doubt in my mind he would beg me to nurse him back to health," Graydon says.

I chuckle because isn't that the truth. OC has a strange kind of connection with Graydon, and even though Graydon tries to constantly fight it off, I know there is no way he would actually leave OC to fend for himself if he really needed help. Graydon puts up a front, but I think deep down...deep, deep down, he has a small liking for OC.

Very small.

Almost minuscule.

But it's there.

"So let's stick with game appearances and no dating shows."

Gretchen nods. "If he keeps driving me insane, then I can't make any promises. Maybe you can talk to him."

Graydon's eyes shoot to her. "Absolutely not."

"Thought I would give it a try." She sifts through some more papers and then pulls out a stapled packet. "Here is your copy of the breakup NDA." She gives it to me, and I can feel the anger spiking through Graydon's body next to me as I take the packet.

I press my hand to his thigh, attempting to calm him down and not make this a thing. We both talked about it, and we both got over it. No need to make it any more of a thing than it already is.

"Maple, I would like to get you into some media training as soon as possible because I'm assuming you two plan on continuing this..." She gestures back and forth between the two of us, and a low growl pulls through Graydon's throat.

"Yes, we plan on continuing this," he says in such a menacing tone that if Gretchen wasn't half the person she is, I'm pretty sure his voice would have split her skin right off her face. "And I don't fucking appreciate the doubt or the contract. I thought we went over this, Gretchen."

To her credit, she remains calm as she shuts the folder on the table. "Graydon, I'm not trying to start trouble. It's my job to put aside personal emotions and ensure everyone is protected in the matter. It's my job to protect the organization as well as you."

"I don't give two shits what your job is," he responds. I smooth my hand over his thigh, wanting to let him know that everything is okay, but I can see that it's doing nothing. "This is my girl, and she's sticking around, so you better get fucking used to it. And if I hear you talk about a breakup one more goddamn time, I will make it my mission to make sure you never work PR in this goddamn city ever again."

That seems to crack her calm facade as she sits taller. "I don't mean harm, Graydon." Her voice cracks. "I have duties handed to me that I have to fulfill, and if I don't, then yes, I would lose my job as well."

"I understand that, but with us, when it's just you, me, and Maple sitting in a conference room, you can show a fucking touch of compassion. This shit is hard enough without someone we're supposed to trust making it more difficult."

She clears her throat. "You're right, I'm sorry. I'm being insensitive."

Well, shit, never thought I would see an apology come from her.

"I don't mean to set you off," she continues. "I just have to make sure we're covered."

"We're covered," Graydon snaps.

"Okay, then, if it's all right with you, I would love to get Maple involved in some media training so if she does run into someone on the streets or at the games who starts asking her questions, she's ready and prepared."

"It's up to Maple if she wants to do that."

I take Graydon's hand in mine. "I would like that," I say. "I don't want to embarrass you in any way."

"You could never."

I chuckle. "You say that now..."

"You couldn't." He kisses the back of my hand as he looks into my eyes. God, he's so sweet. This big lump of muscle who I thought was a total jerk has turned out to be one of the sweetest humans I've ever met.

Tell me how that is possible.

"Okay, then I will send you some times, if that works for you, Maple."

"Yeah, that works."

"Great." She stands from the chair. "I think that's all I needed. Sorry to take time out of your day." She gathers her things and heads for the door. Before she leaves, she turns to us and drops her usual stern expression. "For what it's worth, I like you two together, and I'm glad it turned into so much more. I'm not just saying that because of the PR benefits. I see that you two actually make sense. You complete each other."

She softly smiles and is about to leave before she stops herself.

"Oh, one more thing. We have the PR relationship on lockdown, meaning all prior contracts from it have been shredded since we started this new one. Nothing else is required from that contract since it's null and void. Just wanted to make that clear. You two can just...live your life. We would love for you to share, but you don't have to share everything. What you're already doing is enough, and as popularity increases, the PR will unfold on its own. Just be prepared."

"Thank you, Gretchen," Graydon says, the tension in his voice gone now.

She nods and then takes off, leaving us alone in the conference room. When the door is shut, Graydon pulls me onto his lap.

"How did I know you were going to do that?" I ask.

"This is where you should have sat to begin with."

"That's not very professional, Graydon."

"Like I fucking care."

I drag my index finger over his five-o'clock shadow, letting my nails scrape along the short hairs. "You should. This is your place of work."

"Yeah, never cared about that either." His hand rubs my thigh. "Are you okay? I know that bullshit contract has hurt you before."

"I'm fine," I say.

"Promise?"

"Promise." I smile softly. "Stop acting like I'm about to run off any second. This is where I want to be, with you."

"Okay," he says, but he doesn't smile, and I can see something is in the back of his mind, plaguing his words.

"What are you not saying?"

"Nothing." He shakes his head.

"No, don't do that. You would never let me get away with saying, 'nothing,' so I won't let you. What's happening in your head?"

"I'm just...hell, Maple, I'm sorry that being with me comes with all of this. Contracts and media training and schedules."

"You don't need to apologize. You're worth all of it." I kiss his cheek, then his lips. "So worth it, Graydon."

"It would be easier with someone else."

That makes me pause, and I pull away to look him in the eyes. "Why would you say that? Are you trying to push me away?"

"No." He links our fingers together and stares down at the connection. "I just, fuck, Maple, I feel bad about all of this."

"Well, don't. I knew what I was getting into when I said yes to all of this. Stop trying to protect me, and let me just live this with you."

"It's my job to protect you."

"Says who?"

His eyes find mine. "Says me," he says with conviction. "As your man, it is my job to make sure you're okay and safe. With the season starting and the media attention that we will draw, I want you to know that if you want to back out, I understand."

"Stop saying that," I say, growing angry. "I'm not backing out."

"It's going to be hard, Maple. The fans will be rude and ruthless and—"

"I don't give two shits what they say." I lean back, irritated with him. "You keep saying that the public will hurt me, but this conversation right now, with you pushing me away, telling me I can back out, that's what's hurting me."

"I know, I'm sorry." He sighs out his frustration. "I just, I can't stop worrying about…everything." He drives his hand through his hair. "I'm sorry, Maple. Please…please forgive me. I just want to protect you, and I'm not going about it in the right way."

"You're not." I cross my arms over my chest. "Let me show you just how brave I can be. Okay?"

He nods. "You're right. I'm sorry."

"Thank you."

He pulls me into a hug, then buries his face into my neck, holding me close and kissing me. I push my hand through his hair, holding him tight, letting him know that I can be the rock that he needs, that he doesn't need to be the sturdy one all the time.

After a few seconds, he pulls away and asks, "Can I bring you back to my place and make dinner for you?"

"Only if you do it shirtless."

He smiles softly. "Deal."

# CHAPTER 44
# GRAYDON

"HOW DO YOU FEEL?" HUTTON asks as we set the weights back on the racks.

"Good, ready. How about you?"

"Flexible."

I eye him, causing him to laugh. "Scarlett has been taking me to her Pilates classes this off-season, and at first, I thought it was stupid, as if I needed to go to a class like that, but my man, I've never been more humbled in my entire life. My body was shaking uncontrollably. It was humiliating, but I stayed consistent, and now, I feel more ready than ever for the season to start."

"You're telling me that you've been keeping it a secret this entire summer that you've been taking Pilates classes?"

"Yeah."

"Why?"

"So I could have this moment with you right now, while you watch me attempt to do the splits right in front of you." He starts spreading his legs and lowering his body to the ground.

"What the actual fuck," I say in shock, watching my friend slide closer to the ground, only for him to stop about a foot and a half away and then topple over to the floor. "Uh...that wasn't the splits."

"No, but I was close."

"Not really."

"Pretty close."

"You were closer to the ceiling than the floor."

"Oh fuck off, I was close." He stands. "Watch this." He kicks his leg up toward the ceiling. "Look at that flexibility. Never thought you would see that from me, did you?"

"Honestly, I couldn't have predicted this entire conversation. Consider me surprised."

"You're welcome for keeping things lively in your life."

When I pick up my water bottle and phone and head over to the mats to stretch out, I spot a text on my phone.

> **OC:** Uh…was the plan to announce that you were in a PR relationship with Maple this entire time? [Link]

"What the fuck?" I say as I click on the link, which brings me to an article about Maple and me and how our entire relationship was a fabrication for the media.

"What's going on?" Hutton asks as he comes up behind me.

"Someone let it leak that Maple and I were in a PR relationship."

"Shit, really?"

I pull up my search engine and type in my name and Maple's. When I hit enter, a bunch of articles come up about our fake relationship.

"Fuck." I push my hand through my hair, then quickly dial Gretchen's number.

I pace the weight room as the phone rings.

"I'm handling it," she answers.

"How? Because it's being spread like fucking wildfire."

"I'm well aware, Graydon."

"Who was it?"

"Don't know, but we are looking into it."

I continue pacing the weight room. "This could hurt her. You know that, right? I told her that I would protect her, and this...this is putting a target on her back."

"I know, and I'm going to do everything I can to make sure it doesn't hurt her, but you have to let me do my work," Gretchen says. I can hear her typing on the other end of the phone. "We are working on a statement to dispel the rumor. Because right now, it just says a source close to you let the news out."

"A source close to me?" I ask as I glance over at Hutton. He shakes his head vehemently. "Who the hell is close to me that would give out this information?"

"Who have you told?"

"Hutton, OC, Bennett...those are the only people other than Maple who I talk to. And they wouldn't have said anything. If anyone, it would have been OC, but he was the one who broke this news to me, so it wouldn't have been him."

"Okay, well, I'm going to look into—" She pauses, and then I can hear her swear under her breath.

"What?" I ask.

"My friend over at one of the gossip sites just let me know that the news came from your dad's team."

"What?" I nearly yell, my entire body going stiff with anger. "It was my dad?"

"Looks like it. Someone on his team."

"Are you sure?"

"Yes, this source is reliable."

"I'll take care of it."

"Wait, Graydon," Gretchen says in a panic. "Don't. Don't talk to him."

"The fuck I'm not."

"I'm serious. We need to handle this properly."

"Yeah, and that's with my fist buried in his face."

"No!" she yells. "No, you can't do that. Given the tumultuous relationship you already have with him, there is no doubt in my mind that if you harm him physically, he will take it to the press, and you don't need that right now. Just let me do my work and clear the air. Okay?"

My jaw clenches tight as I fight the need to teach my dad a lesson.

"Graydon, tell me you're not going to go see him."

After a few seconds, I say, "I'm not."

"Thank you. Now does Maple know?"

"Probably not. I can go tell her, though. She's at work, but I can rush over there."

"You know what? Wait. I'm headed over to the facility now. Welcott just messaged me asking what's going on. I think we can nip this quickly if we have a chat with him. See you in twenty in his office."

Then the phone goes dead.

"Fuck," I say as I place my phone on a shelf and then push both hands through my hair.

"It was your dad?" Hutton asks.

"Yeah. Fucking imagine being that vindictive against your son." I shake my head. "Fuck, I am itching to confront him."

"I'm guessing Gretchen thought that was a bad idea."

"You think?" I pace some more, my energy bouncing through me. "She's headed over here, and we're going to talk to Welcott."

"Jesus, maybe you should check in on Maple and see how she's doing."

He's right. I pick up my phone and dial her number. It rings a few times and then goes to voice mail.

So I dial again.

And again.

And again, until finally she picks up.

But instead of her voice, it's a man's.

And not just any voice, but Slutty Little Glasses' voice.

"She is in a meeting right now."

"Well, can you get her? It's important."

"Is it about the article? Because she knows, it's why she's in a meeting, because there is press here at the zoo hounding her."

Fuck…

"First of all, this is none of your goddamn business, and second of all, bring her phone to her…now."

"Can't. She's in a meeting, but I'll be sure to let her know the guy who is trying to disrupt her peaceful life is attempting to contact her."

"You motherfuck—"

But he hangs up.

And if you thought I was angry before, hell has now burned into my bones as a side of fury no one has ever seen takes over.

"Uh…Graydon, I think you might break your phone if you keep squeezing it that hard."

"I'm going to rip him apart."

Hutton clears his throat just as I chuck my phone against the wall, letting it shatter to the floor.

"And here I was worried about your hand breaking it."

I growl, turning on my friend, who now holds his hands up in the air.

"Okay, listen, I know it feels like things are spiraling and that you are losing all control, but I think it's important that we remember—"

"Fuck off," I say as I turn away from him and head up to Welcott's office.

"Yup, saw that coming."

---

I pace the front office, waiting for Gretchen to show up, the image of Slutty Little Glasses answering my girl's phone playing over and over in my head. Was he just waiting for me to call, planning this whole goddamn thing out, laughing 'cause he knew I fucked up?

Probably.

He was probably waiting for the moment to roll in where he could show Maple just how much of a douche he is.

"Stop pacing," Gretchen's voice sounds off as she walks up to me. "I need you calm and collected when we go into that office, or else what I have planned is not going to work."

I pause in my pacing. "What do you have planned?"

"Well, for one, your father and coach are headed this way."

My hands tighten into fists. "Great, can't wait to greet him properly."

Gretchen points her finger at me. "You will not touch him. You will not say a word to him. Do you hear me? I swear to God, Graydon, if you want this to work out in your favor and get your father out of this building and far away from you, then you need to listen to every word I say. Understood?"

The seriousness in her tone snaps me out of my murderous thoughts. "What are you going to do?"

"Just follow my lead." She walks up to Welcott's door and knocks on it.

"Come in," he calls out.

Gretchen looks me in the eyes and takes a deep breath, gesturing at me to do so as well, so I do. And then we release our breaths together. Satisfied, she opens the door, and we both walk in, my dad and Coach Keenan already in Welcott's office.

When my eyes fall on my father, the tension I just released immediately coils at the base of my spine and nearly propels me forward, my fist leading the way, but Gretchen's warning rests firmly at the forefront of my brain, preventing me from making a mistake.

Instead, I take a seat on the couch in Welcott's office, as far away from my father as possible.

"I can't possibly see why we needed to call a meeting," Coach Keenan says. "This PR nonsense is starting to get in the way of my coaching."

"I'm glad you see it as nonsense," Gretchen says as she takes a seat as well. "Good morning, Mr. Welcott. Thank you for meeting on such short notice."

He nods. "Make it quick."

"Of course." Gretchen pulls a piece of paper out of the folder she carried into the office and places it on Welcott's desk. "As you know, the PR relationship has been exposed despite Graydon and Maple being in a real relationship now. The news is damaging but not unfixable. I dug into some of my contacts and came back with this. It's a memo from one of my sources stating that they got the tip from Troy St. John."

My dad stands up, fury raging in his eyes.

"That's preposterous. Why would I ever do that?"

Keeping her eyes trained on Welcott, she continues, "When you brought me onto the job, it became my responsibility to assess all strengths and weaknesses outside of the client I'm focusing on. My team and I did a deep dive into the organization to see what could possibly be tainting the business from the inside, and my team has brought up a series of conversations within your organization, all stemming from Troy St. John and Coach Keenan." She sets down another piece of paper. "We have audio records, but they are written out here. As you can see, Troy and Coach Keenan have been formulating plans to remove Graydon from the team."

Holy shit, how did she get ahold of those?

"What are you talking about?" Coach Keenan asks, now standing as well. "I want to see those records."

"My assistant is emailing them as we speak. They should be in your inbox shortly," Gretchen says, not even cracking a smile. "Given this information, I decided to run beta tests on the importance of the two players, Troy and Graydon. And every test that came back spoke wildly in Graydon's favor." She lays down another piece of paper. "Please note that we tested before the PR relationship and after, and in both instances, Graydon surpassed his father in popularity. But with his newfound relationship with Maple, his popularity has skyrocketed and, as you know, has reshaped the perception the public has of the Foghorns. Now, we have yet to play a game, and given where Coach Keenan's mind has been—trying to get rid of his best player rather than coaching—we will see where the season takes us, but considering the amount of jersey sales and season ticket purchases, I would say you're looking at a positive season, at least in sales. And it's because of Graydon."

"How dare you imply that I'm not focused on my team," Coach Keenan says, but once again, Gretchen ignores him.

"Mr. Welcott, one of the reasons I took this job was because I could see that you were a smart businessman, and you weren't just hiring me to place a Band-Aid on a problem. You hired me because you care about your organization, and you want to see it succeed. With that being said, it is my greatest recommendation that you not only support my efforts in fixing the leak but also consider ridding this team of the disease that's been clinging to the walls of your facility and trying to tarnish your reputation and intelligence as an owner. I recommend you see that Troy St. John is not allowed in these halls and is only on the field when honoring past players—but only if he signs an NDA and walks quietly. If not, we have ways of making sure his reputation takes more than just a hit. And I suggest you look into another head coach. His head is not in the right place."

"Where the fuck do you come off?" Coach Keenan shouts.

Gretchen stands from her chair and nods. "I've taken enough of your time. Please feel free to reach out if you have any questions." And with that, she pauses for me to stand as well, which I do, and together, we head out of Welcott's office and down the hallway, all the way to the locker room, where she finally stops and turns toward me.

"That should be all you need. Good job not opening that mouth of yours."

Still in shock, I tug on my neck and say, "You think he's going to make a change?"

"He's a smart man who cares more about his ego than this organization.

If someone is undermining him, he will get rid of them. Once he hears the audio, you won't have to worry about your father anymore. And given that I've been handling your PR as of late, I would suggest letting the relationship between the two of you die. Don't seek closure, don't seek a conversation. There is nothing of substance that will come from him that will ease the ache I'm sure you have where he's concerned. If I were you, I would just consider him dead at this point."

"He was dead to me years ago."

"Yet you let him bother you. Trust me, Graydon, your significance in this life and this organization outweighs his by tenfold. He means nothing to you. Understood?"

I run my tongue over my teeth, the need to just shove him into a wall and scream at him for everything he's done to me, my mom…Maple, it's overwhelming…

Gretchen grips my shirt, forcing me to look her in the eyes. "Drop it," she says through clenched teeth. "I'm telling you right now, Graydon, fucking drop it. Forget he even exists, because if Welcott takes my recommendation, things will get heated before they calm down, and I need you level-headed, on top of your game, and unfazed by his actions."

I know she's right, but it doesn't make it any less painful.

She lets go of my shirt and takes a step back. "Now, I'm going to be doing some damage control on the relationship news. Don't talk to anyone about this other than me and Maple. We don't need word spreading, because this is a hot topic that is going to be picked up everywhere."

A thought hits me at the mention of not talking to anyone.

"Shit, I think press are at the zoo, trying to speak with Maple. When I called to check on her, that's what her asshat of a coworker said. I'm going to go over there."

"Try calling her before you do."

"Can't. I broke my phone by throwing it into a wall."

Gretchen lets out a deep sigh and then pinches the bridge of her nose. "For the love of God, did anyone see you do that?"

"Just Hutton."

"Okay." Her eyes meet mine. "Control your freaking temper, Graydon, and save the aggression for the field. Can you do that?"

I mull over her words. It's never been that easy for me, ever. I grew up in a household where abandonment hit me every which way. From my dad to my mom—though not on purpose—I've grown to sit in my anger, to wrestle with it daily, to lean on the emotion more than any other. And to just let it go, not to react when something doesn't go my way, well, easier said than done.

"Can you?" she repeats.

"Yes."

"Good." She lets out a sigh. "Okay, can you handle Maple, or do I need to go with you?"

"I can deal with it," I say.

She studies me for a moment and then shakes her head. "No, I'll go with you."

"I said I can handle it."

"And I said I'll go with you." She turns me toward the parking lot. "Follow me."

"I need to grab my shit first."

She crosses her arms and taps her foot. "Hurry up. I'm on borrowed time."

---

I open the gate for Gretchen, and together, we head toward the flamingo building.

There is press hanging around the front of the zoo, but nothing in the back, thankfully. My gut churns from the thought of Maple being hounded by press now. And sure, it will probably—hopefully—die down, but why do they have to be here?

This is her sanctuary. She loves it here, being with the flamingos, and to have that tainted makes me feel incredibly uneasy…and guilty.

We attempt to hide from onlookers, but it's near impossible given my size and the news that's going around today. Phones point at me from all different directions as I make my way toward the flamingos, and I don't even bother hiding anymore, because what's the point? I'm a giant man walking through the zoo in my workout clothes. It's pretty clear who I am and who I'm going to go see.

When we reach the building, I open the door for Gretchen only for her to come up short and stop before I can enter.

Confused, I look up, and that's where I find Slutty Little Glasses, his arms all over my girl and his mouth inches from her head.

White-hot rage encompasses me, and before I can stop myself, I push past Gretchen, walk right up to them, and rip him off Maple with a roar of anger, shoving him a few feet away.

"What the fuck do you think you're doing?" I yell.

"Graydon," Maple says in shock, but I ignore her.

"I asked you what the fuck you were doing." I round on Slutty Little Glasses, giving him no room to run away.

To his credit, he doesn't back down as he lifts his chin and says, "Taking care of her."

"That's my fucking job!" I yell, practically spitting in his face from my anger.

"Graydon, back away," Gretchen says from the side as my fists clench.

"I'm the one who protects her, not you."

"How can you possibly protect her when you're the one causing the harm?" he shoots back, his words creating a tumultuous wave of damage in my chest. "You're the one hurting her."

"Hank, don't say that," Maple says, coming up next to me. "That's not true."

"It's not?" he asks. "Because from what I see, you're crying at work—this not being the first time—over something to do with him. You're being hounded by press, you're panicking so much that you're making yourself sick—"

"You're making yourself sick?" I ask, turning toward Maple, who is clenching her hands together, tears brimming in her eyes.

"Please, Hank, just...stop."

"Wait, what is he talking about?"

Her eyes dart to Hank and then back to me. "I was just...it was a lot to handle this morning. I might have gotten a little sick, but it's nothing that you need to worry about because I'm sure you're worried about enough at the moment."

"I'm worried about you."

"Are you, though?" Hank asks. "Because you're the one who keeps putting her in these situations."

"Who is this?" Gretchen asks, pointing at Hank. "And why is he here?"

"He's a friend," Maple says.

"I was unaware of his knowledge of the situation." Gretchen starts tapping away on her phone while saying, "We need to talk about this privately."

"Why, so you can continue to use her for your benefit?" Hank asks. "Because that's all this has ever been. Using her, using this zoo, taking advantage of an opportunity to make your life better with total disregard for how she's treated."

"You have no idea what you're talking about," I say.

"Hank, please, you're going to make it worse."

"Worse?" His brows shoot up. "How could I make this worse? You were almost attacked out there by some idiotic fan. The press snuck in and hounded you. I care about you, Maple, that's why I'm going to say something, and it's why I'll keep saying something, because no one is seeing what I'm seeing. He's so blinded by what's best for him—"

"All I care about is her," I shoot back.

"If that were the case, then you wouldn't be putting her through this, and all for what? A bunch of broken promises?"

"I haven't broken a promise."

"We really need to take this somewhere else," Gretchen says, but Hank ignores her.

"You haven't? Then what about the donation? The one that was promised her in exchange for helping you out? Phil just told me that money is being put toward merchandise rather than the flamingos, especially now with the painted wall that's gathering attention."

"Wait…what?" Maple asks. "He said that?"

"Yes, so everything you've done…pointless. That's what I've been trying to tell you, Maple, but you've been so…caught up with everything that you haven't been listening. He's hurting you." Hank turns toward me. "You're hurting her, and you're not even realizing it."

"I…I didn't have any idea," I say, his words sinking in.

"Because you're too concerned about yourself. You say you care about her, but do you really? If you cared about her, you would realize that being with you isn't doing her any good. It's only hurting her."

"That's not true." Maple shakes her head and comes up to me, her hand on my chest. "Graydon, that's not true."

I glance down at her, my mind swimming with Hank's words, my own doubts creeping in as well.

"Were you sick this morning?" She looks me in the eyes, and I can tell she's about to lie, so I say, "Tell me the truth."

She wets her lips. "It was just…it was not what I expected this morning. I didn't know that the relationship was going to be thrown out into the wild like that. I thought it was secure information."

"It was," I say, my jaw clenching. "Until my dad thought it was necessary to let it leak."

"It was your dad?" she asks, her eyes still watery.

"Yeah." I take a step back from her and smooth my hand over my jaw. "Fuck…he's right."

"Who's right?"

I gesture toward Hank. "I'm just…I'm a burden for you."

"Don't." Maple steps up, but I take another step away. "Graydon, don't do this."

My eyes find hers, and I can feel myself back away some more, my head shaking, the thought of the pain I've caused her pumping through me.

I've hurt her, in many ways, and this is just another instance. It's not going to get easier than this. It's only going to get harder with every day that goes by. Do I want to keep hurting her?

I don't.

Which means…

"We should go, Gretchen."

# CHAPTER 45
# MAPLE

"NO," I SAY, WALKING RIGHT up to Graydon and pulling on his hand. "Do not leave. Do not do this."

The door opens, and Phil walks in but pauses when he sees all of us. "Um, sorry for the interruption, but we have security pushing people away from the flamingos right now given what's going on." He then clasps his hands together. "Um, I think we're going to send you home early, Maple."

"What? No. I don't need to go home."

He clears his throat and says, "We think it's best that you do and take some time off."

"What?" I ask, shocked.

I can feel Graydon tense next to me, and I can already hear the voices in his head, telling him this is his fault. This is all his fault.

And it's not. It's just the circumstances of the situation.

"It's probably best," Gretchen chimes in. "Until we can get ahold of the story and solidify security here."

"I don't want to leave. This is...this is where I want to be."

"Unfortunately, we are not giving you an option in the matter," Phil says. "Please grab your things. We have security waiting outside to escort you to your car."

I pause because that sounds like I'm being let go rather than taking a few days off.

"Are you…are you firing me?" I ask.

Phil sighs and then shakes his head. "No, but we're in a sticky situation here, Maple. We need to tread carefully. We can't cause a commotion. It will disrupt the animals, and they are always our top priority. If we can't get everything under control, then we will have to—"

"No need," Graydon says. "We're not together anymore. So just let it die down and everything will be okay. It was a PR relationship after all, right? It was bound to happen."

"What? Graydon," I say, turning toward him. "That's a lie and you know it."

He steps away. "Gretchen, make sure she follows the NDA guidelines for the breakup contract."

"Graydon. Stop." I take his hand in mine, but he quickly pulls away. His face remains emotionless as he puts distance between us. "Graydon."

He doesn't look at me.

Doesn't even spare me a glance as he heads toward the door.

"Don't push me away. You don't mean this."

He pauses before he leaves and looks over his shoulder, but not at me. Instead, he looks at Hank. "She won't be hurting anymore."

Then he takes off, and I'm left feeling like my world is crumbling around me.

Because it is.

He's…he's done with this, with us, I saw it in his eyes. The finality was there.

Hank comes up behind me and places his hand on my shoulder. "Are you okay?"

I shrug him off, taking a step back. "Am I okay?" I yell. "Do you think I'm okay? Hank, you just single-handedly made my boyfriend believe that he was a burden on my life. When he's not, he's…been such a blessing. He's made me feel special, wanted, needed. And what we have, it's real, there's nothing fake about it, but everyone seems to have an opinion on the matter, despite it not being their business."

"Maple, let's go—"

I push away from Gretchen, who is trying to take me by the arm.

"No, I don't want to hear it. All I want is to talk to Graydon and for everyone else to step out of our business." I head toward the door but stop in front of Phil. "By the way, if the money that was donated by Welcott does not go to the flamingos, you can bet I'll be writing a scathing article about you, your dishonesty, and how you actually don't care about the animals but rather the bottom line with your merchandise ideas. I'm sure the board of directors will love that."

"Maple," Hank says, but I hold up my hand.

"No. I don't want to hear it. I don't want to hear it from any of you. All I wanted was to help the flamingos, and when Graydon came along, I saw the kind of man he is, the generous, sweet man, and I wanted to help him as well. But all of this…these demands, these needs, the use of his celebrity status, it's gotten out of hand, and frankly, I'm sick of it. He's a good person, and he shouldn't be walking away from a relationship that I know he wants, that he needs, because he's afraid you might fire me."

I gesture to Phil.

"Or because you convince him that he's a burden to me," I say to Hank. "That's none of your business. I knew what I was getting into when I started to fall for him, and I've accepted every aspect of it because I like him and because he's worth it. We're worth it."

With that, I quickly grab my bag and head out the back of the flamingo building, straight in the direction of the parking lot, hoping to catch him before he leaves.

"Maple, wait," Gretchen calls out, but I keep moving forward. "Hold on, let me talk to you."

"No," I snap and move through the employee-only section of the zoo to the parking lot, where I catch the tail end of Graydon's truck leaving. "Fuck."

"Maple, please, can we just talk?" Gretchen asks, catching up to me.

I whirl on her, my anger over the entire situation getting the best of me. "No, the last person I want to talk to is you. You've made this so incredibly difficult, so obnoxiously disheartening, that you are part of the problem."

She juts her head back, her expression full of surprise. "I wasn't—"

"Don't tell me you weren't trying to make this difficult, because you were. From the contracts, to the doubt, to the questioning. It's been a nightmare, but I kept up with it because of him. But now it's gotten so out of control that he's giving up, he's giving up on me." I shake my head. "But I'm not going to let that happen." He's the best man I know, and I've never been in a relationship with someone who cares so much about me. Even to the point of "breaking up" to *help* me. I take a deep breath. "I'm not going to let you get in the way of that."

"I don't want to. I want to help you."

"Oh, just like you were helping me when you told me to sign the breakup contract?"

"I was forced to bring that to you," she says, her eyes narrowing. "Just like there are parts of your job you probably don't like, there are parts of mine that I don't like either, that being one of them."

"I don't want to hear it," I say, unable to process anything she's saying. "I just want to get to Graydon."

I walk toward my car and unlock it.

"I want to help you," she calls out.

"Too late." I get in my car and take off, headed right to Graydon's place to fix this.

---

I pull my knees in close to my chest as I lean up against Graydon's garage door, waiting for him to return. It's been a few hours since I left the zoo, and he hasn't returned. I have no idea where he is or what he's doing, and even though I've tried calling him several times, his phone goes straight to voice mail, and his text messages go undelivered.

To say I'm worried is an understatement.

The sun is setting, the street is calm, just local commuters finding their way home, and there is a slight breeze picking up that ruffles my hair every once in a while. I've shifted a few times on the concrete beneath me because my ass has gone numb, but I don't care because I will stay here through the night if I have to. I want to see him.

Headlights blare down the road, and I perk up, but when I notice it's an SUV, I lower my head back down.

Where is he?

I hope he's okay.

I hope—

The SUV pulls into his driveway and stops short of me. When the lights turn off, I see Hutton sitting in the driver's seat and Graydon in the passenger seat.

Why is Hutton driving him home?

Did he get in an accident?

Panic swells in my chest as his car door opens, and I stand from the ground, brushing off my pants.

When his hazy eyes meet mine, he says, "What are you doing here?" He stumbles out of the SUV and then shuts the door, nearly falling to the ground.

He's drunk.

"Maple," Hutton says, coming up to me. "I'm sorry, I didn't know. The bartender, who is a friend, called me."

"It's okay. Does he have his phone turned off?"

"Broke it," Graydon says, moving past me and to the keypad on the side of his garage door. He types in a few numbers, and it starts opening.

"You broke your phone?"

"He threw it against the weight room wall when Slutty Little Glasses answered your phone."

"Slutty Little...do you mean Hank?"

"Sure," Hutton says as Graydon moves into his garage and starts digging through a bucket that's next to his door. "I don't think he's in a great position to talk right now."

"It's okay. I'll make sure he gets into his place and gets to bed."

"You sure?" Hutton glances at Graydon, who fishes a key out of the bucket. "I'm not sure he wants to be near you right now."

"I don't care about that," I say. "He can push me away all he wants, but it's not going to happen."

"Good," Hutton says, then leans closer. "He needs someone like you."

"I know," I answer.

He offers me a side hug and then takes off as I head toward Graydon, who is struggling to open the door to his house. I press the button to shut the garage door, then take the key from him and unlock the door. He pushes through and then stumbles toward the couch, where he crashes down on the cushions and lets out a deep breath.

While he gains his bearings, I go to the kitchen and pour him a glass of water, bringing it over to him.

"Here," I say, handing him the glass, but he doesn't take it.

"Why are you here, Maple? Didn't you get the hint at the zoo?"

While I was waiting for him, I mentally prepared myself for this, for him to continue to push me away, for him to say things I know he wouldn't normally mean, and not to take offense at them. If I know anything about Graydon at this point, it's that he will do anything to protect the people he cares for in his life, including me. And if he thinks he's protecting me by pushing me away, then he's going to do a damn good job at it, even if it hurts us both.

"Can you please drink some water?"

His eyes fall to mine, dark, dangerous, but also…sad. "I asked you a question."

"And I'm choosing to ignore it."

He shakes his head. "You shouldn't be here."

"Graydon, please just drink some water. I can make some coffee as well—"

"I don't want your coffee, Maple. I want you to leave." His voice is terse, but I stand firm.

"I'm not leaving. Not when you're drunk and saying things you don't mean."

"I wasn't drunk at the zoo and meant every word I said there."

Yup, he's not holding back, but that doesn't matter to me because I can handle it.

At least I hope that I can.

"I'm not going to get into a fight with you right now. Why don't we just get you upstairs for a shower and—"

"Leave me the fuck alone," he says, sitting up and pulling his shirt over his head. He deposits it on the floor and then lies back down on the couch. He closes his eyes and drapes his arm over his eyes.

I stare down at him, wondering how to handle this, how to get him to listen to me, but when I see his breathing even out and his chest rise and fall at a slow pace, I notice that he's asleep, which is probably for the best.

So I pick up a blanket that's draped over the back of the couch, and I cover him with it before heading up to his room, where I turn on the shower and undress. I slip under the hot water and let it run down my body as I allow myself to relax for a moment and feel the anger and frustration pour out of me.

Tears fill my eyes.

The need to hit something pushes through me.

The urge to scream over the situation rises to the tip of my tongue, but I hold back, not wanting to wake or disturb him. Instead, I let my tears flow down my cheeks as I use his body wash to clean the day off me.

After I dry off, I slip on one of his T-shirts and a pair of spandex shorts I've kept here. I brush my teeth and head back downstairs, where I find him still sleeping. I want to climb on top of him, curl into his side, sleep next to him, and let all the worry drain away, but I also don't know how he'll receive me. Instead, I grab another blanket and a throw pillow, and I curl up on one of the chairs.

As I lie there, my eyes on him the entire time, my heart aches thinking about the pain he's feeling, and how unfair his life has been. *His dad leaked the news about how our relationship started.* What sort of person does that to their own son? How can a man so despise his flesh and blood that he can hurt him with such brutality?

I refuse to contribute to that. I know he loves me. I felt it the other night after we visited his mom. I know that I make a difference in his life, that he not only wants me but needs me.

And it's the same with me. He's changed so much in my life, opening my eyes to what love really is, this all-encompassing feeling of happiness where the person holding your hand is your moon and stars, and you go to sleep at night dreaming about them, only to wake up the following morning and crave them.

He's opened me up to a type of passion I had no idea existed, but now that I've had a taste of it, I refuse to let it go.

He can push.

He can hurt me.

But I know none of it's true because I know the way he looks at me, kisses me, loves on me. We have that forever kind of connection that you only find once in a lifetime, and I refuse to let it go despite all the roadblocks.

Nope, I'm going to fight for us, even if it kills me.

# CHAPTER 46
# GRAYDON

FUCK...ME.

My head pounds with regrets.

My stomach rolls with bad habits.

And my body aches with horrible decisions as my eyes peel open, the sun blaring through the windows of my living room like a death ray, attempting to crack my skull in half.

"Fuck," I grumble as I realize I'm on the couch, the cushions doing absolutely nothing to support my battered back. I carefully push myself up and run my hand over my eyes as I attempt to find some clarity.

I blow out a heavy breath and observe the scene.

There's a glass of water on the coffee table, untouched.

A blanket at my feet.

And...

Shit.

Curled up on one of the chairs next to the couch is Maple, her head resting on a throw pillow and a blanket pulled up around her chin. Yesterday's events come barreling to the forefront of my mind as I take in her peaceful face, slumbering in what seems to be a very uncomfortable position.

Hatred for myself billows in the pit of my stomach all over again because I came to the realization yesterday that I'm the problem. I'm very much the problem. As much as it pains me to admit it, Slutty Little Glasses was right—I'm a burden for her. I'm making her life harder.

This entire situation could get her fired from a job she loves.

And in the long run, I'm hurting her.

Destroying the life that she so perfectly crafted for herself.

All for what? To make myself feel better?

I push my hand through my hair, stand from the couch, and walk over to the kitchen, where I start a pot of coffee.

Leaning against the counter, I take Maple in, letting my eyes roam over her and commit to memory this peaceful moment where there is a slight smile on her sultry lips, her stunning face relaxed with nothing bothering her. She's peaceful.

She's perfect.

And if only she could be mine.

The coffee pot beeps, and I catch her stirring, so I turn my back, grab a mug, and fill it up. I'm going to need this liquid encouragement to do what I need to do.

I blow on the mug while I hear her move off her chair and approach the kitchen, her cute feet padding across the floor. Before she can walk up behind me and loop her arms around my waist like she's done in the past, I turn to see her enter the kitchen, her eyes still sleepy and her hair slightly rumpled.

Fuck, I want to pull her into my arms and bury my face in her neck.

"Good morning," she says as she pauses at the kitchen island. Her voice is scratchy, as if she spent the night screaming my damn name, but I know that's not the case. If it was, I wouldn't be putting distance between us right now.

"What are you doing here, Maple?"

"I came to be with you."

"And I told you, we're not a thing."

Her eyes narrow, and I can tell this is not going to be as easy as I thought.

"We're not a thing? As in, we're not dating?"

"That's what that would mean," I say, my voice remaining emotionless.

"Interesting," she says as she props her hip against the island and folds her arms over her chest. "Because last I remember, you really liked me, so tell me where along the way this didn't turn into a relationship."

I blow out a heavy breath and drag my hand down my face. "Maple, don't make this harder than it has to be."

"Did you really just say that to me? Do you really expect me to just roll over, tuck my tail between my legs, and walk away from you after everything we've been through? It doesn't work that way, Graydon. I'm not going to just leave because you're trying to save me from whatever story you're building in your head."

"It's not a story!" I shout, not helping my hangover. "It's real life. The press is hounding you, it's affecting your work, and this is…this won't get easier."

"And you think your feelings are just going to fade away as if I didn't even exist?"

I stare down at my coffee mug, unable to look her in the eyes when I say, "Yeah, it's not like it meant that much to me in the first place."

Silence falls between us, and I can't spare her a look because I know I'll break. I know she'll see right through the lie.

Honestly, the biggest lie I've ever told.

Because that's not how I feel at all.

I fucking love her. I rely on her. I crave her.

I feel like I've found my person. Our souls have connected on another level.

Yet I realize the pressure my job has put on her, the dysfunction of my family, and the demand of my celebrity. I know that it's a lot, and I know deep in my soul that she doesn't deserve to be put through all of that.

She steps forward, closing the space between us until there are only mere inches between our chests.

"I didn't mean that much to you?" Her tone isn't sad, more inquisitive, like she just drummed up an entire plan in her head and is about to best me.

"It was good for what it was," I answer.

"I see." She moves directly in front of me and then, to my surprise, takes off her shorts, then her shirt, leaving her completely bare.

Fuck.

Her hand smooths up my chest, her fingers tickling over my heated skin. She makes me set my coffee down and brings my hand directly to her ass.

My mind screams at me to step away and not to fall for whatever she has planned, but my heart and my body are not listening.

"If I meant nothing to you, then why is your breathing different right now?" Her finger drags over my jaw. "How come your skin is heated?" Her palm smooths over my pec, down my stomach, and right to the waistband of my shorts. "And how come you're hard?" She cups me, calling me out right before she steps away and then lifts herself up on the island counter.

My eyes betray me as they roam over her delicious tits and the way she's pushing her chest out toward the ceiling.

"If this means nothing to you, then I guess you can just watch, right?"

What does she mean…

She brings her feet up to the counter and spreads her legs, giving me a front-row seat to her beautiful cunt. She brings her hand between her legs, and I watch as her fingers slide over her clit. Her head falls back, and she lets out a low, sexy moan.

"Fuck, yes," she whispers as my cock stretches the fabric of my shorts, my muscles tensing. "It's easier to make myself come now. You've shown me what I love. What I…*need*. No one's ever made me feel so sensual before you."

Her fingers circle over her clit, and I watch as she grows wet from the movement, my mouth watering, my jealousy increasing.

Her teeth drag over the corner of her mouth, and her nipples grow hard as she starts to ramp up her movements, her breathing becoming more erratic.

"If you didn't care..." she says and then catches her breath, "then don't touch me. Don't even look. Turn away and let me come on my own." Her eyes land on mine. "Go on, Graydon...oh...fuck." She lets out a deep breath. "Look...away."

She moves faster, her chest heaving, her muscles tensing. She's so goddamn close that I should just let her finish.

I should prove the point and walk away.

But...

Fuck, I can't.

I can't watch her do this without me.

Not when my heart is tearing in two from the thought that she could give herself that much pleasure without me.

In a flash, I push my shorts down, release my cock, and bring it up to her. I pull her close to the edge of the counter, line myself up and then lift her up, letting myself slip inside as I take her hand that she was fingering herself with and slide her fingers in my mouth, tasting her while I lift her up and slam her down on my cock. Her other hand grabs the back of my neck, and she holds on as I pound into her relentlessly.

Her warm, wet pussy clenches around my cock, bringing me to the precipice of my orgasm in a matter of seconds.

"Fuck, Graydon," she moans as she releases her fingers from my mouth and then digs them into my hair. "Harder. Make me come."

I lose all track of what we were talking about, and my only focus is on our connection and how she feels, thrusting in and out of her. It's a goddamn high, this feeling, her clamped around me. Squeezing, tightening, making me mad with need.

"Right there, so close. Give me all of your cock," she says, setting my entire body on fire.

I growl, then thrust even faster, pounding into her, bottoming out on every pulse until she's pulling on my hair and clamping around me.

"Oh my God," she shouts and shatters over me.

Her orgasm is all I need, and I follow quickly after, stilling and spilling myself inside her as the best fucking feeling of my life takes over my body.

We both cling on to each other, letting our breath catch up…and our minds.

Fuck, what was I thinking?

I slide her off me and set her down on the counter only for her to hop off, grab her clothes, and walk away to the bathroom. I slip myself back in my shorts, then push my hand through my hair.

Jesus Christ. Why did I just do that?

Because I'm weak where she's concerned.

Because I have zero control.

Because I'm a goddamn moron.

Here I am, trying to push her away, trying to put distance between us because that fuck at the zoo was right, all I am is a burden to her, and then I go and fuck her in my kitchen.

There is something seriously wrong with me.

After a few minutes, she pops out of the bathroom and heads over to the garage door, where she slips her shoes on. She gathers her things, then walks up to me.

I keep my eyes focused on the ground because I can't look at her.

I can't face her after what I just did.

Her hand lands on my chest, and she quietly says, "Push me away all you want, but it won't negate the fact that I know how you truly feel about me, Graydon. I know deep in my soul that you love me just as much as I love you."

My entire chest seizes from those three words.

"Yes, I said 'love' because I'm not afraid to say it, and I'm not afraid to claim it. I love you, and I will spend every moment I have proving that to you. Proving to you that this is where I want to be. I will not abandon you, I will not leave you. You are who I want to be with, and I don't care about anything else that comes along with it because the only thing I care about…is you." She pats my chest and then loops her hand around my neck, tugging me down to her lips, where she softly kisses me for no more than a second, pulling away before I can even get a good taste.

When she moves away, this sense of loss falls over me, guilt pulses through me, and for a brief second, I consider grabbing her arm, pulling her into my chest, and telling her that I love her too.

But I don't move.

Instead, I watch her walk out the front door, taking my heart along with her.

---

"I'm glad you called," OC says as he walks into my place and hands me a pack of beer—nonalcoholic. "It's all I had in my pantry. I bought it by mistake at the store." He shrugs and then takes a seat in the living room, where Bennett is already sitting.

I stare down at the piss in a bottle and leave it at the front door. I won't be opening those.

I take a seat on the couch in the living room, and I let out a deep breath.

After a few seconds of silence, I say, "I ended things with Maple." OC gasps loudly, clutching his chest. "Or at least I think I did."

"What do you mean you think you did?" Bennett asks in a rational tone.

"No, more importantly, why the hell would you break up with her?" OC asks.

"Yeah, that's a good question too."

I sink into the couch and feel all of the emotion spill from me as I say, "Because I was trying to save her the trouble of being with me."

They pause and exchange looks before Bennett says, "But isn't that something for her to decide?"

"She would never break up with me over it. She would endure the burden until it broke her. She knows too much about me. She's seen too much about my personal life. I know her at this point." I drag my hand over my face. "The only problem is, when I went to break up with her, she wouldn't let me. Instead, I fucked her on the counter, she told me she loved me, and then she left."

OC's mouth falls open while Bennett shifts in his chair, looking uncomfortable.

"You fucked her on the counter?" OC glances at my kitchen. "How?"

"Dude." Bennett smacks OC across the arm.

"Ow, that hurt." He rubs his bicep.

"You get run over by hockey players for a living, and that hurt you?"

"Does it look like I'm wearing pads right now?"

"No, but that was barely a slap."

"You're right. It was a punch."

"Are you really going to argue right now?"

OC still rubs his arm. "No, because I can be the bigger man and move on without a heartfelt apology." He turns back to me. "So how did you fuck her on the counter?"

"Jesus…Christ," Bennett mumbles.

"You know, for a moment, I thought inviting you here might be helpful, but clearly I was wrong." I shake my head, wishing I had just kept to myself, but it ate away at me this morning until I called them over. I was unable to take it anymore, especially since I haven't heard from Maple since this morning.

Not that it should matter. I'm distancing myself…right?

"Don't you dare." OC sits up taller. "You called on the Gladdy Daddies, and we're here to serve. So we can skip the kitchen-fucking question for now, but I would like your technique later. As for the other thing, how do you feel about her saying she loves you?"

"Terrified," I answer, because even though I want to punch OC in the face for how annoying he is, I need someone to talk to about this. And unlucky for me, they are the best ones at the moment, besides Hutton, who was busy with family in town. "Because I love her too, and she called me out on it."

"She did?" Bennett asks.

"Yeah, she did. She said she loves me, and she knows I love her too." I slump enough on the couch that my head leans against the back of it. "I don't know what the fuck to do. Because yeah, I love her, and hearing her say she loves me, it just about tore me in two. But what am I supposed to do with that? Let her continue to love me while she's getting torn apart by the public? I can't let that happen to her."

"Has it happened, though?" Bennett asks. "Besides yesterday with the fake relationship bullshit."

"There have been comments about how she's not right for me."

"That's basic trolling that happens to everyone," OC says. "The other day, I had several people tell me the shorts I wore out to the grocery store were not right for my body. What's a guy supposed to do who has quads like mine?"

I stare at him, my expression unfazed as I say, "You know, I actually hate you."

OC shakes his head. "No, you don't. You love me. Not like you love Maple, but you love me."

I'm about to shove my foot up his ass to really show him how much I "love" him, but then Bennett says, "So you are willing to give up the relationship you have with her because you're worried that she can't handle being with you, right?"

I nod.

"And you won't let her make that decision because you feel like she knows too much about you, and she would never just leave you, right?"

I nod again.

"Okay, well then, just let her be. If that's what you want, then keep your distance."

"And when she doesn't let me?" I ask.

"Then you're going to have to test and see how strong you are when it comes to allowing her to protect herself...while she protects you."

"Whoa." OC turns to Bennett. "Dude, that was really profound." Then he looks at me and thumbs toward Bennett. "Listen to that shit, that's great advice."

"I don't even know what it means. How am I supposed—"

My new phone I got myself after Maple left this morning dings with a message, and I lift it up to see a text from Maple.

"Is that from her?" OC asks, craning his neck forward.

"It is."

"What does it say?"

I swipe on the text and read it to myself.

**Maple:** I missed you at the zoo today. I had to do the dishes myself. Big Hermy wasn't into getting fed by me, and every time I looked at the mural, I thought of you. I took a few pics in front of it for you. Miss you. Love you.

*Does this mean that Phil let her return to work?*

Two pictures follow the text, and they're of her sitting in front of the mural. The camera is at a ground angle, which makes me think she set it up with a timer. In the first, she's smiling and looking so damn adorable that I want to grab her through the phone and pull her into my chest, never letting her go.

The second is of her kissing the camera in front of the mural, and I feel myself sigh from the thought of those lips on me.

"Whatever it says, it's breaking the wall he's tried to erect," Bennett

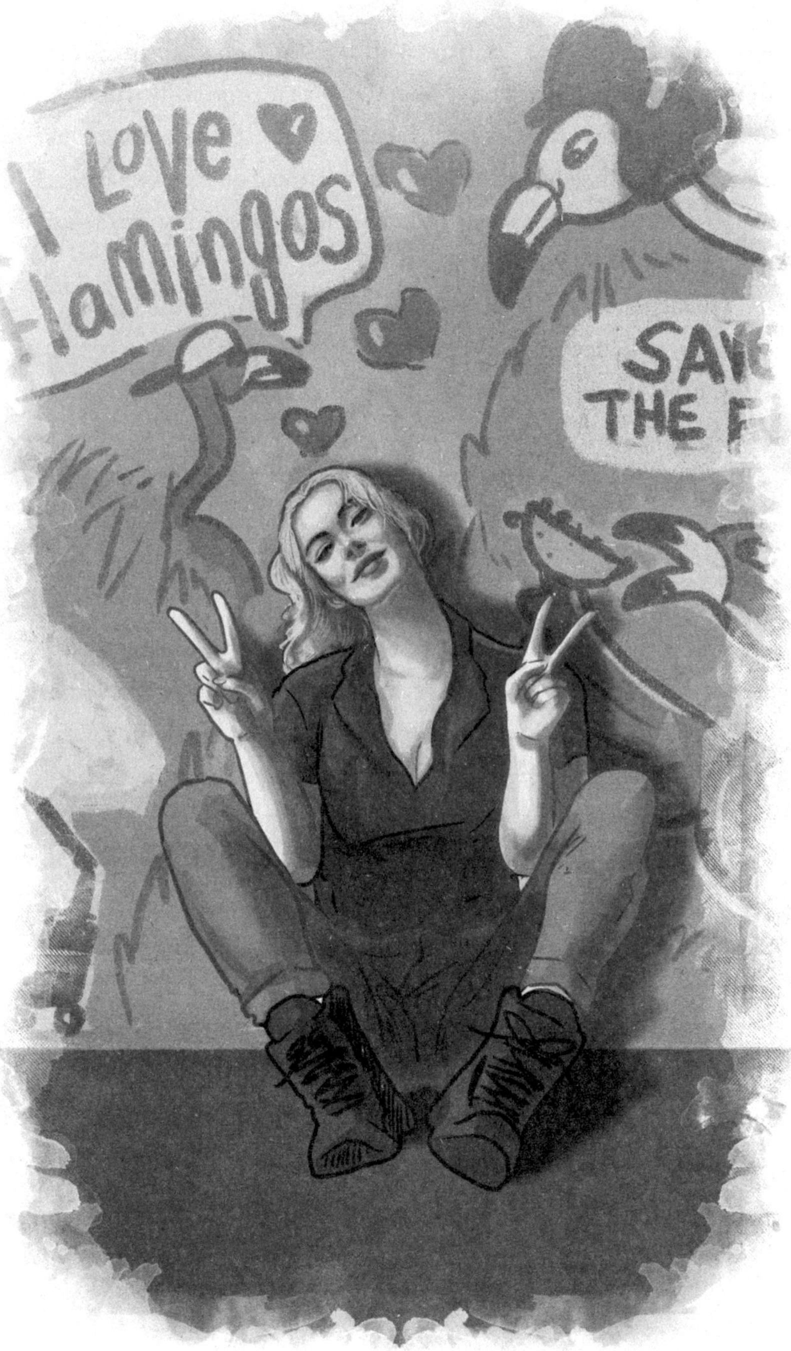
I Love
lamingos
SAV
THE F

says. "I know that look. You can put it off as much as you want, man, but I'm telling you right now, you're bound to give in, especially with that look in your eyes. What you need to focus on is trusting the fact that she's strong enough to handle herself through the ups and downs of what your relationship will bring. That will be the challenge. I wouldn't worry about her. I would worry about yourself."

It's silent for a moment, and then OC chuckles. When we look at him, he motions to Bennett and says, "You said 'erect.'"

I point at the front door and say, "Grab your piss beer and get the fuck out of here."

He nods and stands from the chair. "Yeah, that might be best. I'm adding no value to this gathering. I'll be better next time. Carry on, men."

---

I drop the weights on the weight rack and reach for my phone to skip the song blasting through my AirPods. I'm not in the mood for some pump-up, techno beat. Nope, I've been purely listening to slow songs, mostly covers by Boyce Avenue, but of course that's not something I would ever admit out loud, especially not when I'm benching three hundred and fifty pounds.

When I pick up my phone, I see a text message from Maple. Fucking hell, the way she makes my heart flutter. I open the text and read it to myself.

**Maple:** Remember that kid who you took a picture with at the food trucks? He came by the zoo today and asked to take a picture with me and then stayed to learn about the flamingos. I let him help me feed them. It was incredibly rewarding and I had no idea that my love for you could transfer to so many people in so many good ways. Thank you for giving me the opportunity to call you mine. Xoxo.

Fuck.

I stare down at the text, reading it over and over and hating myself with every second that passes by.

*"Thank you for giving me the opportunity to call you mine."*

That's going to weigh on my chest for a long fucking time.

---

Bennett steps up to the plate, and OC picks up the pizza box in front of us and offers me a slice. I pick one up, and he takes the last slice as we sit in silence, watching the game.

He begged to come over, and I told him he could as long as he stayed quiet. So far, it's been a rather enjoyable evening.

The guy is not half bad when he's not opening his mouth.

Bennett takes a ball, and the announcers talk about his OPS and how he has the highest on the team. How, with every game, he keeps improving, showing up, doing the work, and all with a humble attitude.

Honestly, I'm not surprised.

Just from knowing him for a short period, I can tell that he's a different kind of athlete, one of those that only come around every so often and have it all.

I take a bite of my pizza just as my phone dings with a text, and Bennett hits the ball to right center. He takes off into a run, rounding first and making it to second standing up.

"Jesus, he's fast," I say out loud, then wince at the thought of opening the floodgates for OC to talk.

But to my shock, he just nods and continues to eat his pizza.

Huh, he can take directions well.

Shocking.

I pick up my phone and look at the text. It's from Maple. Of course it is. She's been texting me every day since she left my place a week ago.

**Maple:** Hey, you. Miss you. Miss you calling me beautiful. Miss seeing your face in the morning. Miss you washing me in the shower. Miss you being your overprotective, grumpy self. And I miss being in your arms. Hopefully this won't be forever. Still loving you from afar. Please respond, Graydon. I'm getting worried. Xoxo.

"Is that from her?" OC asks, breaking his silence.

"Yeah." I sigh.

"She cracking your shield?"

"She already cracked it. I'm attempting to patch it up and doing a shitty job."

"Have you texted her back?"

I shake my head. "No. If I do, I know I won't be able to stop."

"I don't know, man. The pain I see in your face, maybe you should just give in. Not sure what the purpose of all of this is at this point. She's not going to stop, and you're only hurting yourself."

Yeah, I know.

But I'm...fuck, I'm scared. The moment I give in, I know that's going to be it. I'm going to be all in, and she's going to be exposed to all of it. And I know she's strong, but is she really that strong?

What happens when I go on away trips?

What happens when people start accusing me of cheating? Because social media is just that cruel.

There are so many unknowns that I just don't know how to handle, and for the life of me, I wish my mom was here to help me.

I wish she could give me some solid advice, anything to help me decide what the fuck to do.

"For what it's worth, not that my opinion matters, but I think you need to give in. Why deny yourself something wonderful like love in your life? Fighting alongside her is going to be so much better than fighting against her."

He keeps his eyes on the TV and takes another bite of his pizza, and honestly, color me shocked because that's the kind of advice I would hear from Bennett, but it came from—

"Dude, come on, that was some good shit, something you would find on a T-shirt. You have to give me credit."

Annnnnnd…there he is.

Grumbling, I say, "Don't call me 'dude.'"

---

**Maple:** I haven't heard from you all week and I'm starting to think that maybe…maybe my love isn't enough. I don't want to think that way, Graydon, I want to believe that you can trust me, that you can understand where I'm coming from, that you can believe in the bond we have, but as the silence grows between the two of us, I'm wondering if I'm pushing you in a direction you just don't want to go. I don't know how to handle this and I thought that maybe I could fix this, but I'm wondering if this isn't mine to fix, that maybe this is for you to figure out. So I'm putting it in your hands, Graydon. If you want me, then you know where to find me. Please know, this is not me abandoning you, or giving up on us, I'm just giving you the option to decide what you want, without pushing you. I love you, always will.

Fuck.

I drag my hand over my face and set my phone down, her words ringing through my head over and over again like a siren, warning me that I'm going to lose her.

Isn't that what I want, though?

To set her free?

For her to finally give in and let go?

I lean back on my couch, my mind racing.

Honestly, I don't know what the fuck I want anymore, but the thought of her not saying those words to me anymore…*I love you*…hell, that makes me feel so much lonelier than I've ever felt before.

---

**Graydon:** Did you see they took away my dad's stadium privileges? And Coach Keenan is on probation? If the team doesn't start winning, he's fired.

**Gretchen:** I did. See what happens when you trust me?

**Graydon:** You sound just like OC, gloating.

**Gretchen:** Please don't compare me to that shoelace.

**Graydon:** Shoelace. LOL. Why is that the perfect description for him?

**Gretchen:** Because it is. Okay, everything is set for tomorrow. I have Maple hooked up with her field passes and seats. After the game, you have to go up to her so we can get the shot we need for socials. But don't answer questions. Got it?

**Graydon:** Uh…what are you talking about? I told you we broke up.

**Gretchen:** And I chose to ignore that.

**Graydon:** We're not talking right now and I doubt she'll be there.

**Gretchen:** She's obligated to be there.

**Graydon:** She is?

**Gretchen:** Yes, and Welcott is expecting a spectacle tomorrow after the game for the start of the season, and I would suggest giving in because, well, you know, he chose our side, got rid of your dad, and is a few games away from firing Keenan.

**Graydon:** Gretchen, I don't want to do that. I don't want to expose her that way. Especially after everything that happened.

**Gretchen:** Not your decision to make. She'll be waiting for you, so don't let everyone down.

**Graydon:** Gretchen…pick up your phone.

**Gretchen:** Yeah, not answering phone calls right now. See you tomorrow.

What the fuck?

I stare down at the text—she'll be waiting for me.

Waiting for me while wearing my jersey, probably looking so goddamn beautiful that it will break me. Not that her text yesterday didn't break me.

*Ding.*

I check my phone, hoping it's Gretchen telling me never mind, but then I see Maple's name.

Fuck.

**Maple:** I know I said I would let you be, let you decide how you want to pursue this, but Gretchen just told me I'm required to be at the game. I won't bother you too much. I'll let them take their pictures and then I'll let you have your peace.

I growl in frustration and toss my phone to the side, driving my hands into my hair before standing from the couch. I pace the length of my living room, warring with myself as I try to find a solution to all of this, where she isn't hurt, I'm not craving her, and everything just…works out.

There isn't such a solution.

Which means I have to decide what I want to do.

Do I want to sit here and deny myself what I really want because I'm trying to protect the woman I love? Or should I trust the fact that she can handle what comes her way and go after her?

Because she's not pushing me. She's not bothering me. If anything, she's reminding me how much she's changed my life these past few weeks…hell, months. She's reminding me about the joy, the lightheartedness, the free feeling of having someone walk by my side, hand in hand, carrying my burdens right along with me.

I glance over at my phone, where I can see her picture on the screen, my jaw tensing, my body yearning.

Fuck…I have no idea what the hell I'm going to do.

# CHAPTER 47
# MAPLE

"GIRL, WE NEED TO TIE up that shirt," Scarlett says as she takes me in.

Thankfully, I was able to get Scarlett's information from Everly, and we've been talking all week. She's been my insider as well as Gretchen, both of them giving me the confidence to keep pushing through and wearing Graydon down—that is, until I broke after the silence got too strong.

It hasn't been easy. There have been nights when I've cried myself to sleep, desperate to hear from him, just a text, any kind of text, but he's gone radio silent. And that silence has destroyed me. If it wasn't for the contract that I signed and the obligation I have to fulfill, there is no way I would be here. I would prefer to be in my apartment, buried in my bed, possibly with Butterfinger Bites surrounding me.

But now, I have to make a spectacle in front of an entire stadium and a pit full of cameras ready to capture a moment between us. A moment that I know is not going to be real, despite how much I want it to be.

And the worst of it all...what if he doesn't go through with the obligation? What if I show up and he doesn't?

Because what if he doesn't walk over to me?

What if he doesn't come to say hi?

What if he leaves me stranded out on the field, cameras pointed at me all alone?

Or worse, what if...what if he comes over just for the cameras, leans in, kisses me, and reminds me of all the love I have for this man, only for him to coldly pull away and leave it at that?

Either way...I'm the one who loses.

But he warned me of this, didn't he? He told me I was going to get hurt. Might as well finally come to terms with that.

"Here," Scarlett says as she pulls a hair tie out of her purse.

I chose to wear one of the jerseys that Gretchen gave me, but it's kind of big. I paired it with some cute jean shorts and white tennis shoes, and I put my hair into two loose French braids to keep it from blowing in my face.

"Turn around for me." I turn around, and Scarlett gathers the jersey in the back and ties it with the hair tie. "I'm just going to slip the knot under the shirt so it will look cute." She does just that and adjusts the shirt so it shows off an inch of my skin. "Is that okay?"

"I don't know. Does it look dumb?"

She smiles and shakes her head. "No, you actually look really hot." She then pulls her phone out and points it in my direction. She takes a picture and shows it to me. The shirt is much tighter, showing off my frame better, which I appreciate, but God, the look on my face is terrified.

"I look so scared."

"Yes, but that's okay. We're not in the public eye just yet."

"This is a bad idea, Scarlett. I'm going to be humiliated."

"Stop that. The minute he sees you, he's going to come back. I know he is."

I shake my head, not so sure of that. "No, he doesn't...he doesn't want me," I say, my voice choking up.

"Don't." Scarlett points her finger at me. "Do not doubt yourself. I know you gave him a choice and trust me, he will make the right one."

"We're ready for you," Corinne, one of the public relations girls, says as she gestures for us to follow her.

My eyes widen as I look at Scarlett.

"You're going to be okay, I promise," she says. "We're about to be in the public eye now. Just smile and try not to be nervous. He'll come over. I know it."

"And if he doesn't?"

"Then we'll wait for him outside the locker room and surprise attack him. I'll go for the jugular, and you can go for the crotch. A one-two punch from us both at the same time will have him rethinking his decisions pretty quickly."

I chuckle and lean into her, grateful I have her for this moment and I'm not doing it by myself.

If she wasn't here, I would for sure have invited Everly, even though Hank suggested he could go with me. I told him that wouldn't be a good idea, and I even had to have a talk with him on Friday about boundaries and that I appreciated him as a friend, but I didn't need him looking out for me. If he couldn't accept my relationship with Graydon, then we couldn't be friends.

He wasn't happy about it, but he said he would work on his feelings toward Graydon. Not that it really matters at this point, but at least I settled that.

Together, Scarlett and I make our way through the tunnel and out onto the field. The pristine quality of the turf, the white lines, the enormity of the stadium, it's…it's incredible.

How can Graydon come out here and play the game he loves every week without getting nervous? Because holy cow.

Not all of the seats are filled just yet, but there are enough fans watching the players warm up that you can hear cheers, catcalls, and mocking jokes coming from every angle. And as I become more and more visible, I can hear those cheers and catcalls increase while a gaggle of phones point in my direction. I just ignore it, though. That's what Gretchen has taught me to do this past week while I took her crash course in media training.

Honestly, given how things started with her, I thought that she was a complete bitch, but in all fairness, she was just doing her job. In reality, she's a really nice person and wants nothing more than for Graydon and me to be happy. She's played a huge part in getting me through this week and preparing me for today, despite what the outcome might be.

"Right over here," Corinne says as she directs us to a sectioned-off part of the sidelines, right near the end zone where the Foghorns are warming up.

"Thank you," Scarlett says as we walk right up to the sectioned-off square.

"Where is he?" I ask, scanning all the players and looking for his number, trying not to look desperate even though I am. I just want to see him, even if he doesn't want to see me.

"Over there." Scarlett points toward the opposite end of the field, where he's bent over, stretching his hamstrings out.

My eyes fall on him, and my stomach twists in knots as he lifts up, his hair just long enough to fall over his forehead before he pushes it out of his face and twists his body, stretching his lower back.

There is a group of fans in the first row of the stands trying to get his attention, holding up signs and footballs, looking for a signature. When he turns toward them—because they're calling out his name—he waves to them, and it's so cute as the little boy in the very front jumps up and down in excitement.

Graydon picks up a football and asks one of the trainers for something. The trainer takes a Sharpie out of his pocket, and Graydon quickly signs the football before handing it to the trainer and pointing at the little boy.

The trainer takes it over to the little boy, who hugs the football and starts crying.

"Oh God," I whisper. "I don't think I can take that."

"He does that all the time," Scarlett says. "One of the few players who don't care about wearing out their autograph for kids. He's one of the good ones."

"I know," I say, staring at him. "It's why I love him."

Just then, he turns toward us, and my stomach lurches when he spots me, his expression morphing into surprise as his eyes narrow in on my shirt, his number in bold on my chest.

"I think it's safe to say he sees you," Scarlett whispers.

"Yeah, I think he does, but he's...he's not moving over here."

"Give him a second. He might still be stretching."

He stands taller, and he says something to the trainer who delivered the ball. The trainer nods, and then Graydon turns his back on me and walks away.

Embarrassment fills me immediately as I realize that even though I told him he could choose his own path, this isn't some magical moment—where he spots me, walks up to me, and kisses me because the minute his eyes land on me, all he can think about is claiming me.

Nope, instead, he walks away the moment I come into view.

"I...I don't think I can stand here and keep a smile on my face," I say, covering my mouth like Gretchen told me to do when talking so people can't decipher what I'm saying.

"Maybe he...maybe he's coming back."

"He went into the tunnel," I say.

"He could still come back."

"Scarlett, come on."

"Okay, yeah, umm, let's just wait a second before we leave. I know Gretchen wouldn't want people to think there's something wrong between the two of you. Then we can go to our seats—"

"And watch the game? There's no way," I say, trying to keep my face neutral. "I can't sit through this game and put on a happy face with all the cameras pointed at me."

"I know, but you already showed your face, so people will be looking for you in the stands. You know what, let me see if I can have Gretchen get us into one of the suites. We can show your face on and off, but you can hang in the back for the most part with me. That way, it doesn't stir any trouble, and from there, you can decide what you want to do."

"Okay, yeah. Thank you."

Scarlett puts her arm around me. "Of course. I'm here for you, girl." She squeezes me, and then we both stare out at the field where Hutton is warming up on the twenty-yard line. He waves to Scarlett, and I'm so caught up in their love for each other that I don't notice the tall figure running in my direction until a cacophony of cheers erupts in the stadium.

"Oh God," Scarlett says just as Graydon stops right in front of me.

My heart skips a beat as he closes the space between us and says, "Hey, beautiful."

Oh God, don't cry.

Whatever you do, do not cry.

"Hey, you," I answer as I stare up at him in complete awe that he came back.

That he's choosing to be near me.

"Thanks for coming to the game."

"Wouldn't miss it," I say as I can feel the cameras and practically everyone in the stadium watching our every move, but it all fades away as I stand there, talking to him.

"Listen, I have a note for you." He takes my hand in his, and he places a folded-up piece of paper in my palm. "Read it privately, where no one can take pictures over your shoulder, okay?"

"Okay," I say, feeling like I'm back in high school where the hunky jock is talking to the nerdy girl who loves animals. "Should I be worried?"

He softly smiles. "No." He glances over his shoulder. "I have to keep warming up or Keenan might have my head. He's already grumbling about how I had to go back into the locker room to grab your note."

"Well, don't let me keep you."

He takes a step back and winks, sending my heart into a tailspin.

"Enjoy the game."

"Good luck," I shout before he jogs off, looking so damn fine in those football pants that I can practically feel my tongue hanging out of my mouth.

"Dear God in heaven, why do I feel like I have an erect dick in my pants?" Scarlett asks.

I let out a laugh and a sigh at the same time, relief flooding through me. Turning to her, I say, "He talked to me."

"He sure did. He even passed you a note. How about we get out of here, and you go and read it?"

"I couldn't think of anything more perfect."

She puts her arm around me and leads the way. "Then let's get out of here."

---

"Let me know if you need anything else," Scarlett says as she sets down some water for me.

"Seriously, Scarlett, you don't need to wait on me."

"I know, but it's more dramatic this way." She winks and then takes off, leaving me in the small conference room she was able to secure for me.

I unfold the paper that Graydon gave me, and I smile as I take in his scratchy handwriting.

Adorable.

Leaning back in my chair, I read his letter.

*Hey beautiful,*

*What the hell am I going to do with you? Here I was, thinking that I could just part from you, suffer the pain of losing you, and regret the decision for the rest of my life, but you just wouldn't let me do that, would you?*

*You clawed and worked your way into my life, never giving up, never running away, never getting scared, and now I'm left here, in my house, needing to make a decision on what to do because I'm going to see you tomorrow, and I know the minute I see you, I'm going to break.*

*Crack.*

*Crumble.*

*Because yes, beautiful, I love you.*

*I love you so damn much that I would give you up, let you walk away, in order to keep you safe, in order for you to be happy. And that has been my intention this entire time, giving you up, attempting to be selfless, but with every day that has passed that I haven't talked to you, this consuming feeling of emptiness has filled me.*

*And do you know what? I realized that even though I'm trying to protect you from what this unlucky life has brought on me, I can't just...walk away.*

*I can't push you away.*

*I can't be that selfless asshole, because I need you, Maple.*

*I want you.*

*I need you in my arms every goddamn day, where I can soak in your goodness. Where I can prey on your sweetness. Where I can devour every last inch of your intelligence, because I'm so fucking in love with you, beautiful.*

*So fucking in love.*

*So please...forgive me for doing this to you because I know this will be tough. I know there will be days when you hate being attached to me and when the media frenzy becomes too much or social media rips into our relationship, but I can't be without you.*

*I don't want to be without you.*

*And if you don't want to be without me, then meet me at the end of the game, at the fifty-yard line, and kiss me.*

*Yours forever,*
*Graydon*

Tears stream down my cheeks as I look over his words...again and again and again until I practically have the entire letter memorized.

He loves me.

He chose me.

That's all I need to know.

That's all I ever needed to know.

Because with that, I know we can battle anything together.

I wipe my eyes, stand from my chair, and open the door, where Scarlett is waiting on the other side. When her eyes meet mine, she says, "Please tell me those are happy tears."

I smile at her and nod. "They are very happy tears."

---

The game flashes in front of me in segments, my mind a fuzzy mess as I watch the Foghorns take the field, the entire stadium erupting for the start of a new season.

A foghorn blasts in the distance during kickoff.

Graydon runs down the opposing team's quarterback...several times.

The Foghorns miraculously score, Hutton leading the charge with a phenomenal catch that brought them to the ten-yard line.

Halftime comes and goes. The boys are in the lead by seven, the score low, but the opposing team is unable to get near the fifty-yard line because the defense is phenomenal.

Graydon intercepts the ball in the fourth just by leaping in front of the quarterback, giving the Foghorns the ball back on their own twenty-yard line.

The ball is passed to Hutton, and he runs into the end zone for another touchdown.

The crowd roars as the time ticks down, and when the game is over, both teams meet in the center of the field and shake hands while Scarlett and I jump up and down, hugging each other over a first-game win.

The offense was shaky.

The defense was unstoppable.

And I think if they continue to tweak and work at it, they might have a fighting chance this season—coming from a girl who knows nothing about football.

"Ahhh, I'm so glad they won. God, Hutton is going to be all over me tonight."

"Really?" I ask with a chuckle.

"Oh yeah, get ready for the postgame adrenaline. You will start looking forward to every Sunday." She winks and then nods toward the field. "Your man is on his way. You nervous?"

I shake my head. "Not even a little."

"Good." She leans in and hugs me. "I'll give you some space, not that you'll really have it with everyone in the stadium watching you, but one less person is better, at least."

She takes off with a wave, and I turn all my attention to the man walking toward me, his helmet in one hand, his sweaty hair not styled in his fauxhawk but more falling over the top of his forehead. His jersey clings to every inch of his torso, and his football pants truly leave nothing to the imagination.

I don't think I've ever seen anything hotter.

Behind me, I can hear people scream, whisper, and talk about how I'm the girl from the zoo, but I block them all out as Graydon walks up to the wall separating the fans from the field.

He looks up at me and says, "Hey, beautiful."

"Hey." I smile, unable to help myself. "Great game."

"Thanks, I had someone watching who I wanted to impress." My cheeks blush, and he nods. "Get over here."

"You want me to climb over this railing?" I ask.

"Yeah, I got you."

And those three words undo me. I know there has never been a truer statement. So I climb over the railing, sit on the side of the wall, and fall into his arms. I wrap my legs around his waist, and he pushes me up against the wall. His smile is so freaking big that it almost brings tears to my eyes.

He caresses the side of my cheek and then presses his forehead to mine.

"I love you, Maple."

I cup his cheeks and whisper, "I love you, too."

"I'm sorry—"

"Don't," I say, my thumbs stroking his cheeks. "Not here…not ever. I understand. I understand everything."

He lets out a sigh as his eyes squeeze shut, and he leans into me even more. "How did I get so lucky?"

"Not lucky, Graydon, just meant to be." Then I tilt his head back and wet my lips before gently kissing him, letting our mouths mold together as the stadium erupts into cheers.

I pull away while Graydon chuckles, his eyes staying on me the entire time.

"I think we gave them a show."

"I think we gave them more than a show. I think we fed them storylines, drama, and everything in between."

He kisses my lips again. "As long as I have you, I don't care what the hell they do."

And then he starts walking toward the tunnel.

"Uh, Graydon, you can put me down."

"Fuck no, you're mine now."

I laugh as he carries me all the way to the tunnel and slightly out of sight of the crowd, then pins me against the wall again and says, "Let me apologize."

"You did in your letter."

"Let me apologize in person." His eyes meet mine, pleading, so I nod. "I know you deserved better than to be avoided all week and I wish I could be smarter, stronger, more emotionally intelligent for you, but it's going to take time for me to learn, to understand just how goddamn strong you are."

"You're not giving yourself enough credit."

"Please, Maple, please just let me say this." I nod and let him continue. "I didn't understand that I've been going through life with this empty hole in my chest. I just assumed it was from the loss of my mother, and yes, that was part of it, but I also think that hole has been waiting for you to come along this entire time, and when you filled it, I got scared. I got scared because I know I'm not perfect. I know that I have anger problems, and I know that I can be too possessive and protective, and that's something I'm going to work on. But I didn't know that the girl in the high-water pants was going to steal my breath away and show me what true love is all about. I promise, moving forward, I will trust you, your instincts, and protect you—when you want me to. All I ask in return is that you love me, beautiful. You continue to love and accept me for everything I am, everything that comes along with my name, and the baggage trailing behind."

I sift my fingers through his hair and look him in the eyes.

"That's not something you ever need to worry about because this love I have for you, it's unconditional. You and me, we will fight the good and the bad together, by each other's sides, because that's what true love is, Graydon. What we have is true love, and I will battle through everything that comes at us because that's how much you mean to me, how much I care about you...and I need you just as much as you need me."

He slowly nods. "Fuck, I love you."

"I love you, too."

And then his lips are on mine again, but instead of the soft, hesitant kiss he gave me out on the field, this is more intense as his hand cups the back of my head and his pelvis drives into mine, a growl parting his lips…

"Hate to break this up," Gretchen says from the side, causing us to pull away. "But the cameras can still see inside the tunnel, and you're giving all of America quite the show. Maybe take the make-out session somewhere else?" Her smile stretches across her face as she looks between the two of us.

"Right, sorry." Graydon sets me down but quickly grabs my hand.

Gretchen's phone dings, and she glances down at the screen. With a giant roll of her eyes, she starts tapping away on her phone.

"OC is watching your make-out session and said I was standing in his way. God, that man is so freaking annoying."

Graydon chuckles. "I don't know…maybe he's not all that bad."

Gretchen raises a brow at him, causing us both to laugh.

"You're right, sorry," he says. "What was I thinking? He's fucking terrible."

"That's more like it." She thumbs toward the hallway. "Now go get showered and changed. I know you have more important things to attend to now."

She wiggles her eyebrows at us and then takes off down the hall.

Graydon turns to me. "Did she just infer that we are going to go have sex?"

"You would be surprised to know that she can actually be pretty chill when you give her the chance to be."

Graydon chuckles. "I'll believe it when I see it." Then he loops his arm over my shoulder. "Let's get out of here, beautiful. There are a million things I want to do with you, and none of them involve a crowd."

# EPILOGUE
# GRAYDON

"DO I LOOK OKAY?" MAPLE fidgets in front of me in a beautiful pink silk dress, one that I helped her pick out from the many that Everly brought over for her to try.

"You look stunning," I say, walking up to her in my all-black suit with a flamingo brooch attached to the lapel.

"Are you sure?" She presses her hands down her sides and over her stomach, where she's just barely showing now.

"Perfect, beautiful," I say and then walk up to her, placing my hand on her stomach, where our baby is growing. "So fucking perfect."

It happened after we won our bid to the playoffs. We celebrated like never before since the Foghorns hadn't been in the playoffs for several years. Maple missed her birth control, we fucked for twenty-four hours straight, and well, here we are.

And I couldn't be happier.

I planned on proposing soon, but Maple said she wanted to wait to get married. She didn't want me to propose just because she was pregnant. I told her I planned on proposing after she told me she loved me, but she still wanted to wait.

And that's fine. I have no problem waiting as long as I know she's mine.

The news broke out to the public that she was pregnant after someone caught us going to a doctor's appointment. I would like to say that we're able to live our lives normally, but that's not the case at all. After our spectacle in the tunnel, the demand for pictures of us only increased. Interviews and spotlights came pouring in, with everyone wanting to know our story, but we made it our mission to keep as much as we could private without taking away from the fans what we started posting to begin with.

So Maple still posts on Flock and Tackle. That's where she posted our baby announcement. It's where she posted a big "fuck you" to my dad when I annihilated his records, even a year early. And it's where I plan on posting the video of my proposal when I finally make it happen.

She did move in with me the week after our kiss in the tunnel because people were hounding her apartment. Hell, they were hounding mine too, so we found a more secure building with a doorman and protection for her so she feels safer.

And now we have a place that we can call our own.

"Okay, then we should probably get out there."

"Are you ready for it?" I ask.

She nods. "I am."

I take her hand in mine and lead her out of the event space in the zoo where we first met and under the bulb lights that line the pathway to the new flamingo exhibit.

It's been a year, and yes, it's not completely finished. The zookeepers' building still needs an overhaul, but the actual exhibit is ready, and given the popularity of the flamingos, they wanted to bring them back as soon as they could.

They expanded the exhibit to twice its original size and added an interactive section where you can pay to feed them at specific hours of the day—handled by the zookeepers, of course—a better viewing area that's unobstructed, and a bigger lagoon. They took the mural I painted and hung it along the side, leading up to the flamingos, and then I and a few artists from local high schools painted around the rest of the exhibit, giving it a cool graffiti look. The zoo covered the murals with UV-protected plexiglass so they won't get damaged.

It came out better than Maple could ever have imagined, and tonight, she gets to celebrate the hard work she's put into this zoo and the advocacy she's done for these birds.

"This feels so weird," she says as we walk through a crowd that's clapping as we approach.

"This is what happens when you do good with your platform," I whisper into her ear. "Be proud of yourself, beautiful."

When we reach Phil, he claps for us as well. After Maple threatened him with a letter to the board of directors, he had a change of heart and put the donation money toward the new facility, which is beating out what any merchandise store could've made, especially with our celebrity behind it. Tickets are sold out for months as well as feeding sessions.

So Phil can suck his own ass...at least that's what I told Maple.

As for Slutty Little Glasses, well, he took off. He found another research project to work on and bolted. Glad the fuck is gone. I don't need him around trying to poison Maple's mind with nonsense. Also, just so I don't look like a douche, Maple did say he changed a lot, and even though he said he would try to accept our relationship, he never did, and I think it's because he had a big old fat crush on her.

Well, guess who fucking won that competition?

This guy.

I step aside, right next to OC and Bennett, who are both dressed up in black suits as well. When they asked what I was wearing, I assumed they were seeing what the dress code was, not trying to match with me. OC smiled like a fool when I growled at him because now we look like three assholes who all tried to twin...or triplet, I guess. He said it was a solid representation of the Gladdy Daddies uniting. I told him he was one incident away from getting cut out of my life.

Of course, that's all talk. I hate to admit it, but I kind of like the guy.

I would never say that out loud, and if someone ever told him, I would deny it until the day I die, but yeah, he's grown on me.

My girl addresses the crowd and thanks everyone for their time, donations, and love for the flamingos. She talks about the importance of saving the birds and how they serve a very important role in the ecosystem. She's poised, collected, and honestly, so goddamn perfect that my heart actually aches from how much I love her.

When she's done, she and Phil cut the ribbon, pictures are taken, and then the party starts, a soiree under the stars with the sounds of the zoo in the background.

"You were fantastic," I say, pulling her into my arms. "I'm so damn proud of you."

"Couldn't have done it without you." She kisses my cheek and then is pulled in another direction, where she shakes hands with some important people.

Her parents, who are really amazing, just like her, are off to the side, talking to a few people, and as I watch them smile proudly over their daughter, the pain I once felt when witnessing the love a parent has for their child no longer exists, as I've spent the last year finding closure. My dad got a job as a GM for the Tigers out in Nashville, something I couldn't care less about, and my mom, well, we have our good days and bad days, but now with Maple by my side, the bad days are easier to swallow.

"Excuse me, are you Graydon St. John?" a man asks while tapping me on the shoulder.

I turn to find a taller man with dark hair, wearing a navy blue suit and a flamingo pocket square tucked into his suit jacket.

"That would be me."

He holds out his hand. "JP Cane. It's nice to meet you."

"Oh, wow. Maple has talked a lot about you and your dedication to saving the flamingos."

He tugs on his lapel with a smile. "Well, it's the least I can do. I thought

I would introduce myself and maybe grab your email or give you my contact information. I'm really in deep with my mission to save the birds, and any advocate I can find, I tend to want to get on my side."

"Oh...uh, sure."

He hands me a business card. "All my information is on there. Love what you've done with Flock and Tackle and would really like to create something like that for the pigeons." He pats me on the shoulder. "We'll be in touch."

And then he takes off. I glance down at the card and then at his retreating back. Hardy steps up next to me and whispers, "Lose the card, man...lose the card."

"I don't know, he sounded nice," OC says. "Maybe I'll join the fight."

"The fight for what?" Maple asks as she loops her arm around my waist, instantly filling me with warmth.

"To save the pigeons."

Maple's eyes widen. "You met JP?"

"Yeah, is that a bad thing?" I ask.

"You didn't give him your email, did you?" I shake my head. "Good, you would never get rid of him." She then tugs on my side. "Can I borrow you? They want to take some pics of us in front of the exhibit and with Big Hermy."

"Of course," I say and then lead her over to the mural-covered exhibit. As the photographer sets up, I turn to Maple and say, "So proud of you."

"Proud of us," she says with a smile as she stares up at me.

"Who would have thought our little social media gimmick would have created this?"

"And this," she says, placing my hand on her stomach.

Possessiveness takes me over as I lean forward and press my forehead to hers. "Wouldn't change it for anything."

"Me either," she whispers and then grips the back of my neck and pulls me down for an earth-shattering kiss.

DISCOVER MORE OF MEGHAN QUINN'S HILARIOUS ROM-COMS WITH A SNEAK PEEK AT

# PROLOGUE
# SCOTTIE

"FUCK OFF, ASSHOLE!"

"No, you fuck off."

"Eat shit and rot!"

God, I love New York City.

There's nothing better than waiting for your breakfast burrito at the corner bodega and witnessing a fight almost break out between a taxi driver and a Postmates runner on a motorbike. Truly chef's kiss.

And it's not just the kerfuffle on the roads that has me tingling with joy. I love the palpable high blood pressure of the collective whole during the morning commute.

The summer humidity, an added obstacle that you slice through during a brisk power walk to your destination.

And the pungent smell of the human race sharing the overworked streets of Midtown.

Spectacular.

*Honk.*

"Watch it, you dick!"

A smile passes over my face as I take a sip of my coffee.

I'm home.

Can't beat New York in the summer.

"Scottie, your order," Vincent calls out as he places my order on the take-out corner.

"Thank you," I say and then point at him with a finger gun as if we're long-lost friends. "Same time tomorrow, my man?"

Completely ignoring me, he goes back to work, scrambling eggs and cooking bacon. It's fine. He'll get to know me soon enough. I plan on stopping by every morning and establishing a rapport, one where I walk up to his storefront, which is decked out in pictures of bagel sandwiches, and he says, "Morning, Scottie. The usual?"

And I'd say, "That would be great, Vincent. How are the kids?"

And he would say something silly, like, "Eating me out of my own house."

We'd chuckle. I'd pay and then stand off to the side, patiently waiting for my burrito while I popped my earbuds in and a classic song like "Dreams" by the Cranberries would start playing.

It would be the perfect opening scene to any New York City–based Nora Ephron romantic comedy, where love is waiting in the wings.

But instead of formulating the well-executed meet-cute where I run into a man in front of an office building, spilling my coffee all over myself only to have him dab at my bosom with his solid-blue tie, I'm going to change the story. This isn't a story about me falling in love with another human.

This is a story about me falling in love with myself.

Yup, being a twenty-nine-year-old divorcée will do that to you.

The only person I want to be in love with right now is me and me alone.

And being here in New York City, the place where I always wanted to live out my early twenties after college, walking the concrete streets, cup of coffee in hand, on my way to my—

"Watch it, bitch." An elbow slams into my cup of coffee, sending the Americano temporarily into the air, only to land smack-dab in the middle of my cream-colored silk blouse.

"Oh my God," I say, pulling my searing-hot blouse off my skin while early morning commuters spare me a wince before continuing on to their occupations.

I glance around, checking for any oncoming men ready to dab my breasts clean, but when not a single person stops to help, I realize I'm shit out of luck.

What was I saying about New York?

Oh right… I love it.

I'm going to keep repeating that to myself over and over again as I carry my burrito in one hand and fan out my shirt with the other. I'll change when I get to work. My company has more than enough polos to spare. I should know; everyone I work with wears one almost every single day.

The only sad thing about getting coffee on my shirt is that I won't be able to drink it now. But hey, it's all part of the experience, right? The New York City experience. Consider this my initiation. My rite of passage. Being a girl from upstate New York, I've always dreamed of living in the city. Not just in my dorm room but on the Upper East Side, so now that I'm here again, nothing is going to stop me from enjoying it.

Not a single thing.

Because this is my new start.

I moved to the city to be closer to my friends, got a job with Butter Putter editing their ad copy and editorials, and now I'm living the single life, trying to regain the confidence I lost when I was married to Matt.

And sure, coffee down the blouse is not the way to start building up confidence, but it's not the worst thing that could happen. It's a conversation starter. Common ground.

Something I can talk about to my new coworkers that I share nothing in common with.

Like I said, nothing, and I mean nothing, is going to stop me from enjoying this new chapter in my life.

Scottie Price is thriving.

She is single.

She's smart, she's charismatic, she's charming.

And she's living out her best Nora Ephron life, falling in love with herself.

Yup, nothing is going to take that away.

Nothing.

# CHAPTER ONE
# SCOTTIE

"MEETING IN TEN," DUNCAN SAYS while knocking on the casing to the door of my office.

"Well aware," I mutter as I press my fingers into my brow. I don't need the reminder.

Another freaking Thursday morning meeting where obnoxious blowhards like to hear themselves speak while absolutely nothing is accomplished.

Great.

It's been three months at this job, and it's like clockwork. We shuffle into the conference room. Brad S carries around a putter like he's King Arthur at the Round Table and talks about the eighteen holes he plans on playing this weekend while Brad F—or Finky—and Chad cheer him on from the sidelines like a bunch of fanboys, frothing at the mouth for the attention of their leader.

Yup, Brad, Brad, and Chad.

The Brads and Chad.

I stare off into the pit of the office. Rows of glass desks, all stacked right next to the other, placed on top of puttable Astroturf flooring. Bobbleheads showcasing a variety of sports heroes are perched atop said desks, jouncing while penis after penis walks by.

Yes, you read that right...penis after chino-encased penis.

To tell it to you straight, I work surrounded by a real sausage fest.

And not just any sausage fest but the worst kind.

It's what the youth are calling...the finance bros.

*Shudders*

Sure, they're not actually "finance bros" given they work for a golf company, but they sure as hell have the aesthetic down to a science.

Every day, I'm subjected to an agglomeration of company-embroidered vests, khaki chino shorts, boat shoes, and polos, all entwining with early morning bro hugs and gentle razzing.

Why does this bother me? Well, besides the fact that they are impossibly annoying to be around, I'm the only woman at the company besides the CEO. She, however, is barely in the office, especially with the launch of a new brand of Butter Putter mini golf courses.

But what really grates on my nerves and has me breathing into my desk drawer like it's a paper bag at least once a week: they're all married.

Every last one of them.

And sure, that's not a bad thing, but if I'm honest, it's not that they're married that's the issue. I'm the issue. It's me. Because I too was once blissfully married.

And at the beginning of my marriage, there was love between me and my ex, there was excitement, there was passion. But as time went on, year by year, I could start to see my husband's interest in me slip. His passion to hold my hand, cuddle, kiss me good night—no longer there. And the love diminished until the last year of my marriage, when it came crashing down after my husband forgot my birthday, leaving me to eat a piece of cake I bought for myself alone at the dining room table while he played video games.

So being in an office building surrounded by men who are happily married...it's...it's just hard. Makes me think of Matt, makes me think of how inadequate I am, how I wasn't good enough to hold his attention.

Not to mention I have nothing in common with them, unless they want to hear about the gum that got stuck on the bottom of my shoe while on a single-lady walk through Central Park over the weekend.

Nor do they care about my Sunday night girl dinner, which consisted of two dill pickles, one single Triscuit, and a cup of applesauce that I ate alone while watching the Menendez brothers documentary on Netflix.

There is a marriage cult, and I'm on the outside, looking in. Heaven forbid they ever find out I'm divorced. I can't imagine the clutching of their embroidered vests, the horror that would wash over their freshly shaven faces.

*Scottie Price, the single one, sequestered in her office, not to go near in case she's contaminated with the "divorcées," a rare condition that could spread if one comes in close contact.*

"You coming?" Finky asks, nodding toward the conference room.

My nostrils flare. "Yes, on my way."

"Good, don't want to be late. Ellison is here today."

My estrogen sonar perks up.

"Ellison is here? Really?"

"Yes. And you don't want to be the last one in the conference room."

No, I don't.

# ABOUT THE AUTHOR

*New York Times*, #1 Amazon, and *USA Today* bestselling author, wife, adoptive mother, and peanut butter lover. Author of romantic comedies and contemporary romance, Meghan Quinn brings readers the perfect combination of heart, humor, and heat in every book.

**Website:** authormeghanquinn.com
**Facebook:** meghanquinnauthor
**Instagram:** @meghanquinnbooks